Bangalore Baloney

A novel by Thomas Itty

For

Barbara, Nathaniel and Alexandra

And dedicated to the memory of my parents
V. I. Itty and Lily Itty

Prologue

December 1994

Everything seemed to happen in slow motion... He saw Gerry point the gun at him and shoot. He could see the bullet coming towards him. He wanted to get out of the way, but couldn't. He felt a sudden, searing pain in the middle of his chest. Then, he was falling backwards. He hit the wall and fell to the floor. He heard Maria scream. In horror, he watched Gerry turn the gun and shoot her through the side of her head. Just before he blacked out, he saw Gerry put the gun to his own temple and pull the trigger...

Swaminathan placed the stub of his boarding pass between the pages of the paperback he was reading and stepped up to the immigration counter at John F. Kennedy International Airport in New York.

"What is the purpose of your visit?" asked the officer. He was a handsome black man in his mid-thirties in a dark blue uniform.

"I'm here to visit my friend," said Swaminathan. "He's in the hospital." He handed over his passport and other documents through the recessed slit in the counter window.

"You don't plan to stay here after that, do you?"

"No sir, definitely not! My family is waiting for me to come back home. I am also a journalist and newspaper publisher. I don't know how they're going to manage while I am away, but I had to come and see my friend," said Swaminathan.

"Where are you going to stay while you are in New York?"

Swaminathan looked inside his address book and told him. The officer flipped through the pages of his passport and examined the documents detailing his finances and activities in India.

"Is this your first time in the United States?"

"Yes sir... but I've always wanted to come here since I was a boy... to visit," said Swaminathan.

"And now your friend is in the hospital... so you've come all the way from..." He looked inside Swaminathan's passport, "Bangalore, India just to see him?"

"Yes, he needs me. I may be of some help to him here... I would like to at least see him and know that he is all right."

The officer looked at Swaminathan quizzically for a few moments. Then, shaking his head, he stamped the passport.

"He must be one hell of a friend!"

Swaminathan nodded, "Yes sir, he is... we've been best friends from the time we were children."

PART 1

School Days

Chapter 1

Swami and Venu meet George

Swaminathan wanted to go to America ever since he saw his first Hollywood movie. He was eight years old. It starred Steve McQueen as a tough detective and featured fabulous urban locations, modern skyscrapers, big jet airplanes, fast muscle cars, beautiful women, smirking villains and exciting high-speed chases.

Swaminathan was entranced. He had never seen anything like it before. In less than two hours, his whole idea of the world changed.

His cousin, Ramesh, who had taken him for the movie, was amused by his excitement. He tousled Swaminathan's hair and said, "Fantastic film, eh Swami? America, what a country!"

When Swaminathan returned home he told his father, "Appa, I want to go to America. Will you take me there?"

"Why do you want to go to America? Tired of India, I suppose, ha... ha..." said his father with a laugh, amused by his son's eagerness.

"Take him if he really wants to go," said his mother, who always assumed her husband could do anything. In her mind, if he was only an assistant bank manager, it was because that was exactly what he had chosen to be at this time.

"Appa, please!" said Swaminathan.

"Swami," said his father, "Do you even know where America is? Get your atlas and come here."

Swaminathan went to his desk, got his school atlas and returned. His father opened it to the world map.

"See, this is India. Where is Bangalore, Swami?"

"Here," said the boy pointing.

"Where is Bombay?"

Swaminathan looked for a moment and pointed, "Here!"

"Good. Now look all the way here… this is America, see? There are two Americas: North and South America. Tell me, where do you want to go?"

"We are South Indian, so we must go to South America," said Swaminathan.

"If you go there you'll find it's not much better than it is here," said his father. "I think you might want to go to North America. See, this is North America."

He added, "Now you have to be specific about which country you want to go to. There is the United States of America and there's Canada. Where do you want to go?"

"United States of America?" Swami asked hesitantly.

"Yes," said his father. "So, in the future you must always say U.S.A. or United States, not just America."

"Appa, will you please take me to U.S.A.?" asked Swaminathan.

"Sorry, Swami, I can't afford to. It costs many hundreds of rupees for a ticket. Even if I could pay for the ticket, where will you stay? You also need a visa to go, they don't let just anybody in."

Seeing the disappointed look in his son's eyes, he said, "Come, Kanna*, let us go to the British Council Library. We'll look at some books with pictures of the United States and other countries. Who knows, maybe someday you will travel all around the world."

◼

When Swaminathan was in the fifth standard, a new student, George Chandy, joined his class at Baldwin Boys' School.

"Did you see the new boy?" asked Venu, his best friend, on the first day of the new term. "I heard he's just arrived from the U.S. His father is a big shot at Larsen & Toubro."

Swaminathan looked at him with interest. "Is he going to be in our section?"

"Yes, I just saw him talking to Mrs. Rozario," said Venu. "He's a pakka** American. You should hear him talk, I couldn't understand a word he said."

"Let's sit next to him in class," said Swaminathan.

They went in early for the first class and loitered near the

*precious one (Tamil)
**100% authentic (Hindi)

doorway until the new boy came in.

"There, that's him," Venu whispered to Swaminathan.

The boy had long wavy hair down to his collar and a very strikingly attractive face. Swami and Venu waited until the boy found a seat, then they rushed and took the seats on either side of him. It was customary that once a boy occupied a particular seat on the first day of class, it was his for the rest of the year.

After they sat down, the two boys began to show off for the benefit of the new student. Swaminathan chewed up half a sheet of notebook paper and threw it at his friend. Venu retaliated by flinging his notebook at Swami. Soon they were rolling around on the floor fighting.

"You dirty rat," Swami told Venu in his best American accent. He had heard the line in an American movie he'd seen recently. "I'll thrash you to pulp after class."

"You haramjadi-karide*, even your mother won't recognize you when I'm finished with you," said Venu, whose source of dialogue was mainly limited to what he saw in Hindi and Tamil films. They followed this with a no-contact, karate fight. After a few minutes, the boys sat down exhausted. Swaminathan looked at the new boy from the corner of his eyes to see if their antics had earned his attention.

The boy was looking straight at him. Swaminathan averted his eyes hastily. A couple of seconds later, he looked again shyly.

The boy smiled. "Hi, I'm George. I just joined this school today. What is your name?"

"I'm V. Swaminathan," said Swami.

"Venugopal here, at your service," said Venu from the other side. He had heard the expression in a Tamil film he had seen recently.

"Nice to meet you both," said George. "What is the first period?"

"Eh?" asked Swaminathan. He was having some trouble understanding the boy.

"He asked what the first period is, buddhu**," said Venu. "I'll tell you! The first period is English."

"It's taught by Mr. Joseph. He's very strict, but he likes me. I had him last year," said Swaminathan trying to draw George's attention from Venu.

"I also had him before," said Venu. "I got ninety in his exam. Swami only got eighty-five."

*bastard-dog (Hindi and Tamil)
**idiot (Hindi)

"You rascal, don't think I didn't see you cheat. Ninety, ha! On your own you wouldn't get thirty-five marks."

"And who wrote the names of all the Indian presidents on the desk before the History exam?" Venu retorted.

"I was just practicing. Don't listen to him," Swami told George. "He's a lousy MGR* fan."

"Swami, it's okay when you insult me, but when you take MGR's name… I'll have to come there and smash your head!"

"Come here if you have the guts, and bring your lousy MGR with you. I'll thrash you both," said Swaminathan. "I saw one of his pictures last month — totally unbelievable! He doesn't look like he can even defend himself against a woman."

"You swine, MGR can defeat any of your American heroes with one hand behind his back," said Venu.

"Ha! Steve McQueen or Clint Eastwood will make him into chutney in two seconds. And James Bond, if he just blows, MGR will vanish," said Swami.

Mr. Joseph walked into the class at this moment. Venu, who was about to fling his eraser at Swaminathan, froze in mid-action.

■

George invited Swaminathan and Venu to his house a few weeks later.

"Appa, this new boy, George Chandy, has asked me to come to his house on Saturday. Can I go?" Swaminathan asked his father.

"Why, is it his birthday?"

"No, just like that. He wants to show us where he lives."

"Why, is he a king? Does he live in a palace?" asked his father.

"No, but his house is in Palace Orchards. He's from the United States of America."

"Chandy… Malayalee** chap, eh? Very smart people, these Malayalees! They eat a lot of fish, that's why. He's from the U.S., eh? They say there are Malayalees everywhere… and they are also so enterprising. There's a joke that when Neil Armstrong landed on the moon, there was already a Malayalee chap selling tea there," he laughed. " What does his father do? He must be a doctor."

"No, he's a big shot in Larsen & Toubro," said Swaminathan impatiently. "Appa, can I go?"

"We'll see. They eat meat, you know. What will you eat if you go

*popular 70s Tamil actor/politician
**people from the State of Kerala

to their house?"

■

Swaminathan woke up early on Saturday morning and got dressed in his best clothes.

"It's only eight o'clock! What are you doing up so early? You're also wearing your new clothes. Where are you going?" asked his mother.

"Amma, I told you yesterday, I'm going to my friend George Chandy's house. I asked Appa for permission."

"It's too early to go to anyone's house. How will you be going?"

"On my cycle," replied Swaminathan.

"Where does he live?"

"In Palace Orchards."

"That's at least five miles away. It's too far to ride your cycle."

"I'm going with Venu. We'll go slowly."

"I don't know, Swami. Did you tell your father you were going to ride your cycle so far away?" his mother asked.

"Tell me what," his father asked, entering the room.

"Amma, please," said Swaminathan.

Seeing the pleading look on his face, his mother said, "Nothing. We were simply talking."

"Radha, is my breakfast ready? I have to be at the bank early today. They're training us on a new check-handling procedure and I have to organize the staff rotation too. Solpam sekram pannu* Ma, please..."

Swaminathan made a quick exit while his parents were talking. A few minutes later while he was taking his cycle from the shed in the back of the house his mother appeared with a small packet.

"You didn't eat anything, so I packed some poories. There's enough for your friends too."

Swaminathan hugged her, "Thanks, Amma."

"Now ride carefully, and come back home before your father returns from work."

"I will, Amma."

Before leaving, he took a rag from the shed and polished his cycle. It was a metallic-red, BSA sports cycle. What Swaminathan really wanted was a flame-red, chopper bicycle he'd seen on the inside back cover of an American comic book. However, that

*make it quick (Tamil)

was a dream that was well out of his reach. At first, his father had refused to even consider buying him a bicycle.

"Why do you want a cycle? Your school is only half a kilometer from here."

"All my friends have cycles, Appa."

"When I was your age, all I could do was clean my father's cycle," said his father. "If you want, you can borrow my Raleigh cycle."

"It's too big, Appa… and ugly."

He didn't mention the fact that he'd been borrowing the old bicycle quite frequently while his father was away from home. It was too big for him to ride in the conventional way, so he rode it standing up and by putting his right leg through the crossbars. After pleading for several months, he had finally convinced his father to buy him the BSA sports bicycle by promising to achieve all sorts of academic honors during the year that he knew were probably far beyond what was possible. He hoped his father wouldn't hold him to his word.

After Swaminathan had finished cleaning the bicycle to his satisfaction, he put the little packet his mother had given him on the carrier and peddled to Venu's house. He stopped outside the gate and rang the bell on his bicycle three times. A few seconds later, Venu's head appeared over the wall.

"Go down the street and wait for me. My father is just leaving," he whispered urgently.

Venu's father owned a pharmacy on Commercial Street. He had a big handlebar mustache and glared at Swaminathan whenever he saw him. Swaminathan often wondered how sick people felt about buying medicines from him. Venu was quite terrified of him and hence avoided any contact with him if he could help it. So, rather than tell his father that he would be going to George Chandy's house, he chose the more diplomatic method of quietly disappearing once his father left. His mother had three other young children to worry about, and usually she didn't know when Venu came or went.

Swaminathan wheeled his bicycle down to the end of the street. A few street urchins around the same age as him were playing marbles in the middle of the road. He watched them enviously.

One of the boys noticed him and spoke in Kannada to the others, "Hey, look at that sissy boy in his clean clothes with his new bicycle."

They all started making faces and laughing at him. Fortunately, Venu arrived just then on an old Atlas Junior bicycle and they both peddled away from the scene quickly before a confrontation or any further embarrassment ensued.

The two boys arrived at their destination a little after eleven o'clock. It was a long, tiring journey. On the way, they stopped for a glass of sugarcane juice at the vendor outside Bowring Hospital. In spite of this, they were both very thirsty and tired when they reached George's house. It was a big two-story mansion with high walls and a big, black iron gate. The boys wheeled their bicycles to it cautiously.

A Gurkha* watchman stood just inside. He saw the boys and asked sternly, "Kyya chahiye?" He was dressed in a khaki uniform and wore a long, curved, khukri knife on his belt.

Swaminathan looked at him closely. The only other Gurkha he knew was the one who patrolled the streets of his neighborhood in Victoria Layout every night, banging his lathi** hard on the gate of each house. Once every month, the Gurkha would go around to each house and collect ten rupees for his services.

"Why should we have to pay that chap just for waking us up in the middle of the night," Swaminathan's father would complain to his wife. "If you ask me, the only reason he bangs his stick so loudly is to warn any robbers that he's coming. Tell me, have you ever heard of a Gurkha catching a thief? Never!"

One day, when the Ghurka was waiting for Swaminathan's mother to get him his ten rupees, Swami asked him about his khukri.

"Ghurka-ji, can I see your knife?"

"No chota-sahib, I am not allowed to take it out."

"What kind of watchman are you if you are not allowed to take out your knife," Swaminathan asked.

"Oh, I can take it out, but I can't put it back unless it has spilled blood," said the Ghurka.

"So what do you do if you have to take it out to clean it," asked the boy.

"Then I cut myself so it has my blood on it before I put it back," replied the Ghurka.

Since then Swaminathan was very careful in his dealings with

Ghurkas. The one outside George's house looked very imposing.

"You talk to him. Your Hindi is better," he told Venu.

"Umm... hum dono George ka dost hai... oose milna aaya hai... we come here... see George," Venu said in his broken Hindi with some English thrown in.

"Kyya? Kisko milne aaya hai?"

"George Chandy saab ko."

"Saab yaaha nehi."

Just then George walked out of the house and said, "Gurkha, let them in. They're my friends."

"Chota saab?" the Gurkha asked. He turned to the boys and said, "Vo, Hindi nehe malum... sirf Angraze aur Kerali!"

"Vo bhola, hum ooska dost hai aur thum humai under aana do," Venu translated for him.

"Teek hai, chota saab," said the Gurkha and opened the gate for the boys.

Swaminathan and Venu had never been inside a house like this. There was a big, well-kept lawn in front. The driveway was tarred and ran around the whole house. There were two shinning cars, a black Ambassador and a white Fiat, under the huge portico. The two boys looked around with open mouths. George was wearing dark-green bell-bottom trousers and an orange full-sleeved shirt with long collars. Around his waist was a wide, brown belt with a big buckle and he had on high-heeled, brown cowboy boots.

Swaminathan had felt positively majestic in his new, dark-brown, striped shorts and flowered half-sleeved shirt that morning but now felt completely humbled in the presence of such regality. He unconsciously wiped his shoes on the back of his leg. He had spent the previous evening washing and blancoing his Keds so they looked pristine white, but they appeared shabby compared to George's fancy footwear.

Venu was dressed, as usual, in crumpled shorts and a half-sleeved shirt with a pair of worn-out leather slippers on his feet.

George led them to a corner of the lawn where there was a glass-topped, metal table and four white chairs.

"Unni!" George called.

A boy who looked to be about eighteen years old appeared.

"Lemonade konduva*."

"Ath enna**, sare?" asked the boy.

*bring (Malayalam)
**what's that (Malayalam)

"Naranga* juice," said George.

"I didn't know you spoke Malayalam," said Swami.

"My parents speak Malayalam at home so I know a little," George replied.

"George, see my Malayalee accent: the mongey climbed the cogonut tree," said Venu. The boys laughed.

"Come, let's go to my room," said George after the boys had finished drinking the lemonade. Swaminathan and Venu followed him through the front door. Just inside was a huge, well-furnished living room with plush sofas, glass side tables, bookshelves, lamps and a showcase with lots of knick-knacks. In the corner of the room there even was a television set.

"Swami, he has a TV, man," said Venu. They both ran up and began examining it excitedly. They had never touched one before.

"We got it from the U.S. but since they don't broadcast here often, we don't use it much," said George. He turned it on, and the screen flickered into a black and white mosaic of dots. The two boys looked at it in amazement."

"I hear they're going to show the cricket test match between England and India on TV next month," said Venu. "Can we come and watch it in your house, George?"

"Of course you can. In the U.S. we have television twenty-four hours a day."

Swaminathan felt a pang of jealousy when George included himself in the citizenry of the U.S.

"What do they show for twenty-four hours there?" he asked.

"Everything... movies, music, children's programs..."

George's room was on the first floor. The boys walked up an elegant spiral staircase. A slim, attractive woman in a starched flowered sari came out of one of the rooms.

"Mummy, these are my friends from school."

She held out her hand, "Nice to meet you. I'm Georgie's mother. And you are...?"

"V. Swaminathan, Aunty."

"K. Venugopal here, madam, at your service."

Swaminathan was enchanted. She was unlike any woman he'd seen in his own family circles. Her hair was cut short and hung loose. She also smelled very nice, like fresh flowers.

"Georgie, I have to go out. Ask Chinamma to make whatever

you boys want to eat, okay? Good to meet both of you. I'm glad Georgie has made friends so quickly." She went out.

"Your mother is very nice," said Swaminathan to George. Venu agreed.

George's room was a treasure trove that went beyond Swami's and Venu's wildest imagination. There was a big four-post bed, a long white desk with George's schoolbooks arranged on it and two tall, white cupboards.

Leaning against the side of one of the cupboards was a guitar. Venu grabbed it eagerly and started strumming the strings.

"Do you know how to play it?" he asked George.

"Yes, I learned a little in my music class in the States."

"They teach music in schools there?" Swaminathan asked in amazement. "Here they only teach boring subjects like arithmetic and biology."

George took the guitar and began playing,

"Imagine there's no heaven. / It's easy if you try. / No hell below us. / Above us only sky. Have you heard this song? It's *Imagine*, a song by John Lennon."

"Yes, I know it… it's a beautiful song," said Swaminathan.

"George, do you know *Dum Aray Dum*?" Venu asked.

"No, I don't think so."

Venu started singing.

"Dum aray dum / Mithu jaya hum / Bolo shobo sham / Hare Krishna Hara Ram. It's from the new movie with Dev Anand and Zeenat Aman, man!"

"Venu, you have a voice like a jackal. Let me show you… George can you play *Love Me Tender*? *Love me tender. / Love me sweet. / Never let me gooo. / You have made my life complete. / And I love you sooo.* Elvis Presley, what a deadly singer!"

"I have several of his records. Here, let me take out my stereo and play one for you," said George.

He went to one of the cupboards and took out what looked like a black suitcase. He opened it, and the two boys were surprised to see that it was actually a stereo. The top half detached into two speakers. The bottom comprised of a record player, tape recorder, and even a radio.

"This is just for you?" Swaminathan asked. All they had at home was an old Murphy radio in the drawing room. After a lot of fiddling on the dials he was able to pick up the Voice of America and Radio Ceylon in the mornings. But this... it was magnificent!

George took out a 45 record and put it on the turntable. Elvis began singing *Love Me Tender*. It was so clear! Swaminathan closed his eyes and let the song permeate into the deepest recesses of his mind. He was in heaven. Except for the few times when he was able to hear albums in the sound booth at the HMV music store on Brigade Road, he had never heard music that sounded so good. And, it did not have the annoying static that accompanied all the content on shortwave radio, his main source of music.

"Do you have any Hindi or Tamil songs?" Venu asked.

"You and your Tamil songs. Is that all you can think of?" asked Swaminathan. Venu punched him lightly.

George opened the other cupboard. "These are my books," he said. There were hundreds of novels, all arranged neatly.

"Hey Venu, I think he has all the *Hardy Boys* here," said Swaminathan. "I started reading the *Hardy Boys* books last year. They're fantastic!"

George opened another cupboard. It contained the best assortment of toys Swami and Venu had ever seen. There were guns, pistols, rubber knives, cars, jigsaw puzzles and even a train set.

"Come, let's play Cowboys and Indians," said George.

"What's that?" Swaminathan asked.

"Have you seen any western films?" George asked.

"I saw *The Good, The Bad and The Ugly*, what a deadly movie," said Swaminathan.

"Yeah, I saw it too. It's a great movie. Have you seen *Stagecoach*?"

"Oh yes," said Swaminathan.

"If you remember, in that movie, there are cowboys and red-Indians. I was thinking we could play a game where we could dress up either as a cowboy or as a red-Indian."

"What is this red-Indian?" Venu asked. He felt left out of the conversation. "Is he red in color?"

"No," said George. "When Christopher Columbus, who discovered America, first arrived there he thought he had come to India. So, he called the people he saw Indians. When he found out that he had made a mistake, he simply changed their name to red-Indians."

"Are they like us?" Venu asked.

"No, they have darker skins than white people, but they're very different from us."

"So why do they call them Indians? We are Indians. Should we call ourselves brown-Indians? Swami is very fair, so he's a white-Indian. George, you are brown, so you are a brown-Indian. I am dark so I am a black-Indian," said Venu giggling.

"Imagine if this fellow Columbus had actually come to India in the first place instead of getting lost, this would be America, would it not?" asked Swaminathan.

His friends could not dispute the logic of this.

Swaminathan and Venu had one of the most exciting afternoons of their lives. Knowing that his guests did not eat meat, George asked the cook to prepare some tasty vegetarian dishes. The boys feasted on iddlys, dosas, pakodas, vadas and ice cream in the large dining room. After lunch, they played every game they could think of. To top it all off, George took them to the garage, and there, to Swaminathan's amazement, stood a gleaming, red, three-speed, chopper bicycle. George allowed his guests ride it for as long as they wanted. Later that evening, the three boys went bicycling to nearby Sankey Tank. Swaminathan rode George's chopper and George rode Swami's BSA. They sat on the grass embankment of the Tank laughing, talking and eating the poories that Swaminathan's mother had packed for them.

When it was time for his friends to leave, George presented each of them with a gift. He gave Venu a red fire truck. For Swaminathan, he gave a miniature of the Statue of Liberty.

Swaminathan went home and placed it on the windowsill next to his bed. It remained there as his most prized possession for many years. Like the real one, thousands of miles away, that provided hope to millions of immigrants, this miniature statue became a symbol for all of Swaminathan's hopes, dreams and aspirations. He would lie awake in his bed at night gazing at the statue that was bathed in the harsh glow of the street lamp outside, and imagine himself in another world: a land of cowboys and red-Indians, John Wayne and Clint Eastwood, beautiful cars and scantily clad women, rock music and 24-hour television — America!

Chapter 2

The Scrimshankers

Venu, George and Swami soon became inseparable friends. They called themselves "The Three Musketeers" at first, but later unanimously agreed that they needed a name that was more unique.

"How about The Bangalore Boys?" Venu asked.

"No, that's too simple," said Swaminathan. "What about something like The Tigers or The Lions?"

"That's too common," said George. "We have to find a name that no one has ever used before. Let's all think about it and have a meeting tomorrow. Each person can pick up to three names. We'll meet in the Graveyard after school tomorrow and decide which one is the best."

The Graveyard was an old British army cemetery that had been abandoned years ago. It stretched out for about half a mile and was flanked by the Bangalore Reserve Police Headquarters on one side and a lake in the other. Because of its location and for the fact that the last burial there had taken place over a hundred years ago, it was always completely deserted. The boys had discovered it one day by accident on their way back home from school and made it their special haunt. They loved playing all sorts of games there and roaming through the rows of un-kept graves reading the epitaphs engraved on the tombstones.

They selected the grave of one unfortunate *"Captain John Saunders of the British Army,"* who had *"Died in Bihar on October 13th, 1764 during the Battle of Buxar at age 34,"* as their regular meeting spot. It was their usual routine to go home after school, change out of their school uniforms, get something to eat, and then meet at the Graveyard from about five to seven every evening.

According to the plaque on Captain Saunders' tombstone, his family in England had erected the fine structure in his honor. It was a large monument about eight-feet long, five-feet wide and six-feet high built of white marble that the years had turned into a pale shade of brown. One side of the structure was covered in darker marble and had the lines, *"He lived with honor, he died with valor,"* engraved on it. The other three sides were open and had round pillars on the four corners that supported the marble roof of the monument. It was a perfect venue for the three boys to meet because it provided shelter from the elements, as well as a secluded spot where they could be on their own.

Assuming that he didn't mind the intrusion at his final resting place, the departed Captain Saunders may have been pleased that someone had finally cleaned up the bushes that had overrun his fine mausoleum. While the rest of the graves in the cemetery were neglected and covered in dirt and weeds, the three boys had carefully cleared the ground in a two-foot perimeter around their little hideaway. They did this, not out of any obligation to the late captain, but because they feared that a snake or chameleon might sneak up on them from one of the surrounding bushes.

The next evening, the three boys met once again above the mortal remains of Captain Saunders. Venu was the first to arrive. He broke off a twig from a nearby bush and cleared away the dirt that had gathered inside the engraved letters of the gravestone. Then, he dusted it with his handkerchief and lay down on it with his hands behind his head.

George arrived next. He crept up silently behind the tomb and said in his deepest voice, "Venugopal, this is your dead friend Captain Saunders speaking. You must buy your friends Swami and George one apple cake each from the tuck shop in school tomorrow."

"George, you scoundrel," said Venu without rising. "I know it's you. I can make out your phoren accent anywhere."

Swaminathan came a few minutes later. In his hand he carried two sliced cucumbers doused liberally with salt and green chilli sauce that he had bought from a vendor on his way. George reached into his bag and pulled out a packet of Marie biscuits. Venu put his hand inside his pant pockets and extracted three ripe polly-mangoes. The boys sat cross-legged on the tombstone, divided the food, and quickly polished it off.

"Okay," said George, wiping his hands on Venu's handkerchief. "What names have you got?"

"Ooo… let me go first," said Venu raising his hand. "My three names are: Sputum… Cholera… and Tetanus." The only printed matter that he could find for reference in his house had been a folder with pharmaceutical brochures belonging to his father.

"What kind of names are those? What does Sputum mean?" Swaminathan asked.

"I think it means spit," said George.

"Who'd have a club with a name which means spit?" asked Swaminathan. "And Cholera or Tetanus. Your names are useless, Venu. Wouldn't you agree, George?"

Venu made a face at Swaminathan. "Okay, let's see what you have then."

Swaminathan pulled out a piece of paper from his pocket and read in a dramatic voice, "Proposed names for our group, by V. Swaminathan: Number one, The Djangos; number two, The Warriors; and number three, The Yanks."

His source of reference was a ragged collection of cowboy and war comics that he kept under his bed.

"I don't like any of your names," said Venu. "I think mine are much better. What about you George?"

"I am submitting only one name for your consideration, but I think you'll like it," said George. "The Scrimshankers!"

"Shimshahwhat?" Venu asked.

"Scrimshankers."

"What does that mean?" Swaminathan asked.

"I found it in the *World Book Encyclopedia*. It means people who don't like to work," George replied.

"Well… it's much better than Swami's names," said Venu.

"It's two times better than your rotten diseases names," retorted Swaminathan.

So, by unanimous consent, it was decided that, henceforth, they would be known as The Scrimshankers. Although Swami and Venu had their doubts if such a word actually existed, they nevertheless agreed that if it did, they personified it exemplarily.

"Let's make a pact with our blood," said George, who had read *Huckleberry Finn* recently.

"What is that?" Venu asked nervously.

"We'll write an oath on a piece of paper and sign it with our blood. This means we have to keep all of each other's secrets and stay friends forever. Here, I have a notebook and a pen." He tore out a piece of paper, unscrewed his pen and started writing.

> "We (Swami, Venu and George) have formed a secret club called The Scrimshankers today, the 4th of February, 1973. We promise to never betray each other. If we do so, may we die at once.
> Signed: Swami, Venu, and George.
> Witnessed by Captain John Saunders (Died 1764)."

He then removed his geometry box from his bag and took out a compass. He pricked his right index finger with the sharp point and signed his name in blood under the oath he had written. He wiped the point on his shirtsleeve and passed it on to Venu who did likewise. Swaminathan hesitated when it was his turn. He was very scared of blood, especially his own. But he didn't want his friends to think he was afraid so he closed his eyes, pricked his finger, and did as they had done. He felt quite faint afterwards but strangely also elated that he had overcome his fear and sealed friendships that would last forever.

George folded the paper carefully and buried it in the corner of the tomb. For a moment, the boys thought they felt the earth move. It may simply have been Captain Saunders turning over in his grave.

■

The Shimshankers got a chance to prove their solidarity and live up to the oath they had signed over Captain Saunders' grave during the second term of the next year. It involved C.K. Ganguli, a prefect in the eleventh standard at Baldwin Boys' School.

CK, as he was known, was a sadistic young man whose main purpose in life appeared to be that of tormenting the juniors in the school. He had been a boarder since his early years and had become almost a fixture in the school because he had failed his grade a few times. He was older than the other students and had a bad reputation as someone not to be tangled with by either student or teacher.

CK was only of medium height, but he was well built and had his school uniform, of navy blue trousers and white shirt, stitched almost skin-tight. The sleeves of his half-sleeved shirt were always rolled up two or three times to show off his well-developed arm muscles. He had closed-cropped hair with a widow's peak in front and usually wore black wrap-around glasses. This had earned him the nickname of "Phantom," because he looked very much like the character illustrated in the popular comic books.

Every morning, from the time he was in the ninth standard, CK would hang around outside the school and harass every boy that was physically smaller than him. He took whatever he wanted from them such as food, comic books and money.

Because of his imposing physique even other seniors, including the prefects, whose duty it was to enforce discipline in the school, were afraid of him. Pratap Kini, the head-boy, and some of the teachers reasoned that maybe his behavior would change if he were given some responsibility. So they made him a school prefect.

If CK was merely a bully before, his new official position turned him into a tyrant. He moved his reign of terror from outside the school gates to inside the school grounds. All the boys, especially the juniors, were terrified of him. Even the teachers were afraid to confront him. It was rumored that he had close ties to some of the notorious goondas from the Johnson Market area.

Between each class, students were given a ten-minute break. This was the time when boys would rush to the tuck shop or make a fast stop at the restroom. Some even played a quick game or two of catch or marbles. It was a time of general pandemonium. The prefects and hall monitors, whose main function it was to keep some kind of order during these breaks, were usually very tolerant to these youthful bursts of exuberance and enforced discipline only when things really got out of hand.

Things changed for the juniors when CK became a prefect. He marched through the hallways like a military dictator handing out corporal punishment for even the slightest offence with sadistic satisfaction. For example, a student running in the halls would be made to do fifty sit-ups holding his ears. Someone coming back late to class after the bell had sounded was slapped hard across the face and made to run around the school perimeter for the rest of the period.

A hushed whisper of, "CK's coming," was enough to send even the bravest boys scurrying off to safer haunts, or turn a classroom full of loud and boisterous young students into one where the only audible sounds was that of forty-odd, trembling, beating hearts.

The Scrimshankers had managed to avoid any trouble with CK before he became a prefect. This was because they always moved around together as a group thereby preventing the bully from picking on any one of them individually. The situation changed when he became a prefect. With the power of his position, and the authority of the school behind him, CK could do as he pleased with any, or all of them, without fear of reprisal.

George was the first one to experience his wrath. One afternoon during break, the boys were playing outside their classroom with a toy gun that George's father had got him from Bombay during a recent business trip. It was a dark-gray plastic imitation of a Luger and fired little, round, plastic pellets. CK saw them playing with it and came over.

"What is that in your hand?" he asked.

"Nothing, sir," said Swaminathan in fear.

"Give it to me."

Swaminathan took the gun out of his shorts pockets and handed it over.

"Whose is it?"

"Mine," replied George.

CK looked at him closely. Then, suddenly, he slapped him hard on his face. "Mine, SIR. I am not one of your friends. You will always call me sir, you hear?"

George fought back his tears, "Yes, sir."

"Where did you get this gun?"

"My father got it for me from Bombay, sir."

"You have a foreign accent. Where are you from?"

"From the U.S., sir."

"Oh, from the U.S., eh? So, you think just because you are from the U.S., you can do anything you want in my country? Tell me, is your father a gangster?"

"No, sir."

"Then why is he teaching you to carry guns?"

"Sir, it's only a toy," said Venu.

CK turned his gaze at Swaminathan and Venu. "Hold out your hands," he said.

The boys complied.

"No, turn them over."

CK took out a wooden ruler from the back pocket of his trousers and gave them each a sharp whack on their knuckles with the narrow side.

"Okay, you can go."

He turned to George, "But you stay."

Swaminathan and Venu left with mixed emotions — relief for themselves and fear for George's fate.

"So, what else do you have from America with you?" CK asked George after the other two boys had left.

"Nothing, sir."

"I'll let you go if you give me something. Do you have any *Playboy* magazines in your house?"

"No, sir I don't know what that is."

"What will you give me then?"

"Nothing, sir," said George.

"What, you're trying to act smart with me? Don't think I haven't seen the three of you before. You guys think you're big shots, eh? Give me five rupees now and I'll let you go."

"No, sir."

"Okay, if you don't have money today, bring ten rupees tomorrow and give it to me."

"No, sir. I'll report you to the principal," said George.

CK slapped him again. "So, you think you're a tough guy, eh... American?"

He took out the gun that he had confiscated and tapped it lightly on his leg. He thought for a moment and then said, "Move back against the wall."

George did as he was told.

"Now open your mouth and close your eyes."

George was forced to comply.

CK poised himself about six feet away from the boy, standing sideways with his arm out, like the Vietnamese military officer whose picture he'd seen in *LIFE Magazine* about to execute a traitor. He aimed the gun at George's face and fired it over and over again until it was empty.

Although only one or two of the little pellets actually found their way into George's open mouth, several struck him on his face. Tears of pain and embarrassment rolled down his cheeks.

CK laughed. "Not bad... I think I'll keep this little toy for myself. If you want to stay out of trouble in the future, you'd better get me something good from your house. And don't even think of sneaking to the principal. He won't believe you. And you don't have any proof. Now get out of here before I kick you... you little American bastard."

When Swaminathan and Venu heard what had happened to George, they were furious.

"That bloody Phantom must be taught a lesson," said Swaminathan.

"But what can we do?" asked George. "I think we should tell the principal. Or, I will tell my father. He'll know what to do."

"If we sneak to the principal or your father, it'll ruin our reputation in the school forever. No, I think we should kill him," said Venu. "I can get some rat poison from my father's shop. We can put it inside an apple cake and give it to him."

"No, I think we should hang him," said Swaminathan. "I saw a film in which Clint Eastwood catches his enemies one by one and hangs them."

"That's nothing. In one of MGR's films, he stabbed one fellow with a knife, then he shot him, and then hanged him," said Venu, not to be outdone. "I think we should feed him rat poison, then stab him with a knife, then shoot him.... and then hang him."

"If we kill him, they'll send us to jail," said George. "I don't want to go to jail over that bastard. We have to think of something else."

Neither of the boys could think of a solution. So, they decided that, for the time being, the best thing to do would be to keep out of CK's way.

They managed to do this for a few weeks, but their luck didn't last. One day when Swaminathan was cautiously returning from the tuck shop, a hand came out of nowhere and grabbed him by the scuff of his neck. It was CK.

"Where are you going, you little chuthia*?"

"Nowhere, sir."

"Where is your house badge?"

*profanity (Hindi) — from vagina

24

The school was divided into houses, named after former principals. Students were supposed to wear their house badge on their left collar at all times. It was a minor infringement of school rules not to do so and, if caught without one by a prefect, usually carried a penalty of a half-hour of after-class detention.

"I'm sorry, sir, I left it at home," blurted Swaminathan.

"Did you leave your cock and balls at home also?"

"No, sir." said Swaminathan.

"Where is it? Let me see it."

Swaminathan turned two shades lighter.

"I-I-I..." he stammered.

"It's okay. I know you don't have any. You're probably a girl. You look like one. Why, there was no seats left in Baldwin Girls, so they put you here, eh?"

Swaminathan's ears turned a deep shade of red.

"Come here and hold out your hand. Let me see if you're a man," said CK.

He took out a pencil from his pocket and put it between the index and middle fingers of Swaminathan's right hand. Then he began squeezing the two fingers together tightly with the pencil in-between them. Swaminathan began to cry after a few seconds. CK didn't stop the torture but continued to squeeze even harder. When he finally let go after a minute, Swaminathan was almost on the verge of fainting.

"See, I knew you were a girl. You cry like one. Okay, you can go now. Oh... and tell your American friend that I'm still waiting. If I don't get something, I'll make all your lives hell."

Swaminathan bore the marks of his encounter with CK for the next week. The impression of the pencil turned blue and remained on his fingers for several days. He could hardly write or even clench his right fist.

The Scrimshankers realized that only a miracle could save them from the evil Phantom. Fortunately, they were given one. It came to them by way of a tape recorder and Mr. Broom, the PT master.

Chapter 3

Mr. Broom

Walter Broom was Anglo-Indian. His father, a British army major, had met his mother, a poor Konkeni* Christian girl, and married her when he was stationed in Bangalore during the last few years of British rule in India. When his unit pulled out of the country a few years later, the Major had left quietly one day without telling his wife anything. The poor woman had tried desperately to contact him, or to at least get papers for her son and herself to immigrate to England.

The British government, who had hundreds of such requests from Indian women at the time, decided that they didn't need this new influx of Indians and half-Indians settling down in their country. The British High Commissioner's Office in Madras ignored any requests she made for information regarding her husband, and finally rejected her application. They questioned the authenticity of her marriage certificate and even the validity of her entire story. Shunned by the British and her own people, as were most Indian women who had been deserted by their English husbands or lovers, Walter's mother settled down uneasily into an Anglo-Indian community in Frazer Town.

Young Walter had a very rough childhood. Frazer Town comprised of three separate communities — the Hindus, the Muslims, and the Anglo-Indians. While they all lived in peaceful coexistence for the most part, there were a few bad elements in each community who were quick to stir up trouble based on their differences. As a youngster, Walter found himself constantly in the midst of such confrontations. Like so many Anglo-Indians

*people from the coastal region
of Karnataka State

in India, he felt a sense of alienation from the dominant Indian culture. They were different. They identified themselves more with their English ancestry than with their Indian one. They talked like the British, dressed like the British, and many of them even looked British. However, as most found out, this did not mean they were welcome in Britain — or in India, for that matter.

Walter's mother, out of desperation and loneliness, had become the mistress of Faiaz Ahmed, a married businessman. Although he paid the rent for the small house on Wheeler Road, he was an abusive man. He visited her two or three times a week. Since he didn't consume alcohol at home, in an effort to keep up the appearance of being religious, he drank heavily when he was with her. Faiaz usually never spent the night there. Instead, he would leave in the middle of the night completely inebriated after beating or verbally abusing her for some reason or the other.

Walter was too young to protect his mother or to provide for her in any other way. Soon, the strain in her miserable life became too much for her to handle. She started drinking throughout the day and sank into a deep depression. One day, when Walter was twelve years old, he came home from school and found out from a neighbor that his mother had hanged herself.

Having no relatives who wanted him, Walter was sent to an orphanage. Chances were that he would have gotten into more trouble there and ultimately turned into a criminal, if it hadn't been for sports. He was always athletic, and as he grew into adolescence Walter discovered that he had a natural affinity for most sports.

The PT master at Clarence Boys' School, where Walter was a student, noticed this quickly. Soon, he was one of the stars of both the school's hockey and football teams. He was also a gifted track-and-field athlete who brought home several sports trophies for the school.

Oddly, despite his English roots, Walter had no interest in cricket. His performances on the hockey and football fields at the inter-school competitions were legendary all over the city. People with no interest in the final outcome of a particular game, thronged to the stadiums just to watch him play. Sports changed his life and gave him a confidence that he had never had before.

When he was eighteen, Walter won a prestigious scholarship to the National Sports Camp in New Delhi. It was there that he discovered his true passions: gymnastics and boxing.

By the time he was twenty-three, Walter was an undefeated National lightweight fighter and one of the most promising members of the Indian Gymnastics Team. He decided to give up boxing to concentrate on gymnastics. For the next seven years he traveled all around the world representing India in major international competitions. His moment of glory came when he won the Silver Medal at the 1966 Asian Games in Bangkok.

Two years later, a training accident broke his right shoulder and ended his career as a gymnast. He could have become a trainer but felt that if he couldn't do it himself he didn't want to be in it. Instead, he got a certificate in Physical Education and joined an exclusive boys' school in Ooty as the PT teacher.

He worked there for a few years and then decided that he wanted to come back to Bangalore where he had grown up. When Baldwin Boys' School offered him a job, he took it at once. At the time of the Scrimshankers' encounter with C. K. Ganguli, Walter Broom had been the PT master at Baldwin Boys' School for only a few months. Although he did not know the boy personally, Mr. Broom was not entirely ignorant of CK's existence.

The motto of Baldwin School in Latin was *"Integritas et Veritas"* meaning *"Righteousness and Truth."* Mr. Broom was convinced that CK's character was antithetical to this lofty ideal and that he was not worthy of being put in charge of young, impressionable children. He had observed the prefect bullying the younger students mercilessly on several occasions and had developed a deep dislike for the boy. Having spent most of his life as an athlete, Mr. Broom believed firmly in sportsmanship, decency and fair play. He hated bullies of any sort.

In spite of his short tenure at Baldwin, Mr. Broom was already one of the school's most well liked and respected teachers. His years on the national team had also made him something of a celebrity. Gymnastics, which had not been a part of the sports program for over two decades, was reinstated and became a source of pride for the whole school.

Every morning, Mr. Broom and some of the students would carry the big wooden horse and springboard outside to a corner of the school cricket field. Until their senior year, all students were required to take two hours of physical education each week. Mr.

Broom devoted much of this time to gymnastics. He would usually start the class by first demonstrating some of the routines himself. This was the part everyone enjoyed.

Mr. Broom's performances were always superb. Dressed in his tight white polyester pants, T-shirt and white Keds, he would run like a daredevil to the springboard, take off with the ease of a bird, perform somersaults or twists in the air with the agility of a sparrow and land perfectly with both feet together on the thick, padded canvas mattress.

Anyone passing by couldn't help but stop and look at this display of rare ability in wonder. The younger female teachers in the school were particularly fond of watching Mr. Broom perform his routines. Many of them fostered romantic fantasies about this soft-spoken, tall, handsome, athletic gentleman.

■

The Scrimshankers held an emergency meeting at the Graveyard the day after Swaminathan's encounter with CK. It was a beautiful Saturday morning. Normally, the boys would have spent their time exploring abandoned old houses, playing cricket, catching butterflies, or looking for buried treasure. Since CK's assault on Swaminathan, however, they realized that they would have to find a way to deal with their tormentor as soon as possible.

Swaminathan and Venu arrived first. They leaned their bicycles against a hedge close to Captain Saunders' grave and sat down in their regular spots.

'I hope George has some new ideas about stopping that bastard Phantom," said Venu. "I wish we could kill him."

Swaminathan agreed. This was the first time he had been physically assaulted in his life. Over the past few days, fear for the prefect had been slowly replaced with anger and indignation.

"Oh, I can picture killing him. But we have to make him suffer as well."

"But what if he kills us first?" Venu asked. "He's bigger than us and probably knows how to do it better than we do."

"Maybe we can pay some goondas to beat him up," said Swaminathan.

"But we don't have any money. I'm sure they charge at more

than hundred rupees."

George arrived just then. He had a backpack slung over his shoulder.

"Hi, buggers*," he greeted his friends.

"Venu and I were deciding how to kill CK," said Swaminathan.

"Forget about killing. I have a better idea. Anyway, do you chaps think you're capable of killing someone? Baloney! It's not like in the movies," said George. "And do you know what the police will do to you if they catch you? They torture you first and then put you in jail. After that they hang you."

"So what can we do?" asked Venu. "We have to do something. That bastard will be looking for us on Monday."

"I have an idea. I'll show you," said George.

He opened his backpack and took out a Philips cassette tape recorder. It was about eight inches long and six inches wide. He also removed a microphone attached to a long thin wire from his bag.

"This belongs to my father. I asked him if I could borrow it for a few days."

"What can we do with it?" Swaminathan asked, puzzled.

"We'll record CK threatening us on the tape recorder and take it to the principal or even to the police. I was thinking about it and I feel that's the only way we can stop him from bullying us."

"But if we sneak to the principal, that will ruin our reputation in the school. I don't know about the U.S., George, but here sneaking about another student, especially a prefect, is considered very cowardly," said Venu. "Everyone will think we are lousy sneaks and have no guts to deal with it ourselves."

"Baloney, why is it cowardly? Isn't he making our lives hell? Look at poor Swami's hand... and my face. Maybe, because you haven't got a beating from CK yet, you're still thinking about your honor. Wait until he picks on you, then tell me if you feel the same way," George told Venu. "Anyway, what else can we do?"

Reluctantly Venu and Swami agreed that the only course of action left was to report CK to the principal.

"Why do we need to tape him?" asked Venu. "Why can't we just complain?"

"The principal won't believe us. CK told me himself that without proof no one will listen to us," said George.

*slang for fellows or chaps —
commonly used in India

The boys racked their brains trying to figure out the best way to put their plan into action. Finally, they decided that one of them would have to deliberately antagonize CK and record the encounter on the tape recorder.

"I wish we could also film him threatening us," said George. "My dad has a small movie camera but I don't know how to use it. Also, the film, and developing it, is very expensive."

"Which one of us will be the person to face CK?" Swaminathan asked. He suddenly realized the full implications of their plan.

"I'm scared to do it," said Venu. "But I don't want to make either of you do it instead of me because of my fear."

"It's going to be scary for all of us, no matter who does it," said George. "Let's draw straws. Whoever gets the shortest straw will be the one who faces CK."

He looked around until he found three twigs on the ground. He then made two of them the same size and the other a little shorter.

"I'm going to hold all three sticks in my closed fist," he told Swami and Venu. "You chaps pick one each. Who ever is left with the shortest stick will be the one to face CK."

George turned away from his friends and mixed the sticks up in the palm of his hands. He arranged it so they were level, and turned around so just the tips of the sticks were visible in his right fist. Swami and Venu both closed their eyes and pulled out a stick from George's hand. Breathing deeply, they opened their eyes to see what they each held in their hand.

George had the shortest stick.

Chapter 4
Encounter with CK

T he Scrimshankers spent the next week preparing for their encounter with CK, all the while making sure they avoided him in school each day. Venu helped himself to four new batteries for the tape recorder from the storeroom at the back of his father's medical shop when his father went outside for a cigarette.

George found an unused BASF tape in his house that he displayed to his friends excitedly. He opened the cellophane wrapping of the cassette and carefully printed the words *"File Under CK: FUCK"* on it.

This made them all laugh for a few minutes despite the stress they were feeling. The boys also practiced using the tape recorder in various surroundings and positions to see how they could get the best possible recording.

"I think, if we want the clearest recording, we need to do it inside somewhere, not outside," said George. "All the sample recordings we made outside have too much noise — like people talking and wind, which makes it hard to hear everything clearly. Also, because we don't want CK to know we are recording him, we need to hide the recorder and mic in a bag," he added.

"Can we cut a small hole in the bag so that the end of the microphone is not covered?" Venu asked.

"I don't want to spoil my school bag by cutting a hole in it," said George. "Anyway, if CK happens to see the mic sticking out, he will realize what we are doing and kill us."

It was decided that George would keep the tape recorder at the bottom of his school bag and cover it with a sweater. The microphone would be taped to the inside so it would have an unobstructed sound path to the opening of the bag. The cassette tape had forty-five minutes of available recording time on each side. George considered buying one that had sixty minutes on each side but decided against it because he had read somewhere that longer tapes were more likely to get jammed while recording and he definitely did not want to chance that happening. The boys spent a few more days testing the recorder until they were sure it was working to their satisfaction. Finally, they were ready.

The plan was that, on Tuesday morning, George would deliberately take out his house badge and walk around the school hallways that CK monitored a few minutes after classes had started. When CK asked him to stop, he would run into an empty classroom nearby.

Meanwhile, Swami and Venu would hide behind the thick bushes outside the classroom. If things got out of hand, they would start yelling for help and go to the principal's office at once.

George would turn the tape recorder on before he ran into the classroom. He would then try to get CK to threaten him, as well as disparage some of the teachers if he could.

This was Swaminathan's idea. "If we can get him to curse out the principal and some other teachers, then our tape will really get CK expelled," he had pointed out excitedly.

"Yes," said Venu. "George, you tell CK that Mr. Broom is not scared of him or his goonda friends. Or, that we heard Mr. Lobo tell Mr. Samuel that CK is the stupidest boy in the school. That will make him very angry and he will curse them both out."

"Okay, I'll try my best, but remember my voice will also get recorded so I can't say anything bad," said George. "Chaps, I'm really scared about doing this... but I know we have to do it, or our days in this school will be really hell until CK leaves the school."

Swami nodded with fear and apprehension.

"Yes, if that ape keeps failing, as he's been doing for many years, we'll finish school before him," he said.

■

On Tuesday morning, the three friends arrived at the school an hour early. Swami and Venu left their school bags in their desks and met up with George in the corridor of the middle-school classrooms. The building that housed this block of rooms had been around since the founding of the school in the late 1800s. It was made of solid granite and stone and featured an open corridor that ran all the way around the building. It also had four cavernous hallways that cut across the length and breadth of the building.

The Scrimshankers were students of the Sixth Standard C Section, which occupied a classroom at the north corner of the block. Their class teacher was Mr. Paul, a kind and portly man in his mid-fifties. He had been nicknamed "Polly-Mango" (Polly for short) by the students because his pear-shaped body bore a striking resemblance to a common local variety of mango called Totapuri — meaning parrot-beak in Hindi and referred to more commonly among English-speakers as "Polly Mango."

Classes started each weekday at eight-thirty in the morning after a fifteen-minute school assembly. All teachers were expected to attend. They usually gathered in the staff lounge half an hour earlier to have a cigarette and a cup of coffee. As the boys expected, Polly was sitting in his favorite wicker armchair in the lounge with a cigarette in one hand, talking animatedly to the attractive Miss Cynthia Benedict. Normally, they would have stood outside the doorway for a little while admiring the beautiful, slim, English teacher with the bob-cut hairstyle who bore a striking resemblance to Jackie Kennedy. Today, however, they had other more pressing things on their mind.

Venu stood at the doorway and gestured to Mr. Paul.

"Sir, can we talk to you for a minute?" he beckoned urgently.

Mr. Paul excused himself from Miss Benedict and came over. He smelled strongly of Old Spice aftershave and cigarettes. He was surprised to see the other two boys outside with Venu.

"What is it boys? Is everything all right?" he asked.

"Yes, sir," said George, "we just wanted to ask you if it would be okay for us to come to class half an hour late. Thing is, sir, we need to finish our experiment from yesterday in the chemistry lab before nine o'clock this morning. Otherwise the lab attendant will throw it away."

"I suppose it's okay, boys," said Polly. "I'll only be reviewing last week's classwork during that period so you can catch up easily. But be sure to borrow someone's notes to keep abreast with the rest of the class, okay."

"Yes, sir, thank you," said the boys and hurried away before their teacher had time to think about things further or talk to Mr. Gopal, their chemistry teacher, who was having a coffee by himself at the other side of the room.

■

Swami, Venu and George stopped at the chemistry lab next. Students were generally allowed to finish what they were working on the previous afternoon if they hadn't completed their experiment. Although they really did not have anything to do there that morning, the Scrimshankers didn't want to be noticed by CK during assembly.

There was no one else there in the lab except for Raju, the lab attendant.

"What are you doing here?" he asked them in Kannada.

"Just finishing up something from yesterday, Raju-anna," replied Venu. His father employed one of Raju's cousin's as a stock boy in his medical shop, so he knew the assistant quite well.

"How is Father?" Raju asked. "Everything okay, no?"

After chatting with Venu for a little while, he went about his morning duties at the laboratory: testing the Bunsen burners, cleaning the tables and checking to see that the glass spigots on the bottles with chemicals were properly closed.

At exactly eight-thirty, they boys left the lab and took a circuitous route to the bushes next to the classroom that they had selected. George waited there with his friends for ten minutes more. He then sauntered down the hallways outside the classrooms.

At first, he thought that maybe CK wasn't in school that day. He ran into Peter Joseph, another prefect at the school.

"Hey Chandy, what are you doing outside class?" he asked George.

"Just going to the toilet," the boy answered.

"Next time, go before class, okay," said the prefect sternly.

George continued walking around. Then, from the corner of his eye, he saw CK reprimanding a couple of younger boys in the corridor between the classrooms. It appeared that CK hadn't noticed him.

George stopped. CK was about twenty yards away down the poorly lit corridor. He was twisting the ear of one of the boys while the other boy did sit-ups in front of him.

George almost felt like calling off the plan and continuing on to his class. But he felt a surge of anger when he saw CK tormenting the other boys. His heart was beating so hard he could feel it against his house badge that he had intentionally removed from his collar and placed inside his left shirt pocket.

He stopped and looked into the dark hallway and shouted deliberately, "Swami, Venu, is that you?"

CK looked up and George could see the anger followed by satisfaction in his face when he realized whom he had nabbed outside on his own.

"You, come here," he commanded.

George walked up to him slowly down the corridor.

"Sir, I was looking for my friends Swami and Venu," he said.

CK smiled at him like a cat that had just spotted a bird with a broken wing lying on the floor.

"You two, get out of here," he told the two trembling boys in front of him.

"And you, come here and stand in front of me," he said to George.

George had his hand inside his school bag. He turned on the tape recorder as he had practiced several times in the last week. Then, on trembling legs he walked towards CK.

The two young boys looked at George with a mixture of relief, fear and sympathy and scurried away quickly before the prefect changed his mind. CK looked at George.

"Where is your school badge?" he asked.

"I forgot it, sir."

"Haven't I warned you last time not to forget it again."

"Yes, sir," said George.

"You chaps think you're very smart, don't you?" asked CK. "I've seen you walking around everyday trying to avoid me. Didn't I ask you to bring me something from your house? What do you have for me in your bag? Let me look."

George knew it would be disastrous if CK looked inside the bag. Instead, as they had planned, he suddenly ran in the opposite direction. CK was caught off guard.

"Where are you going? Come here, saala chuthia," he yelled and began chasing him.

George ran as fast as his legs would carry him into the empty classroom they had chosen. CK was only a few paces behind. As he was running, George could see the frightened faces of Swami and Venu behind the bougainvillea bushes outside.

CK followed him inside, panting. He saw the classroom was empty and that George was inside with nowhere to escape. He chuckled with satisfaction.

"I got you... you little bastard. Hee... hee... hee... Let's see where you go now."

"Sir, please let me go. I have done nothing wrong," said George.

"Then why were you running from me?"

"I wanted to go to my class," said George.

CK approached him quickly and slapped him hard on the face with his right hand.

"You bastard, I'm going to teach you a lesson today," he said.

He went back and locked the door. The classroom had large windows with two sets of big wooden shutters at the top and bottom. CK made sure all the bottom shutters were closed so no one walking past could see what was happening inside.

George was trembling in fear. He felt as though he would piss in his shorts at any moment. But bravely, he stayed focused on the plan.

"Sir, can you tell me what I have done?" he asked, pointed his bag at the prefect.

"I'll tell you what you've done," yelled CK. "You've been annoying me ever since I first saw you. With your foreign accent and expensive things, you think you are better than me. You think your rich daddy is going to protect you? You have a face like a girl... such a pretty mouth..."

George recoiled in fear. He had heard stories about the prefect from some of the boarders in the school. Most of it had not made much sense to him. There was talk that Summan Patel, an effeminate-looking boy in the eighth standard, was CK's "homo."

"If you do anything to me, I'll report you to the Principal," George blurted out desperately.

"And what do you think that old fart, Negative, will do?" asked CK.

The school principal, Reverend Samuel David, had been nicknamed "Negative" by the students. Rev. David's hair and beard were completely white while the rest of his body was almost jet black. Some years ago, someone had remarked that his black and white portrait in the annual yearbook, where he was dressed in a white priest's cassock and black belt, looked more like a film negative than a photo print. Since then, the name had stuck. If Reverend David was aware of his nickname, it appeared that he did not care because he used the same photograph year after year.

"You really think I'm scared of Negative?" asked CK. "He should be afraid of me. I know that kala kutha, spends his evening boozing with the other priests."

"Then, I'll tell on you to the other teachers: Mr. Gopal, Mr. Salim, Mr. Paul, and Mr. Broom,"

CK laughed. "Those chuthias will not be able to do anything. Gopal has to run to the toilet every fifteen minutes because I heard his balls are always swollen. Salim eats biriyani but he behaves like a curd-rice eating weakling, huffing and puffing while pedaling his bike. Polly is a fat saala who tries to speak with a British accent but I know he's from Lingarajpuram, saala Madrasi. And, that chigna Broom is a big loser who couldn't win a real medal in sports. Gymnastics is for sissies — the mather-chuth**."

"Mr. Broom is not a sissy," said George, pointing his bag at the Prefect. He was quite pleased that CK was making disparaging statements about several of the teachers that he had on tape now.

Then, without warning, CK suddenly lunged forward and grabbed George's collar with his left hand. With his right hand, he grabbed George's crotch hard. George began to resist fiercely, but his strength could not match that of the well-built bully. CK kept his hold on George's neck and slipped his right hand inside George's shorts.

"Ahh… does that feel good, you little bastard?" asked CK. He was drooling a little. George could also feel the bully's sour breath on his face.

"Help… help… get the principal," he tried to scream but CK had him firmly by the throat and his cries were weak and futile.

Finally, summoning all his strength, George kicked CK on the shin with his leather shoes. The prefect yelped in surprise and pain. He lost his grip on the boy momentarily. George seized the opportunity and quickly ran for the door, screaming loudly to his friends, or anyone, to save him.

*girlish man (Hindi)
**motherfucker (Hindi)

■

Walter Broom was on his way to the gymnasium after assembly when he heard what sounded like someone crying for help. The terrified voice appeared to be coming from one of the classrooms. Without hesitation, he sprinted towards the source of the sound.

Outside, hidden in the bushes, Swami and Venu heard George's cries for help as well. They ran out frantically and looked around for someone to assist them. Classes had commenced, so there was no one outside. They spotted Mr. Broom on the other side of the field running towards them. Swami sped towards him while Venu ran to the classroom and began banging on the locked door.

Inside the classroom, George had made it as far as the door before CK pounced on him and hurled him across the room. His school bag, which was slung across his body, came loose and burst open. All its contents scattered around on the floor.

CK noticed the tape recorder connected to the microphone.

"What the — !" he exclaimed. "You bastard, what is this?" He suddenly realized what George was doing.

"I'm going to kill you... you chuthia son of a bitch," he said as he approached the boy.

Suddenly there was loud knocking followed by an urgent banging on the door. It was Venu.

"George, are you okay?" he yelled. "Swami is getting help. Don't be afraid!"

CK turned around. He wasn't sure of what to do. He was angry and wanted to hurt the young boy as badly as he could. But he was also aware that there was damaging evidence against him in the tape recorder. He decided swiftly that his first priority should be to destroy the incriminating tape. So he ignored the banging on the door and concentrated on getting to the recorder.

George was more frightened than he had ever been. He knew that the situation had gone beyond anything he or his friends had anticipated. However, he tried to focus on the plan and the satisfactory denouement of this deliberate encounter and entrapment of the bully. He knew he could not let CK destroy the tape.

So, before CK could get to the recorder, George grabbed it, tucked it under his chest and curled up in a ball on the floor. The prefect reached him and tried to get it from him, but George held firm with all his strength.

"Give it to me, you bastard," said CK, pummeling him on his back with his fists. But George held on to it bravely.

Now the banging on the door got louder and much harder.

It was Mr. Broom. "Open this door at once," he commanded.

CK continued punching George and trying to get his hands on the tape recorder. George screamed in pain but refused to let go.

The door suddenly flew open with a well-timed, solid kick from Mr. Broom. He rushed inside. He saw the prefect on top of the young boy. He jumped over two rows of desks and was by the boys in a flash. He grabbed CK by the scruff of his neck and threw him across to the back of the class.

"What's going on here?" he demanded.

CK picked himself up swiftly and analyzed the situation.

"This boy was bunking class and breaking school rules so I was just punishing him lightly," he said brazenly.

Mr. Broom saw George's limp form on the floor and knelt down beside him.

"You call this punishing him lightly? This boy is hurt. Go and get the matron," he commanded Venu.

He turned to CK.

"We don't allow prefects in the school to hand out severe corporal punishment — you know that. What were you doing beating up this young boy so badly? Go and sit on that chair in the back until the principal gets here."

CK looked angry and defiant.

"I don't have to take orders from you... you dingo* bastard," he told Mr. Broom insolently.

For a moment, Walter felt a rage that threatened to overtake reason. His every impulse was to give CK a good licking right there — one that the bully would never forget. But he restrained himself and instead walked over coolly to the prefect. He stood half-a-head taller than CK so he was looking down at him when he said quietly, "You, sit down now... or I will knock you down. Am I clear?"

CK tried to stare down the PT teacher, but he couldn't. With exaggerated bravado, he sauntered over to a chair and sat down defiantly.

*offensive term for "Anglo-Indian"

By this time, several other teachers, including Principal David had rushed to the classroom. Swaminathan, after quickly appraising Mr. Broom of the situation, had run to the principal's office as well as to the teacher's lounge and begged for assistance.

CK became subdued and less belligerent when he saw there were several more adults in the room now. Nurse Mary Grace, the school matron, had been summoned by Venu and was examining George. Before he was taken away to the school's infirmary, George opened his arms to display the tape recorder he had guarded so valiantly. He gave it to the principal.

"Sir, please listen to the tape in this. It will explain everything. Phantom... I mean this prefect, CK, has been bullying us for several months. Ask Swami and Venu, they'll tell you..." He fell back on the stretcher, unable say anymore.

Principal David consulted with Swami, Venu and Mr. Broom for a few minutes. He then walked over to CK.

"For now, I think you'd better leave the school grounds, Ganguli," he said quietly. "I am suspending you until the school board investigates the matter. If we feel it is required, we shall bring the police into the picture. Do you have anything to say?"

CK was clearly out of his element now. However, it was not in his nature go away quietly.

"Yes," he said, "I have something to say... Fuck you... fuck you... and, especially, fuck you!" he said, pointing one by one to George, Principal David and Mr. Broom.

He then squared his shoulder and walked out insolently from the classroom.

■

A few weeks later, the school board unanimously decided to expel C.K. Ganguli from the school. They had heard the entire recording made by George along with the testimony of Venu and Swaminathan.

Several more boys in the school came forward with other horrific accusations about the prefect. There were complaints of beatings, torture, robbery and abuse from several of the juniors.

The police were called, in but Ali Khan, the Superintendent for the Richmond Town district told the principal that they did not have enough evidence to arrest C.K. Ganguli.

"If we don't have any real proof that he actually abused the boys, the judge will automatically just dismiss the case. This recording just has galia* about the teachers on it. Your school name will simply be dragged up in the mud in the newspaper headlines," he said.

George's parents were very shocked and upset to hear what had happened. His mother's brother Abraham Verghese, who the family called "Ebby," was a high-ranking member of the Bangalore police but at George's insistence, and the principal's assurance that every avenue had been pursued, they decided not to ask the police to further investigate or publicize the incident.

There was, however, one person who felt very strongly that justice had not been done in this matter and that CK could not be simply allowed to walk away without being taught a lesson. He decided he had to do something about it.

*curses (Hindi)

Chapter 5
Walter Broom vs. C.K. Ganguli

C K was playing billiards at the Ace of Spades, a social club on Serpentine Street, when Walter Broom walked in. It was a week after the school had sent a letter to Arthur Pias, his appointed guardian at the Methodist Mission, stating that he was being expelled from the school. CK was livid at this because it was going to affect his existence. Until then, he had enjoyed free room, board and schooling since he was seven years old.

CK had been abandoned by his parents in the slums of Calcutta, and would most probably have ended up as a victim of his circumstance if a Methodist charity group hadn't found him and taken him in. He spent a few months at an orphanage in Calcutta and was then sent to Baldwin Boys' School in Bangalore, which was also affiliated with the Methodist church.

Pias had always suspected that the boy had an evil streak in him. Because he had nowhere else to go, CK even spent weekends with the priests and staff at the Methodist Mission Home. Whenever he was there, many residents complained that money was missing from their rooms. Others said they had seen him abusing the younger boys, or smoking in the lavatory.

As he grew older, CK became friends with many of the ruffians in the area. He even stopped going to the Mission on weekends, or during school vacations, as he was supposed to and instead hung around in the bars and billiard parlours with the petty criminals of the area. However, he always showed up promptly every Sunday evening to collect his weekly stipend of fifty rupees from the Mission.

A few days after he received the letter from the principal of the school, Mr. Pias terminated C.K. Ganguli's sponsorship as well. He had called the Bishop and explained the whole situation to him. He convinced him of the ramifications to the Mission of associating with such a character. CK had turned eighteen years of age a few months earlier, so he was not legally a ward of the Mission anymore.

Arthur Pias was not someone who usually enjoyed doing such tasks, but he felt a strange gloating feeling inside that went against his better nature when he passed on the bad news to CK.

"Ganguli, I'm sorry, but we are going to cancel your scholarship here. The accusations against you are too serious. I hope you find your way in life but it cannot be here or with this organization. The Bishop has kindly instructed me to give you two hundred rupees to help you at this time. After that, you are on your own, I'm afraid."

"You chuthia bastards," responded CK angrily, "I'll find a way to get back at all you mother-fuckers someday!" Then, thumbing his chin, he stormed out. However, he made sure he stopped at the accountant's office to collect his two hundred rupees before he left the premises.

CK moved in with Yusuf, a petty criminal in the area, who rented a room at the Langford Boarding House. He left most of his belongings at the godown* of a marble dealer on Hosur Road who owed him a favor. The room had two beds so Yusuf didn't mind his new guest. His rent would still stay the same and maybe his guest would give him money now and then, or at least pay for food sometimes.

Although his activities always tended to veer towards dishonesty and deception, CK was surprisingly rather good with his money. In spite of the fact that he was a full-time boarding student, he had been involved in all sorts of minor criminal endeavors in the past few years. This included scalping cinema tickets, pick pocketing, black-marketing liquor and working as an enforcer for Naseer Rehman, the dada** who controlled most of the juvenile street beggars in the Bangalore Cantonment area.

CK always lived very frugally and saved as much money as he could. In a little more than three years, he had squirreled away almost 30,000 rupees. Not trusting banks, he kept it hidden in several locations all over the neighborhood. After living for free

*basement/warehouse
**underworld don (Hindi)

and collecting a stipend from the Methodist Mission for so many years, the very thought of spending his own money on room and board annoyed him. He blamed all his present misfortunes on Walter Broom. So, he reacted in surprise and anger when Mr. Broom walked into the Ace of Spades.

"You chuthia, I'll kill you…" he exclaimed when he saw the PT teacher.

"Ganguli, you better be careful that you don't get into deeper trouble that you are already," said Mr. Broom coolly.

Amarnath Raj, who owned the Ace of Spades club, quickly intervened. He didn't want a fight to break out inside. Although most of his clientele tended to be criminals and crooks, he wasn't very proud of this fact. Amarnath had always wanted to be a respectable businessman. Unfortunately, none of his more socially acceptable ventures had been successful, and this was all he had now. He wished he could attract a better class of customers to his establishment — customers like Mr. Broom.

"Ganguli-bhai, keep your anger in check, yaar," he said. "There are police constables at the methai shop next door."

"I haven't come here to fight with you now," said Mr. Broom to CK. "I know how angry you are and how much you hate me. I have to admit that I feel the same way. So, I have come here with an offer, Ganguli."

"What offer? Do you want to suck my cock?" asked CK.

"No, even better," said Mr. Broom. "I'll fight you."

"What? I thought you didn't want to fight here, saala."

"Not here, Ganguli, not today. But how about on Saturday at Joe's Boxing Gym on Berlie Street?"

"Why at the gym? Why can we do it in some field?" asked CK.

"Let's do this like gentlemen, even though you're not one," said Mr. Broom. "Also, if we fight on the street, the police can get involved. Instead, if we do it in the boxing ring, it will be a match. You'll have a chance to thrash me without getting into trouble with the police. We'll keep fighting until only one of us is left standing."

CK thought about this offer for a moment. He was confident he could beat the gym teacher. In his mind's eye, he pictured the bruised and bloodied face of Walter Broom as he smashed him into the ground, again and again. He even felt a little aroused at the thought.

"Do we have to fight with boxing gloves?" he asked.

"Yes, otherwise it would be a street fight, which is illegal," said Mr. Broom.

CK had never boxed in his life, although he had used his fists fighting on the streets since he was eight years old. Just a few weeks ago, he had punched out a young boy who was holding out on the money he got from begging on the streets for Naseer Rehman. CK had knocked him unconscious with one punch to the side of his head. Days later, the boy was still incapable of speaking clearly.

"Okay, you bastard," he told Mr. Broom. "I'll fight you anywhere. You'll wish you hadn't thought this up, you lousy dingo."

"Good. Then it's next Saturday at five o'clock in the evening at Joe's Boxing Gym on Berlie Street," said Mr. Broom. "If you don't come, everyone will know you for the coward you are," he added.

"Oh, I'll be there. When you have had time to think about it, you come back here and beg me to suck my cock instead," said CK.

Without saying any more, Mr. Broom turned and left the club. Amarnath Raj, who was listening, let out a sigh of relief and anticipation.

■

The next day, the school was abuzz with the news that Mr. Broom would be fighting CK in a boxing match on Saturday. Joe's Boxing Gym was located only a few blocks from the school and most of the students wanted to be present for this unprecedented fight. This was even more exciting than a boxing match between Mohammad Ali and George Foreman, as far as they were concerned.

The Scrimshankers were overjoyed with the outcome of their plan and ecstatic thinking about what was going to happen. Things could not have turned out better. CK had been expelled from the school, and on Saturday he would also receive the thrashing he so richly deserved.

"I can't wait for Saturday," said Swaminathan. "I told my mother it was a school boxing match."

"I spoke to my parents about it, and my father said he will take us all there in his car," said George.

"I told my mother I am coming to your house, George," said Venu, who had no intention of telling his parents any more than they needed to know.

The principal and teachers at Baldwin Boys' School talked about the matter. They decided to allow the boarding students who wanted to attend the fight to gather in the school hall on Saturday afternoon at four o'clock and walk together with a few resident teachers to the venue. The day scholars would have to ask their parents to take them if they wanted to attend the event.

Like the students, most of the teachers also felt that CK deserved some form of punishment for his bullying and abuse. Many had unpleasant personal experiences with the prefect in the past. Mr. Broom personified all their collective anger and hopes for retribution. There were also those who wondered if Mr. Broom could indeed take on C.K. Ganguli.

"What if that Ganguli manages to defeat Broom in the ring?" Mr. Gopal, the chemistry teacher asked. "It would literally be a blow for the school. We will become the laughing stock of the City," he told the principal in the teachers' dining room during lunch.

"Even if I wanted to, I don't think I can stop this fight," said Rev. David. "Broom will go ahead with it whether we approve of it or not. Since they are not fighting on the school grounds, and because Ganguli is no longer a student here, it has nothing to do with the school anymore."

"My money is on Broom," said Mr. Paul. "He seems to be a very chalu* fellow."

"Yes, but Ganguli is a street thug," said Mr. Aziz. "I'm not sure Broom will be able to beat him so easily."

"Well, it promises to be an interesting match," said the principal.

Miss Cynthia Benedict nodded dreamily. "I think Walter will make us all proud," she said.

Unknown to the others, she had been in bed with him the previous evening in his tiny apartment at the edge of the school grounds. She had felt the taut, hardness of his body as they made love. She could somehow tell that just beneath his polished exterior and gentlemanly manners, he was someone who could be every bit as dangerous and tough as C.K. Ganguli.

■

The day of the fight arrived, and it promised to be an exciting one for the whole neighborhood. Almost everyone in the area had heard about it. The gamblers and bookies had been focusing on

*capable (Hindi)

just this event for the past few days. It appeared that C.K. Ganguli was favored to win by the punters with four-to-one odds against Mr. Broom. They reasoned that a middle-aged PT teacher and gymnast could not be a serious challenge to a young, seasoned street fighter and thug like Ganguli.

Joe Fernandez, who owned the gym where the match would take place, had set a ticket price of five rupees for anyone who wanted to watch the event inside. The gym featured two boxing rings with three rows of seating all around. However, because Joe anticipated a large crowd for the fight, he had removed one of the raised stages and moved the other one to the middle of the room. He had then taken out all the folding chairs and made it a standing-only event. He estimated that about three hundred people could fit inside.

Because it was a Saturday, the Scrimshankers met in the morning at the Graveyard. They could barely contain their excitement. Swami and Venu had told their parents that they would not be coming home until late in the evening. The plan was that they would go over to George's house in the afternoon and ride in his father's car to the event. They discussed what they thought would happen at the fight as they sat on Captain Saunders' gravestone.

"Mr. Broom will finish CK off in a few minutes," said Swaminathan.

"Yes," said Venu, "that Phantom will wish he was in the deep, dark jungles of Africa after this."

"I wonder what CK will do," said George thoughtfully. "He's a sly crook, so I'm sure he'll have something up his sleeve."

"I hope Mr. Broom is prepared for some cunning golmal* from him," said Venu.

At quarter-past-four in the afternoon, the boys all jumped into the back of George's father's shining car, a tan-colored Standard Landmaster. They loved riding in the car. Among the three boys, only George's father owned a car. Swami's father used a Vespa scooter, while Venu's father drove a Vicky moped.

The Landmaster was a big, solid and roomy station wagon. To Swami, the best thing about it were the turn signals — two little lighted arrows next to the front doors that popped out and flashed when they were turned on.

George's father, Mohan Chandy, was a jovial, handsome, slim man with straight black hair combed back and a pencil-thin

*trickery (Hindi)

mustache. He reminded Swami of Alain Delon, the French actor from the recent movie, Red Sun, with Charles Bronson. He had gone to work that morning, but was now in leisure clothes. He wore a woven synthetic, short-sleeved, knitted shirt that had a black and white hounds-tooth pattern, narrow black trousers and black suede loafers. He looked very dashing. Swami and Venu liked him very much. George and he always got along well with each other. Mohan Chandy also talked to the boys like they were older, and not just insignificant children as most adults they knew did.

He smiled at the Scrimshankers, "Are we ready to go?" he asked.

"Yes, Uncle," said Swami and Venu.

"Dad, thanks for taking us," said George.

Swami and Venu were awed by the easy friendship George had with his father. Neither Venu nor Swami could imagine talking to their fathers' the way George spoke to his.

"So, what do you think, boys? Will your Broom sweep the floor with that Ganguli fellow? He appears to be a very capable chap."

"Yes, Uncle, I think CK will become chutney," said Venu laughing.

Everyone laughed too. On their way to the venue, George and his father discussed the Vietnam War and other events that were taking place in the United States. Swami and Venu listened to them intently while happily looking out of the window of the big car as they drove through the city.

■

When they got to Berlie Street, there already appeared to be a throng of people in the vicinity of Joe's Gym. George's father parked his car on an adjacent street, and the four of them walked up to the gym.

"Hmm... five rupees each? I suppose he has to make some money too," Mr. Chandy said as he handed twenty rupees to the man at the entrance.

The gym had once been a social hall and occupied over 2,000 square feet of space. The ring had been moved to the middle and people had already begun standing around it. George's father led the boys to a vacant spot right next to the ring. The contingent of students and teachers from Baldwin Boys' School hadn't arrived yet so there was still a lot of standing room at the gym. C. K. Ganguli was there and was pacing around nervously at one corner of the ring. Next to him, as his assistant, stood Rafiq Ali, a butcher from Johnson Market, who claimed to be a relation of Haji Mastan, the notorious Bombay underworld smuggler and don.

CK was wearing tight black shorts and nothing else. He was barefoot, and his body glistened with oil and sweat. He had the stocky build of a weightlifter with well-defined muscles that rippled under his skin. The spectators looked at him in awe as he flexed his muscles and stretched himself against the ropes.

The gym filled up quickly as more people, including the boarders from the school, came inside. Fernandez had offered Principal David a special bulk rate of three hundred rupees for the entire school group. Over hundred students and teachers who resided at the school had elected to come.

The referee for the match was going to be none other than Joe Fernandez himself. He had also hand-picked three judges for the event: Kaleem Durani, a well-known youth politician from the area; Brigadier Ebenezer Kamat, a retired army officer who had boxed for the Services team; and Arvin Kumar, an official with the Sports Selection Committee at the Bangalore Kanteereva Stadium. The judges were sitting at a long table on metal chairs in a cordoned-off area just below the stage.

Promptly at a quarter to five, Mr. Broom arrived with his friend, Major Prakash Sinha, a boxing trainer for the Sainik School. Mr. Broom was wearing a white tracksuit and white Keds. He unzipped and removed the top of his tracksuit to display a white singlet vest. At the center of the front of the vest was a dark blue emblem in a circle about six inches across, with the words, "All India Boxing Championship 1962" and a drawing of two fighters inside.

If C.K. Ganguli had viewed Walter Broom only as a failed gymnast, this emblem should have given him a few clues to the PT master's capabilities in the boxing ring. However, CK either did not notice it or, as was more likely the case, wasn't impressed by it. He glared at his opponent from across the ring.

Mr. Broom looked around at all the students and teachers who had come to see him fight CK. He raised his hand in acknowledgement and smiled at them.

The two fighters put on boxing gloves supplied by Fernandez from his gym. They were standard ten-ounce gloves made of brown leather, and well used. CK flexed his gloves and punched the air still glaring at Mr. Broom, who appeared relaxed, unconcerned and calm, as if he was also only present as a spectator at the event.

Fernandez walked to the middle of the ring. He held a small megaphone that he had borrowed from one of his friends who supplied equipment for political rallies.

"Welcome to all you ladies and gentlemen," he began in a dramatic stage voice, although except for Miss Benedict and two or three female teachers there were no other women present.

"We are going to witness an exciting boxing match today between Mr. C. K. Ganguli, in the right corner, and Mr. Walter Broom, in the left corner. This fight will be conducted according to the Marquess of Queensberry rules. The match will have three-minute rounds up to a total of twelve rounds. If a knock-out is not achieved by the end of twelve rounds, the judges will decide who is the winner."

He turned to both the fighters and read from a small card, "There will be no hitting below the belt, holding, tripping, pushing, biting or spitting," he continued. "You are also prohibited from kicking, head-butting or hitting with any part of the arm other than the knuckles of a closed fist including hitting with the elbow, shoulder or forearm, as well as with open gloves, the wrist, the inside, back or side of the hand. Do you understand, and are both of you ready?"

"Yes," said Mr. Broom. CK just nodded his head. He hadn't even been listening to the rules.

"I'm going to rip that bastard's head off in the first round itself," he whispered to Rafiq Ali as he walked to his corner.

Fernandez rang the bell on the side of the ring and announced, "Round number one."

CK charged like a tethered bull that had just been released from his cage and took a gigantic right-handed swing at the side of his opponent's head. Had it landed, it may have caused serious harm to the teacher. Unfortunately for CK, it didn't.

Mr. Broom moved his head and torso back at the last moment. CK did not have a chance to check himself on time. He punched only air. The momentum put him off balance. He fell down heavily but he quickly jumped back up. Many of the spectators who were there to cheer Mr. Broom laughed and clapped. CK's supporters, which included a motley group of petty crooks and gamblers from the neighborhood, appeared a little worried. They had money on him in this fight.

With a smile that didn't reach his eyes, Walter Broom waited patiently for his opponent to get back up. The two fighters then jabbed, punched and blocked without doing much damage to each other for the next few minutes.

Finally, with a sudden burst of energy, CK attacked the teacher again with a quick right-and-left combination. Neither reached their target. Mr. Broom was much faster than his attacker. He stepped aside nimbly and jabbed CK a quick uppercut with his right hand. The blow hit CK squarely in the middle of his chest and sent him flying back against the ropes. As he bounced back, Mr. Broom stepped forward and punched him hard with his right fist in the middle of his face. CK yelped in pain and surprise. His nose started to bleed.

The bell went off just then. Referee Fernandez called out time and sent the fighters back to their corners. Mr. Broom sauntered over to Major Sinha, and the two friends spoke quietly as if they were on coffee break at the canteen.

CK walked slowly to his corner. Rafiq Ali was not impressed with his performance so far.

"Aare bhai, you didn't hit him even once," he exclaimed. CK glared at him angrily.

Fernandez sounded the bell. "Round number two," he said.

CK was more cautious now. He circled around the ring slowly following Mr. Broom. He felt a little out of breath now. He realized that it would not be easy to take down the teacher. He looked once more at the emblem on Walter's vest and it began to suddenly make sense to him. He felt betrayed. He had expected an easy victory, but this fight wasn't going as he had planned. Then rage took over. *He was going to beat up this chuthia. Nothing would stop him.*

He attacked again fiercely. Mr. Broom was dancing lightly on his feet with his left hand crossed firmly across his chest in a classic defensive stance and making small taunting jabs with his right fist. CK rushed him with both fists flailing wildly. He was very strong and decided he could over-power the teacher with brute force. He was wrong.

Mr. Broom pivoted on his feet like the gymnast he was. As CK reeled off balance, he jabbed him with a hard left on his right cheek. Then, as CK was trying to regain his footing, Mr. Broom hit him again with a solid right hook on his chin. The blow knocked CK backward and on to the ground. The crowd of Mr. Broom's supporters roared. The gamblers and goondas shook their heads silently in disapproval and disgust.

CK got to his feet groggily. Fortunately for him, the bell ending the round went off just then. He walked back to his corner slowly. He realized he couldn't defeat the PT teacher in a fair boxing match. He had come prepared for just this eventuality. He nodded to Rafiq Ali.

As planned, CK sat down on the stool in his corner while Rafiq Ali threw a towel over his hands. Then Rafiq's hands dipped quickly into his bag and stealthily pulled out a stubby, tightly wrapped roll of coins. He swiftly put his hand under the towel and put it into CK's right glove. He then pulled out a short strip of adhesive tape and stuck the roll to the inside of the glove. This was something CK had learned while fighting in the streets: a roll of coins inside the fist could increase the power of a punch many times over. It would feel as hard as an iron fist on the teacher's face and cause severe damage. His new strategy now was to wait for the right opportunity and then hit just one hard blow somewhere on Mr. Broom's head that would knock him out completely.

The bell rang for the third round. CK got up wearily but with a new vigor. He parried with Mr. Broom waiting for his opportunity. He smiled to himself thinking about how it would feel when he hit the teacher on the side of his head.

Mr. Broom appeared calm and relaxed, except for the fact that he had a dangerous glint in his eyes. He had known that something had changed as soon as he felt CK's right glove on his fist. Every quick jab now appeared to have much more power than before. Having done his own share of street fighting, Mr. Broom realized exactly what CK had done. He was suddenly overwhelmed with anger and disgust at the actions of C.K. Ganguli. He had heard details of all the bullying and abuse that the Prefect had inflicted on the young boys in the school. He looked straight into CK's eyes and shook his head disapprovingly.

At that moment, CK realized that Mr. Broom knew about the roll of coins hidden in his fist, as well as maybe a lot of things about him he had told no one else. He felt like his life was spiraling out of control. Everything was moving in slow motion. He could hear the shouts and cheers of the spectators supporting Mr. Broom. This had turned into a B-rated movie where he was the lousy villain who was being thrashed by the handsome hero. He snarled like a cornered rat and launched one last desperate attack at the PT teacher.

"*I just have to hit him in the head once,*" CK told himself as he lunged at Mr. Broom with his right fist.

Instead of moving back, however, this time Mr. Broom stepped forward and ducked under CK's punch. The momentum carried CK's body over Mr. Broom's head. The PT master stood up suddenly, and CK found himself sailing over Mr. Broom uncontrollably. He landed heavily in the dirt and sawdust on the wooden stage.

He got up unsteadily. The back of his neck hurt. His vision was a bit blurry. He could see Mr. Broom smiling mirthlessly at him. He lowered his head down and charged madly, intending to butt the Master with his head and then punch him out. He didn't care about observing the Marquess of Queensberry rules anymore.

But once again, Mr. Broom wasn't where he should have been. He stepped quickly to his right, and as CK went past with his head down he kicked him hard with the bottom of his left foot squarely on the buttocks. It appeared that the master had also decided to disregard gentlemanly boxing rules.

The kick sent CK flying all the way across the ring and left a dusty impression of Mr. Broom's Keds on the back of his black shorts. Most of the spectators, including those on CK's side, were now laughing loudly and cheering. CK got up painfully and turned around to face his opponent in shame and humiliation. He saw the teacher coming towards him, and for the first time in his life he felt something he had never experienced before — fear!

Mr. Broom stepped up and jabbed CK with his left fist a few times until CK was against the ropes. Then, keeping him pinned, he punched him on his chest and face repeatedly. CK could feel each punch exploding on his body. He tried to bring up his arms to defend himself but they didn't seem to have any strength left. He felt his nose break and blood streaming down his face. He could barely see now because his eyes were cut and swollen. He wanted to punch Mr. Broom at least once with his loaded right fist but the PT master had his arm trapped in a vice-like grip. Then, with a final roundhouse punch to the side of his head, Mr. Broom sent CK crashing to the floor.

Referee Fernandez stepped up to the fallen C.K. Ganguli and looked at Mr. Broom in wonder. He waited a few moments and then began to count slowly.

"One... two... three... four... five... six... seven... eight... nine...ten!"

CK hadn't moved. "The winner by a knockout is Mr. Walter Broom," he announced to the judges as well as the spectators.

CK appeared to be completely unconscious. He lay on his back with his arms splayed out on the floor.

"Get this man some medical attention," said Mr. Broom to Fernandez. "And check inside his right glove. You'll find a roll of coins taped there," he added.

The referee opened up CK's right glove and was astonished by what he saw.

"This is unacceptable," he told the judges. "This man was cheating as well. He has a roll of coins taped to the inside of his glove. This is against all boxing rules."

There was angry murmuring from the crowd, including the gangsters, punters and chamchas*. They looked for Rafiq Ali but he had quietly disappeared from the scene.

The students and teachers were cheering wildly. They stared in surprise and delight when Miss Benedict, unable to contain herself, ran up and embraced Mr. Broom.

Someone had called the police. The criminal elements among the spectators slunk away silently. A doctor looked over CK and declared that he did not need to go to the hospital. But he appeared disoriented and confused by what was happening around him.

However, a few minutes later amidst the celebration, CK managed to disappear stealthily and unnoticed. Mr. Gopal later claimed he had seen CK limp painfully into a waiting auto-rickshaw and speed away into the night, wearing nothing else but his black shorts.

Indeed, no one in Bangalore who was acquainted with C.K. Ganguli ever saw him again. It was rumored that he had found a job on a fishing trawler headed for Australia. Some claimed he had gone to Bombay and become an enforcer for Chota Ibrahim, a ruthless Mafia don. Others said that he had joined the French Foreign Legion.

*sycophants (Hindi)

Chapter 6
Wonder Years

The next few years were ones of discovery and wonderment for the Scrimshankers. Adolescence is usually a magical and exciting time. These are years when the true joys of living are revealed and previews of what life has to offer are experienced for the first time. The human condition in all its glory, majesty, anxiety and absurdity, becomes abundantly clear as an unavoidable part of existence. It is a time when lifelong interests in literature, history, philosophy, science, mathematics, music and theology are forged, when young mortals begin their quest to reach for the stars and beyond. And, it all usually begins with the wonderful world of books and music.

George always had copious amounts of books at home. When he was a child in Long Island, New York, his mother had enjoyed going to all the yard sales in the neighborhood. She always made it a point of buying every age-appropriate book she could find. As a result, he had acquired all the children's classics as well as the complete series of both the *Tom Swift* and *Hardy Boys* books.

When his family relocated to Bangalore, George had brought along most of his books with him. Later, when he met Swami and Venu, they introduced him to Enid Blyton novels. He had completed reading the entire *Famous Five* and the *Adventure* series in less than a year.

George's father was an avid reader of pulp fiction, particularly of the hard-boiled crime and adventure variety. There were bookshelves full of Mickey Spillane, Alistair MacLean, Desmond Bagley, Leslie Charteris, Perry Mason, Raymond Chandler,

Dashiell Hammett, Ross MacDonald and James Hadley Chase in the house. George had also discovered a suitcase of more adult paperbacks by Harold Robbins, Nick Carter and Ted Mark in the bottom of his father's bedroom cupboard.

■

Although Swaminathan did not have many books at home, his father, R. Venkatasubramanian, or Venkat as he was known, had always taken him to the British Council Library every Saturday morning since he was quite young.

The goal of the British Council in its charter was outlined as *"promoting abroad a wider appreciation of British culture and civilization by encouraging cultural, educational and other interchanges between the United Kingdom and elsewhere."*

The library was a godsend for the people of Bangalore. There were no other libraries that had the same selection of books and periodicals anywhere else in the city.

Venkat loved books, even though he was not a very prolific reader himself. His main reading material was the *Reader's Digest* he received in the mail each month. It usually took him two weeks to complete an issue from cover to cover. His hobby, and a source of immense pride and joy for him, was the shelf of *Reader's Digest* Volumes he had put together in the drawing room. These were arranged in chronological order and boasted every issue ever published since January 1961. To preserve and protect them, he had hardbound every six issues into volumes at the local printer. It was one indulgence he permitted himself. Each year's volume was bound in a different colored Rexine and had the dates printed in gold on the spine.

Swami had been explicitly prohibited from removing any of the volumes from the shelf without his father's permission. He did so quite frequently, however, when his father was away. Once, while eating a ripe Alphonso mango and laughing uncontrollably while reading the *"Humor In Uniform"* section of the April 1969 issue, he had inadvertently stained the entire spread with sticky mango juice. Fortunately, his father wasn't aware of it yet.

The British Council Library was located next to St. Mark's Cathedral, above the popular Koshy's Restaurant. After their morning tiffin* every Saturday, Venkat would take Swami to the

*South Indian term for snack
between meals

library on his Vespa scooter. Father and son both enjoyed this outing very much. Swami loved sitting behind his father on the scooter and hugging him around his waist as he breathed in the comforting and familiar smell of dhobi*-starch and talcum powder on his father's shirt as they zigzagged their way through the crowded streets.

Ever since he was a young man, Venkat always dressed in exactly the same way: in white. Whether he was at the bank, at home, or elsewhere, he always wore his self-imposed uniform of starched white trousers, white half-sleeved shirt, thin black belt and black leather shoes with laces. He also usually carried a black, gold-capped, Parker fountain pen clipped to his left breast pocket.

"I used to always wear a white shirt and white pants when I was a boy in school. When I came out, I missed it so much that I decided that I would continue wearing it as my uniform for the rest of my life," he told Swami.

"A uniform gives a person pride, discipline and humility. Our beloved Mahatma Gandhi wore only a white dhoti for most of his life for this very reason," he added with fervor. Venkat loved to talk about his years as a young boy during the freedom movement.

"It was a time when Gandhiji inspired all Indians to have pride and patriotism," he reminisced. "I was quite young, but I still remember the excitement and hope during the years after independence. These days, I'm not sure what has happened to all that. Now, we have an Emergency put in place by another Gandhi that is curtailing our freedom. I am sure the Mahatma would be very disappointed with the developments in our country."

Prime Minister Indira Gandhi had declared a state of emergency a few months earlier. Many civil liberties, including the freedom of the press, had been suspended. Several opposition leaders, including the popular labor organizer, George Fernandez, had been arrested and reportedly even been beaten by the police. Swami was very much influenced his father's strong political views and passionate outrage.

"You mean even the newspapers cannot write the truth about what is happening?" he had asked indignantly.

"Yes," said Venkat. "Until this Emergency is lifted, the Press is not allowed to write what they want about the government. This goes against the basic rights in a democracy like ours," he added,

*Indian laundry service

fuming with anger.

■

Entering the British Council Library was like stepping into another world. It was hard to imagine, once inside, that right outside there existed the chaos and incongruity that are part and parcel of every Indian city. One could usually find: A few cows sprawled on the footpath outside amidst a heap of dung and hay... Vendors with little baskets attached to the back of their bicycles selling guavas, sliced cucumbers, roasted peanuts, mangoes and confectionery... Executives in suits and ties walking past nimbly avoiding the garbage, mud and excrement on the streets... Shaggy-haired intellectuals reading newspapers and smoking as they made their way leisurely to Koshy's Restaurant for their daily rendezvous with friends... Pedestrians, cyclists, auto-rickshaws, motorbikes, scooters, and cars vying with each other amidst a cacophony of horns, beeps and shouts... Young barefoot children dressed in rags chasing each other on the street while their parents worked at a construction site nearby carrying loads of stone sand and cement like Sisyphus up and down rickety ladders with little metal troughs balanced precariously on their heads... A group of cheerful lepers squatting outside the big wooden gates of the majestic St. Mark's Cathedral displaying their missing digits and bandaged hands while begging for alms from people passing by... Half-naked young mothers in thin saris with babies on their hips with their emaciated breasts exposed selling newspapers and magazines to motorists at the traffic light...

These sights and sounds are so common and pervasive in Bangalore, that most of its denizens are quite immune to them. They might instead look at a Western tourist with his camera pointed at this mise-en-scène and wonder in surprise what amongst it would merit capturing on film for posterity.

Inside the library, however, the discipline and order of the British Raj was still impeccably maintained. There was a large sign posted just inside the doors that said, "SILENCE," and underneath it to emphasize the point, "Please Do Not Talk." Swaminathan knew from experience that even a slight whisper could attract the ire of the vigilant librarians at once. It was rumored that repeat offenders were barred from ever coming back.

Swaminathan loved the smell of the new books in their tight, clear, cellophane wrapping. Sometimes he liked to loiter around near the counter where the library assistants wrapped the new hardbound books in cellophane. He was fascinated by the way they measured, cut, wrapped and sealed each book. Several times, he had tried doing the same thing with his textbooks using a plastic bag from one of the sari shops. The results, however, were not entirely satisfactory.

Swaminathan's initiation into the exciting world of books began with the *Noddy* series by Enid Blyton when he was in the fourth standard. After that, he was hooked. By the time he was in the eighth standard, he had read all the Enid Blyton mystery novels, as well as most of the other British schoolboy series in the library, such as *Billy Bunter, Jennings, William* and *Biggles*.

He usually took home seven books, the maximum number allowed by the library, with him every Saturday. Every night, after the rest of his family had gone to sleep, he would sit up in his bed with a pile of books on one side and some tasty savories, like mixture, roasted peanuts or masala chips on the other side, munching abstractly and reading hungrily.

■

Venu was never very interested in reading novels. He found them to be rather boring. For him, just getting through his English literature assignments was hard enough. When Swami once asked him to go to the British Council Library with him, Venu retorted, "Why would I get more books to read if I don't have to?"

He was, however, very fond of pouring over his science books, particularly his biology textbook, and looking at the diagrams of human body organs. He also enjoyed browsing through the medical and pharmaceutical literature that came to "Get Well Medicals," his father's medical store that was located at the end of Commercial Street.

From the time he started going to the eighth standard, his father made Venu work every evening at the medical shop. He had to manage it completely on his own for a few hours while his father went home to rest and to eat his dinner. In a short time, Venu had become quite familiar with all the medical and household products carried in the store.

Only a few of the customers that came to buy medicines at the store actually had prescriptions from a doctor. Instead, as was the common practice in India, people usually just described the ailment to the person behind the counter of the medical store who gave them what he thought was the best medicine for it. Venu's father, M. Krishnachandra, had given him loose instructions on what could be handed out for most of the common illnesses that people came seeking treatment for.

"For simple fever of less than two days, give one strip of Crocin. For more than two days, add a strip of Tetracycline. If they also have cough and chest congestion, add a bottle of Waterbury's Compound. Any cuts, rash, itch or burns give a tube of Burnol. For anything else, tell them to come back after an hour or two."

Krishnachandra was a very stern and serious man. He did not talk much to his wife and children or even his relatives, friends and acquaintances. He was conservative and old-fashioned in his views. He believed that a man was the provider for the family and that the woman was the caretaker. Children were supposed to simply obey adults without asking any questions. He had no patience for even the smallest bit of disobedience from his children.

One day, while Swami and George were waiting outside the school for Venu, they were shocked to see his father slap him hard across his face when he got down from the Vicky moped. When they asked him what had happened, Venu said it was because he had been fidgeting and moving about on the seat of the moped while his father was driving him to school. Both his friends were shocked because neither of their parents ever slapped them on their faces even for much more serious offences.

Life wasn't easy for Krishnachandra. In addition to Venu, he had three other young children. Although his medical shop was on one of the busiest streets in the Cantonment area, his income was barely enough to provide for his family.

Furthermore, an enterprising businessman, Rajendra Kumar, had recently started another pharmacy and convenience store at the other end of Commercial Street. He called it "Bharat Pharmacy & Mini Mart." The new store was gaudily designed and decorated in bright lights and colors. It boasted a much larger selection of both pharmaceutical and home products. Kumar's shop also featured air-conditioning inside, which he announced proudly in big, red letters on the modern, self-closing, glass doors.

In comparison, Krishnachandra's store was dimly lit and dingy. It had furniture and shelving that were over thirty years old and had been left behind by the previous owner. Without available capital or a healthy cash flow, Krishnachandra was unable to increase his product variety or improve the décor of his store to match the offerings by his competitor. He knew he would be losing customers slowly to the new store and resigned himself to just hanging on for as long as he could.

Venu enjoyed the time he spent in charge of the medical shop. When there were no customers, he did his homework or read *Amar Chitra Katha* comics, which retold stories from the great Indian epics, mythology, history, folklore, and fables.

Although most people would consider Krishnachandra's practice of leaving his young son alone in the medical shop to dispense medicine to an unsuspecting public to be irresponsible and even dangerous, Venu was a very capable and conscientious pharmacist. He made it a point to read all the information he could find on the drugs he handed out. He often felt like a doctor when people came in with ailments hoping for relief. He listened gravely to them and gave them the appropriate medicine judiciously and with much sympathy for their condition.

Many customers also came in for common household items like bulbs, batteries, glucose biscuits, razor blades, chocolate bars and hard-boiled candy. Every now and then, someone would come in and shyly ask for a box of Nirodh, the government subsidized, condom brand. These packs were easy to identify because they had a large inverted red triangle on them. Venu's father told him it was for "family planning" and left it at that.

Some nights, the Scrimshankers all hung out together at the medical shop. Although Venu could not allow friends to help themselves to the chocolate bars or other sweets at the store, they had found a way to at least have some of the Dubble Bubble Gum from the big glass jar on the counter.

As part of a sales promotion strategy by the manufacturer National Products, ten-percent of the Dubble Bubble pieces in the jar were white while the other ninety percent were pink in color. If a customer got a white piece of gum, he was allowed to pick another piece for free. The gum was wrapped individually with a twist at the ends of the wrapper. It was relatively easy for the boys to open the gum wrappers slightly, take out all the white pieces and put the rest back. They loved chewing up two to three pieces together and blowing the biggest bubbles they could. Customers, however, may have wondered why they never had any luck in picking a white piece of bubble gum at Get Well Medicals.

■

Music also played a very important role in the lives of the Scrimshankers by the time they were in their adolescent years. George had taken a liking for rock music at a very young age.

Mohan Chandy had come to the U.S. as an engineering post-graduate student from Bangalore in the early 1960s. He had quickly developed a taste for American popular music. In a few years time, he had acquired a large collection of albums by artists such as Jim Reeves, Nat King Cole, Frank Sinatra, Andy Williams, Sam Cooke and Elvis Presley. This was the soundtrack for George's early years.

As he grew older, George developed his own musical tastes. He particularly loved the music of The Beatles and The Rolling Stones, who he saw as opposite sides of the same coin. The Beatles were clean-cut and their music had beautiful melodies and lyrics while The Stones offered an edgier and more dangerous view of life with equally melodic tunes and fabulous lyrics.

By the time George came to Bangalore, he was quite an expert on rock music and had a large collection of records. He had also started learning to play the guitar. In addition to the basic musical instruction he received in public school since the second grade, he had taken a year of private guitar lessons at the Rob Evans Music School in Hicksville. He could play most of the open chords on his guitar and had started to teach himself scales from a book his mother had picked up at a yard sale.

When he met Swaminathan, he knew he had found a kindred spirit. Both boys shared the same passion for rock music.

Unlike George, however, Swaminathan never had easy access to the kind of music he loved. He managed to find it nevertheless. For rock music fans in India, the 1960s and the 1970s were years of unfulfilled musical desires. Most of the youth in the country could not afford to buy records from the music stores. Even those that could afford it had to be satisfied with the meager selection of albums that were released each year. There were only a few record stores in Bangalore that sold rock music. One was HMV Records, a subsidiary of the popular His Master's Voice Company in England.

From the time his mother allowed him to venture out on his own, Swaminathan spent as much time as he could at the HMV store on Brigade Road. It had a small section devoted to Western music that usually featured about twenty to thirty albums. They ranged from classical to pop, instrumental, rock, reggae, Motown and disco.

At first, Swami had to beg his father to go along with him. This was because he needed an adult present to request one of the soundproofed booths inside the store. These music booths had gramophone players that output sound that was infinitely better than anything he could listen to elsewhere.

Swaminathan usually picked two to three records to listen to, but the sales clerks were the only ones who could touch either the records or the gramophone. Much to his consternation, they would usually play each song only for a minute or less before going on to the next.

After a while, the employees at the HMV store recognized the fact that Swaminathan was only interested in listening to the records and would not be buying anything. So most of them looked on him as a nuisance and ignored him when he came inside. Fortunately, one day he befriended Llewellyn Martin, a young Anglo-Indian, who worked at the store.

Llewellyn played guitar and sang in a cover band named The Chiefs that performed at the Catholic Club and other venues all over the city for dances and functions. He worked part-time as a sales clerk at HMV.

The innocent, unbridled enthusiasm he saw in Swaminathan for rock music amused and interested him. He began chatting with the boy and soon realized he was talking to a walking encyclopedia of rock music.

Swaminathan was not merely satisfied with just listening to rock music: he also wanted to know everything he could on the subject. One evening, while walking with his parents on Brigade Road, he stopped at Iqbal's Books, which was literally a hole in the wall between a shoe store and a restaurant, where the proprietor had dumped a mountain of books. Most of them were without covers. They were "stripped" books that had been reported unsold to the publisher in the U.S. or Britain and supposed to have been destroyed. They had somehow made their way into Iqbal's store.

While his parents went shopping to another store, Swaminathan browsed through the hundreds of books that had been dumped on a thick canvas sheet on the ground. He had discovered a squat paperback titled, "*Rock Encyclopedia Volume 1.*" He looked through it with excitement by the yellow light of an oil lantern that hung at one corner.

The book did not have any photographs in it but it listed almost every rock band and artist in the world in alphabetical order with a few paragraphs about each of them in small print. When his parents returned to collect him, he persuaded them to part with the ten rupees needed to purchase the book.

In a few months, Swaminathan had read through the entire book several times and knew a little about every band and artist featured in it. His other source of rock music information and news came from the *Junior Statesman* magazine. If his father's hobby was the *Reader's Digest*, Swami's bordered on obsession with the *Junior Statesman*.

JS, as it was called, was a weekly, tabloid-sized magazine started in the late 1960s by *The Statesman* newspaper in India. It came out every Saturday and cost sixty-five paise. The magazine targeted the urban youth in the country and featured an eclectic collection of news stories and information. It was the only Indian magazine of its kind that covered two topics that mattered the most to Swaminathan, rock music and Hollywood movies. Every issue also had a poster as the center spread, which the magazine referred to as the "blow-up," and usually featured rock musicians, actors, cricket players, starlets and athletes.

Swaminathan kept every issue of *JS* he had ever purchased in pristine condition on the bottom shelf of the metal Godrej almarah in his room. Unlike some of the other boys he knew, who detached the blow-ups and pasted them up on their walls, Swami kept every one of his intact and inside the issue.

He guarded his *JS* magazine stash fiercely and forbade all his family members from touching his collection. Each Saturday evening, he walked over to the Higginbottham bookstore where he bought the latest issue and didn't go to bed until he had finished reading it completely.

Swami never shared his *JS* magazines with anyone. So, his parents were very surprised one day to see him give his entire collection to George to take home in the dickie of his father's car.

"Since you have come to India only recently, you must read my entire collection of *JS* to find out what is happening here," Swaminathan told his friend. "We too have rock bands here, like Atomic Forest and Human Bondage, which they have write-ups about in *JS*!"

George was the only one who understood Swami's need to share everything of value both tangible and intellectual in his life with him. He was touched and honored by the gesture.

Swaminathan's knowledge of rock music served him well when he met Llewellyn Martin, at HMV Records.

"So you really like rock music, eh?" the sales clerk asked the boy.

"Yes," said Swami, "but we don't have a gramophone at home and I don't have any records."

"So you just come here to listen?" asked Llewellyn.

"Yes, what to do…?" said the boy.

"Who's your favorite band or singer?" the clerk asked.

"The Beatles and John Lennon. Do you know the Beatles first drummer, Pete Best is an Anglo-Indian?"

"Yes," said Llewellyn. "Name three famous singers who are originally from India."

"Easy! Engelbert Humperdinck, Cliff Richards, and Freddie Mercury. Do you know Freddie Murcury's first band was called The Hectics when he lived in Bombay?"

"Who wrote *Sweet Caroline*?"

"Neil Diamond."

"What is Bob Dylan's real name?"

"Robert Zimmerman."

"Which band wrote the song *Good Vibrations*?"

"The Beach Boys."

"What about *Satisfaction*?"

"The Rolling Stones."

"Who buried Eleanor Rigby in the song by a famous band?"

"The Beatles song?" asked Swaminathan. He was stumped. He had only heard the song once on the radio and was only vaguely familiar with the tune and lyrics.

"I don't know," he conceded.

"Okay, that wasn't fair on my part. You have to listen to a song many times before you know the words," said Llewellyn. "It was Father McKenzie. This is how the verse goes," he sang… "*Eleanor Rigby died in the church and was buried along with her name. / Nobody came. / Father McKenzie wiping the dirt from his hands as he walks from the grave. / No one was saved...* We perform this song with my band sometimes," he added.

"What deadly words," said Swaminathan, "Do you know that this song was written completely by Paul even though they always said that all the songs are written by Lennon and McCartney."

Llewellyn was impressed. He felt a sense of kinship with the boy. Most of the other sales clerks in the store knew less about the records they sold than this little chap. He searched through the music rack and dug out *Revolver* by The Beatles.

"Come with me," he told Swaminathan.

They went to the back of the store where there was another little booth with a gramophone and speakers set up.

"We use this to check the records when they first come in. I listen to the entire album here many times if I like it," said Llewellyn.

He put on the record and adjusted the volume. The cool opening countdown followed by the wonderful, electric, sounds of *Taxman* filled the little room. Llewellyn let Swami sit in the booth by himself and listen to the entire record from start to finish. Swaminathan never had experienced listening to a whole album on his own before.

From that day onwards, whenever he was in the store, Llewellyn, who also happened to be the store manager's nephew, allowed Swami to listen to the store's copies of albums in the sound room if it wasn't in use. He could not believe his good fortune. Unfortunately, a few months later, Llewellyn moved to Bombay when his band was offered a job playing every night at the Taj Hotel.

A third and equally important source of light in Swami's otherwise bleak musical landscape came from radio. It included the Voice of America and Radio Ceylon.

The Voice of America, or VOA, as it was known, was started in the late 1930s by the U.S. Federal Communications Commission to "reflect the culture of the United States and to promote international goodwill, understanding and cooperation." By the 1950s it had become primarily a propaganda tool for the U.S. State Department in their efforts to thwart communism all over the world. Despite this, it was a window into the world of American culture, music and events. For Swaminathan, it allowed him access to a variety of music from the U.S. for free.

Radio Ceylon, broadcasting from nearby Sri Lanka, was Swami's other source for the latest news and music in English. Because of the lack of quality, English-oriented, programming on Air India Radio, it had become very popular in India. It broadcast a mixture of western pop music and world news in English every morning from six to ten.

Swaminathan's father had installed a large Murphy tube radio in the drawing room that picked up both VOA and Radio Ceylon signals on the medium-wave and short-wave bands quite clearly. Venkat liked to listen to the news every morning and again at night from eight to half-past-eight. The rest of the time, he allowed his son to listen to whatever he wanted.

Swami usually turned on the big radio as soon as he woke up in the morning. It took almost five minutes for the valves to warm up and come to life. Once it did, it offered a magnificently deep sound that was comforting to the boy.

He would sit sleepily in the darkness, huddled in his blanket, with just the glow of the radio twiddling the two knobs in the front, moving back and forth between the sultry voice of Shirley Perera on Radio Ceylon and the high-energy announcements of Cliff Groce on VOA, until his mother woke up and chased him away to get dressed for school.

■

Venu had come in contact with rock music much later than Swami or George. His family only listened to the Tamil and Hindi programs broadcast on All India Radio on the little transistor radio at home. Although he had become best friends with Swami in the second standard, he had not shared his friend's devotion to western music or movies. He liked watching Indian movies and listening to the popular film songs on the radio.

When the duo expanded their friendship to include George,

Venu was exposed to even more rock music. Nothing interested him very much until he heard The Eagles for the first time in the seventh standard. He was in George's house with Swami when he noticed the record on the bed.

"What is this album, George?" he asked.

"Wow... buggers, this is a great new album," said George. "My dad bought it for me just last week from Bombay. Even you might like it, Venu."

The cover featured a dazzling blue sky with some cactus bushes. On the top of the album was a small image of an eagle with its wings spread with the words, *"Eagles,"* inside it. The back cover had a larger image of an eagle with the names of the ten tracks on it. That was all.

Venu was intrigued by it for some reason. "Can you play it, George?" he asked.

"Yes, George, play it. I was reading about them in *JS*. They are a deadly band," added Swami.

"Let's go to the living room," said George, "so I can play it on the big stereo."

They walked through the spacious house to the living room where George's father had his solid-state Grundig stereo amplifier, turntable and speakers that were almost as tall at the boys. George took out the record carefully from its sleeve, put it into the turntable, turned on the stereo amplifier and delicately placed the needle on the rotating disc. Since his parents were not home, George turned up the volume so it was almost at the maximum. The down-stroke of an acoustic guitar filled the room, followed by the most wonderful song Venu had ever heard. George took out the record sleeve and passed it to his friends. They saw that the words of the songs were printed on it.

The three boys huddled around it and read the lyrics as they listened to every song on the record one by one: *Take It Easy, Witchy Woman, Chug All Night, Most of Us Are Sad, Nightingale, Train Leaves Here This Morning, Take The Devil, Early Bird, Peaceful Easy Feeling, Tryin.'* It was unlike anything Venu had ever heard. He was captivated by the melody of the songs and the wonderful harmony displayed by the vocalists.

"Can you play it again?" he asked George after they had listened to both sides completely.

George was only too happy to oblige. The three friends sat huddled together with their eyes closed listening to the music, hearing it as individuals but also subconsciously filing away the moment in their minds as a unique shared experience, somehow also knowing they were forging a bond that would last their whole lives.

Chapter 7

First Experiences

I f the preceding few years had stimulated their intellectual curiosity, the Scrimshankers were now at a stage in their adolescence when another natural inclination, girls, and an unavoidable physical transformation, puberty, were unleashed together during the most stressful time of their young lives so far, their ICSE final examinations.

For boys, the years comprising and immediately following puberty are years of excitement, bewilderment, confusion, anxiety, hope, frustration, realization and embarrassment. Hormonal signals moving swiftly from brain to gonads... stimulated libidos... morning wood... facial hair... change in voice... muscle development... strange sensations... nighttime ejaculations... uncontrollable obsessions.... Mother Nature saying, "Welcome to manhood, bugger... and good luck on the final examination!"

It was the Scrimshankers' last year at Baldwin Boys' School. The terrifying Indian Certificate of Secondary Education, ICSE, exam loomed closer with every passing day. It was their first national exam. Much of the time during the year was dedicated to reviewing all the subjects in preparation for the exam.

Of the three boys, Swaminathan usually scored the highest marks. Since the seventh standard, he was always among the top three students in all his subjects. He had a natural inclination for physics and mathematics. Because of his voracious reading habits, he was also a very good writer. His English essays were impeccable and Mr. D'Souza, the tenth standard class master, often read them out aloud to the class as an example of what was expected from top students.

George was very bright but rather easygoing in his attitude to school and exams. He spent most of his time playing his guitar, drawing or writing songs. Although he performed above average in his class exams, he did not seem to be the least bit interested in doing exceptionally well in school. On the other hand, he could spend hours on end sketching pictures in his notebook, practicing music scales or learning new chords on his guitar.

Venu did very well in the science subjects but had difficulty in the language classes, particularly Hindi. As a native Tamil speaker who could also write in it fluently, he was confounded and annoyed at having to learn another Indian language.

"Why should we South Indians have to learn so much Hindi," he exclaimed angrily one day to his friends. "I can speak it quite well but writing in the correct grammar is so bloody hard."

"It's the national language, that's why. Everyone in the country has to learn it," said Swaminathan. "I read somewhere that forty-one percent of people in India speak Hindi or some dialect of it."

"I agree with Venu," said George. "If I could choose Malayalam as my second language, I would do so much better on my exam."

"I think they should allow students to take their mother tongue as their second language," said Venu. "The chaps who speak Hindi at home have an easy time the way it is now. It is not fair to us Southies."

"Yes, that's true. Just look at the guys who get the top marks in Hindi in our class: Jyothi Singh, Ajit Thakur, Govind Verma, Raj Goenka — all North Indians! I bet they don't even need to study. We have to struggle just to pass!" said Swaminathan.

"Yes, I don't know how I will ever be able to answer essay questions about the short stories and poems in the ICSE," said George. "I bought the book with English translations but I can't even understand the questions on the tests — so how can I write the answers, that too in Hindi."

"I think we need to go for Hindi tuitions, otherwise we'll fail in the exam," said Venu.

"I've heard that the best place is with a guy named Mohiuddin, who teaches from his house on Langford Road," said Swaminathan. "He used to write the questions for the ICSE Hindi exam. Now he is retired."

"Maybe, he can still get us some questions and hints for the exam then," said George.

"I'll ask Pratap Kurien, who goes there, about the details and we can sign up for the tuition class," said Venu.

"You know, buggers," said Swaminathan. "I've heard that Mohiuddin's classes are co-ed and there are lots of students from all the girls' schools who go to him as well."

"Let's register quickly then," said George.

■

It had only been a short while since the Scrimshankers became interested in girls. Over the past few years, they had seen and felt the changes taking place rapidly inside their bodies. They began to see things in the world they hadn't noticed before: movie posters with pretty heroines... schoolgirls walking past in skirts that were a few inches above their knees... Miss Benedict's cleavage when she bent to pick something from the floor... the exposed soft curve of Miss Mohini's hips as she stood next to their desk in her sari during the geography class... and, a strange but uncontrollable, exciting hardness between their legs that came on suddenly and threatened to make itself known and embarrass them almost everywhere.

They didn't talk about these feelings to each other at first. Then one day George asked his friends casually, "So, do you chaps shag* yet?"

Swami and Venu were caught unawares. The both flushed in embarrassment.

"I... I... what about you George?" Swaminathan asked.

"I've been doing it since I was fourteen," said George.

"Well... I... I've also been doing it now and then since last year," said Swami shyly. "What about you Venu?"

"No, I've never done it," said Venu.

"Baloney, I don't believe you, Venu," said George. "Maybe you do it without knowing what you're doing, but it's still shagging. I was reading that every male does it."

Although he was dark, Venu's ears turned a deep shade of red. Truth was that he had been masturbating quite regularly for the past two years. He was ashamed to admit it, however. It somehow felt as though what he was doing something very bad. Sometimes, he looked through advertisements in the *Illustrated Weekly* until

*common term in India for
"masturbate"

73

he stopped at one that had the photograph of an attractive woman. Most times he thought about some Hindi or Tamil actress in his mind while he masturbated.

George wouldn't let it go. He couldn't believe that Venu did not masturbate.

"Venu, you can tell us. Don't be shy. It's nothing to be ashamed about. We are your best friends."

"I... I... don't," he said firmly but his face betrayed the lie.

They were in the school canteen after class. There were only a few students around. Suddenly George got up and started singing loudly, "*I shag, I shag. / I have a shag rag. / I keep a shag bag. / I shag...* See, Venu, I'm not ashamed to tell everyone. You shouldn't be afraid to admit it to us."

He then grabbed Swami's hand and the two of them began dancing around the room singing, "*I shag, I shag. / I have a shag rag. / I keep a shag bag. / I shag...*"

Venu had to laugh. George was fearless and wasn't embarrassed to do anything. Swami usually followed George's lead in such situations.

"Okay, buggers, I'll admit I shag too, okay, but I'm not going to sing that silly song with you guys here, okay?" he said.

But George just grinned and grabbed Venu's hand, pulled him up and forced him to dance with Swami and him while they sang, "*I shag, I shag. / I have a shag rag. / I keep a shag bag. / I shag...*"

The other boys in the canteen looked in amusement at the three friends singing their mad song and laughing uncontrollably. They wished they could have a friendship like that.

A group of teachers walked in just then. One of them asked, "Practicing for the school play, eh, Chandy?"

"Yes, sir," said George. "Master Bates is the main character."

"He plays on his organ a lot," added Swaminanthan.

The Scrimshankers ran out of the canteen laughing uncontrollably. The teachers shook their heads in puzzlement and exasperation as they walked over to the tea counter.

"George, I know what a shag rag is, but what's a shag bag?" Venu whispered to his friend when they were unlocking their bikes at the cycle shed.

"Oh, it's a brown paper bag with pictures of beautiful women that I cut out of my mother's magazines. I call it my shag bag," said

George, laughing.

Swami and Venu were amazed that they were talking so openly about something they had been so ashamed of before. But somehow it didn't seem shameful anymore.

■

"So you chaps want to take Hindi tuition for the ICSE, eh?" asked Mr. Abdul Mohiuddin. He was dark and extremely fat, with a thick black mustache and badly dyed, longish black hair. He sat on a large armchair that was almost filled up by his bulk.

The boys had gone to see him the next evening at his house on Langford Road. It was an old colonial bungalow with a large flower garden in front and a spacious veranda leading up to the house. Mr. Mohiuddin had just finished his last tuition class for the day. There was a pleasant smell of biriyani coming from somewhere inside the house.

For most of his life, Mr. Mohiuddin had earned a pittance as a Hindi teacher and exam writer for the board. However, after he retired, he found he could increase his income more than tenfold by just giving private tuitions. He charged each student one hundred and fifty rupees per month for three days of tuition per week. Each session lasted an hour. He conducted four separate sessions each day with approximately twenty-five students in each group. His first session for the day started at three-thirty in the afternoon, just after the schools closed, and the last session went on until eight-thirty at night.

"Okay, you fellows can start tomorrow in the fourth batch. So, you will come on Tuesday and Thursday from seven-thirty to eight-thirty in the evening and on Saturday from twelve to one in the afternoon. My goal is to make you pass the ICSE. We will concentrate on just that. I have devised a special method of preparing students so don't worry about passing anymore. But I don't put up with slackers, you hear?"

He paused for a moment and continued with a very stern expression, "If I think you are slacking off, I will kick you out of my class. Is that clear? No student who has taken tuition with me has failed the ICSE in Hindi. I have a reputation to hold up. Am I very clear about this?" he asked the boys.

"Yes, sir," they said.

"Bring one hundred and fifty rupees each with you when you come tomorrow."

■

Mr. Mohiuddin's tuition classes were every bit as hard and boring as the Scrimshankers had dreaded it would be. In addition, not one of the twelve girls in the class appeared to be either very attractive or even remotely interested in anything but performing with honors in the ICSE. Most of the boys, on the other hand, looked like they were backbenchers from various schools in the city that just wanted to scrape through the exam.

On the first day, Mr. Mohiuddin split up the Scrimshankers so they were nowhere near each other. He grinned knowingly and said, "What, you though I would let you chaps sit together? Now, stay in the same seat for every class, so I can connect your names and faces to that spot."

The students were put in two groups on adjacent sides of the large room on metal folding chairs. The tutor sat in the middle on his amply padded armchair with his back to the wall. Swami and Venu were on one side but in different rows. George was in the back row on the other end of the room.

Mr. Mohiuddin's method of preparation involved reading each of the stories and poems in the syllabus from the textbook slowly in Hindi and then explaining it in English, one paragraph at a time. Next, he read out some questions and answers he had made up which he had the students take down verbatim in Hindi in their notebooks. Lastly, he pointed out certain key words in his questions that he had the students underline.

"For the exam, all you have to do is to memorize my questions and answers," he said. "If you do that, I guarantee you will perform well. They may change a few words here and there but as soon as you recognize any of the key words in the questions, just write everything you can remember from the answers I have given you."

This seemed like a reasonable strategy to the Scrimshankers, even though it looked like it would be a very long and arduous process. In a few weeks time, they finally began to feel optimistic that they would actually pass the exam. However, each hour they spent with Mr. Mohiuddin was intolerably and excruciatingly boring.

They looked for any diversion to keep things interesting. Even Mr. Mohiuddin's poor jokes began to sound funny to them. The girls in the class started looking more attractive and interesting as the class dragged on. Venu, who sitting behind Aarti Chinappa, a bespectacled, studious girl, suddenly noticed that she had rather shapely calves... George furiously scribbled lyrics to new songs in the back of his notebook... Swaminathan slowly replayed entire movies he had seen recently, scene by scene, in his mind while appearing to look interestedly at the tuition master.

One night, Ashwin Varma, a boy from St. German's School, brought a *Rasvanti* magazine with him to the class. The Scrimshankers had never seen a pornographic magazine before. Ashwin was sitting next to George. Five minutes before class started, he nudged George and passed him the magazine.

In the absence of any quality pornography, *Rasvanti* had become quite popular in India among a certain class of people. It was published anonymously in English as well as in several regional languages. The erotic magazine was printed in dark brown ink on cheap newsprint and measured about eight inches tall by five inches in width. It usually had the close-up of a voluptuous woman's breast on the cover.

The inside pages contained only text and featured sexually explicit short stories written in questionable English. A popular recurring theme was that of a young man being seduced by a mature woman, who initiates him into the joys of sex. Each issue contained only twenty-four pages and was saddle-stitched with just one staple. Since it was an underground magazine, it did not contain any information about the publisher or where it was sold.

George looked inside the magazine that Ashwin had passed him. The first story was named, *"When The Major Was A Minor."* It detailed the sexual experiences of Major Rathore, an Indian Army officer and his housemaid, when he was just a teenager. George had never read erotica before. He quickly began to feel an uncontrollable throbbing in his pants. He hurriedly gave the magazine back to Ashwin.

"What, you've never seen a *Rasvanti*?"

"No," said George.

"I got it from my driver — I don't know where he gets it from. It's only two rupees. Go ahead and read it during class. Enjoy, bugger!" He passed the magazine back to George.

Mr. Mohiuddin entered the room. "Today, we are going to cover the short story by Munshi Premchand called *Boodhi Kaki*," he said. "This is the most important story in your syllabus. I will guarantee you that there will be at least two to three questions from it in the ICSE exam. That's why I asked you to read it at home."

George slipped the thin *Rasvanti* magazine between the pages of his textbook and started reading.

"Premchand used his stories to talk about injustices in society," said Mr. Mohiuddin. "Boodhii Kaki ek tatha anya kahani hai. It is a great story that looks at greed and the abuse of elders by their relatives. Who can tell me what happens in the story? Miss Preeta?"

A chubby girl dressed in the Sophia's School uniform stood up and said in a sing-song voice, "Boodhi Kaki's husband passed away one day, and she was all alone with no children of her own to take care of her. Her only relative was Budhiram, his wife Rupa and their two children…"

Meanwhile, George was reading about Major Rathore: "*I want to share my experience, which happened with our maidservant, when I was young, which is hundred-percent true. Believe me friends, I am not just cooking up some fantastic cock and bull story and writing it here. Our maid's name was Gulshan. She was some thirty years old lady and she was little dark. The key thing to be noticed in her was her boobs. She had very big boobs. She always wore her sari below her waist, so her navel could be seen clearly whenever she bent for sweeping or wiping the floor. By looking at her back, one could easily notice that she never wore a bra because she always wore see-through blouses…*"

"Budhiram and his wife tricked Boodhi Kaki into giving them her house by promising that they would take care of her for the rest of her life. As soon as they got ownership of her house, they started treating the old lady badly — so sad… no?" said Miss Preeta looking around. "They wouldn't even give her any proper food to eat…"

"*On that day, Gulshan came to my house wearing a green color sari, green color blouse and yellow color petticoat. On that day, I was wearing a white T-shirt and black shorts and no underwear. Gulshan, as usual started wiping the floor with a piece of wet cloth.*

While wiping, Gulshan lifted her sari up to her hips so that it does not get wet. However, her petticoat was still down covering her legs which prevents me from watching her sexy legs..." George read.

Miss Preeta continued: "Budhiram and his wife, Rupa, were very mean to Boodhi Kaki. Only their daughter, Laadli, was nice to the old woman. One day, they had the engagement of their son. The whole village was invited, but when Boodhi Kaki came out, Rupa scolded her and locked her up in her room...."

In George's world, Major Rathore also continued his story: "*She told me to start with a French kiss because she likes the taste of French kiss very much. Therefore, I locked her lips with my lips and started kissing her. Our tongues were playing with each other. After five minutes, we broke the French kiss and we started kissing each others body parts for ten minutes with the clothes on the body. After kissing each other for ten minutes, I pulled the blouse down from her breasts and out came two big watermelons. I started sucking her boobs like a small baby...*"

Miss Preethi was getting emotional now. Her voice faltered. "They don't feed Boodhi Kaki the whole day, and she is very hungry. Laadli takes a small packet of food to her, but she is still hungry. So at midnight, she goes outside with Laadli to where the leftovers from the feast are and begins to eat the crumbs of the kichori on the plates. Rupa wakes up from her sleep and, not finding her daughter in the house, comes outside looking for her. She finds the old lady and young girl sitting together eating the leftovers. Rupa is really moved and ashamed by this scene and realizes how badly they have treated the old woman. She falls at Boodhi Kaki's feet and begs her for forgiveness and serves her the best food from the kitchen..."

George was also getting to the end of his story. "*Now my lust was fulfilled. Now both of us were exhausted. Therefore, we decided to take some rest. We decided to sleep for some time with naked bodies. After getting up one hour later, we went inside the bathroom to take a bath. While taking a bath, we rubbed and washed each other's body parts with soap and water,*" narrated Major Rathore.

"What is Munshi Premchand trying to say with this story?" asked Mr. Mohiuddin suddenly. "Thank you Miss Preethi — good summary."

"Mr. Chandy, can you continue?" he said, pointing to George

who was in the back row.

By now George had an erection that was threatening to tear the seams out of his trousers. He stood up, but realizing his situation, quickly pulled out his shirttails out of his pants to cover his embarrassing bulge.

"Sir, Major Rathore... wanted to... I mean... Gulshan..." He fumbled for words. He was confused and disoriented.

"Who is Major Rathore or Gulshan? There is no Major Rathore or Gulshan in the story. Were you not even paying attention to Miss Preeta just now? Have you not read this story at home like I asked you?"

Ashwin Varma was giggling softly to his left. Venu and Swami looked at him with sympathy from across the room.

"Sir, I have a question," said Swaminathan trying to get Mr. Mohiuddin's attention away from George. "Is Boodhi her first name or is it because boodhi also means old woman in Hindi?"

The tutor held up his palm and glared at him. "I haven't finished with Mr. Chandy yet. Go on, Chandy."

"Sir, I wasn't well, so I did not read the story completely," said George.

"Okay, sit down. But I'll tell everyone once again, I won't put up with slackers, hear... If you can't do your homework, don't bother coming to class. Is that clear?" he asked George.

"Yes, sir," said the boy and quietly slipped the magazine back to Ashwin. He recounted the story of the *Rasvanti* magazine to his friends later and they roared with laughter. They were disappointed that they hadn't known about it in class earlier, to appreciate the hidden fun in the episode while it was happening.

■

By the middle of the year, the Scrimshankers were quite interested in girls. In fact, it was the only thing they usually wanted to talk about.

George had been blessed with a handsome face and a slim, athletic physique ever since he was a boy. That, coupled with his American accent, mannerisms, style and clothing made him stand out among his peers in the city. The girls riding in the public buses sometimes shouted out to him as he rode past in his red American chopper bicycle. He had become known as "Handsome Boy" to many of the girls in the various schools in the city. George was not sure how to react to the girls, however, so he remained as clueless about them as his friends were.

Swaminathan was tall, fair and lanky. He had sharp features and the intelligent face of a scholar. He wore black, horn-rimmed spectacles that made him appear even more studious than he was. He was awed and intimidated by girls, even though they occupied his thoughts day and night. He wished he had George's magnetic attraction for girls. No girl appeared to be interested in him. He was physically a little awkward and unsure of how to go about initiating contact with the opposite sex.

Venu possessed his own simple, charming way that endeared him to certain types of girls. If George was a hit with the girls from convent and missionary schools, Venu appealed to the girls who attended the state and local schools that taught in the vernacular rather than in English. He never missed an opportunity of chatting up a girl from this broad group in a mixture of English, Tamil, Kannada and Hindi. He could not be called handsome in the traditional way, but he had a very pleasant face, ebony complexion, stocky build and an attractive smile. Although he never had any actual physical contact with a girl yet, he was very comfortable interacting with them and even referred to several of them as his girlfriends.

The boys often had conversations about the girls from the various schools in the city. Swaminathan liked to look at everything from an academic and theoretical perspective. Because of his practical ineptitude with girls, he had chosen to become a student on the subject instead. He had recently purchased a book named "*Everything You Ever Wanted To Know About Sex But Were Afraid To Ask*" and had read it from cover to cover a few times. By the middle of the term, he considered himself an expert on sex, in theory at least.

"Which school in Bangalore do you chaps think has the best girls?" he asked his friends. They were in George's house.

The Chandys' residence, which had been provided for them by George's father's employer, was a large two-storied mansion with gardens both in the front and back of the house. It had a six-foot high, solid cement wall embedded with broken glass on top, all around the property. There were two metal gates, one in the front and one in the rear of the compound. The property also had an outhouse with three large rooms near the rear entrance. The family's cook and maid occupied two of the rooms. The third was vacant. George had convinced his parents to let the Scrimshankers use it as their clubhouse.

They had spent a lot of time furnishing it with bits of furniture from the main house. It had an old sofa set, side tables, a lava lamp that George had taken from his room, an old record player and shelves with books and magazines. They had a few posters on the walls: The Beatles, The Rolling Stones, Bob Dylan, Jimi Hendrix and even one of Farrah Fawcett. The Scrimshankers spent most of their spare time there. They played games, listened to music or just chatted.

"Christian schoolgirls only or parachutes as well?" asked Venu.

While the girls from the Christian schools wore one-piece dresses that ended two inches above their knees, those from the more traditional state educational institutions wore a separate blouse and a long skirt that ballooned out from waist to feet. The boys referred to them as "parachutes."

"What do you mean by the best girls?" George asked.

"Let's stay with the Christian schools in the Cantonment area for now," said Swami. "Best means overall ranking — both beauty and brains."

"My girlfriends are all parachutes," said Venu, "but it may become too hard to count all the schools then."

"So which schools are we comparing?" George asked.

Swaminathan took out his notebook. "Let's write down a list," he said. "There's Baldwin Girls, Bishop Cotton Girls, Cathedral School…"

"How about Sacred Heart and Sophia?" Venu asked.

"Okay, let's only stick with those," said George. "Even though I'm from Baldwin, I think Cotton girls are the best. The ones I've watched in the debates and music competitions in our school are really smart and pretty. Their school captain, Archana Singh, is fantastic-looking as well… she looks like a model, you buggers! Roopa Paul is such a fantastic singer. She comes to St. Mark's with the boarders every Sunday, but they leave the Church as soon as the service is over. In sports, their captain, Anupam Soodhi, is the best hockey player in the girls' inter-school tournaments, and she has great legs! So I'll pick Cotton's girls. Sorry Baldwin girls."

"Call me loyal, but I am sticking with the girls from our sister school," said Swaminathan. "Maybe it's their uniform, but they look so much better than the Cotton girls in their uniform. I like the Sophia uniform too — they have the brown and tan checkered blouses and dresses. It is more interesting than plain white, but once, near Mayo Hall, a girl from that school yelled at me for almost hitting her cycle, so I don't like them anymore. Sacred Heart girls remind me too much of nuns with their all-white uniforms, and Cathedral girls look too much like aunties to me."

"Baloney! Swami, all-white is so virginal; that's a definite turn-on," said George, "and the Cathedral girls who you call aunties are really hot too. Lots of Anglo-Indian girls there, they're so beautiful. I've seen some very cute Sophia's girls too... damn, they are all beautiful."

"I like all girls too," said Venu, "but unlike both of you, I like traditional Indian girls. All the girls from the Christian schools are too mod for me. I prefer parachutes to mini skirts. When more is hidden, there's more to imagine."

"Okay, let's agree to disagree," said Swaminathan. "Actually, I like all girls too. I was just trying to be loyal to Baldwin. Hey Venu, do you know what the missionary position is in sex?"

"No, what is it? Is it when someone talks about Jesus while having sex?"

"No buddhu. I was reading about it in the book I told you about. The missionary position is the most traditional sexual position — man on top, woman on her back with legs spread out."

"Oh, yeah? What are the other positions?"

"Oh, there are so many," said Swami. "I'd really like to get my hands on a *Kamasutra*, the sex manual written by Vatsyayana in 400 BC. It was first translated into English in 1883."

"Yes, I was reading about it in one of my parent's magazines. They say it lists hundreds of sexual positions. Those ancient Indians were really randy bastards, eh?" said George.

"Yes, but now we are such prudes." said Swami. "It's a word that means being excessively concerned with modesty and such. Bloody hypocrites, that's what we are now."

"I don't know Swami, I'm someone who likes girls to be modest... not show everything off like some of the Americans you see in magazines," said Venu.

"Hey, don't make fun of my people," said George jokingly. "I agree with Swami. I think Indians are hypocrites today. Many of my own relatives are so closed minded about girls. Some of my cousins in Kerala are not allowed to wear pants or skirts that are above the knees? What baloney! To think we are the same people that came up with the *Kamasutra*!"

■

The next few months revolved mainly around cramming for the ICSE examination. School days were spent reviewing for the exam with teachers while evenings were spent on Hindi tuitions, reading their textbooks or solving math problems. The Scrimshankers studied together whenever they could. George's parents didn't mind him studying with his friends but Swami's and Venu's fathers were against the idea.

"What is this combined study nonsense?" asked Venkat to Swami. "You chaps just want to have fun. I like your friends but I think studying on your own is better. Keep your social activities to a minimum until the exam is over."

"If you go out of this house for anything but school or to the shop until your exams are over, I will thrash you," was Venu's father's reply when he asked for permission to study at George's house.

However, the boys still managed to spend time together in the days leading up to their exams. They hung out after school for at least an hour each afternoon before going home to study. It was their routine to stop at Fatima's Bakery for a quick snack after school and chat for a bit but the impending exam always hung over their heads like a black cloud.

Even George realized he had to take things more seriously. He only played his guitar during his study breaks now. Swami woke up at four-thirty every morning to study but, usually, his mother would come in with a steel tumbler of piping hot coffee at five-thirty and find him fast asleep with his head on the thick *Charles Farro* geography textbook. Venu had less time than his friends to study because his father still expected him to put in time at the medical shop each evening. His only option was to read his textbooks when there were no customers.

Finally it was the week of the exams. The first exam was English, followed by History, Biology, Geography, Physics, Chemistry, Mathematics, and finally, Hindi. The exams lasted a fortnight but it seemed like an eternity. As they finished each exam, they rejoiced in the fact that they would never have to look at those particular textbooks again.

The newspapers reported that a girl with aspirations of becoming a doctor had hanged herself after doing badly on the biology exam. Another student was caught cheating with bits of notes hidden in his socks. He was immediately marked failed in the ICSE.

Then suddenly, it was over. All the pent-up anxiety, fear and trepidation were released in jubilant celebrations on the last day of the exams. George and Swami burned their Hindi books in the Graveyard on their way home. Venu couldn't add his books to the fire, because his father had explicitly told him to sell it to the second-hand bookstore the next day.

The boys decided to celebrate the completion of the ICSE exams by going for a movie and dinner together on the final day. Even Venu's father had, reluctantly, given him the evening off. The plan was to see the film *Airport 77*, followed by dinner. It was the first time they would be going out so late at night entirely on their own. Usually, the only opportunity the Scrimshankers had of going to a nice restaurant was when George's parents, at his insistence, invited them along to places like Blue Fox, Top Kapi or Canopy.

After going home to change out of their Baldwin School uniforms, hopefully for the last time, the Scrimshankers met at five-thirty in the evening at Lido Theater. The movie was starting at six-thirty but there was already a long line of people for the middle-seats.

There were four tickets prices at Lido: The balcony seats, which were on the first floor, cost seven rupees. Next were the last ten rows on the main floor that cost five rupees. This was followed by the middle-seats that cost three rupees. Seats in the first four rows, known as "buckets" because they did not have any padding and usually simulated the experience of sitting in an empty bucket, cost one rupee and fifty paise.

The Scrimshankers usually sat in the bucket seats when they went for movies together. They didn't mind the seats or the colorful audience that usually occupied the section and shouted loudly at every opportunity, or threw coins at the screen whenever there was a good scene or dialogue.

The boys pooled their money when they were together. George was usually the only one with cash, but he never hesitated to share what he had with his friends. He would much rather go for a movie with Swami and Venu and sit in the bucket seats than spend his weekly pocket money of ten rupees just on one balcony seat for himself. It was even enough for samosas or chicken puffs during the interval.

Swami only got ten rupees for the entire month. Venu got nothing from his father even though he worked every evening and on weekends at the store. Now and then, his mother would give him a few rupees quietly. He also managed to keep some of the change left over from the rum and cigarettes his father sent him to purchase.

The boys had all been saving their money for this special evening for a few weeks. Swami and Venu had twenty-five rupees each while George had fifty rupees with him. They decided to watch the movie in the better seats because it was a special day.

"You know, we should see *Airport 77*. This way, we'll remember the year we finished our ICSE always," said Swaminathan.

His friends agreed. It was a remarkable coincidence that a film with that year in its title was playing right then. It was past nine o'clock when they came out of the movie.

"What a fantastic film," said Swaminathan. "It was so realistic. How is it to fly in a plane, George?"

Swami and Venu had never traveled in an airplane before. The nearest they got to the experience was watching planes take off and land from the little enclosure a short distance away from the main building at Bangalore's HAL Airport. Most of the planes that flew in and out of the airport were domestic flights to Madras, Bombay, New Delhi, Hyderabad and Mangalore. They were mainly smaller passenger planes: Fokker Friendships, Caravelles, Boeing 727s and even the odd Dakota or two. The airport shared a runway with HAL, the government aircraft testing facility, so spectators could occasionally also see Russian MIGs or French Mirage fighter jets taking off and landing.

"I came here in a Boeing 707 jet," said George. "The plane was a little smaller than the 747 jet in the movie. It was fantastic, buggers. It took more than a day to get here, with one stop in London and another in Cairo. I was much younger then but I remember they had a big screen in front where they showed children's movies all the time. The adults watched other movies on screens in the aisles. We came by TWA. I saw the pyramids and Sphinx from the air, as we were landing, but we only stayed in the airport. We couldn't go out."

"The first *Airport* movie took place in a 707 plane," said Swami. "That was also a deadly movie."

"Where do you chaps want to go for dinner?" asked George.

"What are our choices?" asked Venu.

"Well," said Swaminathan, "let's look to keeping it under twenty rupees each. You are the expert, George. Where can we go for that much money?"

"I think our best choice would be a Chinese restaurant or a Kaka joint."

Since Swami and Venu had become friends with George, they had both started eating meat. They were beginning to acquire a taste for it now.

"So, what places are there?" asked Venu.

"From where we are now, we can go towards Brigade Road and go to Impy or Chin Lung," said George.

"Let's go to Impy's," said Venu. "Their biriyani and chilli chicken are really good. They ordered food from there for my neighbor Selven's birthday. It was fantastic."

The boys got on their bicycles and pedaled the two miles to Brigade Road. Imperial Restaurant, or Impy's as it was known, was attached to Imperial Hotel on Residency Road and catered to a wide range of customers. It was operated by Kerala-Muslims, or Kakas as they were called, who were well known for their non-vegetarian restaurants in every neighborhood of almost every big city in South India. They served a staple variety of Muslim-influenced cuisine such as parothas, biriyani, chicken, lamb, beef, egg and brain curries. Their prices were very reasonable and the food was excellent. Patrons ranged from auto and bus drivers to day laborers and businessmen — anyone who wanted reasonably priced, good, non-vegetarian food. The eat-in clientele were mainly men. Women and families usually got the food parceled to take home. The boys left their bikes at the two-wheeler stand and walked up Residency Road to Impy's.

George suddenly asked his friends, "Do you chaps want to do something we've never done before tonight?"

"Like what?" asked Swaminathan.

"You don't want to look for a prostitute, do you" asked Venu.

"No," said George. "I was thinking more about smoking and drinking."

"I… I don't know George. It smells a lot," said Swaminathan.

"I can have a fag. I don't mind. I've smoked my father's cigarettes before," said Venu.

"I've also tried my dad's," said George. "It's not a big deal. How about some rum, too? I've tasted it from my father's cabinet. It's nice. If we drink it slowly, it won't hit us much."

Normally Swami would have vetoed the idea, but since it was a special night, he decided to go along with his friends. George went to a paan shop and picked up a packet of Wills Filter cigarettes. His father sometimes smoked it although he usually preferred foreign brands like Marlboro, Rothmans or John Player Special. Swami's father did not smoke and Venu's father smoked only unfiltered Charminar cigarettes.

They went inside Impy's and found a comfortable booth.

"Ooru cheria rum bottle and three Thums Up," George told the Malayalee waiter. "Penna ooru chilli chicken inum dry aaite kondouva."

Because of a trade dispute, the government had banned Coca Cola in India, but an enterprising Indian manufacturer had created Thums Up as a replacement cola drink. If the waiter thought the Scrimshankers were too young to be consuming Thums Up with hard liquor, he didn't show it. He had gotten used to boys much younger than they were, who worked at the auto mechanic shops, coming in and drinking until the wee hours of the morning.

George opened the pack of cigarettes and offered it to his friends. They took one each and lighted up solemnly. Swami started coughing at once.

"Here, I'll show you how," said George. "You take in the smoke and hold it in your mouth. Don't let it go into your lungs until you've got used to it. See, like this…." He demonstrated.

Swami tried again. This time he blew it out without inhaling any of the smoke. The three friends sat smoking quietly for a few minutes. They felt liberated and excited, like they were beginning a new phase in their lives.

The waiter arrived with the rum, Thums Up and a plate of chilli chicken. This was the first time Swami and Venu were drinking alcohol.

"Okay, pour about three fingers of rum into the glass, and then fill the rest with Thums Up," instructed George. "Then drink it very slowly. Don't gulp it down quickly. Also, eat some of the chicken while you are drinking; otherwise it will hit you badly."

His friends did as they were told. At first, Swami didn't feel anything. "*The rum just makes the Thums Up taste better,*" he thought to himself. Then, he began feeling a strange sensation, a little light-headedness at first, followed by a strange warm glow that spread all over his body. He felt happy and talkative.

"I'm having the best time so far, chaps," he said. "I think I did well enough to pass the Hindi exam easily. What about you fellows? How did you do?"

"Yes, I may scrape past the exam," said George. "I wrote everything I could think of, even if it wasn't required, but my grammar and spelling must have been awful. I just mugged whatever Mohiuddin gave and spat it out at the exam — probably badly though!"

"Yes, I think I did okay too. I'll pass," said Venu.

"Hey, don't you chaps think it was a fantastic idea to raise the plane with balloons in *Airport 77*? That Jack Lemmon is such a deadly actor, one of my favorites… such a comedian too," said Swami. Then he and George went into a long conversation about the movie they had just watched.

If George and Swaminathan were feeling talkative after half a glass of rum each, Venu had become more silent and a bit morose, as well. Even though he liked his friends very much, he sometimes could not relate to them.

George was so carefree. It was as if he did not have a worry in the world. His parents gave him money whenever he wanted it and were very lenient with him about everything. To add to it, he had a very attractive appearance that drew people, especially girls, to him. Venu was a bit jealous of him.

Swami was different from George. He was studious, reserved

and shy. But in many ways, he was just like George. They always liked the same music, movies, books and girls. Swami would do anything for George. He was also less timid when George was around. He did things he wouldn't do otherwise — like drinking rum, smoking or eating meat. His friendship was reciprocated because George was willing to do anything for Swami as well.

Once, during Mr. Gupta's Hindi class, in the ninth standard, the teacher hauled Swami up for not doing his homework. He made the boy come to the front of the class. The teacher was a strict disciplinarian who insisted on total participation and dedication from his students. He was quick to hand out corporal punishment.

Mr. Gupta made Swami stand facing the class next to the blackboard. His lesson for the day was a poem by Kabir, the eminent Indian poet from the fifteenth century, called *Kasturia Mrig Ko Ang* or translated in English as *Of the Musk Deer*.

"Kastori kundali baso... Musk lies in the musk deer's own nave," the teacher read from the book, which he held in his left hand. He walked slowly up to Swaminathan and caught hold of the boy's right earlobe.

He continued to read, *"Kasturi kundal base, mrig dhoondhe van mahi,"* while he twisted Swaminathan's ear slowly tighter and tighter. "Here is the English translation of the second verse: *'In man himself the Master dwells, / But man, deluded, knows not this, / So similar to the musk deer who, / Again and again the grass sniffs."*

Swami's eyes were beginning to tear with pain and embarrassment as Mr. Gupta kept twisting his ear harder. Suddenly, George stood up and in a loud voice said, "Sir, you stop that, okay?"

Mr. Gupta was startled. He had never before been challenged like this. He let go of Swami's ear, closed his book slowly, placed it on his desk, and walked over to George. He was fuming with anger. George was still standing up. He was nearly as tall as the teacher, and he didn't flinch from Mr. Gupta's gaze. The entire class thought that the Hindi master was going to slap George.

For a moment, it looked like the teacher would punch George. He opened and clenched his fist a few times. Then he remembered what he knew about George... his encounter with C.K. Ganguli... that his father was a big shot... that he was from the U.S... that he would not take any physical punishment lying down like some of the other boys.

So, barely holding his anger in check, he asked as calmly as he could, "Chandy, what is your problem?" through clenched teeth.

"Sir, our parents don't send us here so you can abuse us," he told the teacher cooly. He didn't seem very perturbed. It was as if he was just having a conversation with his equal.

"Okay, let me look at your homework then, Chandy," said Mr. Gupta. He looked through George's notebook muttering and shaking his head disapprovingly.

"What does, *'Kabir koji Ram ka…'* in the third stanza mean?" he asked George.

"I wasn't sure of that, sir," said George.

"We went over it in the last class. You were supposed to analyze it for your homework. Instead you have written some nonsense, just filling up a page without understanding anything." He flicked his finger at George and said, "Out, and take your friend with you. Both of you can stand outside the classroom for three periods."

Swami and George didn't mind standing outside. They whispered to each other and spent their time watching all the activity going on. The gardeners trimming the hedges... Mr. Broom conducting gymnastics classes... Parents coming in to register their sons at the school... Dangerous-looking hawks circling overhead and suddenly diving to scoop up a rat or discarded morsel of food... The younger boys playing marbles during their break... The canteen cook frying bondas outside in a big steel vat…

Venu sometimes felt that his two friends only hung out with him because his friendship with Swami had preceded the arrival of George. Although he got along well with both the boys, his situation was completely different from theirs.

George's family had a lot of money and influence in the city. Swaminathan's father was also now the assistant director at the bank's head office. He received a good salary and many perks, such as a nice house and even a brand new Ambassador car.

Meanwhile, Venu's lot in life had basically remained the same: the strict and abusive father, the timid harried mother, working for nothing at the medical shop. He looked at his friends laughing, carefree, innocent — the way all children should be.

He then thought of his own life, of the secrets he did not even share with his friends: his father's alcohol fueled rage, the abuse that was a common occurrence in his house, his mother's tears.

He was ashamed of it all. He had never invited his friends over to his house. He was afraid they would not want to be his friends if they knew.

As the alcohol took hold, Venu began to slowly feel better. He took another large gulp of the rum and shook out a cigarette from the pack and lit it. He looked at Swami and George and felt a surge of love for them suddenly. What did he have to offer them but his simple friendship? They both had everything they needed. Yet, through the years, they had steadfastly been his friends and always included him in everything they did. Maybe someday he could be their equal. He was going to amount to something. Someday, he told himself.

He lifted his glass. "Hey, buggers, let's have a toast to our friendship. I just want to tell you both how much I appreciate what we have together. Thank you for being my friends."

George raised his glass, then reached out and squeezed the back of Venu's neck with affection. "I too would like to thank you both. I have really enjoyed our friendship," he said. "Here's to us!"

"Yes, here's to the Scrimshankers," said Swami. "The best friends on earth."

The food they had ordered came to the table: chicken biriyani, chilli chicken, lamb fry and Kerala parottas. George ordered another quart of rum. The boys were now a little inebriated. George and Swami began debating loudly whether George Harrison or Eric Clapton was the better guitar player.

Suddenly, Venu said, "That bastard… I'll show him someday"

"Who," asked Swami startled.

Venu looked at his friends with a slightly glazed expression. He lit another cigarette. "My father, that's who," he said. "He's a real arsehole. He beats my mother. He beats us all, that bastard!"

In spite of their condition, George and Swami realized Venu was serious. All they could do was look at him with sympathy.

"I don't want your pity, okay?" Venu said, slurring slightly. "You chaps don't have any idea what it is to live my life. That bastard has been beating us all since we were children. He makes my mother work like a servant and sometimes even beats her when he's drunk. He gets me to work at the medical shop and doesn't pay me. Do you know, I stole twenty-five rupees from his purse last week so I could come here with you today?"

Then a shrewd expression came over his face, and he said, "Forget it, I don't know what I'm saying. Let's have a good time tonight, okay? Who cares about yesterday or tomorrow?" He clammed up suddenly and stopped talking.

They finished dinner, paid the bill, and walked outside unsteadily. When they reached the corner near the cycle stand, Swaminathen suddenly vomited all over the footpath. A few minutes later, Venu and George followed suit. They three boys leaned back, relieved, only when they had thrown up most of what they had eaten and drunk that evening.

A well-dressed man passing by looked at them, stopped, and exclaimed angrily, "Bloody drunkards, who do you think is going to clean the footpath. Why do you drink more than you can, idiots? You are a bloody disgrace to this country!"

The Scrimshankers all looked at him sheepishly. "Sorry, Uncle... it won't happen again," said Swami. "We are first-time drinkers..." He realized he had some difficulty speaking clearly.

The man looked at them in disgust and walked away shaking his head.

It was already eleven-thirty at night, but the boys were in no state to ride their bicycles home.

"Let's walk up Brigade Road," said George. "They have a cart on M.G. Road that sells coffee and tea."

The friends bought three steaming hot cups of coffee in little plastic cups and sat on a cement bench on the raised walkway that ran along the Army Parade Ground and Mahatma Gandhi Road, the most well-known road in all of Bangalore. They wanted to wait out the effects of the alcohol before they rode their bikes back to their respective homes. Swami and Venu lived relatively close to each other so they could go home together, but George had to make his way home alone in the opposite direction.

As they were sitting on the bench, talking and smoking, two uniformed police constables approached them with the intention of harassing and collecting some money from the boys. One of them asked, "Neevu yenu maduthideera--?"

Looking at George and observing his long hair and jeans, he added in broken English, "What you boys doing here? You drinking? I taking you to police station... stand up you bugger, you..."

Before George could react, Venu stood up instead. These were, after all, his kind of people.

"Sar...yenu madhilva... we are not doing anything... simply talking... avaru chikkappa* DIG of police Varghese..." He pointed to George.

It was true that George's mother's younger brother, Abraham Varghese, was the Deputy Inspector General of the Bangalore police. He had tremendous influence in every government office in the city and just the mere mention of his name was usually enough in such a situation.

The policemen were suddenly more respectful. "Sorry saar," they told George. "Tappu aytu**."

George did not know what they were saying, but he nodded. When the policemen left, the boys walked back to the cycle stand, took their bicycles and went their separate ways.

*mother's younger brother
**made a mistake (Kannada)

Chapter 8
The Start of a Long Recess

The Scrimshankers had six months without classes to look forward to after their final exams. This was because, while the first to tenth grades ran from January to December, junior college, as the 11th and 12th grade were known, followed a June to May calendar. All students looked to this long recess with anticipation right from their middle school years. Parents tried their best to keep their children occupied during these months. Those who could afford to do so, sent their sons and daughters abroad or to visit relatives in far away places... Business owners introduced their offspring to what would probably be their futures by making them work in their shop or office... Europhiles registered their children in foreign language classes at places like Max Mueller Bhavan or Alliance Francaise... Those that wanted their kids to have something practical to fall back on enrolled them at institutions such as a Dawar's Secretarial College, where students learned the fundamentals of typing and Pitman's shorthand...

For the Scrimshankers, it was generally understood that Venu would be working at his father's medical store for much of his recess. For Swami and George, however, their horizons were wide open; the possibilities were endless.

"You lucky buggers," said Venu woefully one morning. "I have to work every day from ten in the morning until eight every night. You get to roam around all day."

"I know," said Swami. "Can you ask your father to at least let you have the weekends off?"

"I asked, but he won't listen," said Venu. Although he had

revealed a little about his abusive father to his friends when he was drunk, he never brought it up again. For their part, Swami and George had acted as though they never had the conversation with him. They didn't want to pry or embarrass their friend and left it to Venu to decide when he wanted to talk about it again.

"So, what are you chaps doing for the next few months?" asked Venu.

"Well, I'm going to the U.S. in March for my cousin's wedding for three to four weeks," said George. "Other than that, I don't know."

"Wow, George, you are so lucky," said Swami. "I wish I could go to the U.S. too."

It was just before Christmas. It had been two weeks since their ICSE exams. The Scrimshankers loved the city during this time of year. Although Swaminathan and Venu were Hindus, their friendship with George had exposed them to a culture and lifestyle that they did not have access to before.

Most non-Christians in India who were educated at the convents and missionary schools usually had some knowledge of the Christian religion. This was because prayers, scripture classes and even church services were usually part of every school day. Non-Christians could opt out of these activities if they wanted.

George's parents were both Malayalee Orthodox Christians, but they had decided long ago that they preferred a more moderate religious experience. The family attended St. Mark's Cathedral, which was part of the Church of South India and incorporated Anglican and Protestant doctrines in their services.

George had been in the St. Mark's youth group since he arrived in Bangalore. He also attended Sunday school and all the other social activities at the Church with his parents. As churches did all over the world, St. Mark's provided a complete social experience for its members. In addition to spiritual guidance and religious instruction, it also delivered social interaction, philanthropic outlets, as well as sports, fun and recreation for the whole family.

The Hindu and Muslim youth in Bangalore did not have this in their temples and mosques. So, those that had Christian friends joined them in the myriad activities and programs at churches all over the city. For the past few years, George had taken Swami and Venu to church picnics, talent contests, fundraisers and potluck dinners, as well as to the annual St. Mark's Fete. Because of the church's liberal views and inclusive philosophy, the boys also felt very much at ease attending services on Christmas, New Year's Eve and Easter. None of the Scrimshankers were particularly religious but they all liked the experience of being at St. Mark's.

George, in particular, liked hearing and singing the beautiful hymns that were part of every service. The church boasted of one of the few antique grand pipe organs in the world. Installed in 1923, it had towering flues and reeds that were over a story high. The church choir was one of the best in the city, while their organist was reputed to be one of the leading pipe organ players in the world. City residents belonging to every caste and creed flocked to the church every December for the carol service.

The annual fête was another yearly event that drew thousands of people from all around the city to St. Mark's for three days of fun, food and carnival games. The event was organized and run by the church's many associations, including the youth fellowship. George usually helped out at the "Fish-the-Bottle" stall. Players had to put a ring around the long neck of a beer bottle using a fishing pole. Swami and Venu joined their friend at the stall, every year. They enjoyed interacting with the visitors, particularly the pretty girls from the city's schools that came in groups to the fête. The girls seemed mainly interested in flirting with George at the stall but he seemed unaware of his magnetic sexuality and rarely responded to them. Or, maybe it was just that he didn't feel right about being singled out for attention while his friends were ignored.

St. Mark's Cathedral was right opposite the Bangalore Cricket Stadium. During important matches, the youth group exploited the church's sprawling grounds to make money for their programs by providing car and two-wheeler parking for visitors to the stadium. They charged five rupees per car and two rupees for a scooter or motorbike to park for the whole day. This was less than half the cost of parking at the stadium's parking facilities. Most patrons returned time and time again because it was cheaper and more convenient. Plus, the church's youth were always present on site unlike the attendants at the other lots, who disappeared once they collected their fee. Swami and Venu usually joined George whenever the St. Mark's youth group ran the parking lot. They enjoyed being together and chatting with each other all day.

One day, when the Scrimshankers were helping out at the parking lot, a middle-aged man with his pregnant wife and son returned early to collect his car. The boys were surprised because it was only noon on the second day of the five-day test match. The game usually went on until five-thirty every afternoon.

"What happened, Uncle?" George asked. "Is everything okay?"

"Yes," said the man, "but my wife is not feeling so good so we are going home early. She's due any day now."

"So sorry, Uncle — I mean congratulations, but sorry she's not feeling well," said George.

"I say, you boys, would you like our tickets for the test match? They are good tickets. It cost one hundred and fifty rupees for each ticket, but we won't be able to come back anymore."

The boys could not believe their luck. They got permission from Ben Solomon, the head of the youth group, and went in together to watch the match. They had never been to a cricket match before. The seats were fabulous and located in front of the player section with an unobstructed view of the pitch. They even had a up-close look at all the players as they walked past. The match was between India and their arch-rival, Pakistan. It was an exciting four days that ended in a win for India.

"Whether there is a God or not, I think I'm happy we decided to help out at St. Mark's," said Swaminathan. "What a deadly match and what deadly seats!"

The other institution Swaminathan and Venu got a chance to visit now and then because of George was the Bangalore Club. Founded in 1868, it was the oldest club in the City. Its members were the cream of Bangalore high-society. The Club still retained its distinct Britishness even years after the Raj had disappeared, if merely for snob value. Past members included Winston Churchill, who still owed an unpaid bill for thirteen rupees as stated in the ledger in the main hall, and the Maharaja of Mysore, who had once rode an elephant into the Club. It was practically impossible to become a member anymore. However, because of his position and influence, Mohan Chandy had wrangled a membership after years of trying. This included being sponsored by three members who had not endorsed another individual for membership to the Club in five years.

The Bangalore Club had sprawling colonial-style buildings

that were spread out over several acres. It included a well-stocked library with the latest novels, magazines and comic books, a good-sized swimming pool, two restaurants with full bars serving various cuisines, a food bar that offered casual dining every evening on the huge lawn, sports facilities for badminton, tennis, squash, billiards, table tennis and bridge, and a well-stocked store for provisions.

During British rule, the brass sign outside the main bar had once said, *"Dogs And Indians Not Allowed Inside."* After Indian independence in 1947, the club management had changed it to, *"Dogs And Women Not Allowed Inside."*

The Scrimshankers loved the Christmas season particularly because they got to experience it in George's world. This included St. Mark's Cathedral and the Bangalore Club. Now that their exams were over, the boys could enjoy the holiday season with carefree abandon.

■

It was a Saturday evening, and Swami and George were at St. Mark's Cathedral for the annual Christmas carol service with Mohan and Sheila Chandy. Venu was at work. George was wearing faded bell-bottom jeans that were tight on the thighs but flared at the bottom, a white T-shirt with a peace symbol on it and open sandals. His hair was long and wavy and he was beginning to develop a wispy beard. He looked like a handsome hippy. Swami was next to him in tailored bell-bottom pants, a big collared half-shirt with long tight sleeves, as was the fashion, and kholapuri slippers. He had changed his glasses to ones that was squarer and in a larger frame the day before. He thought he looked quite mod in them.

Reverend M.M. Koshy, the pastor of the church, stepped up to the mic and said in a very pronounced Malayalee accent, "Dearly beloved parishioners in Christ, I am very happy to welcome you to tonight's service of nine lessons and carols. Let us turn to page twelve in your prayer books."

George nudged Swami, "Did you hear that? He said tolve!" They both smiled. On the seat to the right of Swaminathan, sat a tall, dark girl in a short black skirt and a red blouse. Her name was Mona Philip. George knew her slightly because she had been in the church's youth group until a few years ago. She was now in her early twenties.

Swami had been glancing at her slyly from the corner of his eyes since she had come and sat down next to him. She leaned over and smiled at George. Swami noticed that the top button of her blouse was open and he could see the top of her bra and a hint of her breasts. Because the church was very crowded for the carol service, everyone on the pew was sitting very close to each other. Mona's thigh was touching Swami's lightly. It sent a sexual current through his entire body. He felt an uncontrollable hardness developing in his pants. She had nice thighs and legs, he thought to himself.

George and Swaminathan liked the same type of girls while Venu's tastes were a little different. Like most traditional Indian males, Venu preferred women with fat thighs, or thundering thighs, as George called it, and wide hips. Swami and George, on the other hand, both liked girls with slim thighs and narrow hips. Mona's legs were long, narrow and lovely. Swami couldn't help but glance at them every few minutes. She also had very nice breasts he noticed... "*just the right size and shape.*" As George had at Mr. Mohiuddin's tuition class, Swaminathan now felt his erection threaten to get out of control.

"*Why did I have to wear my old underwear today?*" he cursed at himself silently. It was loose around his skinny thighs and he was afraid his semi-hard penis would slip out from the side. He tried to unobtrusively push it back inside, but instead, pushed it out more. He could feel the foreskin peel back. This heightened his arousal even further. He quickly covered his crotch with an open prayer book. Mona was sitting very close to him. She may have not been aware of this but even though her thigh was barely touching his, he could feel a burning heat from it.

"*Let us hear again from Holy Scripture the tale of the loving purposes of God from the first days until the glorious redemption brought us by this holy Child; and let us make this house of prayer glad with our carols of praise,*" read the pastor.

By now, Swaminathan could think of nothing but the presence of the young woman sitting next to him. The burning heat he felt from where her thigh touched his had become a red-hot flame. It was now shooting signals straight to his penis. He was aghast when he suddenly felt something sticky on his upper leg. He looked down and saw that there was a small, round, wet, sticky patch on his right thigh. His erection also seemed very visible.

He stood up quickly embarrassed and flustered. "I… I have to go to the bathroom," he told George and rushed out.

The toilets were in a row behind a small rose garden. It was dimly lit. His erection was still very strong. He suddenly felt a sudden pain in his scrotum.

"Oh God, maybe there's something wrong with me," he thought.

He urinated with difficulty with his still-erect penis. It got a little less turgid after that. He went into a stall with a mug of water and tried washing the sticky discharge from the head of his penis. However, a lot of the water fell on his pants in the process. Now it looked like he had urinated on himself. He dried it as much as he could with his hands, left his shirt untucked and returned to his seat. George looked at him curiously when he sat down but didn't say anything.

The choir was magnificent. They were singing *O Little Town of Bethlehem*, but Swami could not help but let his thoughts wander again to the girl on his right. It appeared she had moved closer to him. He felt another erection slowly come on and the same pain in his testicles again. *"Maybe he should have shagged in the bathroom and got rid of his arousal,"* he thought himself.

He tried to think of something else to divert his mind. It was hard. He browsed through the *Book of Common Service*. Maybe if he read something boring, it would help. He flipped through the pages and saw a section titled, *The Burial Service*. He started reading…

"Here is to be noted, that the Office ensuing is not to be used for any that die unbaptized, or excommunicate, or have laid violent hands upon themselves…." Although he didn't know what the first part meant, he understood the last part was probably referring to suicide.

"So, what happens to the corpse then? Where do they bury such people?" he asked himself. He continued reading, *"The Priest and Clerks meeting the Corpse at the entrance of the Church yard, and going before it, either into the Church, or towards the Grave, shall say, or sing, 'I AM the resurrection and the life, saith the Lord: he that believeth in me, though he were dead, yet shall he live: and whosoever liveth and believeth in me shall never die…'"*

He slowly forced his mind to digress from Mona to death and

funerals instead. *"Why do the Christians bury their dead?"* he wondered.

He remembered his grandfather's funeral when he was ten years old. It was his only up-close experience with death. He had been terrified. They had got the body home in a stretcher. His father and the priest had bathed it, and immediately tied a white band tightly under the chin to the top of his grandfather's head and closed his eyes.

Ramesh, his older cousin from his mother's side, who was standing next to him, had kept a non-stop commentary going throughout the entire proceedings. He leaned down and put his mouth near Swami's ear and whispered, "They tie the face so the mouth stays closed... The body has to face south with arms by the side... They can only put white clothes... They put some rice in the mouth now..."

When they got to the cremation ground, he continued, "This place must be near a river... The body must again be facing south on the pyre because that is the direction of the dead... Your father has to perform the ceremony because he is the eldest son... He has to walk around three times so the spirits don't follow him home... He is now sprinkling ghee and water on the body... This is the last part... Your father is putting flame on the body of your grandfather and whoosh... see!"

It had taken several hours for the body to burn. To Swaminathan's horror, about half an hour after his father had set fire to the body, it suddenly sat up. Quickly, his father took a long stick and beat it back down into the flame.

"Don't worry, it's only natural... gas and such..." whispered Ramesh. "Now your father is going to break the skull with the stick to let out the spirits from grandfather..."

Thankfully, his erection was gone now. They were at the eighth lesson. "Let us listen to St. Matthew chapter two, verses one to eleven... where the wise men are led by the star to Jesus," said Reverend Koshy.

Mona was now leaning away from him. He glanced at her face closely for the first time. He was disappointed. Her face didn't match her lovely body. She had features that were disproportionate. Her nose was too wide, her eyes too small and her lips too full. One day, when he was about ten years old, he had heard his older cousins, Ramesh and Shekhar, talking about an ugly girl they knew who had a beautiful body.

"Here's what I always tell myself when I see girls like that: cover the face and enjoy the base," said Shekhar.

Swaminathan had imagined his cousin covering the girl's face with a handkerchief while he did something enjoyable with her base. He didn't understand fully what that meant then, but the expression had stayed in his mind. He recalled it now as he glanced at Mona. Then he felt angry with himself for thinking about her in that manner. *"How would he feel if someone judged him the same way? No girl probably wanted either his face or his base!"*

The service had almost ended. Reverend Koshy was giving the benediction in a sing-song voice, punctuated even more by his strong accent, "May he who, by his Incarnation, gathered into one, things earthly and heavenly, grant you the fullness of inward peace and goodwill, and the blessing of God Almighty, the Father, the Son and the Holy Spirit, be amongst you and remain with you always. Let us sing *O Come All Ye Faithful*. It's found on page twenty-two."

Swaminathan liked the tune of the hymn. He was not used to singing, but he hummed along. George was singing loudly. He had a beautiful voice but he had never been interested in joining the church choir.

After the service, they stood outside the church and had coffee and cake while George's parents socialized with other members of the congregation. Swami narrated his predicament in the church and his mishap in the toilet.

"Bugger, my balls began to hurt. I hope it isn't anything bad," he told his friend.

George laughed loudly and slapped his thigh. "Haha... Swami... it is too funny... that too inside the church!" He laughed more. "Don't worry about your balls. It is called blue balls."

"What's that?" asked Swami.

"Oh, it's nothing to worry about. When you get a serious hard-on, with no ejaculation afterwards, it causes cum to gather in your balls or something. It's a temporary condition; once you piss it out, you're okay. It's happened to me several times. I'm surprised you haven't read about it in your sex manual."

Swaminathan remembered suddenly... yes... how could he have forgotten? It was called vasocongestion, *"a prolonged dull aching pain caused by unsatisfied sexual arousal in males..."* It was towards the end of the book. He felt relieved.

When they told Venu about it later, he said, "Thank God! I thought something was wrong with me too. Blue balls, eh... but my balls are so black, I'm sure they'll never turn blue."

■

Swami and Venu often accompanied George to the Bangalore Club. Mohan Chandy allowed his son to sign for snacks at the swimming pool or in the lawn of the Club. They usually had chips, soft drinks or their favorite, a mango ice cream bar.

That year, George asked his friends to come with him for the New Year's Eve party. It was one of the most exclusive events in the city. Only members of the club and their guests could attend. Swaminathan's father, Venkat, did not like the idea of his son going to the Bangalore Club at all.

"It is a very elitist institution," he told Swami. "During the British days, they did not allow Indians to even enter the club. Now, they only allow some types of Indians. If Gandhiji walked in today in his usual clothes, he would be thrown out of the Bangalore Club," he said angrily.

The Club, like its many counterparts all across the country, had indeed carried its British traditions to absurd lengths. All members and visitors were required to adhere strictly to a formal Western dress code for entry to the main building of the club and for formal events and parties. Even Indian-style formal wear was prohibited. Kurta-pyjamas, dhotis, lungis and slippers were guaranteed to keep the wearer out of almost all the buildings in the Club at any time.

Most of the members of the Club didn't mind these archaic traditions. A large percentage of the permanent members had been grandfathered in because their families had belonged to the Club for decades. The Club did not represent the new social order in India, but rather an elite, traditional upper class from an earlier era: nawabs, princes, queens, and other royalty... British expats who had decided to continue living in India even after Independence... the English-speaking, public-school educated, cream of Bangalore society... top industrialists and heads of foreign companies... socialites, famous personalities and artists who were markedly

European in their outlook... or collectively, as Venkat categorized the Club members, "Indians who act more British than the British themselves."

Even the newly affluent were not welcome at the Club, if they did not have the right connections, background or pedigree. A spokesman for the Club was quoted in the local media as saying that the institution was, "proud that the club's members were sophisticated and conservative in their style."

The newer members were thankful that they had somehow made it into the Bangalore Club. They now viewed themselves as belonging to the elite social class they both hungered to be in and despised before. They accepted the traditions of the Club as a reward of their hard-won membership to the esteemed institution.

Those that were denied membership to the Bangalore Club had no choice but to settle for the more egalitarian Bowring Institute that was about half a mile up the road. It had the same colonial past as the Bangalore Club but right from its inception the Bowring Institute had been dedicated to "*philanthropic, intellectual and secular values.*" Subsequently, there was less snobbery there.

"If you want my opinion, it's okay... but it's no Bangalore Club," was what most Bangalore Club members would say when asked about the Bowring Institute.

Swaminathan's father had recently become a member of the Bowring Institute as a perk for his promotion at the bank, but he usually did not attend any of the parties or gala events there. On a couple of occasions, he had taken his wife and son there for snacks. Venkat was still true to his Gandhian ideals of humility and service. He disliked ostentatious behavior of any sort.

George and Swaminathan were waiting for Venu outside the entrance of the Bangalore Club. Because Venu and Swami were not members, George had to personally sign them in at the gate. Venu arrived in an autorickshaw. He was coming straight from the medical shop.

George and Swami were wearing formal clothes but when Venu got out of the auto, they realized that he was not dressed in keeping with the rules of the club. He had on crumpled tan-colored cotton trousers and a short, green cotton kurta with slippers on his feet.

"Bugger, they're not going to let you in like that," said George.

"Sorry, I went to the shop like this and came straight from

there. Don't worry about me. You chaps' go on in. I'll go home," said Venu.

But George wouldn't hear of it. "We all go in or none of us goes, okay?" he said.

His parents were already inside by then, so the Scrimshankers walked up to the entrance on their own. As they had expected, the steward who was on duty outside the hall refused to let Venu in if he didn't change his clothes.

He would not even look at Venu, but only spoke to George with a haughty expression on his face, "You are a member here. You should know the rules. This is a club for high society, not riff-raff you know."

Swaminathan was incensed. "How dare he call Venu riff-raff," he told George. "You should complain about him."

George knew how hard his father had worked to become a member of the Club. He didn't want to create any trouble there.

"It's okay," he told Swami. "You chaps wait in the car park. I'll speak to my dad and meet you there in a few minutes." He left his friends outside and went inside the hall to look for his parents.

When he saw his father, he explained what had happened and asked him if he could have permission to go somewhere else that night.

"Okay, but be careful and come back here before one o'clock. I'll drive your friends home too." He took out his wallet, extracted some money and gave it to George. "I will tell mummy but you be careful and don't do anything naughty."

George met his friends and showed them the money his father had given him. It was sixty rupees — enough to have a nice dinner and even ice cream.

"Let's walk towards M.G. Road," he said. "We can find a place to eat and then go for ice cream to Chit-Chat or Lakeview. But we have to come back here by about one o'clock."

It was only a little after nine at night and the boys knew they had ample time for a nice evening. "You know buggers, I think we'll have a much better time on our own than at that stuffy club," said Swaminathan. He was beginning to understand and appreciate his father's perspective on elitists.

The Scrimshankers walked the two miles from the Bangalore Club to Mahatma Gandhi Road. It was a beautiful night.

There were Christmas and New Year's lights and decorations everywhere. George stopped at a roadside vendor and bought a pack of cigarettes. This was the second time they were smoking. Swaminathan bought some mint chewing gum so they could chew it later to disguise the smell of the cigarettes. The boys all lit up and puffed like experienced smokers — although George was the only one who could inhale without coughing.

"Chaps, do you want to have a nice thali?" George asked. "I am suddenly feeling like eating some good vegetarian food. Let's go to Airlines Hotel."

Venu and Swami agreed wholeheartedly. The boys changed their route and turned on to Lavelle Road instead. They passed a girl in a short dress wearing heavy makeup standing in the semi-darkness.

"That's a prostitute," Swami whispered to his friends.

"Happy New Year," said George to her cheerfully. The girl looked at him and smiled. His friends hurried him along before he said anything else.

The Scrimshankers had a wonderful time at Airlines Restaurant sitting outside smoking, eating and talking about movies, music and girls. At eleven o'clock they left and walked down M.G. Road to Lakeview, an ice cream parlor that served the most delicious sundaes. They each ordered a Merry Widow. It was three scoops of chocolate ice cream on a bed of chocolate cake with hot chocolate sauce, nuts and a chocolate wafer on top.

As the clock struck twelve, the Scrimshankers hugged each other and welcomed in the New Year. The revelry outside started: people began cheering... motorists honked and stopped to shake hands with the crowds on the street... drunks yelled nonsense and lifted their bottles to toast everyone... A fight broke out when a man in the crowd, under the pretense of shaking the hands of occupants in a car, fondled the breast of one of the women in it.

"We should be getting back to the Club," said George. "My dad will be worried if we don't show up on time."

The walked back slowly, chatting and enjoying the celebrations going on around them on the streets. George's father was still inside dancing with his wife when they got there, but seeing that the boys were tired he decided to leave at once.

They drove back slowly, first to Venu's house, then to Swami's and then back home. They were stopped several times by revelers who wanted to shake their hands.

It was almost two o'clock in the morning when George got into his bed. For some reason, he felt happy, but also pensive and introspective at the same time. It was the start of a new year. He thought about the past and the future. He tried to look ahead at what life would bring him, but it didn't appear to be very clear. He lay awake thinking for a while. Then an idea for a song began to take shape in his head. He picked up his guitar and strummed a G chord, then an F chord, then the progression G-D-F-C-D. The lyrics came to him slowly and he began singing softly.

> I can't wait forever. I ain't got the time
> Got to keep on moving got to stay in line
> Don't be disheartened if I move too fast for you
> Got to do it all before my time is through
>
> Time will show what's ahead down the road
> Time will show if we've been there before
> Time will show what happens to our soul
> Time will show what you and I do not know...

He took out his notebook and quickly scribbled down the words he had sung along with the chords on the page. He knew he had the crux of the song in his head. He would finish it later. He put away his guitar and got back into his bed. He was too tired to masturbate, like he usually did every night, so he went to sleep right away.

Swami also stayed awake for a long time thinking about all sorts of things. Like George, he was also very creative, but his talent lay in writing prose. He had dreams of being a reporter and starting his own magazine someday or even becoming a novelist. Every time he thought about it he was filled with excitement. He lay in bed trying to think of what he would have to do to make his dream a reality.

Venu snuck in quietly to the room he shared with his younger brother. He slept on the bed while his brother slept on a mat on the floor. His mother opened the door of the house for him without making a sound. He could hear his father snoring in the next room.

"Appa seriya kudichtu thoongaraya?" he asked his mother. After consuming his usual quart of rum, his father was dead to the world.

"Kanna, ne sapitya?" his mother asked. Venu told her he had eaten. Then he hugged her and said, "Happy New Year, Amma," and kissed her on her forehead. Although she was still quite young, her hair had turned almost completely gray.

Venu lay in bed thinking about his life for several hours. He wished his father were more like Swami's or George's. He was not really a bad man but rather simply a weak person who had let his life's failures make him seek refuge in alcohol and self-pity. It resulted in his cruel treatment of his family. Venu knew that he would have to take control of his own life and make something of himself soon if he wanted his situation to change. He could not count on guidance or encouragement from his father. The next few years would be critical but he would find a way to do it. It was almost morning when he finally fell into an uneasy and restless sleep.

Chapter 9
Coffee and Cigarettes

The next few months flew by quickly. Venu worked almost everyday at the medical shop. Swami and George spent their time together... loafing around on Brigade Road, M.G. Road or Commercial Street... listening to music or talking about politics, music, art, books and movies in their club room at George's house... watching almost every English movie they could, including reruns from the 1960s and earlier playing in decrepit old theaters in far away corners of the city... sitting on the sidewalk at the corner of Brig's and M.G's girl-watching... smoking and chatting over cups of strong coffee at Koshy's... sharing bottles of beer at the seedy Chin Lung Bar just to watch the live rock band, The Mustangs, perform there...

Venu joined them when he could, but his father kept him on a very tight leash. Krishnachandra did not like his son's friends very much.

"Those boys are going to spoil you," he told Venu. "I don't want you mixing with them. They come from families with money, position... different value system, not at all like us. That boy, George, has long hair and wears such strange clothes. He must be smoking, drinking and taking some drugs. Swaminathan used to be a nice boy but the other boy, George, has spoiled him. Now he wants to spoil you also. Venda, ne avarkuda pogatha..."

Venu had considered standing up to his father many times. *"What value system,"* he wanted to say, *"Where you beat your wife and children and drink so much you don't even know what you are doing?"*

However, he always decided against it at the last minute. He knew he could not stay in the same house anymore if he challenged his father. He had a sense of responsibility to his mother and brother and sisters as well. By staying at home, he felt he was keeping an eye on his father and making sure he did not go too far.

He also found it was a better strategy to just keep his father ignorant of his comings and goings. By half past nine every night, Krishnachandra would be too drunk to care where Venu was. During the day, when his father was in the shop with a customer, he would suddenly say, "I'll be back soon," and disappear for a few hours.

Swami and George would meet him at a restaurant nearby where the friends would drink coffee, chat and smoke. Since the night at Impy's, the Scrimshankers had all started smoking regularly.

George usually smoked a whole pack of ten cigarettes everyday. He even smoked at home in the shed behind the servants' quarters sometimes. Swami was more disciplined. He bought only five loose cigarettes every morning and kept that as his limit for the day.

Venu was a sporadic smoker. He rarely bought his own cigarettes but bummed one or two from his friends when they met him for coffee. If he couldn't meet them, he sometimes smoked a cigarette after lunch on his own in one of the side streets near the medical shop.

At first, the Scrimshankers only smoked *Wills Filter* cigarettes. But after a few weeks, they realized that they also needed something cheaper as an alternative when they were low on cash.

The tobacco industry is arguably one of the oldest industries in India. By the mid-1970s, the country was the second-largest producer of cigarettes in the world. Indian Tobacco Company, ITC, was the biggest manufacturer with more than eighty percent of the market share.

Their product line extended from the premium brands, *India Kings* and *Classic*, to the mid-priced *Wills Filter Navy Cut* and *Gold Flake*, to their value-priced brands, *Capstan* and *Scissors*. The other tobacco companies were much smaller and included Godfrey Phillips, a subsidiary of Philip Morris that made *Four Square* cigarettes, Golden Tobacco, makers of *Panama* cigarettes and Vazir Sultan, whose brands included *Charms* and *Charminar*.

All the tobacco companies advertised heavily, and each of the brands had a very loyal base of users. Among the affluent and educated class, the ITC brands were the most popular. The poor in the country smoked beedis, a thin cigarette made by wrapping tobacco in a tendu leaf. They were strong and very inexpensive. The sales of beedis far outpaced that of cigarettes in India.

A few weeks after they started smoking, George and Swami decided to buy one cigarette of each available brand from a paan shop nearby and test them all out to see which ones they liked the best. After taking puffs and passing cigarettes back and forth all day, they came to the conclusion that they liked *Wills Filter* the best, even more than the higher priced *India Kings* or *Classic* cigarettes. *Capstan Filter* was their second favorite and *Charminar Unfiltered* was their least preferred brand. They tried smoking beedis as well but did not like the taste or smell, even though it was very cheap.

Swami's parents had become a lot more lenient with him since he had completed the ICSE exam. They allowed him to spend the whole day with his friends if he wanted. His curfew time was usually ten o'clock at night.

On some nights, George, who appeared to have no curfew, and Venu, who sneaked away when he could, accompanied Swami home. The boys ate a hearty vegetarian dinner there and then spent hours talking and smoking on the terrace. Sometimes, after telephoning his mother, George even slept over at Swami's house when it got very late.

Swaminathan had recently purchased a cheap Reynolds guitar with the intention of learning the instrument. The boys usually took it with them to the terrace. George tried to teach Swami a few simple chords, or he played and sang popular songs, as well as some of his own. Swami and Venu were in awe of George's ability to play guitar, sing and write songs.

"How do you come up with these songs?" asked Swami. "They are so fantastic. If you record them and put out an album, I am sure you will be famous abroad."

One day, while they were studying for a world history exam in the tenth standard, George had come up with a song called *From There To Here*. It cleverly encapsulated everything from their textbook and even personalized the concept of history in a remarkable way at the end.

From there to here has been thousands of years, if you're counting
From dinosaurs and Neanderthals we've been evolving
It's been a long time from there to here but it's not clear
If we've learned from our mistakes and our tears

The pharaohs believed they could live forever in their mausoleums
You can find their shriveled bones now in the museums
It's been a long time from there to here, but it's not clear
If we've learned from our mistakes and our tears

The Crusades were about killing each other in the name of religion
Then they added a little pain and torture at the inquisition
It's been a long time from there to here, but it's not clear
If we've learned from our mistakes and our tears

The Dark Ages, the Renaissance and the Age of Reason
Were followed by the news at ten on television
It's been a long time from there to here, but it's not clear
If we've learned from our mistakes and our tears

From there to here my life is just a drop in the ocean
As I look back now, I am filled with mixed emotions
It's been a long time from there to here, but it's not clear
If I've learned from my mistakes and my tears

Songs just came to George and flowed out of him. He often told his friends that he had no idea where they came from.

"You know something, I can't even take credit for the songs I write, because I think it's coming from somewhere outside me and just being channeled through me."

George had plans of being a singer and songwriter but he was still in the process of honing his craft. He did not have a master plan yet, but he wanted to start performing soon.

◼

Venkat, Swami's father, had slowly risen through the ranks in the bank where he worked. The year before Swami completed his ICSE, he had been promoted to Assistant Director of the bank and moved into the head office on the top floor of the Unity Building. The position came with a big increase in his salary as well as many perks. However, Venkat was essentially a simple man who did not like the trappings of wealth or luxury. The family now lived in a big house in a desirable neighborhood, courtesy of the bank. It had expensive furniture, but it was sparsely furnished to reflect Venkat's simple tastes. They had a nice dining table and cushioned wooden chairs, but Venkat and his wife still preferred sitting on a mat on the kitchen floor while taking their meals.

As his savings grew, the only visible difference in Venkat was that he indulged Swami more. He allowed him to purchase a good stereo for his room as well as lots of records, books and clothes. Over the years, Venkat had realized that his son was essentially a good and responsible boy, as well as an exceptional student. He was very proud of him. Now as Swami was approaching adulthood, he decided to let him have a little freedom so he could learn about the world.

Unlike Venu's father, Venkat was quite fond of George. He was always very respectful when he came to their house. Venkat had also seen a marked change in his son since the two boys became friends. He had become more confident and outgoing. Venkat had met George's parents on a few occasions and thought they were very nice people as well. They appeared to be free from airs and pretentions, in spite of the fact that Mohan Chandy held a high post in such a big company and his wife's brother was the Deputy Inspector General of Police. The Chandys always made it a point to come inside and chat with Venkat and his wife for a few minutes or even stay for coffee and snacks when they came to pick up or drop off their son.

Venkat suspected that the boys had started smoking and drinking a little. But he decided not to reprimand or punish his son unless it got out of hand. One of Venkat's best friends, Murthy, had always been unreasonably strict with his son, Arvind. After his pre-university, the boy had gone away to the Madras Christian College for his BA. As soon as he was out of his father's reach, he had started smoking, drinking and taking drugs — all in excess. Now he was a charas and heroin addict, well beyond any help or intervention. Venkat believed it was Murthy's controlling nature that had turned his son into someone who could not handle his vices in moderation.

"Amma, children slowly need to learn how to control their appetites and desires," he told Swami's mother one day when she informed him that their son's clothes smelled of cigarettes. "If we are always going to tell him *'do this and don't do that,'* then how will he know what to do when he moves away from us or when we are gone? No, Radha, I know he's a good boy and will never go too far astray."

However, he spoke to Swami one day about the matter. "Kanna, you have finished your school now and have a long vacation. You have been studying very hard so I am going to be lenient with you during your holidays. But I want you to also be responsible for what you do from now on. Don't do anything bad. A little smoking or drinking is okay; all boys will try, but please do not use any drugs because once you are addicted you will have a hard time breaking the habit. You know about my friend Murthy's son Arvind. See what happened to him."

"Appa, I will promise you that I will never take any drugs," said Swami.

■

Swaminathan usually carried only brand-new rupee bills in his pocket. His friends were envious of this. Since Venkat worked at a bank, he always brought home cash for the family expenses in new, one-rupee, five-rupee and ten-rupee notes. It was something he had done for many years. At the beginning of each month, he would give his wife several bundles of stapled new notes with the brown paper band and sticker from the central bank still on it.

Each morning after breakfast, Swami's mother gave him five, crisp, new, one-rupee bills from her almarah. The money smelled of fresh ink and new paper and even clung together. His friends loved to smell and touch the notes.

"This is the smell of money, buggers," said Venu. "I hate all the old notes that I have to handle every day. When I get a job I'm going to get my full salary every month in new one-rupee notes like this."

"When I was younger, I used to put my initials somewhere on all the money I spent to see if I would ever get the same notes back. So far none of them have come back to me, not yet at least," said Swami.

"In the U.S., all money is in the same size and color, unlike in India. When I was in New York, I once gave a twenty-dollar bill instead of a one-dollar bill and the storekeeper didn't even tell me.

I was so upset," said George.

"I'm glad India has some things that are better than in the U.S.," said Swami. "However, it is nicer to have all your money in the same size when you carry it in your pocket or in a purse."

Although his new allowance, of five rupees a day, was a substantial increase in his finances, Swami had to budget it so the money lasted him all day until he got back home at night. He usually met up with George somewhere in the Cantonment area around mid-morning. Sometimes they stopped off at HMV records or one of the music stores that sold pirated cassette tapes of the latest music.

The easy availability of cassette players and tapes was the best thing that had happened recently for music lovers in Bangalore. Although the tapes that were released by the record companies in India were few and far between, an entire cottage industry had mushroomed up around this new technology of manufacturing and selling music on cassettes. Hundreds of little booths began sprouting up in street corners and under the staircases of shopping centers all over the city. They sold pirated pre-recorded cassette tapes of all the latest releases from the U.S. and Europe for as little as twenty-five rupees. Audiophiles who wanted better quality sound went to custom recording stores that transferred music from original records straight to high-quality, metal-coated cassette tapes. This cost about hundred rupees for one hundred-minute cassette that usually fit two albums. Swami had made several such tapes recently.

George had quite a large collection of records that he had got with him from the U.S. In addition, his father often traveled to Singapore and Europe on business. He picked up the latest albums that George asked for during his trips.

Recently both boys had developed a passion for the songs of Bob Dylan. "What deadly lyrics!" said Swami, "I was listening to *Blood On The Tracks* last night, George. I heard it from start to finish without stopping."

"Yes, I've started to write better lyrics since I started listening to Dylan last year," said George. "It's funny, but I never liked him at first because I didn't think he was very musical, but when you start to play his songs on the guitar, you realize how melodic and complex they are."

"If I had written *Blowing In The Wind*, I wouldn't want credit for doing anything else in my life," said Swami. "What a song, none better!!"

The two boys usually followed a routine now. They met in Koshy's for coffee and a couple of cigarettes by ten or eleven o'clock in the morning, walked around Brigade Road or M.G. Road, had lunch somewhere, saw a matinee movie sometimes, hung around in one of their houses for a few hours, had dinner together outside, maybe a coffee after that and went home by ten or eleven o'clock at night.

Occasionally Venu joined them after work for an hour or two. His father usually went home and started drinking around seven every evening. By ten o'clock, he had drunk himself to sleep. Venu closed the shop at eight o'clock and then met his friends for a little while before heading home. His mother had given him a house key, so he let himself in silently without waking his father.

■

"Do you know what 'Capstan' stands for," Swami asked his friends one evening.

It was just after nine o'clock at night. The three of them were having their last cup of coffee for the day at Koshy's Restaurant, which had become one of their regular haunts, before going home. He showed them the red, white and blue packet of *Capstan Filter* cigarettes. The Scrimshankers only smoked it when they didn't have money for *Wills Filter* cigarettes.

"It's the rotating thing on ships that pulls up the anchor when you turn it slowly," said George.

"Okay, that is one meaning but I was talking about an acronym, like CIA stands for Central Intelligence Agency."

"You tell us, Swami," said Venu. "I'll never guess."

"CAPSTAN stands for, 'Can-A-Prick-Stand-Twice-A-Night?'" Swami said laughing. "And here's something even better: if you read it backwards." He pointed to the packet, "it is NATSPAC, 'No-A-Twice-Standing-Prick-Always-Collapses.'"

His friends laughed loudly. "Where did you hear this?" asked George. "It's so funny."

"From those old Anglo-Indian and British retired military guys who come here in the mornings to smoke, have coffee and chat together," said Swaminathan. "Like we will probably be doing in fifty years."

"You mean the oldies who sit at that corner table?" asked George pointing.

"Yes, they are quite interesting chaps, actually. I was sitting at the next table from them when I was waiting for you the other day, George. They were having a conversation on World War Two postal acronyms. One of them said that soldiers used them to spice up the postcards they sent to girlfriends back home."

"Like Capstan?" asked Venu.

"Yes, they wanted to write dirty things to each other but because everyone could see what they wrote on a postcard, they had to use secret acronyms. Just a bit of relief to get through the terrors of war, I suppose. Let me see if I remember some of the others they mentioned: how about Egypt?"

"Tell us," said Venu.

"Eager-to-Grab-Your-Pretty-Tits." When the woman wrote back, they used acronyms too — here's another one, China…"

"What does that stand for?" George asked, "Something with Cum…"

"No," said Swami, "Come-Home-I'm-Naked-Already."

"Swami, I don't know how you remember this stuff after just hearing it once," said George, "You are a walking, talking encyclopedia of knowledge, of both necessary and unnecessary information," he added, laughing. "You should become a reporter or writer, start a newspaper or magazine or something."

Swami looked at him earnestly, "You know, George, I am seriously thinking about just that."

Chapter 10

The Ides of March

March promised to be an eventful month. Their exam results were going to be announced around the middle of the month and George was going to the U.S. for three weeks at the end of the month. The Scrimshankers were all a bit nervous in anticipation of their exam results. They would have to apply to junior colleges as soon as they had their transcripts in their hands. The boys had already narrowed down their choices to three institutions: St. Joseph's College, Christ College, and Bishop Cotton School. They could also continue on at Baldwin School for the eleventh and twelfth grades, but none of them wanted to do that. They had decided that they would prefer a change of scene for the next two years.

Venu hadn't told even his friends yet, but he'd decided that he wanted to become a doctor someday. He had been interested in medicine from a young age, and for the past few months, he had been thinking seriously about it as a career. He knew he would have a long and difficult road ahead of him. He did not think he was brilliant, like Swaminathan, who was exceptional at whatever he put his mind to academically, or rich and connected like George, whose family had influence almost everywhere in the country. No, he did not have money, influence or genius, but he had determination. His immediate goal was to get into the science group at St. Joseph's College. If he did really well there in the final exam, it was possible that he would get admission to some medical college. But right now, that was just a distant dream.

Mohan Chandy wanted George to go to Bishop Cotton Boys'

School. It was a very prestigious institution. He was friends with the principal and also had a lot of influence with the school's governing body. He knew he could get admission for his son if he just passed the ICSE exam. George was confident that he would get reasonably good grades in his final exam but he was not sure what he wanted to do in junior college. His only real interests were music and drawing.

Swaminathan was confident that he had excelled in the ICSE exam and could get admission into any junior college in Bangalore. His dilemma at this point was deciding which subjects to take. His father had suggested that he take a commerce and business stream so he could complete a degree in accounting and join a bank after that. On the other hand, many of the teachers in his school had advised him to stay on a science and mathematics focus because of his excellent grades and to apply for admission at the Indian Institute of Technology, one of the most prestigious colleges in the country.

However, Swaminathan had decided that he wanted to become a reporter and publish his own newspaper someday. His goal was to get a broad education in his junior college years that would help him develop both his skills as a writer and as a journalist.

The exam results were supposed to be announced on the fifteenth of March. The date was not lost on the Scrimshankers, who had studied every line of *Julius Caesar* for their English Literature exam.

"Beware the Ides of March," said Swami to George over the phone in his best British accent on the evening of March fourteenth. He tried to imitate Sean Connery in his mind. It sounded very authentic. One of Swami's lesser-known talents was that of mimicking and doing impressions of people. He was very good at it. One day he had called George and mimicked a CIA agent from the U.S.

"Is this Mr. George Chandy?" He put on a strong American accent.

"Yes."

"This is George Kennedy calling from Washington." He mimicked the actor George Kennedy from the Airport movies.

"Yes," said George, "how can I help you?"

"Well we are looking to recruit people for the CIA. You are a

U.S. citizen, correct?"

"No, wh… who is this? How did you get my number," asked George.

"We know everything about you Chandy…" Then, unable to control himself, Swami had burst out laughing. But it was so believable that it took a few seconds for George to realize that he had been fooled.

Another time, he imitated MGR's assistant and called Venu on the phone. MGR was a Tamil film actor and politician who inspired a fanatical following in his state. Venu was an ardent fan and supporter.

Swami and George were in the Chandy residence feeling bored one day. "Hey, Swami, let's have some fun with Venu," said George. "You do a terrific Tamilian accent. Why don't you call him at the shop and pretend to be MGR or something?"

Venu did not have a telephone at home so when his friends needed to contact him they called the medical shop. Swami dialed the number of Get Well Medicals.

"Yes, hello… Get Well Medicals, Krishnachandra speaking," said Venu's father at the other end.

Swami changed his voice, "Yes, my good saar, this is Arumugam calling from Madras. Can I speak to one Mr. Venugopal at this number?"

Venu's father was puzzled. He didn't know that Venu knew anyone in Madras on his own. He passed the phone to Venu.

"Yaaro Arumugum from Madras," he said.

When Swami picked up the phone, Swami said in a thick Tamil accent, "Venugopal, this is Arumugam, Mr. M.G. Ramachandran's assistant. I want to give you a ticket for his latest picture *Netru Indru Naalai*. You meet me in thirty minutes in Kamat Restaurant by Commercial Street."

Venu was fooled for a few seconds; the voice did not sound anything like Swami's. But he put two and two together. Because his father was next to him, he said, "Okay sir, thank you for the information, but not interested."

He kept a serious expression, even though he felt like laughing. Instead, he said, "Annayo sales call… nothing important…"

When he met up with his friends later he laughed and told Swami, "I knew it was you bugger, but good job. You should have spoken in Tamil, not English, and maybe I would have believed you."

When Swami called George warning him of the Ides of March, his friend wasn't surprised, or fooled. Over the years, he had gotten used to people with strange accents calling him. It was very entertaining, however.

"Why would you think a soothsayer would have a British or Scottish accent like Sean Connery?" he asked. "Wasn't he an Italian?"

"Okay then, bewareee the Ideees of a Marcheee..." said Swami in his best Italian accent.

George laughed. "Are the results really coming out tomorrow?" he asked.

"Yes," said Swami, "they're posting it in school at ten o'clock. We'll get the actual transcript in the mail only by next week though."

■

The next morning, the three Scrimshankers were at Baldwin Boys' School a little after ten in the morning. They parked their bicycles at the cycle stand and walked to the office building. Several of their batch mates were already milling around outside the big stone building. Some were coming down the stairs smiling. Others were obviously disappointed.

"Great job, Swami," said Rajan, who was in their class. He had already seen Swami's score while looking for his.

"Looks like you maxed the exam as usual," said George punching his friend playfully on the shoulder. They went up the steps to the hallway where the results were posted on the notice board. All three craned their necks over the other students.

George let out a whoop, "Chandy twenty points! Not bad, buggers, if I say so myself."

The ICSE was graded with a points system. There were six subjects and students were given a grade from one to six on each. Points from one to three were considered excellent with one being the highest. Four through six were passing. Seven was a failing grade. An aggregate of up to twenty-one points for the six subjects was considered a first class.

"K. Venugopal, sixteen points," said Swami. "Great job, Venu!"

His friend's face was shining. He was relieved and happy.

Finally, he looked for his — then he found it: V. Swaminathan, eight points.

"Swami, bugger, you got eight points — fantastic! Must be the highest scores in the school," said George. He hugged his friend.

They looked at the individual grades. Swami had all ones, except for Hindi in which he had a three.

"I have to telephone my father," he said.

They went to the office and asked Miss Rozario if they could use the school telephone. Swaminathan was a hero in school that day. Everyone in the bursar's office had heard that he had scored a remarkable eight points in the ICSE.

"Of course, Swami, you can use the phone," said Miss Rozario smiling. "Only Rahul Mishra got higher marks than you. He got seven points, but he's from the North, you know, so it was expected that he would do well in Hindi."

Swami called Venkat in the office, "Appa, I got eight points in my exam," he said excitedly as soon as his father picked up the phone.

On the other end, Venkat's was overjoyed. He had expected Swami do well but he knew that this was an exceptional score.

"Nijamavaa? I am so proud of you, Kanna. I don't know what to say. God bless you my dear boy. You must call Amma and tell her also. She must hear from you. I will go to Kamat Sweets and buy some ladoos for the entire office. Swami, I am so happy!"

Swami called his mother and shared the news with her. She cried with happiness.

George telephoned his father next. Mohan Chandy was delighted and relieved. He knew his son was intelligent but he was generally not a hard worker when it came to academics. He had not expected much more than a passing grade from him.

"Georgie… wonderful news, son. I am so proud. Wait, mummy is here… Sheila, Georgie ke first class onde!"

"Wow! Congratulations… ente makane*… daddy and I are so proud of you. Come home a little early so we can celebrate, okay?"

Venu did not have a telephone in his house, although there was one in the medical shop. He thought about calling his father but decided not to. The only person who he wanted to share the news with was his mother.

*My son (Malayalam)

"Swami, George, I'll just go to my house. I want to tell my mother. I'll see you chaps later, okay."

"No, we'll come with you," said Swami.

"Yes, let's stop at All Saint's Bakery and buy a cake for your brother and sisters," said George. "My treat; I still got a lot of money left over from my birthday. It's for my twenty points in the ICSE. I still can't believe it — I even got a four in Hindi."

George bought a plum cake from the bakery and the boys pedaled to Venu's house in Cambridge Layout. It was a small two-story building with a low cement wall and little gate at the side. The exterior walls were stained with mud and rainwater. The house had once been painted in pista-green but over the years the elements had faded it down to almost white. It still had patches of green showing here and there. There were dense money-plant vines growing all over the compound wall and the sides of the house.

An old man in a blue, checkered dhoti and white banyan sat on a little wicker armchair on the narrow balcony upstairs, apparently just watching the activity on the street below. He was a retired government officer who now lived with his son's family in the first-floor apartment.

Venu nodded to him respectfully. "How are you, Uncle? We got our ICSE exam results. All of us got first classes," he said. He was clearly still excited about his grades.

"That's very good news. God bless you all," the man replied. "We need smart young people like you in this country. Bloody politicians and crooks are spoiling what we all fought so hard for during independence!"

He started to go into a rant on the subject of corrupt politicians because he usually had no one to talk to during the day. However, seeing that the boys were in a hurry, he just waved to them and picked up a newspaper from the floor and started reading it.

A boy who appeared to be a few years younger than Venu with similar features as him was playing with a blue rubber ball in the narrow pathway inside. He was wearing the white uniform of Frank Anthony's Public School, which was located only a few blocks away. It was just after noon and Venu's brother and sisters were at home for their lunch break.

"One minute chaps, I'll come back now," said Venu. He had never invited his friends inside his house, even though they had known each other for several years. Swami and George leaned their bicycles on the wall outside and sat down on some granite slabs that the workers from the construction site next door had left on the footpath.

Venu went inside the gate. He tousled his brother's hair and said, "Cake sapadia, Ravi?" He opened the front door and put the cake on a little table in the kitchen. He unwrapped the box, took a knife and cut the cake into a few pieces.

"Where are Priya and Mallika?" he asked his brother. Hearing their names, the two younger girls came running out from the back of the house.

"Venuanna," they screamed. Venu hugged them both and gave them each a piece of cake.

His mother was washing vessels in the kitchen. She turned around and smiled when she saw him. For a moment, her son saw the beautiful woman she once had been. Then it disappeared as a look of concern appeared on her face.

"Ella seriya, Venu?"

"Yes, Amma, everything is so wonderful," said Venu smiling, "First class kitaittatu. I got sixteen points… it's a very good score. Swami got eight points… that brilliant bugger. George got twenty points… very good for all of us. Amma, I am so happy!"

His mother stopped what she was doing. "Venu, what good news!"

She sat down on the chair. Her legs were trembling. Her eyes welled with tears. Only she knew the effort and dedication it had taken for her son to perform so well in the exam. She thanked God everyday for Venu and for having him in the house, especially now that he was older. Krishnachandra was still drinking every night, but he had been less abusive since Venu had grown up.

One night a few weeks ago, Venu had returned from the shop to find Krishnachandra ranting and raving about something in front of his terrified family. His eyes were glazed and he was standing up and shaking his fist in the air. Venu had stepped up to him, held his arm firmly and put him into his armchair, in spite of his father's resistance.

Then he said quietly said, "Appa, if you are drinking, sit in the chair and don't get up, otherwise something bad may happen to you. Do you understand?" He looked straight into his father's eyes.

Krishnachandra tried to stare down his son but he saw something that he hadn't noticed before: Venu was no long afraid of him. He averted his gaze and muttered to himself, but even in his inebriated state he knew his years of abuse and domination would soon be over.

"Okay, Amma, I'm going now. My friends are outside. George got some cake for us. It is on the table," said Venu.

"Aaiye, tell your friends to come inside and have some snacks."

In all the years that Venu had known Swami and George, he had never introduced them to his mother or asked them to come inside his house. Unlike her husband, Venu's mother liked his friends. Though she hadn't talked to them directly, she knew about each of them in detail from her son. When he was younger, he spoke incessantly about everything he and his friends did together. Even when he was older, Venu still shared things about his friends with his mother: that George would someday be a famous singer and guitarist; that Swami was so clever he could finish the arithmetic test in half the time that everyone in the class took and still get every answer correct.

"Amma, I have the best friends," he would tell her. His mother was grateful that he had at least found friends who were there for him. It broke her heart that he had the misfortune of being born as the son of a drunkard. She had heard about all the wonderful things Swami's and George's fathers did with them. Venu had none of what they had, but they always included him in everything they did.

"No, it's okay. We have to go," said Venu.

But his mother was insistent. It may have been that she felt a sense of hope in the future, both for herself as well as her children for the first time in years.

She said, "Venu, I want to meet your friends. Please ask them to come in. Give me one minute to put some things away and call them inside."

"Okay, Amma, I'll ask them."

Venu went outside. His friends were sitting outside talking.

"Shall we go?" asked Swami when he saw Venu.

"My mother wants you chaps to come inside. But only if you want — you know our situation. We have a very small house, so I haven't called you inside before. But if you don't mind, I'd like you to come in for a little while."

Swami and George were very surprised but they didn't show it.

"I will be glad to come in, but only if your mom makes some nice dosas for me. I really like the ones you used to bring to school for lunch," said George.

"I'll be honored to come inside, Venu," said Swami.

The boys locked their cycles and went inside. The room they entered was a small narrow sitting area. There were two cushionless wooden sofas and a side table. One one wall, were large, framed, sepia prints of what was probably Venu's grandparents. Attached to the other wall, was a little shelf that contained the images of Lord Krishna and Lord Ganesh along with pooja accoutrements: a tray, incense sticks, a bell, a lamp, water container and spoon, and red kum kum powder.

Venu's mother and siblings were lined up just inside the door in single file, as if they were in a receiving line to welcome dignitaries at an important event. "Please come inside," said his mother with her hands pressed together palms touching and fingers pointed upwards in front of her chest in the traditional namaste greeting.

"Vanakkam, Aunty," said Swami returning her greeting the same way with his palms together. "How are you?"

"Hi, Aunty," said George. "Venu tells us you will be making some fabulous dosas for us to eat."

Venu's mother smiled. It was hard for anyone not to like George immediately. He had an open, innocent and direct way about him that endeared him to most people.

"And who are these pretty little school girls?" he asked Venu, looking at the girls who were now hiding behind their mother's sari. "You go to FAPS, eh?" he said, looking at their uniforms.

"Chaps, this is my sister Priya, who is twelve years old, and this is my other sister Mallika, who is nine years old. Girls, these are my two best friends George and Swami. Yes, they go to Frank Anthony's. They are on their lunch break now."

The two girls blushed and hid behind their mother even more. "You know my brother, Ravi, right? He's thirteen now." The boy stepped forward and shook their hands.

"Okay, you children can go inside now."

Venu's mother said, "Please sit, I will come back soon."

The Scrimshankers sat in the little room and talked about their exams and their plans for the future.

"Which junior colleges will you chaps be applying to?" Venu asked. "Swami, you don't need to apply. They will all come to your house to ask you to join their colleges."

"Yeah, bugger, what fantastic marks you have," said George. "My father wants me to go to Bishop Cotton. I wouldn't mind, but they make you wear a school uniform even in the eleventh and twelfth standards. All PUC institutions don't have that requirement. I would rather go to Christ College, but it's quite far away. My father has promised that he'll get me a motorbike once I get a license next year."

"I wouldn't mind going to Cotton's," said Swami. "The school is really good and I've heard they have the best facilities — beautiful campus too! Their girl's school is right next door as well, not like Baldwin."

"I would really like to go to St. Joseph's for the PUC," said Venu. "After that, I haven't told anyone yet, even my family, but I want to do medicine — if I have the marks required for admission, that is."

"Wow, a doctor. Dr. Venugopal... hmm it has a nice sound to it," said George. "You should definitely do it."

"Yes Venu, you will be a wonderful doctor," said Swami.

"Come, let's go into my room," said Venu. He led them inside through the main room of the house. There was a small kitchen on one end and a partitioned area with a Chinese screen, for his sisters, on the opposite side. There were two curtained doorways in the middle of the room. Venu led them through one.

His room consisted of a small bed, a long metal desk with two metal folding chairs and a wooden cupboard. George and Swami sat on the bed while Venu remained standing. "This is nothing like your rooms, chaps, but I manage," he said.

The desk was divided in two with a strip of black electrical tape. Venu's books were on the right side, neatly arranged between two bookends. He had an old mug filled with pencils and cheap ballpoint pens. The little fire truck that George had given him years ago was on one end. The left side of the desk was much messier and contained his brother's schoolbooks.

"This is a nice room," said George. "Very comfortable bed," he said, laying down on it.

Venu's mother entered and beckoned him outside. He came

back a few seconds later. "My mother has made some snacks for us: dosas, pakodas and coffee. We can eat here."

A few minutes later, his siblings appeared through the door with stainless-steel plates of food that they passed along solemnly to the guests. George sat cross-legged on Venu's bed and ate with gusto while Swami sat on the chair at the desk. Finally, Venu's mother came in with small, steel cups of steaming hot South Indian coffee.

"That was so good, Aunty," said Swami. "My mother's dosas are good, but your dosas are great!"

"Yes," said George. "I love good dosas. Can we come back again, Aunty?"

"Yes, please," said Venu's mother smiling. "Venugopal, bring your friends whenever they want."

Venu laughed. He felt pleased and relieved that his friends were comfortable in his house. *"I shouldn't have expected anything less from them,"* he thought to himself.

Swaminathan was not a stranger to accommodations such as this. When he was much younger, their house was very similar. As his father had risen higher and higher in his position at the bank, their quarters and grown larger and larger. But he never forgot their humble beginnings. Even now, because of his father's simple way of living, they did not have a very extravagant lifestyle.

For George, on the other hand, coming inside Venu's house was a revelation. He had never known anything other than a comfortable and luxurious life. His father had always held managerial positions since he was born, even in the United States. When they came to India their position had been instantly elevated to the top social bracket. His parents hobnobbed with the cream of Bangalore society. But here in Venu's little room, none of that mattered to him. He was happy that his friend had finally invited him in. He felt quite at ease here in this humble home. In fact, he even envied Venu a little because he had a younger brother and two sisters. They apparently looked up to their big brother. *"That must be a nice feeling to have,"* thought George. He saw the pride and love in Venu's mother's eyes for her son's achievements. He also realized the tremendous effort it had taken on his friend's part to do so well in the ICSE exam.

Their brief visit to Venu's house had given George and Swami a better understanding of their friend. Seeing where he lived: his room, his mother, his brother and sisters, had filled in the missing pieces of what they knew about him.

"Come, chaps, let celebrate today," said Venu. "But I have one more stop to make. After that we can enjoy — maybe go out for dinner."

The boys said goodbye to Venu's mother and siblings and followed him as he led the way.

■

They rode their bicycles to Commercial Street. "I want to go to the medical shop for a few minutes and talk to my father, if that's okay with you both," said Venu. "You chaps can come with me… please."

This was also the first time Venu had asked his friends to come inside the medical shop when his father was still there. Usually, they waited until Krishnachandra had left before they came inside to hang out with Venu.

They parked their bicycles at the public cycle stand at the end of the street and walked to Get Well Medicals. Krishnachandra was surprised to see his son with his friends.

"Venu, is everything all right? If something was wrong you should have phoned."

"Everything is fine, Appa. You know my friends Swami and George."

"Yes… yes… how are you boys?" Krishnachandra was still surprised and caught unaware by their visit.

"Appa, I just wanted to come by and tell you that I got a first class in my ICSE exams… sixteen points… it is a very good score. My friends also did very well, Swami got eight points, the second highest in our school. If you take out Hindi, it's the highest score. George also got a first class."

"Th… that's very good news Venu… congratulations to all of you."

"Thank you, Uncle," said Swami and George.

"Appa, one more thing," said Venu. "Tonight we are going out to celebrate, so I will not be able to work this evening. Also, please give me thirty rupees so I can go to the cinema and have dinner with my friends."

Krishnachandra didn't know how to respond to this. He had no choice but to open the cash register, take out the money and give it to Venu.

"Thank you, Appa," said Venu.

Then, unexpectedly, he went up and hugged his father. Krishnachandra was taken aback. It was the first time his son had hugged him in a long time. Instinctively he put his arm around the boy and hugged him back.

Venu and his friends left soon after that, but Krishnachandra stood like a statue in the same spot for several minutes until a customer walked in and broke his train of thoughts. Still, he couldn't stop thinking about what had happened even several hours later. He felt something that he couldn't quite put his finger on: it was a mixture of shame and remorse... as well as pride, hope and love for his son.

"God bless you my son. May you have the life I never could," he thought to himself.

Chapter 11
Vacations And French Exposure

The following week was a hectic period for the Scrimshankers. They had to send in their applications for admission to junior colleges. The process involved essays, transcripts and letters of recommendations. The boys were glad when it was finally done. Now, they just had to wait for a few weeks to know about the status of their applications. They celebrated again, but this time it was tinged with a bit of sadness because George was leaving the next day for three weeks in the U.S.

"What do you chaps want me to get for you from there?" asked George.

"Can you get me a pair of Levi jeans, George?" asked Swami. "My waist is twenty-eight inches and length is thirty-two inches, but only if you have extra space in your suitcase."

"No problem," said George. "Venu, how about you?"

"No, nothing… I don't even know…" said Venu.

"Well you must want something," said George.

"Actually there is something. Can you get me a checked red and white shirt with studs for buttons… like a cowboy shirt you see actors wearing in movies? My size is medium."

"Okay, no problem," said George. "I'll write to you from there and also try to call you on the phone. I'm only going for about three weeks, so don't bother writing back because I will be back home before I get your letters."

Venu and Swami went to see George off at the airport. They squeezed into the front seat of the white Ambassador car with Sundar, the Chandys' chauffeur, while George and his parents sat in the back. After they had said their goodbyes at the entrance of the airport, the boys went upstairs to the viewing area and watched the plane, a Boeing 727, take off for Bombay. Then, Sundar took them back to George's house, where they had left their bicycles.

■

The next few weeks passed very slowly for Swami because he did not have George for company. Venu still worked almost every day at the medical shop. Swami changed his daily routine He only left home only after lunch now. He would sit alone at Koshy's or sometimes watch a movie and then spend a couple of hours with Venu at night. A week after he left, George called Swami at home.

"How are you buggers?" he asked. "It's quite expensive to call, so I won't speak for too long. It's nice to see all my cousins here after so long. I've sent you a letter two days ago, I hope you get it before I come back."

Swami could sense that George missed his friends too, even though he had such fantastic things to see and experience in the U.S. The next week he received George's letter. Surprisingly it had taken only nine days to reach him. It was a long letter. He opened it at once and started reading:

Dear Swami and Venu (Fellow Scrimshankers),

How are you buggers doing?

We had a pleasant journey here. As you know, our Indian Airlines flight left on time at 3pm (I think I saw you chaps standing upstairs on the balcony from the window of the plane, but maybe it wasn't you!). We landed in Bombay at 5:30pm at the domestic terminal. A bus picked us up and took us to the Centaur Hotel. I think it is a 4-star (almost close to a 5-star hotel I would say).

We had dinner in a nice restaurant at the hotel. They even had a live band playing there. After dinner, we went up to our rooms and went to bed by 8 o'clock. This was because we had to wake up by 4:30 in the morning to catch our Air India flight to London. Another bus picked us up and took us to Sahar International Airport. This time, buggers, it was a Boeing 747. It is a huge plane — much bigger than the 707. The flight took off at 7 o'clock in the morning. It took over 10 hours to arrive in London. They kept serving food: breakfast, lunch and dinner. I didn't sleep at all... but watched movies the whole time. I saw The Deer Hunter, The Eyes of Laura Mars and Superman (they are all fantastic movies).

We couldn't go out of the airport in London because we were there for only 4 hours while they refueled and cleaned the plane. We took off again for New York. I tried to stay awake but I fell asleep in the middle of Midnight Express (which is a deadly movie about two guys who get caught smuggling heroin into Turkey and they are put in prison). I woke up in the middle of Force 10 From Navarone (Swami, I know you are a big fan of Alistair MacLean's books). The movie was good, but not as good as Guns of Navarone, which we saw at Imperial Theater last year. Again, food and drinks kept coming throughout the journey. I must have had at least 5 cans of Coca Cola.

We arrived in New York at 4:00 pm and passed through customs and immigration. Because I am a U.S. citizen, I can come and go as I please. My parents only have a green card. My Uncle Sam was there at JFK airport to pick us up. He has a Chevrolet Impala. It is a very comfortable car. It took us over an hour to drive from the airport to their house in Bloomfield, New Jersey. They live in a nice house with lawns in the front and back of the house. I met my cousins Sophie (who is getting married) and Solomon (who is two years older than me) for the first time in five years.

My dad and mom have been given their own bedroom on the first floor but I'm sleeping in the basement on my own. It's not bad, actually, because it's quite big and has a TV in it. My cousin Solomon has an old guitar (which is nowhere as good as my Martin), but he doesn't play, so it is understandable. It took me a while to tune it so it sounds halfway decent. If I get the chance I'll put in some new strings.

We went to the Willowbrook Mall yesterday. It is the closest shopping center to my aunt's house and is in a town called Little Falls. Buggers, you will be amazed at the size of this place. It has big department stores like Bamberger's, Ohrbach's and Sear's as well as smaller store, music stores and a food court with over 25 small fast food restaurants. First thing I did there was purchase the items you chaps wanted.

I also bought several albums, including Fleetwood Mac's Rumors, Steely Dan's Aja, Billy Joel's The Stranger, Neil Young's Decade, Slowhand by Clapton, Running on Empty by Jackson Browne and the Grateful Dead's Terrapin Station. We can listen to it together when I get back.

How are things in Bangalore? I miss it even though I'm having an exciting time here. I'm going with my dad to New York City tomorrow. That will be the highlight of my visit here. We are going to spend the whole day there seeing all the sights.

My cousin Sophie's wedding is next week and we will be returning back to Bangalore the week after that. My aunt and uncle asked me to stay here for longer, but I would prefer to return soon. Have you received any news on the applications we sent out for admission to junior-colleges? It will probably take a few weeks more I think.

I'm hoping to pick up an electric guitar while I am here — possibly an American Stratocaster (like the one Jimi Hexdrix played) and maybe a nice microphone. I'm seriously thinking of performing when I get back.

The worst thing is that I can't smoke. I had one in the back of the plane coming here — I bummed it of some young French guy (it was an unfiltered Gitanes... yuk!). Since I got to my aunt's house it's hard — it would have been nice if my cousin Solomon smoked, but he seems like a sida-sada* sort of guy. I took a couple of fags from my dad's pack and smoked while taking a walk — he smokes Marlboro's here. I still like our Wills Filter the best... so light one up for me!

That's all for now. More when I see you buggers soon...

> You friend in G-Major,
>
> George

P.S. The girls here are awesome!!!!

Swaminathan smiled when he finished reading the letter. It

---

*on the straight and narrow/
innocent person

appeared that George was having a wonderful time in the U.S. *"Wow, imagine walking around in New York City,"* he thought. *"I wonder if he will walk across the 59th Street Bridge singing Simon and Garfunkel's 'Feeling Groovy'?"*

George did a wonderful rendition of the song on his acoustic guitar. Swami sometimes tried to sing harmony with him, but his voice was a far cry from Paul Simon's.

He reread the letter again. Signing off in G-Major was clever, Swami thought. George always said how much he liked the key of G.

"G is known as the people's key," George had once told him. "Most people can sing comfortably in it, and it has a very pleasant sound to the human ear. I usually start writing most of my songs in G-major, then change the key to suit the melody and my vocal range."

He showed Venu the letter when they met later that evening in Koshy's. The both envied their friend for being able to travel to the other end of the world and experience things they couldn't even dream of.

"Looks like the bugger is having a good time," said Venu.

The boys each lit up a *Wills Filter* cigarette and toasted their friend. Even if they couldn't live his fantastic adventures first hand, they could at least do so vicariously through his letters and stories.

"To George," said Swami, lifting his coffee cup. "The lucky bugger!"

"Yes, to George," said Venu. "The luckiest bugger on earth!"

■

George was back in Bangalore a few days later. He got Swami and Venu everything they had asked for, plus so much more: chewing gum, candy, nuts, chocolates, t-shirts, stickers, pens and books. The Scrimshankers sat in the clubroom in George's house, listening to all his new records and feasting on American junk food for days.

George filled in his friends on all the exciting places and things he had encountered on his holiday. He showed them photos of everything.

"I loved New York City the best," he said. "You can literally feel the excitement when you are there. My dad took me to the Empire

State Building, the World Trade Center, Wall Street, Central Park, Metropolitan Museum of Art, and even to Greenwich Village — it is a very Bohemian place. Bob Dylan got started there!"

"This is so wonderful. I almost feel like I have seen these places myself now," said Swaminathan studying the photos intently.

A few days later, the Scrimshankers finally started receiving their admission letters from the various institutions. Swami was the first to get admission.

"Dear Mr. Swaminathan: We are pleased to inform you that you have been selected for admission to the PUC Science program at St. Joseph's Junior College." The next day he got a similar one from Bishop Cotton.

Mohan Chandy had already put in a word at the diocese, so George got admission to Bishop Cotton the day after Swaminathan got his. Venu was accepted at Christ College the next day but there was no reply from St. Joseph's.

"Looks like I'll be going to Bishop Cotton," said George. "I don't think St. Joseph's wants me."

"Yes, me either," said Venu. "You're a lucky bugger, Swami. You can go anywhere."

"I know how much you want to go to Joseph's, Venu. I wish I could transfer my admission to you."

"So, Swami, do you want to come to Cotton's with me?" asked George.

"You know something, I wouldn't mind, since neither of you are going to Joseph's anyway," said Swami. "Venu, who knows, if a few more students who are offered admission at Joseph's don't accept, they may offer you a seat!"

He was right. A few weeks later, Venu received a letter from St. Joseph's College saying that he had been selected for the PUC science track at the institution.

The Scrimshankers were excited at the prospect of moving into a new stage in their lives. They sent in their letters of acceptance, paid the required tuition advances, provided all the necessary documentation and registered for their classes. After that, they realized they still had two more months left before the term started.

"I'm getting quite bored of just wandering around all day," said

Swami. "Let's do something — maybe join a course."

"Like what," asked George? "Are you already sick of not having to study everyday? Bugger, that's what most people look forward to when they graduate."

"No, I don't want to mug like we had to for the ICSE: the height of Mount Everest, the date of the Battle of Plassey, or the names of every bone in the human body. No, I want to do something interesting."

"Hey, you know something," said George, "Amit Sodhi told me that the French classes at Alliance Francaise are quite interesting. They also have French movie screenings every Saturday. Bugger, there is a lot of nudity in those movies!"

"Okay, let's check it out then," said Swami.

George and Swaminathan made it just in time for admission to the final eight-week session of French lessons at the Alliance Francaise, before their term at Bishop Cotton School started. The classes ran for two hours each weekday morning at ten o'clock.

The aim of the Alliance Francaise is stated as *"promoting French language and culture around the world."* It was founded in 1883 by a group of eminent French intellectuals, including the scientist Louis Pasteur and writer Jules Verne. Since then, it has grown to over a thousand locations in one hundred and thirty-five countries. The boys were pleased to see several of their Baldwin School classmates at the Alliance Francaise.

"Hey, chaps, where's the third musketeer?" asked Naveen Matthews when he saw the boys.

"Venu has to work at his father's medical shop," said Swami. "How are the classes here, Naveen?"

"It only started yesterday, so you didn't miss much. You should check out the magazines in the library. Two words: frontal nudity," said the boy. "The French are so open about sex. Every magazine has at least ten pages of tits in it — and I'm talking about both the ads and news articles."

When George and Swami went to the library, they found all the chairs were occupied by male students who had been studying French for only a few days but were now apparently proficient enough in it to be reading thick glossy magazines written completely in French. George noticed Prakash Badrinath, who had been in their eighth standard class section, carefully remove a page from one of the magazines and quietly slip it into his folder.

"Tits or ass?" he whispered to the boy.

"Ass… and what a nice one at that," said Prakash. "This is the best place in Bangalore to get some good shag material."

"Hi, Swami," said Arjun Nanjappa, another boy from their class. "I heard you maxed the ICSE. Where are you going for your PUC?"

"George and I are going to Cotton's for the ISC," said Swami.

"Lucky buggers! Their girl school is right next door. Come this Saturday evening for the movie here. It's called *Le Train* starring Romy Schneider. Someone who saw it before said it has some terrific nude scenes in it," said Arjun.

After a week there, the boys were glad they had decided to attend classes at the Alliance Francaise. Their teacher was a funny little Frenchman name Pierre Louvere. He said he had opted for teaching rather than joining the army for two years as was required of all males in France.

There were thirty students in each class. They sat in single rows on two sides of the narrow classroom while Pierre walked up and down looking at their notebooks or explaining the lesson. The class had more girls than boys. Some of them were quite pretty.

One day, a girl with her hair cut short like a boy's, with ample bosoms and tight jeans, smiled at George before classes started. She was sitting on the opposite side of the room from him. There was a vacant chair next to her. George was next to Swami.

He nudged Swami and said, "That girl is smiling at me, bugger. What should I do?"

"Why don't you go sit next to her?" Swami said.

"And tell her what?"

"I don't know… that her hair looks nice?"

"After that, what?"

"Ask her if you can see her after class."

"If she says no, then what will I do? I'll have to sit there like an idiot for the whole class feeling awkward."

"Okay, then don't go. Smile at her and ask her to come and sit next to you."

"Really, you think she'll do that?"

"Sure, why not."

"Okay, bugger, I think I'm going to go and sit next to her!"

"Go for it, George."

"You wouldn't mind if I left you alone?"

"No, I think it will be entertaining for me to watch you."

"Okay, then wish me luck."

"Good luck, George."

Just then Vinay Gokuldas, a boy they knew from Mohiuddin's Hindi tuition class, who was sitting next to Swami, ran over quickly and sat next to the girl.

"Shit, that bastard Vinay… he must have been listening. I heard he's quite slick with females. He used to always flirt with the girls during tuitions," said George.

Vinay had made contact with the girl and was busy chatting and smiling at her. "I don't know why he's so good with girls," said Swami. "He always smells of Brylcreem."

"Bugger, I missed my chance. I know she was smiling at me," said George. "Look at him, the lousy bastard is laughing at me."

Indeed, Vinay was talking to the girl, but every now and then he would turn and look at George with a triumphant smile on his face. Just then Pierre entered and started the lesson.

"Repeat after me, Comment allez-vous? It means Ow are you…"

During recess, Swami and George went outside the building for a cigarette. The same girl with short hair was near the gate talking to a well-built, older boy on a Royal Enfield motorcycle. He had his arm around her waist in a proprietary sort of way.

"George, I think it was good you didn't go and sit next to her. Otherwise that guy would probably have been looking for you after class," said Swami.

"I would just say, Je ne comprends pas! See… I'm learning French."

Then suddenly they saw Vinay Gokuldas come charging out of the building looking for the girl with the intention of continuing the conversation he started inside. He saw her with her muscular boyfriend on the motorcycle and just as quickly turned around and ran back inside. George and Swami laughed out loudly in delight.

That Saturday, they took Venu along with them for the screening of Le Train at the auditorium at Alliance Francaise. The place was full. The audience seemed to be predominantly male even though there were actually a much larger number of females registered for the classes.

"Looks like the word has gotten out that there are nude scenes in the movie," said Swami. "What a bunch of desperate sex maniacs."

"Unlike us, who are here for art and culture, right?" asked George.

The three friends laughed. *Le Train* turned out to be a serious film about people fleeing Nazi Germany. Romy Schneider was beautiful as Anna Kupfer, a young Jewish girl who has a brief romance with a fellow passenger. It was, however, not what the audience was expecting.

Half the auditorium walked out after the first fifteen minutes when they realized it was going to be a war movie. Those that stayed, however, were treated to a rare cinematic experience that explored war, death, human dignity, love and female sexuality from the French perspective. And yes, the males who had waited long enough enjoyed a brief glimpse of Ms. Schneider's lovely breasts.

"Not a bad movie," said Swami. "Do you remember the scene where they just show the close-up of Romy Schneider's ear and mouth while she is sitting in the train? I got such a hard-on from that... and there wasn't even any nudity there. These French directors are the masters of sexuality."

"I like the scene where she pulls down the top of her dress and throws water on her underwear. You could see her breasts so clearly... nips and everything. She's so sexy," said George.

"Sorry, I think I fell asleep after the first fifteen minutes," said Venu.

Chapter 12
On Straight On

Bishop Cotton Boys' School, where they had registered for the eleventh and twelfth standard, was everything that Swami and George hoped it would be. It was right in the center of the Cantonment area in Bangalore and close to the Bangalore Club, M.G. Road, Brigade Road, Commercial Street, and not too far from where they lived. The campus was much bigger than Baldwin School. It had four large sports fields, a big auditorium, a basketball court, swimming pool, library, gymnasium and even a little chapel. Many of the buildings were made of solid granite and intended to create the ambiance of Eton, Harrow or some other public school in England.

The school had a proud tradition of excellence in education that dated back to the Victorian era. It was founded in 1865 by Reverend S. T. Pettigrew, the Chaplain of St. Mark's Cathedral, based on the model established by Bishop George Edward Lynch Cotton, one of the founders of the British Public School system. Rev. Pettigrew's intention was to provide an education for children of British army officers that was comparable to that of the best public schools in England. The administration of the school was taken over by the Brotherhood of St. Peter in the early 1900s. After Indian independence, it was passed on to the diocese of the Church of South India.

The school's motto was *"Nec Dextrorsum, Nec Sinistrorsum,"* which was Latin for *"Neither to the Right Nor to the Left"* but *"On Straight On."* It was repeated in the refrain of the school song, penned by Rt. Rev. Herbert Pakenham-Walsh, the school principal in 1915. Although the school did not have many British teachers or students by the 1970s, it still celebrated its archaic British public school traditions. This included the wearing of robes, gowns and mortarboards by the principal and teachers, canings and corporal punishment to enforce discipline, rousing school and house songs sung every day during assembly, celebration of the Feast of St. Peter at the end of June, and fireworks every November fifth for Guy Fawkes Day. Notable alumni of the school included England's cricket Captain, Lord Colin Cowdrey; current Indian test player, Brijesh Patel; former Chief of Army Staff, General Sir Frank Simpson; former Governor of Madras, Norman Majoribanks; the Chairman of the Indian Atomic Energy Commission, Dr. Raja Ramanna; the Indian Army Chief of Staff from 1956-1961, General K. S. Thimayya; as well as film actors, pop singers and politicians both in India and England.

Students from the fourth standard up to the twelfth standard could attend the school as either boarders or day-scholars. Boys from kindergarten to the third standard went to Bishop Cotton Girls' School first, which was across the street, and transferred to the boys' school in the fourth standard. Similarly, in the eleventh standard, girls who wanted to continue on at Bishop Cotton transferred from the girls' school to the boys' school for the ISC program.

Since George and Swami were joining the school in the eleventh standard, they were automatically seniors at the school and got respect from their juniors for this status. However, they still had to wear the school uniform of dark green trousers, white shirt, green and gold striped tie, dark green blazer with gold fringes, black socks and polished black leather shoes. The girls in the class wore dark green skirts instead of pants. The rest of their uniform was the same as that of the boys. The teachers who taught the eleventh and twelfth grades were mostly lenient and easy-going with their students. The curriculum was rigorous but interesting. Swami and George soon fell into a routine of classwork and other activity in the school.

The two boys usually went to the back room of Ali Baba, a small café opposite the school, for a smoke and coffee during class breaks. They had to be careful though: being caught smoking by a teacher while in school uniform was a serious offence and could result in expulsion.

Sometimes George took Swami with him to the Bangalore Club, which literally shared a wall with the school. They played billiards or just hung around on the lawn and swimming pool watching the pretty schoolgirls who came there on their own or with their parents.

St. Joseph's College, where Venu had enrolled for the pre-university program, was only about half-a-mile down the road. The Scrimshankers usually all got together for lunch or in the evening after classes.

The biggest change in the recent past had been in Venu's life. Since the day he got his ICSE results, there had been a marked difference in his father's behavior. Krishnachandra had started drinking less. When he did, he made it a point to go inside his room and do it in private without disrupting the lives of his family. On the days that he restrained from drinking, he was sociable and pleasant to everyone at home. One Saturday evening, he even took his wife and younger children for a Tamil movie — something he hadn't done in years.

Venu was surprised by his transformation, but also a little wary. He couldn't believe that his father had changed so much. However, he decided that he would encourage this new behavior in whatever way possible. He told his mother and siblings to do the same. He began interacting with Krishnachandra more: asking his opinion on things that he hadn't before; making small talk with him at the store; talking to him about his classes; having lunch with him at the Kamat Restaurant on the corner when they were working together at the store; or engaging him in conversation in the evenings, so he wouldn't begin drinking.

Since the day when his son had hugged him unexpectedly, Krishnachandra had realized that he needed to change his ways. Life had been hard for him since he was a child. He had begun his marriage and family with good intentions but when life got hard he had turned to alcohol. He never actually remembered the physical abuse he inflicted on his wife and children the following day, although he had some recollection of getting out of control. He started to examine the responsibility he had to his family as a husband and father more clearly. Venu had managed to get a first class without any help or encouragement from him. He was ashamed of this and did not want to repeat it with his other children.

For the first time, he began to realize that Venu could possibly be the savior that the family needed: the one who could move them all to the next social level. His daughters were getting older and would soon have needs of their own. Who would marry them if the only thing they had was a drunkard for a father? But what could he do? Could he just stop drinking and change his life around? He felt an irresistible urge every night. It was strange, he never thought about drinking during the day. But every evening, the pull was too strong for him to overcome. Unlike most alcoholics, Krishnachandra did not get happier or seek company when he started drinking. On the contrary, he drank on his own and slowly got more morose and angry when he did, until the point when he turned violent and lashed out at his wife and children.

Recently, he had been trying to not to drink at all. He knew that once he took the first sip of alcohol, he couldn't stop until he was completely drunk. He tried to go out in the evening for a walk with his wife and children, so that when he returned he was tired and would go straight to sleep. On some days, thought, he just couldn't hold back his demons. So, he started locking himself in his room with food and alcohol when he got the urge to drink. He came out only the next morning when he was sober.

Venu realized how important the next two years were for him if he wanted a seat in a medical college. He would have to get over ninety-eight percent in his PUC final and perform exceptionally well in the medical college entrance exams to get admission that was solely based on merit. He decided to take his studies very seriously. His friends understood his predicament, so they did not pressure him to join them on their jaunts after school, but he tried to at least have a coffee and cigarette with them everyday.

■

George and Swami had both decided that they would not be pursuing traditional careers if they could help it. Swami had started working at the school's newspaper, *Green and Gold*, as a reporter. It was published every month and featured school-related articles as well as local news and events. From the first day there, Swami realized that gathering and writing news was something that he really enjoyed. The newspaper had a staff of about twenty students, including writers, photographers, editors and layout artists. They were all carefully chosen from high achievers, ranging from the seventh standard right up to the twelfth standard, by the faculty advisor and the editor. Swami's top-scoring ICSE credentials as well as his ability to write quickly and succinctly made him an automatic candidate for a writer's job at the *Green and Gold*. Professor Asha Thomas, the faculty advisor for the newspaper, had already singled him out for the position of editor-in-chief in the near future. The current editor, Andrew Doraiswami, had graduated the year before but had stayed on at Professor Thomas' insistence because there did not appear to be anyone to take his place.

Swaminathan enjoyed being involved in every aspect of the publishing process. The newspaper was printed on letterpress. This meant that all the news stories had to be composed in galleys one letter at a time by hand at the printer. Photos, illustrations and advertisements required engraved blocks that needed to be ordered separately and given to the lithographer.

A few months after he joined the *Green and Gold*, Swami had become an indispensable member of the team. In addition to writing and editing many of the news stories, Swami also helped in taking the typed articles to the printer, sizing photos and line drawings for blocks, collecting advertising material from the agencies on film and taking it to the block maker and checking the galley proofs'. He especially liked hanging around at Brindavan Printers, the company that printed the *Green and Gold* newspaper. He loved the smell of new paper and fresh ink and felt like a publishing mogul when he was there.

"Bugger, I feel like Gareth Brendan in *Dreams Die First* when I am at the printers checking the galley proofs and making decisions on the headlines and lead stories," said Swami to George.

While George was in the U.S., he had picked up a copy of *Dreams Die First*, the latest Harold Robbins novel, for Swami. The book told the story of a Vietnam Vet who is given a small failing newspaper by his wealthy uncle and manages to turn it into a very successful pornographic magazine. It was full of sex, drugs and the seedier side of publishing. Both boys had read the book and enjoyed it very much. As a publicity stunt, the publishing company had released a limited edition cover that featured a beautiful woman wearing a lace adhesive bra and panty that could be removed by the person purchasing the book. George had bought the book in New York City, wrapped the cover in brown paper to get it past the custom inspectors at Bombay's Sahar International Airport and presented it to Swami triumphantly. Of course, they found that when they removed the bras and panties on the cover, what was beneath was in soft-focus and not really any great revelation at all.

■

Like Swami, George had found a way to indulge his calling too. His father knew the owner of Melody Restaurant, an open-air bar and food establishment on Brigade Road. With the help of Mohan's introduction, George had convinced R. T. Sundaram, the owner, to allow him to perform there two nights a week. He was not interested in getting paid, but rather just wanted the opportunity of playing before a live audience.

After impressing R.T. at an audition, George began performing at Melody from seven-thirty to nine-thirty on Wednesday and Friday nights. His parents had realized that this was extremely important to their son so they allowed him to do it even though he was still a full-time student in high school.

"As long as you get good marks in your studies, we will let you follow your dreams of singing and playing music. But if you start doing poorly on your tests, you will have to stop at once," Mohan Chandy told his son.

George was actually quite clever and capable of doing well in school if he wanted to. He made it a point to keep abreast of his class assignments and subsequently performed above his parent's expectations.

The restaurant had its own amplifier and speakers. George also took along his trusty old Martin D-35 as well as the Shure SM58 vocal microphone and his new Starburst Fender Stratocaster that he had purchased at the Sam Ash store on Utica Avenue in Brooklyn a few months ago. With his long hair, wispy beard, faded denim shirts and bell-bottom jeans, George looked like a young Cat Stevens. He had already written over a dozen songs on his own with several more in various unfinished stages. However, he soon found that the audience at Melody Restaurant was not very receptive to original material. He would try to slip in one of his own songs between the Beatles, Cat Stevens, John Denver, and Crosby, Stills and Nash.

"Here's a song I wrote called *From There To Here*," he would say and begin singing it. The women were usually quite nice and cheered him on. They men, however, would lose interest quickly if it weren't a popular song.

"Play something we've heard, bugger," one of them would yell out.

"The audience in India is not ready for original songs," he would tell Swami sadly. "They judge a musician by how well they can sing the latest popular song. Baloney, I tell you, I pour my heart and soul into writing and performing my songs, and they would rather hear *Country Roads, Here Comes The Sun* and *Sounds Of Silence*. I will have to go to the U.S. to make it, then if I come back, they'll love my songs here."

However, George was a big hit when he played covers of popular songs. People slowly began coming to the restaurant just to watch him perform. Even R.T. realized his value and began paying him fifty rupees a night for his shows. As the months went on, George got more and more comfortable performing in public. He started interacting with his audience and even started adding his own songs to the playlist on a regular basis. The regulars soon began to think that some of his songs were actually hit tunes from the U.S. or England and even began singing along with him.

One of the first songs he had ever written was called *Distant Thunder*. It was in a minor key and had sad, soulful lyrics that seemed to appeal to many people. However, he never let on that the song was his to his audience at Melody. They appeared to appreciate it more when they thought a popular songwriter from England or America wrote it.

"Ladies and gentlemen I think I hear a distant thunder," he would say and perform the song.

> *My mind was filled with wonder*
> *When I heard the distant thunder*
> *And I saw you standing in the moonlight*
> *Your eyes were shining ever so bright*
> *You looked at me and I wanted to say...*

But I found the words wouldn't come my way

Ooo ooo the distant thunder
Oh yes, oh yes, it makes me wonder
Ooo ooo the distant thunder

I held out my hand and you came to me
And I found it was like in a dream
We were two lovers on that night
As we walked together in the moonlight
The rain outside and the night so gray
Now this is all I want to say...

Ooo ooo the distant thunder
Oh yes, oh yes, it makes me wonder
Ooo ooo the distant thunder

It's been many years since that fateful day
We got married and I lost my way
You took up with another man
I shot you dead in a desperate plan
So they locked me up now they want my life
To the gallows I go for killing my wife

Ooo ooo the distant thunder
Oh yes, oh yes, it makes me wonder
Ooo ooo the distant thunder

Goodbye... don't you cry. Tomorrow I'm gonna die
An eye for an eye. Tomorrow I'm gonna die
I loved her once, don't you know
But my love for her to hate did grow

George had been inspired to write *Distant Thunder* after listening to *I've Just Got To Get A Message To You*, by the Bee Gees.

"Swami, you've got to listen to this Bee Gees song closely, bugger," he told his friend one day. "You don't realize he's writing the song as he's waiting to be executed... what deadly lyrics! What a great tune. Barry, Maurice and Robin Gibb are such excellent songwriters. They were performing their own songs and recording them since they were fifteen..."

"George, someday they'll be saying the same kind of things about you and your songs," said Swami.

Chapter 13

First Kiss

St. Peter's Tide is celebrated with pomp and circumstance every year on the 29th and 30th of July at Bishop Cotton. According to school history, when the board had contemplated the closure of the school in 1906, St. Peter's Brotherhood, a missionary order in India, had stepped forward and saved the institution. Because of this, even after the school was transferred to the diocese of the Church of South India in 1948, the role that the Brotherhood of St. Peter had played in its existence was never forgotten. The annual tribute to it became the most important function, as well as a tradition, of the school year.

Faculty, staff and students prepared for several months to host the event. Alumni from all over the world came to Bangalore just to attend the two days of activities. The first day's festivities started with breakfast in the large mess hall of the Boys' School... followed by a treasure hunt... lunch... a football match... evensong services at the Girls' School... and ended with the popular St. Peter's Social. The social was held at the Boys' School Hall and usually went on until one or two in the morning. Alumni and students who woke up on time, after the previous night's revelry, could attend the 8:00 A.M. Holy Eucharist Service at the beautiful St. Peter's Chapel at the Boys' School. This was followed by a rousing game of cricket between the present Cottonians and the Old Cottonians. The celebrations ended with high tea and the annual general body meeting of the Old Cottonians Association.

For most of the current students, St. Pete's Social, as it was called, was the most important event of the entire two days. Unlike their counterparts in the West, most teens in India did not have the opportunity to interact with the opposite sex frequently. Schools were segregated by gender and cultural mores made it impossible for girls and boys to freely mix with each other. This was especially true for Hindu and Muslim students. Christian teens had it a little better of because could attend mixed youth groups, dances, picnics and other activities organized by the church or its affiliates.

As a result, most of the students had never danced, or even had a lengthy conversation, with a member of the opposite sex before. St. Pete's Social gave the boys and girls in the school an opportunity to mingle with each other in a venue that was acceptable to their parents.

The social was open to current students of the boys' school from the tenth standard to the twelfth standard and for the girls' school from the ninth standard upward. Alumni of any age could attend the event every year. George and Swaminathan had been looking forward to it since they joined the school.

"I've been told by Gopinath, who's been in Cotton's since the fourth standard, that the St. Pete's Social is fabulous... a very classy affair," said Swami.

They were having lunch with Venu at Casa Piccola, a newly opened European restaurant that was next door to their school. It was the first of its kind in the city and served western food like pastas, meatballs and potpies.

"You lucky buggers, I wish I could come," said Venu.

"You can... just show up, people will think you're an alumnus. You could be, since students who graduated from the tenth standard last year and are doing their PUC now are Old Cottonians," said George.

"Yes, but students in our age group know me. They'll think I'm desperate. I don't care so much about the girls. I just want to have fun with you chaps," said Venu.

"I'm sorry you can't come, Venu," said Swami. "However, George, I too have a problem. I don't know how to dance."

"I can only do a halli dance, like they do on the street during weddings and funerals," said Venu.

"Dancing is quite easy," said George. "I've attended a few dances at the Church and the Club. When I was younger, I used to dance with my mom at home all the time. My parents are very good in both formal and modern dancing. I heard that at the St. Pete's Social most people don't close-dance. Actually for students, it is not allowed. Can you imagine? Those desperate buggers in our school would be pawing at the girls if they were allowed to touch them!" he said laughing. "But don't worry, Swami, I'll teach you. Come to my house this evening."

■

When Swaminathan arrived at George's house later that evening, his host had already got everything organized. He had moved the furniture out of the way in the living room. He had also borrowed some dance and disco music from his cousin, Annie, since all his records were only folk, country and rock. Among the ones George got were two that he knew would be played over and over at the St. Pete's Social that year: both were produced by Biddu Appaiah, an old Cottonian who had gone on to fame and fortune in England as a songwriter and music producer.

Biddu, as he was now known, had written the song *Kung Fu Fighting*, which sold eleven million copies for singer Carl Douglas in the U.S. and Europe. He was also the songwriter and producer for the latest disco sensation in England, Tina Charles. It was a safe bet that his songs would be heralded as being written by an OC and played several times at the event.

"I'm going to play these disco records and show you some simple dance moves," George told Swami. He put on a Tina Charles record.

"First, listen to the rhythm. Almost all disco music has a 4/4 beat… count from one to four… move your head and body to the beat…"

He showed a simple dance move and asked his friend to try it. At first Swami was a little embarrassed. Dancing freely was something he had never done before. After a while, he began to get into the groove. George danced with him.

"Keep shifting your weight from one foot to the other, and keep your elbows bent," he instructed. "Keep your legs loose, and bend your knees slightly. Now move your feet. If you are dancing with a partner, then don't move around too much; if you're on your own, go for it…"

Swami was beginning to feel more relaxed and less self-conscious.

"Okay, now we can go to the next stage," said George dancing around his friend. "Try moving your hips to the music... like this... slightly in the direction of your foot... yes, like that. Lastly, if you really want to look like you are a really good dancer, throw your arms in the air and keep them loose. It'll look like you're really comfortable dancing... that's it, bugger."

The boys practiced dancing for over two hours, until George's parents arrived home from a party they had gone to.

"Sheila, looks like we can continue the party here!" Mohan Chandy said and pulled his wife to the middle of the living room. The couple were both very good dancers and they showed the boys some wonderful dance moves including *The Hustle*, *The Bump* and *The Twist*.

"You know, Swami, when they play *Kung Fu Fighting*, do some of the moves I showed you but also throw in some martial arts gestures. That will really impress the girls," said George.

The Chandys and Swaminathan danced for another hour until it was time for him to go home.

◼

St. Peter's Day arrived. They were in George's house late in the afternoon. Swami did not own a suit or even a sports jacket other than his school blazer. Fortunately, George had several. He usually wore a suit and tie to church and a blazer for some of the other events he went to with his family. Swami and he were around the same height and build — although, while Swami was skinny, George was wiry and muscular.

George had decided to wear his tight black suit, a frilly white shirt with puffy sleeves, a skinny black tie and high-heeled black boots. He took out all his other jackets and blazers from his closet and laid them on his bed.

"Choose whichever one you want," he said.

Swami picked a dark green, ribbed, polyester jacket that had a gold lining inside and fit snugly. He had worn his tight-fitting black flared pants with brown boots. His hair was getting longer too, and he combed it to the side.

George looked like a young movie star. His long, wavy hair was brushed back and fell almost to his shoulders. He went to his father's room and came back with a bottle of Brut cologne, which he sprayed, liberally on Swaminathan and himself.

"Dy-no-mite!" he said looking at himself in the mirror. He had watched several episodes of *Good Times* when he was in the U.S. recently.

The boys arrived at the event at eight o'clock. It was being held in the school hall. Loud disco music was playing inside but the only people dancing were a few of the older alumni who were there with their spouses.

The center of hall was cleared for dancing and there were two long rows of metal chairs on both sides of it. Usually, it was used for indoor school events like plays, music competitions, award ceremonies and school meetings. It had a large raised stage on one end. The hall had been built in the late 1800s and was part of what was known as the Hall Block of the school. It included classrooms, restrooms and masters' quarters. It was rumored that there was a secret passageway under the stage to the hall in the girls' school almost half a mile away.

The stage in the hall was set up for the social as well. A large cloth banner with the words, "Welcome Past & Present Students," was pinned to the satin curtain above the large embroidered school shield with the school's motto *"Nec Dextrorsum, Nec Sinistrorsum"* below it. Four desks were set up in front of the curtain on the stage to sell tickets for food and beverages at the event.

The schoolgirls were all sitting on one side of the room while the schoolboys were on the other. Many of boys were looking intently at the girls, trying to spot the attractive ones and then hoping to summon up the courage to walk over to the other side and to ask them to dance. So far, no one had taken the plunge. George and Swami joined the group of boys.

"Let's just walk across and ask one of the girls to dance," said George.

"Okay, you go first, and I will follow you," said Swami.

George scanned the row of girls on the other side. He noticed one girl that stood out. She was very fair with hair that was cut fashionably short up to her neck and wearing a short, dark blue sleeveless dress with a white collar. From across the room it appeared that she was slim and had decent sized breasts.

"I'm picking the girl in the blue dress with the white collar," said

George to Swami.

"Okay, I'll pick the one next to her," said Swami.

Without hesitation, George walked across the room bravely. All the other boys looked at him enviously. Swami followed a few paces behind.

George approached the girl. Close up, he could see that she was even prettier than he first thought.

"Excuse me," he said, "may I dance with you?" He held out his hand.

The girl hesitated for a moment. Then she reached out, held his hand and walked with him to the middle of the dance floor.

Swami tried the same technique as his friend. His heart was racing fast and his palms were sweating. He walked up to the girl he had picked and asked, "Excuse me miss, will you dance with me?"

However, it appeared that he had made the wrong choice. She was a tall, pretty girl with flowing long hair wearing a full-length, red dress. She shook her head, "No, I'm just sitting here. Maybe later, sorry!"

Swaminathan was flustered and embarrassed. He tried asking the girl next to her, but she refused too. He kept going down the line one by one. After about five refusals, one girl finally agreed. He looked at her gratefully, but she was not his type at all. She was short and heavyset, with her hair tied back tightly in a short braid. She had on a loud flowery dress that ended a few inches below her knees. Swami stepped aside and followed her to the dance floor.

He could see George dancing with his partner. *"They looked like such an attractive couple,"* he thought to himself. Then he looked at his own partner. She appeared to be a rather vigorous dancer. She was shaking her hips and moving her feet rather quickly. Swami tried to keep pace with her.

George was taking in the beauty of the girl he was dancing with. The music was quite loud, and he had to lean in close to her ear to speak to her. She smelled very nice with the subtle scent of some expensive foreign perfume. He was glad he had popped a mint Chiclet into his mouth before going over.

"I'm George. What's your name?" he asked.

"I'm Jennifer," she said.

"Great... very nice to meet you," said George. He wasn't sure what to say after that, so he just danced for a little while. He was a very good dancer and moved naturally without being embarrassed or self-conscious. His partner also appeared to be familiar with dancing.

"You dance well," he told her.

"Thanks, so do you," she replied

They danced some more. The music suddenly stopped. A short, dapper man in a three-piece suit walked up to the stage and picked up the microphone.

"Good evening, ladies and gentlemen, alumni and present Cottonians, my name is Farook Rashid, and I am the president of the Old Boys' Association. I am absolutely thrilled to welcome you all to our annual St. Peter's Social. I have a few small announcements to make before we continue with the fun and dancing. Food will be sold in the hallway outside. We have chicken biryani, chicken curry, parotas, kebabs as well as some vegetarian dishes such as pani puri, veg biryani, channa, paneer kurma and chapatti. You have to come up to the stage and buy tickets for the food you like, and then take it to the stalls in the hallway where you can pick up the food. The servers will not... I repeat the servers will not accept cash... only tickets."

"Farook stop talking yaar, and put the music back on," shouted an old boy from the back of the hall.

"In a minute," said the president, unperturbed. "Next, regarding alcohol, we have a full bar in the classroom next door. However, only alumni will be sold alcohol, and you have to pay cash only. We have beer, whiskey, rum and gin and some imported wine. Students will not be permitted to buy or consume alcohol at this event. Teachers will be watching to enforce this rule strictly. Thank you for your patience and have a wonderful time tonight. Let's get this celebration underway with a song written by our very own old Cottonian, Biddu Appaiah. Here's Tina Charles singing 'Dance Little Lady Dance.'"

The music started, and everyone resumed dancing. George and Swami nodded at each other. When his partner's head was turned away, Swami pointed to George and made a thumbs-up gesture. Then he pointed to himself and made a sad face and a thumbs-down sign.

George laughed. He had to admit that his dance partner was

definitely deserving of a thumbs-up. He was enjoying himself immensely. Suddenly, he felt someone tapping him on the shoulder. He kept dancing. Jennifer was smiling at him. The tap became harder. Someone was pawing at him. He turned around. It was an earnest looking student from the tenth standard. He was a prefect named Sudhakar or Sudhir or something.

"Sorry, may I cut in?" he asked. George was annoyed, but there was nothing he could do.

"Okay, see you," he told Jennifer. He looked into her eyes and he was pleased to see that she looked disappointed. He went and sat down on one of the metal chairs. By this time, most of the boys had screwed up the courage to ask a girl to dance.

George watched the people who were dancing. Very few of the boys could dance well. Some just slouched and moved their feet out of sync with the music, others looked like they were jogging. Some were making exaggerated moves that did not match the music or their partner's rhythm. Swaminathan was looking good though. George was proud of his protégé. He looked at ease. As expected, they played *Kung Fu Fighting*. Swami was in his element now, chopping, kicking and keeping in step with the music!

George looked for Jennifer in the crowd. The tenth standard prefect was still dancing with her. George made up his mind. It had been about twenty minutes since he was tagged. He walked over purposefully and tapped the prefect on his shoulder firmly. "Sorry, Sudhir. I'd like to cut in, if you don't mind," he said.

"Sudhakar, not Sudhir," said the boy. "No problem, thank you Jennifer," he said lowering his head with an arm flourish.

"Thanks for coming back," said Jennifer. "That boy didn't talk at all."

"No problem," said George. "Say, do you want to sit down, maybe have something to eat and drink?" He was afraid that someone else would decide to cut in if they kept dancing.

"That would be nice," said the girl. "We usually have dinner in the mess at eight, but we came here instead, so we didn't eat."

"So, you are a boarder?" George asked.

"Yes, are you a boarder? I don't think I've seen you before. We come to your school for chapel in the morning."

"No, I'm a day scholar. I just joined Cotton's in the eleventh standard. Before that I was in Baldwin."

"My cousin-brother goes to Baldwin. His name is Allen Rego. He's in the ninth standard now. Do you know him?"

"No, I graduated almost two years ago. Maybe I'll remember him if I saw his face. What would you like to eat? I think that chap said there was biryani, some chicken something, paneer something…"

"If you don't mind, I'll have a biryani. Everything else is too messy to eat. Here let me give you money."

"No, not a problem… my treat. What would you like to drink? I think they have Fanta, Limca and Thums Up."

"No, I insist we go Dutch," said Jennifer. "Here is ten rupees. Can you get me a Limca and a biryani?"

George led her to a corner where there were a couple of chairs. He took out his jacket and put it on the chair.

"I'll leave my jacket here, okay?" he said.

He wanted to make sure that other male students with roving eyes would not think the girl was available. He pushed his way through the hoard of people to the stage, stood in line, purchased coupons, then stood in line again for the food, and returned to Jennifer.

When he came back balancing the plates and soft drinks in his hand precariously, he was grateful to see she was still where he had left her.

"I had to tell a couple of chaps that I was waiting for you. Thanks for getting the food," she said with a smile.

"Not a problem… the line was so long…"

He sat down next to her and passed over one of the plates. They both started eating. He looked at her closely. She was really quite beautiful, with even white teeth He couldn't believe he had lucked out so much that evening. He looked for Swaminathan. He was still dancing with the same short girl.

The biryani was quite good. Jennifer appeared to be hungry. She finished her food quickly. So did George.

"Good food," he said. "This is authentic Hyderabadi biryani."

"Sorry, I was so hungry. The food is so tasty."

They continued eating and talking. She told him her name was Jennifer Rego. Her parents lived in Dubai, that was why she was in boarding school in Bangalore. They were originally from Mangalore, and her grandparents still lived there.

Mangalore is a port city about two hundred and fifty miles from Bangalore that dates back thousands of years. It was an important hub for the spice trade and, for hundreds of years, there had been a steady stream of merchants and conquerors from Europe and the Middle East trying to stake their claim on the region. Many of the Catholics that migrated to Mangalore, like Jennifer's family, had come from Goa, where they faced persecution for their religious beliefs. It was said they were the descendants of the Aryans who had come to India from Iran. Jennifer certainly looked like she shared this ethnicity. She was very fair with delicate features, but she also had a strong nose.

George had always found Mangalorean girls very attractive — especially the Catholic girls, who were quite fashionable and easier to talk to than traditional Indian girls. Jennifer appeared to be the personification of the best of everything he imagined of that particular community.

George was not a complete stranger to mingling with the opposite sex. He was aware that most girls found him attractive, and he had spent enough time in church and other social activities that were co-ed to be comfortable in such settings. However, this was the first time he was in the company of a girl that he had chosen and invited to join him on his own. It was a nice feeling to be sitting there and talking to such a beautiful girl. He didn't want it to end.

He told Jennifer about his life: that he was from the U.S. and had come to Bangalore when he was twelve; his passion for music and songwriting; his best friends, Swami and Venu.

"There's Swami," he said pointing to his friend, who was still on the dance floor. "That guy is quite a good dancer now. Can you believe he had never danced until last week when I showed him some moves?"

Jennifer laughed. *"She had a nice laugh,"* he thought.

The music stopped while Farook Rashid came on stage again to make some more announcements. George saw Swami thank the girl he was dancing with and return to the boys' side of the hall. He wanted to talk to him.

He got the opportunity when Jennifer excused herself to use the restroom. He left his jacket on the chair and quickly rushed over to Swami.

"Hi, bugger, you were dancing for almost an hour. You're dancing quite well."

"Thanks, George, but I kept dancing because no one would tag me. I couldn't just tell her that I didn't want to dance with her anymore. She's a nice girl. Her name is Lakshmi and she's a Tamilian Brahmin like me… but no sparks. It's like dancing with my sister, if I had one. Anyway, you're a lucky bastard. The girl you're with is the most beautiful girl here — there, she's coming back!"

"Thanks, Swami, I'll better go. I really like her. See you later. Find someone else, there are so many pretty girls here." Then he hastily went back to his chair.

"It's such a beautiful night outside," said Jennifer to him when she sat down. "It would be nice if we could take a walk. I have only seen your school along the path we take from the front gate to the chapel."

"I'll be glad to show you around," said George.

He put on his jacket, and they walked outside. All the students had been explicitly cautioned, in a class notice the previous week, that boys were not allowed to stray far from the hall with girls during the social. But he didn't worry about that now. If a teacher spotted them, the consequences would just be a small price to pay. The moment was too exciting to be dampened with thoughts like that.

Fortunately, as they walked away from the hall, there was no one there to stop them. Mr. Prakash, the PT master, who had been on duty outside, had gone inside to get some food and use the toilet. George and Jennifer were both wearing dark clothes so it was hard to see them once they had crossed the large football field behind the hall. It was exhilarating to be completely alone with a beautiful girl in the darkness.

"Let's walk this way," he said, pointing to a little path that ran along the trees and hedges. Jennifer held his arm as they were walking. George could smell the shampoo in her hair and her perfume. It was thrilling.

"This is our gym on the left," he said happily. "It has a swimming pool on the other side. These are the fourth and fifth standard classrooms. This is our sickbay and pharmacy — the nursing matron lives inside. The sick dorm has ten beds, and there are also four rooms with single bed. On the right side, you will see the tower block. It has classrooms on the ground level and student dorms on the first floor. On the left is the fourth-eleven field, and further down are our science labs…"

They were now a long distance away from the school hall. "Let's sit here for a little while," said Jennifer as they reached a secluded area. They sat side by side on the low wall of the fourth-eleven field. The spot they had chosen was overgrown with bushes. Unless someone came right up to them it would be hard to see them sitting there.

Jennifer suddenly leaned towards George and held his hand. It was so natural and electrifying at the same time. He squeezed her hand gently. Then she turned towards him with her face upturned. George had never done it before, but he kissed her gently on her lips.

She returned his kiss. They kissed for a few minutes. All sorts of things were happening to him now. The feel of her soft mouth against his was unbelievable. *He tried to not think about the little naughty monster in his pants that was now straining to get free.*

Jennifer stood up suddenly and turned so she was facing him. She bent down and kissed him again. He stood up and held her around the waist. Involuntarily his hands went to her breasts. She pushed them away gently. After a few more minutes of kissing — it was getting more passionate now — he tried again. This time she moaned slightly when he caressed her breasts. He slipped his hand down her blouse from the top. He could feel her bra. He navigated under it so he could feel her naked right breast. He felt her nipple; it was small and hard. Jennifer was moaning and pressing herself to him.

Suddenly, she pushed him away abruptly and said, "We must go back. The boarders will be leaving at exactly eleven-thirty."

It took George a moment to come out of his present state. "Whaa… of course. We must get back. Sorry I didn't mean to…"

"No, George, I enjoyed myself tonight. I think you are a real gentleman, and so very handsome. Thank you for showing me your school." She leaned up and kissed his lips again.

They walked back cautiously to the hall. Mr. Prakash spotted them this time. "Come here. Where did you go?" he demanded? "You know boys and girls cannot go off on their own."

"No, sir, the ladies room at the hall was full, so I was just showing her to the latrines in the next block."

Mr. Prakash looked at them suspiciously, but he let them go. *"They were such a beautiful couple,"* he thought to himself. He had seen George perform at the music competition a few weeks earlier and win the first place. *"Very talented bugger… his kind would have no shortage of girls."*

Then he noticed a couple of students hide beer bottles in their jackets and sneak away to the bushes on the other side of the field. He followed them silently. He had work to do.

George said goodbye to Jennifer inside the hall. The girls' school boarders were lining up to leave.

"Can I see you again sometime? Do you come outside the school anytime?" he asked her.

"My guardian lives on Hayes Road, I visit them on weekends usually, but it will be hard to meet you. I come to the boys' school chapel on weekdays too, but it's hard to meet or talk because we all sit together on the other side."

"Can you call me? Here's my phone number…579295…" he realized he didn't have a pen or paper.

"I have to go," she said Then she squeezed his hand and ran away to join her group.

George was in seventh heaven. He was walking on clouds. The past few hours had not yet been registered and assimilated into his long-term consciousness. He felt a song come on: *"I don't need any of this… there is nothing I would miss, but your kiss…"* He wished he had a pen and paper to write down the lyrics. He saw Swami sitting by himself in the corner.

"How are you, bugger?" he asked. He was euphoric and bursting inside to blurt everything that had happened with Jennifer to his friend. But he stayed calm.

"Well, I danced with a couple of other girls," said Swami. "It was okay, but no real interest on both sides generally. Finally, I just danced with myself. You know, I realized that I love to dance. It is so liberating when you stop worrying about how you look to others. What about you, bugger? You disappeared with that girl. I was looking for you."

Then a knowing look came to his face. "You dirty bugger, don't tell me…"

"Baloney, nothing dirty, Swami, but we kissed, and I felt her breast from inside her clothes. It was fantastic; I thought Mr. Johnson would unzip my fly on his own and come out!"

Like most boys of that age, the Scrimshankers had all named their penises. While George had chosen the more traditional Mr. Johnson for his penis, Swami had named his James, after James Bond, and Venu had named his Naga, after the snake god.

Swami was beside himself with excitement. He kept pacing around in delight. He appeared even more excited than George.

"Tell me everything, bugger," he said. "How does it feel to taste a girl's lips, especially ones as beautiful as Jennifer's?"

George told him of his experience briefly, but he didn't feel right sharing the more intimate details, even though Swami was his best friend.

Swaminathan understood, too: that ultimately, friendships take a back seat to stronger natural bonds that are far more exciting and meaningful; that the sexual drive is stronger than any other human need; that desire and love can drive people to do things they would never do otherwise.

It was almost three o'clock in the morning when George finally got home. He picked up his guitar, and the song that had begun in his mind a few hours ago flowed out easily. He thought of Jennifer.

If I wake up in the morning and the sun doesn't shine
If I have you by my side, it's all right
If the rivers stop flowing and the mountains crumble down
If I have you by my side, it's all right
I don't need any of this
There is nothing that I'd miss
But your kiss...

If the earth it stops turning and there's panic in the land
If I have you by my side, it's all right
If the prophets start proclaiming that the end is at hand
If I have you by my side, it's all right
I don't need any of this
There is nothing that I'd miss
But your kiss...

If I wake up in the morning and the sun doesn't shine
If I have you by my side, it's all right

He set the alarm for six-thirty and went to bed. He hadn't even told Swami of his plans. When the bell went off, he woke up, had a bath quickly, dressed in a nice pair of pants and a blazer, and peddled furiously to the school. Jennifer had said that she attended the services at the boys' school chapel. *There was a special service for St. Peter's Tide that morning!*

He got to the school at seven-thirty. The Holy Eucharist service was starting at eight o'clock. He left his bicycle in the stand and tried to think of the best place to position himself as the boarders from the girls' school arrived. He decided to wait outside the Chapel. It was a lovely little structure with a small wooden gate, a white picket fence, rose bushes and hedges with assorted flowers. A narrow path lined with red bricks led from the gate to the quaint chapel. It looked like it would fit in perfectly in an English countryside.

"I'll wait just inside the gate," he said to himself. *"This way, I can walk alongside the girls and give Jennifer my note."* He put his hand inside his jacket pocket and felt the small sheet of paper on which he'd written a short note: *"Hi, call me as soon as possible at 579295. Thanks, George."*

He sat on a little wooden bench among the hedges and waited. Students, alumni and teachers started streaming in from the mess hall after breakfast slowly and entered the chapel. Finally, George saw the long column of boarders from the girls' school in the distance. He felt his excitement grow as they approached him.

They walked past him. They were three in a row. They were dressed in their school uniforms and were wearing blazers, even though it was quite warm. The column was arranged by age. He looked intently at the last few rows. He didn't see Jennifer. Several of the girls noticed him and smiled. He looked very handsome and dashing as he lounged nonchalantly against the picket fence.

Finally, they had all gone past. He was disappointed. There was no sign of Jennifer. George had no intention of attending the service if she wasn't there. So he returned to the bicycle stand, took his chopper and rode back home. Then he went back to sleep.

Chapter 14
A Little Romance

George celebrated his seventeenth birthday the following month. His father had promised to buy him a motorcycle as soon as he got his two-wheeler license. Swaminathan's cousin Ramesh owned a Lambretta scooter and offered to teach George how to ride it and also go with him to the RTO for the road test. As someone who could do wheelies and other daredevil tricks on his chopper bicycle, learning how to ride a scooter wasn't very difficult for George. The license for all motorized two-wheelers in Bangalore was the same. So, people usually took the road test on scooters or mopeds, because they were easier to drive, and then bought a motorbike once they had their license.

George didn't think he would have a problem getting his license. He had already spoken to his uncle, Abraham Varghese, who was the DIG of the Bangalore police.

"Ebby-Chachan*, I'm going for my two-wheeler license next week. Can you put in a word?" he asked. His uncle's house was next to the Governor's mansion on Race Course Road. George was there visiting with his parents.

"Daddy said he'll get me a Jawa motorcycle once I pass the test and get a license."

"Have you learned to drive properly?" asked his uncle. "If you want, I can ask one of my fellows to teach you. Some of the chaps in my division are on the city's Motorcycle Daredevils Team!"

"No, Ebby-Chachan, I have already practiced and studied for the test. But if you just show up, you know how it is here. They want money to let you pass and get the license."

*older relative or brother
(Malayalam)

"Okay, no problem Georgie-boy. I will tell Shivshanker, my assistant, to meet you there. You're going to the Indira Nagar RTO, correct?"

The next week, George showed up with Ramesh at the Bangalore Regional Transport Office in Indira Nagar.

"Thanks for teaching me to drive the scooter and bringing me here," he told Ramesh.

"No problem, bugger. This is better than counting money in the bank the whole day."

Swami's father had got Ramesh a cashier's job at the bank. He had called in sick to accompany George to the RTO. He also needed to transfer the ownership of his second-hand scooter to his name while he was there. He had talked non-stop about it since they left: about how many times he had to come to the RTO, that the policemen there had made him run from pillar to post each time. They wanted a hefty bribe that Ramesh wasn't willing to give.

George looked around for his uncle's assistant. He saw a dark man in a police uniform and sunglasses waiting by the door of the office.

"Sar... neevu Shivshanker... DIG Verghese's assistant?" George asked in his broken Kannada.

"Yes sir, I am Shivshanker," the man said in fluent English. "Please give me your application."

George handed him his completed application. Shivshanker went inside the room and came out half an hour later.

"This is your temporary license. You will get the permanent license in the post in one month."

George was very surprised that he did not even have to do a road test. "Thank you sir," he told the assistant. "Also Mr. Shivshankar, can you help my friend with transferring the ownership of his scooter? He has come here many times but has not been successful. If you want, I can phone my uncle..."

"That's not necessary. Give me the papers," he told Ramesh. He left them again and returned a short while later. "Okay, all done. You can come and pick it up at three o'clock. Here's the chit," he said.

George slipped him twenty rupees. "Please have a coffee, sir," he said and left with a grateful Ramesh.

"I can't believe it, bugger... I tried on my own for three months...

nothing… now in fifteen minutes I got it. Thanks George, I thought I was helping you, but you have helped me more," said Ramesh.

■

Once he had his driving license, George was able to buy his dream bike: a 250cc Jawa motorcycle. The history of Jawa motorcycles began when Frantisek Janecek started manufacturing Wanderer motorcycles in the Czech Republic in 1927. A few years later, he rebranded the machine with the name Jawa, derived from the first two letters of the words Janacek and Wanderer. It was introduced in India in 1960 as a 250cc single cylinder air-cooled engine with a twin exhaust.

By the mid-1970s, Jawa was the most popular motorcycle in the country. In addition to acquiring a cult status among the youth, it also won the market war against the more powerful British Royal Enfield motorcycles, as well as Lambretta and Vespa scooters. Yezdi Motors bought the company in 1974 and the name was changed to Yezdi. However, the older Jawa motorcycles still remained popular even several years later. Owners swore that it was the best motorcycle for Indian conditions. It required little maintenance and did not cost as much as the motorcycles of British lineage to buy, maintain and repair.

George had his eye on the 1974 Roadking model. He found a second-hand bike advertised in the Deccan Herald for Rs. 5,000. He went with Swami to Rajajinager to see it. The owner had modified the bike to suit his tastes. It was painted in dull black metallic paint all over, including the twin exhausts, gas tank and handlebars. The Jawa logo was embellished in gold on the gas tank and there were subtle gold accents on the exhausts and sides. It was exactly what George was looking for. He took it for a test drive and decided to buy it right away.

The next day, he was cruising down M.G. Road on his new motorcycle. He took it to a repair shop in Ulsoor and got it serviced. The mechanic told him it was in perfect condition and would give him many years of service. George was very pleased with his purchase.

He certainly looked very dashing as he rode his motorcycle in his black jeans, black t-shirt, brown bomber jacket, black boots and Ray Ban aviator glasses. He had also bought a used American

Electro Pro helmet and had painted it in dull black.

"Georgie come lately, there's a new kid in town..." he sang to himself as he rode his motorcycle around the Cantonment area. He was hard to miss. Men and women noticed him. All he now needed was a girl to ride pillion with him.

◼

It had been three weeks since the St. Pete's Social. George had become a regular worshipper at the daily morning service in St. Peter's Chapel... with the hope of meeting Jennifer and giving her his note. He saw her everyday, but other than smiling at each other, there was no opportunity for them to meet or talk. The girls' school students all sat together in the pews on the front right side of the chapel. The teachers from both schools sat on the front left side, while the boys' school students sat behind everyone in the available rows. The chaplain was Father David, the last living member of the Brotherhood of St. Peter in India.

George had considered leaving Jennifer his note in one of the hymn books. However, he reasoned that it would be hard to alert her about it and he didn't want some other girl to read it. So far, there was really no chance for him to speak to her because the girls were herded in and out by Miss Robinson, a stern middle-aged spinster who was the matron for the senior boarders in the girls' school.

Finally, he decided that he would have to take a chance. He managed to get a seat just behind the last row of girls. The morning service was only thirty minutes long so he had to be quick. Jennifer was two rows in front of him.

"Jennifer..." he whispered urgently.

She turned around, as did many of the other girls. He quickly held out his rolled-up note to her. To his relief, she took it at once. Some of the girls stared at them in shock. Others smiled. Fortunately Miss Robinson was too engrossed in singing, *Love Divine, All Loves Excelling,* to notice what had taken place just a few feet away from her.

Once he knew Jennifer had his note, George joined in singing the hymn loudly as well. Miss Robinson looked at him approvingly. He had a lovely voice. Wesley was one of George's favorite hymn writers. As a songwriter himself, it was his habit that whenever he liked a particular song, he would try to find out who had written it and when. Glancing through the hymnbook one day at St. Mark's he had noticed that Charles Wesley had penned many of his favorite hymns in the mid-1700s, including *Arise My Soul Arise, Lo He Comes With Clouds Descending*, the Easter favorite, *Christ The Lord Is Risen Today*, and the Christmas standard, *Hark, The Herald Angels Sing*.

■

Jennifer called George at his house the next morning. It was only seven o'clock and he was still asleep.

"Georgie…" his mother shook him awake. "There is a telephone call for you — some girl named Jennifer… edukuno… or shall I tell her to call later?"

"No, Mummy, it's very important," he said and ran in his pyjamas to the phone downstairs."

"Hello, Jennifer. Thanks for calling. I've been trying so hard to give you my number…"

"I know, I wanted to talk to you too," said Jennifer. "I don't have much time. I told the matron I was calling my guardian. Can you come to the back gate on Residency Road this evening? I will try to meet you there at five-thirty. I usually go for a walk with my friends on the school grounds. I can talk to you for a few minutes.

That evening, George parked his motorcycle at St. Joseph's College, which was close by and loitered around outside the back gate of Bishop Cotton Girls' School. The walls were over ten feet high and the small gate did not give much visual access to the inside of the school. For many of the Cotton schoolboys, beyond the walls there existed the Holy Grail of so much of their longing. Beautiful girls who were so near… and yet so far.

"Imagine how many pretty ninth, tenth, eleventh and twelfth standard girls there are on the other side of those walls," Swami told George one day while they were walking past.

"Is it really true that all the schools are co-ed in the U.S.?"

"Yes, most schools are," said George.

"Why don't they just join the boys and girls schools here? It's not fair that chaps our age in the West get to spend all day in school looking at girls while we have to imagine what they look like across high walls and big gates…"

Jennifer appeared from a little trail along the side of the wall on the other side. They looked at each other across the big black iron gates. There was no watchman there because this entrance was always locked and rarely used for thoroughfare.

Jennifer looked beautiful. She was wearing a very short white skirt, a green blouse and white Keds. She had beautiful, long legs. She looked a little flushed.

"Hi, George," she said. "I was practicing hockey, but I snuck out. I don't have much time."

George reached out and held both her hands with his. She let him for a few minutes, then she pulled back. "We have to be careful. The teachers and matrons sometimes come this way."

"I've been thinking of you everyday. Can you meet me outside?" asked George. "I've got a new motorcycle. We could go somewhere."

"This weekend, maybe — I'm going to my guardian's house. I could make up some excuse and meet you," said Jennifer. "Wait for me at the bottom of Hayes Road on Saturday at ten o'clock in the morning."

She smiled at him and went back the way she had come.

■

George was waiting in front of the petrol station at the end of Hayes Road on Saturday morning. He was wearing a blue and white plaid flannel shirt with snap-on buttons, tight blue Levi's and black boots. He had come up with a plan for spending the day with Jennifer. A few minutes after ten o'clock, he saw her walking down the road in his rear-view mirror. She had on a short denim skirt, a sleeveless white blouse and white Keds. She carried a small jute bag with her.

She saw him and ran over. "Quick, let's get out of here, George," she whispered and climbed behind him, sitting sideways. She held him around the waist and pressed herself to him so she wouldn't fall.

Her touch was electrifying. George quickly started the motorcycle and took off like a bullet on Richmond Road. Jennifer had her face on his back so she would not be easily identifiable to someone who knew her. He could feel her breath through his shirt. It sent shivers down his spine.

She relaxed a little only when they were a few miles away. George pulled into Tiffany Restaurant, which was usually quite empty during the mornings but still served a good Western breakfast.

"I thought we could first stop and have some breakfast and coffee while we decide what to do," said George. They went inside.

The restaurant was quite popular for lunch and dinner. It had a circular dance stage and even an area for a live band. However, it had a deserted look now and there were no other customers. A tired-looking waiter wearing black pants, a white shirt, black tie and a black vest approached their table.

They both ordered eggs with sausage and coffee. George looked at her closely and reveled in her beauty. He could feel Mr. Johnson rise up in approval as well.

She had her hands on the table. He reached out and held them. She didn't resist but rather looked straight into his eyes. He rubbed her hands gently. In his pants, Mr. Johnson cheered!

"I have a plan for today," said George. "Let's go to Nandi Hills. Have you ever gone there?"

"No, but isn't it far away? I have to get back to my uncle's house by six o'clock."

"It only takes an hour by motorbike. We can easily come back by six o'clock," said George. "The best thing about my plan is that we can walk around there freely without worrying if anyone will see us," he added.

Jennifer agreed that it would be best if no one she knew saw her with George. So they had breakfast and drove the thirty miles to Nandi Hills in George's motorcycle.

At 4,851 feet above sea level, Nandi Hills is one of the highest locations in the Bangalore region. In the mid-1700s, the Muslim emperor Tippu Sultan constructed what he thought was an impregnable fort of solid rock on top of the hill. However, on 19th October 1771, the British, led by General Charles Cornwallis, were successful in storming the fort and defeating Tippu's army. In the 1800s, the fort became a summer home for the British Governor Lord Cubbon. When India got independence from the British, it was converted into a hotel and restaurant. Since the 1960s, Nandi Hills has also become a popular picnic destination for the people of Bangalore City. Getting to the top requires travelling up a treacherous narrow road that has over thirty sharp hairpin-bends, before finally arriving at the Cubbon House Hotel.

Some of the popular tourist spots at Nandi Hills include: Tippu's Drop, a sheer cliff where the ruler, allegedly, interrogated his prisoners before pushing them off; the Secret Passage, which runs from the fort to the plains below; the Bridle Path, which soldiers used to enter the fort, and; the Amrutha Sarovar, a fresh water lake, and a beautiful botanical garden with rare plants and trees.

George and Jennifer arrived at the top of Nandi Hills only after noon. It had been a long journey. The hairpin-bends were difficult to navigate and George had to drive slowly all the way up. They washed up in the restroom at Cubbon House and had lunch at the restaurant there. After that, they walked leisurely around the scenic location.

Jennifer seemed liberated and uninhibited since she had left the city. She hugged George tightly on the motorcycle all the way to Nandi Hills. Once there, she held his hand and leaned against him as they walked around. Even though it was a Saturday, the place was not very crowded. They spotted a few families and some of the gardeners now and then, but it appeared they were almost entirely on their own. They stopped and kissed when no one was around. A couple of times, she allowed him to slip his hand under her skirt and caress the exciting curve of her buttocks through the smooth fabric of her panties. The experience was absolutely thrilling to George.

They walked up to Tippu's Drop and looked down. It was a sheer cliff that went down hundreds of feet. The actual ledge had been cordoned off with a high wall because it had become quite a popular destination for people, including couples, who wanted to commit suicide.

They visited the lake and the botanical gardens. Then, George saw a small ledge by the side of the hill that was over the wall of the fort and almost hidden from view.

"Let's go and sit there," he said.

He led the way as they climbed over the wall and walked the short distance to the ledge. It was a perfect spot for lovers. No one would be able to observe them without climbing over the wall. The view was beautiful from there as well.

They sat down on the ledge and leaned back on the wall of the fort. There were bushes on both sides. The front had an open view of the magnificent plains far below. The grass beneath them was dense, soft and comfortable. After they had admired the scenery for a little while, George put his right hand around Jennifer's shoulders and slowly drew her towards him. She didn't resist. They kissed again. He slipped his hand under her blouse and unhooked her bra. Her breasts were ripe and firm with small hard nipples. He could feel her heart beating fast as he caressed her breasts.

They kissed for a little while. Then, she suddenly turned around and mounted him so she was sitting on his thighs and facing him. She hiked her short skirt up around her waist. His legs were stretched straight in front of him and his back was against the wall. She unbuttoned her shirt, removed her bra and unbuttoned his shirt as well. They kissed, but now their naked chests were touching. Then slowly she reached down and unbuttoned his pants and pulled down his fly and his underwear. Mr. Johnson sprung out like a jack-in-the-box. She began to guide him to her...

"Wait," he said, "I have a Nirodh."

The previous evening Swami and George had gone to see Venu at the medical shop. When George had told him of his plan to go to Nandi Hills with Jennifer, Venu had taken a pack of Nirodh from the shelf and given it to him.

"Just keep this in case. Don't do anything without it," he said. "I've heard Dr. Gaythri next door talk to my father about the increasing number of young girls who get pregnant. It ruins their lives, so be careful, bugger."

"Yes," said Swami, "I was reading in my book that at this age girls are the most fertile. Jennifer can get pregnant from just one touch of your Mr. Johnson."

So George opened the little pack and quickly slipped the slippery condom over Mr. Johnson. An impatient Jennifer guided him in from the side of her panties. She was soft and moist. She moved up and down, gently first, then harder.

Then she whispered in his ear, "Don't worry; I'm not a virgin. Let me show you how..."

In a few minutes, George couldn't control himself any longer... he ejaculated. It went on for several seconds. His face was between her soft, fragrant, beautiful breasts, and he could feel her vagina contract as if to suck more and more out of him.

"I'm sorry," he said, "I couldn't control it. This is my first time."

"Don't worry," she said, "I had an orgasm too. I was really excited by you."

They lay back together in post-coital bliss. He held her tightly. He took in the warm musky smell and the glow on her face. He kissed her gently. He took out a cigarette and lit it.

"Can I have one too?" she asked. He was surprised, but he found he was aroused when he saw her smoking.

"Are you shocked that I'm not a good girl like you thought? she asked him.

"No," he said. "You are exactly as I hoped you would be."

Half an hour later, he felt Mr. Johnson start stirring again. She felt it too and climbed on top of him again. He opened up another packet of Nirodh.

This time they made love slowly. He deliberately slowed everything down in his consciousness so he could enjoy the present moment for all it was worth. He took notice of every detail: the curve of her hips, her naked breasts, her small brown nipples, the dark tangle of hair between her legs, the expression on her face as she closed her eyes and achieved orgasm. He ejaculated only after she was completely satisfied.

She held on to him. She was perspiring lightly. She looked beautiful and radiant. He suddenly had a thought.

"Capstan is wrong," he said laughing. "Yes it can, it can stand twice a night!"

"What?" she asked.

"Nothing, just a joke I remembered."

He lay back and pulled her close to him. They fell asleep in the warm late-afternoon sunlight. When he woke up it was four o'clock. He shook her awake gently.

They both adjusted their clothes and climbed back over the wall of the fort. They walked back to Cubbon House, hand-in-hand. After using the restroom and washing up, they headed back to the city.

It was a little past six when George dropped Jennifer off at the end of Hayes Road. She got down from his motorcycle and ran up the street without turning back.

George met Venu and Swami later that night. He told them what had happened briefly, but did not go into details. It had been one of the most exciting days of his life. Making love to Jennifer was everything and more than he had imagined.

■

Jennifer and George's romance lasted only for a few more months. It was difficult for her to meet him outside. However, one day she called and asked if he would like to go somewhere for a couple of days and stay the night. They decided to go to Madras. They took the Brindavan Express train from Bangalore Cantonment station. George got the tickets and met Jennifer outside the train.

"I told my guardian that I was going with the school team for a debate competition," she said. "I have to come back tomorrow night."

They sat together in the 2nd-class, air-conditioned carriage of the train holding hands. George wanted to kiss and touch her all over the whole journey, but the compartment was full of people. Mr. Johnson complained for the entire trip. They got to Madras in the evening and checked into Woodlands Hotel. Both George and Jennifer looked older than their years, so they had no trouble getting a room.

"Are you from Ceylon?" the bellboy asked them as he showed them to the room.

"No, actually, I'm from the U.S.," said George truthfully.

As soon as they were alone, George and Jennifer were on each other hungrily. They tried everything they could possibly think of sexually for the next several hours. At midnight, George went downstairs and got biriyani from a street vendor downstairs. They ate, and then went at it again.

The two, hardly slept a wink that night. They made love as many times as Mr. Johnson could manage to rise up, and then lay naked in each other's arms.

Towards morning, Jennifer stirred and said softly, "George, there is something I must tell you…"

"What?" he asked.

"As you know, I'm graduating in two weeks. Once school is over, I'm going back to Dubai and maybe to the U.K after that. I probably won't be returning to Bangalore for a long time."

George was silent. He wasn't sure how he felt about this revelation, or even how he was expected to react to the news. So, he just held her close and revelled in the moment of having this beautiful naked girl in his arms.

A few weeks later, Jennifer left for Dubai. George waited for her outside the school gate the evening before she was leaving. She held his hand through the gate and said, "I will never forget you. Thank you, George. You are really a very handsome and nice boy."

George watched her wistfully as she walked away. She promised to keep in touch, but George somehow knew she wouldn't. They had enjoyed each other's bodies a few times. It was beautiful, but he didn't feel sad. Neither of them had really fallen in love.

As she turned around to wave at him for the last time, he captured a snapshot of her in his mind. Somehow, he knew that this was only the first among many similar wonderful experiences that he would have during the course of his life.

Chapter 15

The Home Stretch

T he Scrimshankers were now in the last few months of junior college. Venu spent most of his time studying. In the past two years, he had become a top student in all his pre-university classes. He would have to be in the top two-percent of his class to apply to medical school, and perform exceptionally well in the entrance exams, as well as in the personal interview.

"I am not going to worry about everything right now," he decided. His goal was to just focus on one hurdle at a time and perform to the best of his ability. *"The universe will take care of it when the time comes. For now, the only thing I can do is study hard, so why think negative thoughts at this stage?"*

He still went to the medical shop every day but his father was very flexible with his hours. In the past year, Krishnachandra had stopped drinking completely. He was trying to make up for all the years that he had neglected his family. He now closed the shop every night at seven-thirty and spent time with his wife and children. One day, when Venu came home, he could hardly recognize his mother. She had dyed her hair black, and she looked a good twenty years younger.

"Your Appa asked me to color my hair. Does it look good?" she asked him.

"Yes, Amma, you look beautiful and young," he told her.

"Appa and I are going to Madras on Saturday for Murugan's marriage. It's the first time we are going out of station in more than ten years."

"I'm happy that Appa has stopped drinking," said Venu. "I had forgotten how he was before, Amma, I pray he will never drink again."

As luck would have it, Krishnachandra's business had also started doing better. The proprietor of the other medical shop down the street had been arrested for selling spurious medicines a few months earlier. Once the word got out, his business had plummeted and customers had started coming to Krishnachandra's store instead.

Venu had taken him to see Swami's father, Venkat, at the bank. Based on his recommendation, the bank had extended Krishnachandra's line of credit so he could carry a more extensive selection of products. He was also able to perform some much-needed renovations to the store. Krishnachandra was finally beginning to see a light at the end of the tunnel.

■

In addition to now being the editor of *Green and Gold*, Swaminathan had also taken a part-time job at *The City Register*, a local weekly newspaper. He started off by reviewing rock records and covering youth-oriented musical events in the city.

The City Register was owned and run by Darius and Zenia Unwalla, a Parsi couple who had migrated from Bombay five years ago. Darius had worked for *The Times of India* as an editor, while Zenia had been the business manager at Hindustan Thompson. The newspaper's office was in the basement of a six-floor building on Infantry Road.

Although the Unwallas had experience in both essential aspects of a newspaper, reporting and advertising, it appeared that they did not have the business acumen to do it successfully on their own. They usually operated on a seat-of-the-pants paradigm: from week to week. The newspaper always had a serious cash flow problem. Things had gotten so bad that the owner of the company that printed the newspaper would only start his presses rolling on an issue after their check had cleared. It was not unusual for Darius to run to the printer with hard cash minutes before the deadline for printing an issue.

Some pay periods, the staff of *The City Register* did not get their salaries, although they usually received the money at some point in the next few weeks. For Swaminathan, however, it was a wonderful experience. In addition to the Unwallas, the newspaper had three reporters, two editors, three layout artists, two photographers, two advertising executives and a bookkeeper. There were also several freelancers and part-time reporters like Swaminathan who were paid based on the word count of their articles.

Most of the full-time editors and reporters were old timers who had worked at some of the largest newspapers in the country. Compared to their earlier remuneration, they were paid a pittance at *The City Register*. Most of them were in their retirement years, but bad decisions, alcoholism or a desire to continue doing what they loved had brought them here. To Swaminathan, they were a treasure trove of knowledge. He made it a point to spend as much time as possible in the office, sometimes late into the night, even though he didn't really need to be there at all.

His favorite staffer was Ram Murthy, a curmudgeonly old man in his seventies who had once been an ace reporter for the *Deccan Herald*. He was now the senior news editor for the paper. Swami's articles usually never made it to his desk — he held disdain for entertainment news. However, he had recognized the talent in Swaminathan and had slowly warmed up to the boy. He allowed Swami to look at his edits on the news articles before he sent it to the typesetter.

"All news stories should resemble an inverted pyramid," he said. "The most important parts of the story should be first, followed by the less important, and so on and so forth. This way an editor can just cut the story from the bottom and it will still make sense. Sometimes it is because he thinks it is unnecessarily long. Other times, in the layout stage there is no more space left so it must be done."

The entertainment editor was the erudite Javed Iqbal, who had once been an editor at the *Junior Statesman* in Calcutta. Swami could hardly believe that he was working alongside a luminary such as this. Although he had descended into the lowly ranks of *The City Register* because of a drinking problem, Javid still had a nose for what readers would like.

"I was reading your review of the Spring Festival in Christ College last month," he told Swami. "Your article was a straight up report of the colleges, the songs, who won awards, etcetera. However most of our readers are over thirty-five. What do they care about who won some college music award or the other? Instead, you could have written the article from the perspective that the Spring Festival brings together over 100,000 students from all over the country every year to Bangalore and fosters understanding and tolerance for people from other backgrounds. Add a human element. Interview the people who went to watch, the performers, the organizers — then you have a story that anyone will read, not just the families of those whose names are mentioned in it."

Rajendra Prasad was the art director. He was a surly fifty-something designer who had lost his job at Sistas for harassing one of the secretaries. Swami did not like him. However, he was friendly with Manjunath, the layout artist who explained the process of specing type and creating page layouts. He worked on a large light table with a T-square and triangle, cutting and pasting the typeset galleys on to large boards pre-printed in light blue. Swami always retyped his articles himself after Javid edited them, even thought there was a typist on staff to do it, and proofed it himself at the typesetting stage. He also was present when it was imposed into the layout.

The senior advertising salesman was Shiv Kumar, who was now in his sixties but at one time had worked for *The Standard*. He was one of those unfortunate people who had lost their jobs when the paper closed down a few years ago. Swaminathan learned about selling space from him.

"Developing a customer is like getting a girl to marry you," said Shiv. "You have to reel them in slowly. Even after you get them you still have to take care of their every need; otherwise they leave you."

Swami enjoyed sitting across from his desk and hearing him make his sales pitch to prospective customers.

"The difference between *The City Register* and *The Deccan Herald* is that they try to target everyone in the city. We only look for a certain kind of readership, which is why our circulation is lower. That means you get your ad seen by only the thirty-five to sixty age group of affluent and educated readers." Of course, Shiv did not mention the fact that the circulation was low simply because they couldn't get more people to buy the newspaper.

Finally, the most important lesson in Swami's education about the world of newspaper publishing came from the Unwallas themselves, by observing what they were and what they were not. He learned that every business needs at least four to six months of working capital in the bank, as well as discipline and honesty in all financial matters to succeed.

Although the Unwallas may or may not have been deliberately dishonest, what mattered was that they had developed a reputation as people who could not be trusted to pay their bills or honor their commitments. It was not unusual to find irate creditors in the office looking for the couple while they hid in the back room or sometimes even absconded from the City until they had the money to pay off their debts. Swami vowed he would never run a business that way.

■

George was performing two nights a week at Melody Restaurant. However, a few weeks earlier, he had stumbled onto another opportunity that utilized one of his other passions: drawing. He was at Koshy's Restaurant waiting for Swami one afternoon, but his friend was at *The City Register* and was delayed by over an hour. George was getting bored, so he took out his notebook and started sketching the water glass and sugar bowl that was in front of him with his pencil. Soon, he was lost in the sketch.

Suddenly, a man at the next table spoke to him, "Excuse me, can I look at what you're sketching."

"Oh it's nothing… I'm just passing the time," said George. He showed the man his sketch.

"This is very good," said the man. "You have an innate grasp of light and shadows. Are you an artist?"

"No, I just draw to pass time and because I like doing it," said George.

"Have you thought about doing commercial art?" asked the man.

"You mean like ads?"

"Yes, but also other things: retouching photos, creating layouts…"

"No, I don't know anything about that," said George.

"Would you like to learn?" the man asked.

George looked at him closely for the first time. He appeared to be in his mid-forties. He was short and of medium build with a receding hairline and a French beard.

"Hello, I am Kalinga Rao, but you can call me Kal. I have a small advertising agency and creative studio on Church Street called Dimensions. If you like, you can come and pay us a visit. I may be able to offer you a part-time job."

The next day George went to see Kal. He was curious. Dimensions turned out to be a small three-room office on the first floor of a large office complex. In addition to Kal, it consisted of two layout artists and a copywriter.

Kal had been an account manager at Lintas Advertising for over twenty years. He had started Dimensions solely on the basis of one client, Manmohan Pharmaceuticals, that he had been able of take with him when he left Lintas. It was a reasonably sized account and was enough to maintain his small staff.

Recently, however, he had acquired a couple of new clients, so Kal was on the lookout for some fresh talent. He had seen George drawing on the table next to him at Koshy's and had been drawn to him for some reason. The boy looked almost like a male model and had an easy confidence about him. When Kal looked at his drawing, he knew George was a good artist as well. He had spent a lot of time with graphic designers to recognize real talent when he saw it.

He introduced George to his staff. "This is Shekhar and this is Devraj; they are both commercial artists. This is Ronny, our part-time copywriter. I do everything else: service the clients, place the advertising in the media, handle the printing and production, as well as get the coffee. Would you like to join our team?"

"Yes, but I'm still a student in the twelfth standard at Cotton Boys. I will graduate in a few months. Maybe then…"

"I'll tell you what, you come and work here on Saturday morning and on school holidays. Once you graduate, you can come everyday. How does that sound? And here's what I'll pay you." He wrote an amount on a piece of paper and passed it to the boy.

George looked at it and agreed, even though he wasn't worried too much about his salary right then.

"Okay then," said Kal, "the first thing you can do is get us all some coffee." He gave some money to the boy.

The next Saturday, George started working at Dimensions. The world of advertising art was something he had never considered before, but now it piqued his interest. He realized that in spite of the modest set up, Kal and his staff were very good at what they did. Over the course of the next few months, they taught George everything he needed to know about commercial art: from using a T-square and triangles, cut-and-paste methods, line drawings, typography, airbrush techniques and photo retouching, layout, print production, halftone screens and so much more.

Swaminathan was spending all his spare time at *The City Register*, so George was glad he had something to do as well. He found he enjoyed this new world of advertising art. He began to spend more and more time at the agency, including an hour or two after school everyday and all day on Saturday.

Kal opened the door to his advertising agency promptly every morning at eight o'clock. He was a Kannadiga Brahmin who followed the rituals of his religion quite seriously. He usually arrived every morning with a handful of jasmine flowers, wrapped in a leaf and tied with string, which he had bought from a street vendor on M.G. Road on his way to the office. He had a small pooja ledge set up in the reception area of the office. He took off his shoes, lit a few incense sticks, placed his flowers and performed his pooja seriously with chants and meditation. This daily ritual lasted about half an hour. If George arrived at work while Kal was in the middle of his pooja, his boss would offer him a little sweet prasad, the ritual offering he made to the gods.

After his pooja, Kal had another ritual as well. He took out one of his Panama filter cigarettes and removed all the tobacco out of it from the top. He then fished out a small ball of pure, Kerala ganja wrapped in foil, that he had bought from a dealer near Ulsoor Lake the previous evening. He threw away three-fourths of the tobacco from his cigarette and replaced it with an equal quantity of ganja. He mixed and ground the ganja with his thumb on the palm of his hand along with the tobacco and then refilled it back into his cigarette, packing it tightly.

After that, he leaned back in his chair and smoked the joint. His staff usually arrived in by nine o'clock. Kal was usually in good spirits by the time they got there. He repeated the same process every evening after his employees had left. If it had been a stressful day, he smoked two joints.

At first George was surprised to know that his boss smoked ganja. However, he soon concluded that it did not really have a detrimental effect on Kal. In fact, it seemed to make him both relaxed and focused at the same time. George decided that he would like to try it as well. However, Kal refused to give him any from his stash or even let him have a toke.

"You're too young, bugger," he told him. "Don't do something until you know what you are getting into. I promised to teach you about advertising and commercial art, that's my duty. This is something else. I don't want to be the person who introduced you to ganja."

When he told Swami about it, his friend was livid.

"George, do not start taking drugs, okay? Smoking is fine, but drugs… never. I promised my father that I would never take drugs."

George didn't say anything. He wasn't sure if he felt the same way — especially about grass.

George soon became good friends with Kal as he got to know him better. Right from the start, Kal had recognized that the boy was bound for something much bigger than working at Dimensions. He was happy to teach George all he knew about advertising and he genuinely liked his company, but he knew his protégé would be with his agency only for a short time.

George soon became a very good commercial artist. His photo finishing was even better than the full-time artists. Much of what Dimensions did as an agency involved product images that needed to be airbrushed before they could be converted into film separations and imposed into the negatives for platemaking. George was very good at retouching photos of machinery, pharmaceutical bottles and household products in painstaking detail. He first pasted tracing paper on the photo with rubber cement. Then he cut out small masks and airbrushed highlights on to the photo. His overall sense of shadows and detailing was exceptional.

Soon Devraj and Shekhar were asking him for advice. They also realized that George wouldn't be at Dimensions for very long, so there was no competition or jealousy involved where he was concerned. The young secretaries in the building were enamored with George's looks and made excuses to drop in late in the afternoon, just so they could chat with him. Some days, he brought along his guitar to the office and sang for them.

Kal was a bachelor and he enjoyed this newly found attention from the fairer sex for his office, even if wasn't directed at him. He encouraged the women to come by anytime they wanted — especially when clients were supposed to show up.

"Having some pretty women in the office is good for business, no," he told George.

"So why don't you just hire a pretty receptionist?" George asked.

"What, and not do any work all day because I'm only looking at her? George, you're a handsome bugger. You have no idea what it is like to be ordinary looking. I have often considered an arranged marriage but I have been against it always. However, if I can't find someone soon, I may have no choice but to throw my principles out of the window."

As a bachelor, there was also one more routine that Kal maintained. Every Monday afternoon, he visited a brothel in the City Market area. George found out about it one day when he arrived at Dimensions after school. It was around four o'clock. As he was parking his Jawa in the parking lot, Kal pulled up too. They walked upstairs together and Kal went to use the latrine while George sat down on his art table.

Suddenly Kal came rushing out. He was very perturbed. He kept repeating the words, "Oh shit... oh shit... oh shit..." to himself.

"Kal, are you okay?" George asked.

"Yes, but I forgot something. I have to go back!"

"What? Where?" George asked?

"Come inside my office, and close the door." George did as he was asked.

"I haven't told you this but you know a man has needs, right? So, I have been going to this brothel near Mysore Road every Monday afternoon for the past five years. Today, as usual, I took out my thread and hung it on the bed post before the girl came inside, and you know what, bugger, I forgot it there!"

George had learned from Swami about the meaning and importance of the Upanayana, or sacred thread, for Hindus. The initiation ceremony was usually performed when a boy was anywhere from seven to thirteen years based on his caste. Brahmins could get their sacred threads earlier than other castes. The Upanayana symbolized the coming of age as well as the point in time when a boy could begin his studies towards achieving the ultimate transcendental stage of being a Bramachari someday.

"Don't worry, Kal. Why don't you go back and get it?" George asked. "I'll come with you if you want." He had never been to a brothel before. He didn't even know they existed in Bangalore.

"Okay, if you don't mind coming with me," said Kal. "Then let's go now. It will take almost two hours to go and come back with the traffic near City Market. You're sure you don't mind, right? I can't believe I left it there... shoo..."

George hopped on the back of Kal's Royal Enfield motorcycle and the two set off up Residency Road, to Race Course Road, through Mysore Road, and finally to some small gullies and back roads of the City Market region.

After several twists and turns through the narrow streets, George had no idea where he was anymore. The Scrimshankers usually never left the Bangalore Cantonment area and he was coming here for the first time in his life. Kal stopped his motorcycle outside a nondescript, two-story house.

"You wait here. I'll come back now," he said.

"No way, I'm coming with you. I've never been inside a brothel. I need the experience — just to know what it is like, Kal. I'm a songwriter..."

"Okay, but if the police or anyone show up, just stay with me, and don't say a word, all right?"

They walked up a stairway located along the side of the building to the first floor. A narrow corridor ran around the whole floor. A middle-aged woman in a purple sari was sitting at a desk in the first room facing the open doorway. It was no more than the size of a closet with space for nothing more than the desk and a small Godrej almarah.

The woman recognized Kal and said, "Neevu... eh, you're come back again so quick already? You got your friend also?"

"No, amma, I left my thread on the bed this afternoon. I just want to take it from the room and go back," he explained.

"Room 9, elva. There's no one there now. Go and take it," she said.

George followed Kal as he walked down the corridor. The cement wall on his left was about waist high and he could see the busy activity of vendors, pedestrians, bicyclists, scooters, motorcyclists and cars below. On his right was a row of small rooms. The ones that were occupied had a thin curtain across the door. Those that were currently unoccupied had the curtain pulled up and tucked into the tight metal spring that was stretched across the top of the door.

As he walked past, George tried looking inside each room unobtrusively as possible. He was very curious. Through the gap in the side of the curtain of the first room he could see a man furiously pump the woman beneath him. She seemed to be bored and even smiled cheekily at George as he walked past. In the next room, he could make out a naked man sitting on the bed with his legs on the floor while a woman knelt in front of him. He could see her head bobbing up and down. The man's eyes were closed. The other rooms also had various such acts in progress. In one room he could see two naked women with one man.

The rooms after the sixth one were vacant. Some of the prostitutes were just sitting and chatting in the unused rooms. Others were combing their hair or putting on make-up. A few smiled suggestively at George.

"You pretty boy, you want to come to me," asked an attractive young woman. She looked like she was about eighteen years old with a girlish face. She was wearing only a petticoat and blouse. She opened her blouse and showed him her small round breasts. Her nipples were large and brown.

"Th... thank you, not today... maybe some other time," George replied. *"If I can ever find this place again,"* he told himself. He was revelling in the experience, however. *"Wait till I tell the buggers about it,"* he thought to himself.

When Kal got to Room 9, he found his thread was still hanging on the post of the bed. He retrieved it gratefully and slipped it into his pocket.

They thanked the Madam in the purple sari, got back on Kal's motorcycle and returned to the office. It took them over an hour to get through the rush hour traffic.

George recounted his experience to the other Scrimshankers as they had coffee in Koshy's that night.

"Chaps, there was something about it that was important for me to experience. I am sure that, as a writer, you will feel the same way, Swami," he told his friend.

"Somebody, I don't know who it was, said that you've got to try everything once — otherwise, how will you know what's out there and what you want for yourself? I don't think I want to have sex with a prostitute, but going there with Kal gave me a peek into a world I would never have seen otherwise."

"You're right, I suppose," said Swami. "However, you will be the guy who will experience all these things. I will have to be satisfied reading about it in a book or magazine and listening to your escapades," he said smiling.

"Do you think you can find your way back?" Venu asked.

"Not a chance in hell," said George.

Then, just like that, it was the end of their school years. Swami and George had to take the ISC national exam. This time, they were relaxed and more or less ready for it. The past two years had revealed what they wanted to do with their lives. Academics did not make them nervous anymore. Both boys were sure their futures would not be determined by their grades in either this exam or any other coursework after that.

For Venu, however, it was a different matter. He had been studying for his PUC exams since his first day of class. He was completely focused on performing exceptionally well in the finals and in the entrance exams of the medical colleges he had selected. Things were much better at home now, and he no longer had the mental anguish of his earlier life to deal with anymore. He could instead focus only on his goal of getting into medical school and realizing his dream of becoming a doctor someday.

PART 2

From There
To Here

Chapter 16

Follow Your Dreams

Their ISC exam results were announced a few weeks later. As expected, Swaminathan had performed exceptionally well. He had the highest grades in school. George also had a first class. However, both had already decided that they didn't want to go to college, at least not right away.

"Appa, I would like to continue being a full-time reporter and put off college for a while. Can you allow me to do that?" Swami asked his father. "I already have top marks, so if I want I can always get admission even after one or two years. For now, I like nothing more than being a journalist."

Venkat thought about this for a while. He already knew how much his son wanted to be a reporter and work in a newspaper. Deep in his heart, as a young man, he had also wished to be a journalist and write about injustices and corruption, but he had ultimately chosen a safer career path.

"Okay, Swami," he said. "I will allow you to follow your dreams for two years. After that time, if I feel you are not making any headway, you will have to go to college, do a BCom and get a good job."

Swami agreed happily. George also spoke to his parents about postponing going to college. Mohan had wanted him to continue his education in the U.S. However, George had not taken the SAT yet, so he would not be able to apply for the next academic year anyway.

"Dad, I already have a job. I make 1,500 rupees at Dimensions as a graphic artist and also five hundred rupees performing at the restaurant. That is more than what most graduates are making nowadays."

Mohan had to agree that George was right. Like Venkat, a part of him was also very happy that his son had an exceptional raw talent in the arts. When he was young, pursuing a career in music or drawing would have been unthinkable.

"Okay, son," he said. "But promise me you will get a degree someday. There are so many things you will learn in college that you will not become aware of your whole life otherwise. I would like you to get a Liberal Arts undergraduate degree in the U.S. Then, you can focus on whatever you like. I went straight to the IIT after my school, so I never had a chance to learn about things like art-appreciation, philosophy, literature or psychology. As long as I am alive, you can study as much as you want."

"Thanks Dad," said George. "I promise I will get a Liberal Arts degree someday. But for now, my career in music and commercial art are both beginning to take off. I can't even tell you how happy it makes me when I perform or paint."

"I know, son, Mummy and I are very proud of you. It was not easy moving here from New York and adjusting, but you never complained. You can do anything you set your mind to, George, remember that, not just music or drawing."

■

Venu got his PUC exam results a week later. He had a ninety-eight percent average and was among the top twenty-five students in the state. He was ecstatic. He had never thought that he was capable of performing so well in his exams. His friends were overjoyed. They knew how hard he had worked for two years to achieve this feat.

"Great job, bugger," said Swami. "I think you will be able to get admission in a good medical college with these marks."

"I don't know," said Venu, "I still have to do the entrance exams next month. A lot depends on that, plus the interview..."

"Don't worry, Venu," said George. "You have done everything you could. Now just relax and do the entrance exams. We'll help you with preparing for the personal interview."

Venu had gone from studying for his PUC finals to studying for the entrance exams without a break. *"I can relax after my exams. I only need to do this for a few more weeks,"* he told himself.

Performing so well in the PUC final exam had empowered him as well. He remembered what Swami had once told him: *"Doing consistently well in studies is simply a matter of deciding where you see yourself when compared to others and then making sure you get there, and stay there. Once you start getting top marks, you won't want to settle for anything less. It becomes a habit. So you start studying more than others, attending all your classes faithfully, checking your answers twice… going beyond what you learn in class in all your subjects. Then, before you know it you are a brilliant student!!"*

His family was proud beyond belief, but they only understood the true meaning of his achievement when they saw his name published in the *Deccan Herald* as a rank student. Neighbors and friends from all over the state and beyond called to congratulate them.

Lying in his bed the night the results were announced, Krishnachandra felt tears of joy and pride run down his face. He hugged his wife and said softly, "Devika, I have never done anything to deserve this happiness. Please forgive me for everything. I will try to be a good husband and father from now on."

But his wife had gone to sleep. She was tired after a day of unusual excitement. She had served sweets, savories and coffee to the steady stream of visitors. It was an exceptional honor to get a rank in the state exam. Everyone who lived close by wanted to come and personally congratulate Venu.

Krishnachandra had closed the medical shop and left a sign on the door that said, *"My son achieved a rank in his PUC final exam, so I have gone home to celebrate with my family. Please come tomorrow. Thank you. — Proprietor."*

The whole family had stayed home that afternoon and evening to accept felicitations. Many relatives gave Venu money. It was also the first time Venu had told his parents of his ambition of becoming a doctor. They could barely comprehend what they heard. It was so much more than they had ever imagined for one of their own.

■

Venu applied to take the entrance exam at three medical colleges: Christian Medical College in Vellore, St. John's Medical College in

Bangalore, and the state-run Bangalore Medical College. His first choice was CMC, but he had heard admission there was virtually impossible, especially since he was a Hindu. The same thing was a factor in St. John's, where Catholics were given preference. But he was optimistic. He had not expected to even make it to this point a few years ago.

He had to take the state test to apply to the Bangalore Medical College. The other two colleges required him to take their own private entrance exams as well as attend grueling personal interviews. The CMC test was generally considered to be the hardest. It was three hours and ten minutes long and consisted of three-hundred questions — sixty questions each in Physics, Biology and Chemistry, as well as one-hundred and twenty questions on general ability and current events. Results were calculated using the Stanine grading system, developed by the U.S. Army in the 1940s.

There were times Venu wanted to give up. The pathway to his dream appeared too long and arduous. But something kept him going. His friends encouraged him in any way they could.

"Remember that if someone else can do it, so can you," said Swami.

"Yes, Venu," said George. "You have already proved that you can do as well as anyone else in the PUC. Don't worry about these entrance tests. I know you will do well and get into all three medical colleges."

The entrance exams for each of the three colleges were in a span of less than two weeks. Venu took them all and came away with the feeling that he had done very well. He was finally able to relax. He spent the next few days sleeping until noon and then going out with his friends for movies, drinks and dinner. Since Swami and George were also both working now, the Scrimshankers usually only met in the evenings.

At first, it felt strange to Venu that he was able to wake up in the morning and not have to worry about studying for an exam. After a week, he started going to the medical shop from ten until five every day and then spending the evenings with his friends.

"When will you get your notifications from the medical colleges?" Swami asked.

"I think they said it will take three weeks at least," replied Venu.

"I am nervous for you," said George. "I can only imaging how you must be feeling. Hang in there. You'll get in, Venu!"

There was still no news even after three weeks. Then, in the middle of the fourth week, Venu got a letter from the Karnataka Medical College Testing Board. He had performed well enough in the exam to get into several state colleges. They gave him a fortnight to accept the offer. Venu was happy but also disappointed. He had really wanted to go to CMC or St. John's. At the end of the week he still hadn't heard from the other two colleges.

"Well at least I know I can go to a medical college," he told his friends. "I knew I would have a problem in the Christian colleges because I am not a Christian," he said.

On his way home that night, George had an idea. He remembered that his father knew a lot of people with influence in the protestant educational institutions. When he got home, he talked to his father about Venu and how he had really wanted to go to CMC.

"He has the marks, Dad. He got a rank in his PUC, plus he thinks he has done really well in the entrance test. But he feels he will not get admission because he is not a Christian. Can you do something?"

Mohan knew several people in the Vellore CMC Admissions Board. In fact, his cousin Jacob and his wife Molly, in addition to serving on the Board, were also in charge of a foundation that generated a lot of money for the college. He knew that George would not have come to him unless it was very important to him. He had never asked Mohan to intervene on his behalf before for anything.

"I'll see what I can do," he told his son.

The next day, he called Jacob. "Just see what the situation is. This boy Venugopal has top marks, but if he is being rejected only because some Christian boy with lower marks is being given admission, then please see what you can do. Nalla cherikan ah... I have known these boys for years. He has a very good character and is a hard worker."

George did not know if it was because of his father's call but the next week Venu got a letter inviting him to come for a personal interview at CMC in Vellore. He never told Venu that he had asked his father to use his influence with the admissions board.

■

Venu was a little nervous about the personal interview. He was a bit shy about speaking in public or being in the spotlight.

"I wish I was like George," he thought to himself. *"That bugger can just stand up anywhere and talk or sing."*

Swami and George helped him prepare. They sat across from him at Koshy's and interviewed him.

"Why did you decide to apply to CMC?"

"What are your plans after you graduate?"

"Do you think medicine is a higher calling? Why?"

"If you saw a man and a child with wounds of the same nature, who would you try to save first? Why? Why not the other?"

They grilled him for over an hour until he was comfortable answering rapid-fire questions. They also suggested additional points he could include in each question.

"Okay, bugger, I think you are ready for your interview," said George.

In fact, the actual interview at CMC was a little easier than the one with his friends. It was conducted by a panel that consisted of just three Board members. Venu was not as nervous as he had thought he would be. The questions were all rather simple and straightforward.

Surprisingly, his final question was whether medicine was a higher calling or not. He answered it splendidly because he had already discussed it with his friends. He talked for over five minutes on the topic.

Two weeks later, Venu received an acceptance letter from the college. He had never been so happy or excited in his life.

■

Soon, it was time for Venu to leave for Vellore. Swami and George came to his house in the morning to say goodbye. An old yellow and black Ambassador taxi was parked outside. Venu and his family were loading his luggage into it. His friends rushed to help. Krishnachandra was going along with his son in the taxi and coming back the next day.

Once he had admission to CMC, the next hurdle for Venu was to somehow find a way to pay for almost five years of boarding, food and tuition. His parents had told him they would help him as much as they could, but he didn't know if it would be enough. By his estimation, it would cost about 50,000 rupees to complete the MBBS program. He wondered if he could get a loan. Maybe he could ask Swami's father if something like that was possible.

One evening as he was sitting at home looking through the forms, dates and deadlines for submitting payment to the college, his mother and father came into the room. His mother held a brown paper bag in her hand.

"Venu, you have never asked us for anything, but we want to do whatever we can. I sold all my gold and jewelry yesterday. We got 45,000 rupees. Please put this in the bank and use it for your studies."

Venu looked at her with tears in his eyes. "Amma, you shouldn't have. It's all you have…"

"Your Amma even hid it from me during my drinking days. She's a very sensible woman, so please take it. I will arrange for the rest somehow, for your expenses," said Krishnachandra.

"I promise you I will study as hard as I can," said Venu.

The taxi was finally all packed to leave. Venu bent and touched his mother's feet and hugged her. She had tears in her eyes. He said goodbye to his brother and sisters. Then, he turned to his friends.

"Bye chaps, looks like the Scrimshankers are breaking up," he said.

His friends hugged him. "No, bugger, we're here always. When you want to spend time with us, just show up, Doctor Venugopal," said George.

"Yes," said Swami. "Venu, we are very proud of you. All the best in your studies."

Everyone waved goodbye as Venu and his father got into the back seat of the taxi and it drove away.

■

Vellore is known as the Fort City, even though it is actually only a town compared to other big cities in the region. It lies along the banks of the Palar River in the state of Tamil Nadu and is approximately midway between Bangalore and Madras.

The fort there was built in the sixteenth century by the British and was subsequently the site of the Vellore Sepoy Mutiny of 1806, that preceded the more infamous Sepoy Mutiny in Meerut in 1857. The sepoys in the British Madras Brigade in Vellore Fort revolted when they were told they could not wear any religious or caste markings on their bodies. The British commander had replaced turbans with hats, ordered beards to be shaved and religious jewelry to be removed. The new hats were made from the hide of cows and pigs, which was a defilement of Hindu and Muslim religious beliefs. It was rumored to be the first step in the process of converting all the sepoys to Christianity. The Indians in the Brigade had already experienced prejudice and humiliation from the British officers and soldiers for many years. This was the last straw. At daybreak on July tenth, the sepoys attacked the European barracks and killed fifteen officers and over hundred soldiers. British reinforcements were sent from Madras to quell the rebellion. Over eight hundred sepoys and hundreds of British soldiers were killed in the fierce fighting that ensued. The sepoys finally surrendered. The British commander ordered the summary execution of over a hundred sepoys. The Vellore Mutiny is considered the starting point of an era of resistance to British rule in India.

In 1900, Ira Sophia Scudder, an American, and one of the first women graduates from the medical college at Cornell University, arrived in Vellore as a missionary and decided to build a hospital there. She called it Mission Hospital. In 1918, she added a medical college for women to the hospital. It was upgraded to a university in 1947 and men were allowed to study there as well. The college was renamed Christian Medical College and the hospital became part of the college. In the years that followed, CMC Vellore became known as one of the top medical colleges in the country, and the hospital soon developed a reputation for providing the best quality care.

Venu arrived at the college hostel and was shown to his room in the large granite four-story building. He met his roommate, Joseph Varkey, who was from Madras. Classes at the college would start only the following week, so this gave the new students a few days to acclimatize themselves to what would be their home for the next few years.

Krishnachandra bid his son goodbye and left in the taxi right after helping him move his luggage to the room. They would have to drive through the night to make it back to Bangalore by morning.

"Seri… I'll leave now Venu," he said. "Your amma will be waiting to hear how everything went."

"Okay, Appa, thank you," said Venu and hugged his father.

"If you ever need anything call me at the medical shop. Even otherwise call me now and then, please…" Krishnachandra told his son.

Venu had dinner in the mess hall and returned to his room. He unpacked his things and even though it was only about nine o'clock, he went to bed. It had been a long and tiring day.

■

He was woken up only a few hours later by a loud knocking on the door. "Come out! Come out! Come out!" a voice yelled.

There appeared to be a lot of activity going on in the corridor outside. Venu looked at his wrist-watch. It was only eleven-thirty. He saw Joseph hurriedly pull on his trousers. He did the same.

"Oh my God… they're going to rag us," said Joseph.

"What?" Venu asked. He had been too busy with all the college formalities to think about ragging at CMC. He knew all about the practice though. Every student that ever went away to school or college in India has experienced some form of ragging. The Scrimshankers had all been day students until now so they never had to deal with it before, although they had got a taste of bullying from C.K. Ganguli at Baldwin.

Ragging in India is considered by many to be a legacy of the British Raj and a carry-over ritual from British military and public schools. The practice was institutionalized in the educational models they set up in India over they years. Proponents claimed that the goal of ragging was to make the individual feel weak without the strength of his peers to support him and to instill a sense of social hierarchy among newcomers to a group. College ragging in India typically involved mild verbal and physical abuse as well as public embarrassment. However, it was sometimes known to escalate into extreme cruelty and torture.

Venu's heart was racing as Joseph opened the door. There were a few seniors outside.

"All you buggers… come downstairs to the quad at once," one of them commanded.

The boys went down to the open rectangular area in the middle of the hostel. All the freshmen students were pushed to the center of the quad. The seniors stood around them in a circle.

"Okay, everyone sing the national anthem," said a senior. Those who didn't know the words had to run around the quad a few times. For the next hour, the new students were made to do a series of embarrassing things for the entertainment of the seniors.

"Bark like a dog!"

"Act like you're drunk!"

"Stand on one foot!"

"Lie down on the ground and pretend that you are swimming."

Like the other new students, Venu did as he was asked. He had heard that students who resisted were singled out for more extreme ragging. He noticed that there were a handful of seniors that were the ringleaders. Most of the others seemed almost embarrassed and ashamed to be taking part in this humiliating activity. However, it appeared that none of them had the courage to question their peers as to why they were doing this to the newcomers.

Many psychological studies have been conducted on what is known as mob mentality. Some findings postulate that people lose their individual morals when they are part of a mob and do things they would not otherwise.

The closest ringleader to where Venu was standing was a tall, fair North Indian with a mustache. He was the one giving orders to the new students in that section of the quad. Venu tried to avoid eye contact with him. But the senior singled out Venu and Joseph.

"You two come here," he said. They both went to him.

"Take off your shirts."

"Now you wear his shirt, you wear his... actually, wear it backward."

"Take out your pants... now perform a silly dance in your underwear... no, more silly than that..."

"From now onwards until the end of this week, you must always call me Sir and salute me when you see me, is that clear?"

"Okay, get back in the group."

Another senior yelled, "Everyone bray like a donkey, and run around with your eyes closed." Many of the new students bumped into each other to the hilarity of the watching seniors.

Then it was over — for that night at least. The new students still had to put up with ragging until the end of the week. The seniors could pick on them anywhere and at anytime. Surprisingly, most colleges in the country allowed the practice and considered it as a benign rite of passage.

The next day, when Venu was at the mess hall in the morning having coffee, two seniors approached him and asked him to drink it through his nose with a straw. Fortunately, it was lukewarm. Later, when he was returning to his room, he walked passed the open doorway of a senior's room.

"Hey, come here," said one of the students in the room. Venu saluted and went inside.

"I was away visiting family last week, so I had to miss my classes," said the senior. "My friend Ranganath here was good enough to give me his notebook. I would like you to sit at that desk and copy all the notes from his book into mine."

Venu had to sit there for the next few hours and copy a week's worth of notes into the senior's notebook. Over the next few days, he had to stoically put up with several other embarrassing tasks that the seniors had concocted for the new students: dressing in women's clothes, wearing make-up, reading pornography aloud and swimming in his underwear in the fountain.

His worst experience occurred one night as he was returning to his room after dinner at the mess hall. Three senior students stopped him. Venu saluted them one by one.

"Come with us," said one of them. It was the same North Indian student with the mustache that he had noticed the first day. Venu learned that his name was Dev Puri. He was one of the worst of the raggers, and most freshmen stayed clear of him.

Venu was taken to a big building that was part of the college. He saw that it was the mortuary. He was led through the doors. "I wonder what they want me to do now… but this can't be good," he told himself.

"Okay, what's your name?" Dev Puri asked.

"K. Venugopal."

"You're in luck, K. Venugopal. This is you final ragging task. After this you will face no more ragging from anyone. You can tell the other seniors that Dev had told you this, okay?"

"Thank you, Sir," said Venu.

"But you have one more task to do." He took out a small bag of loose hard-boiled sweets and gave it to Venu.

"I want you to go inside that room. There are twenty metal trollies inside — each has a corpse on it. You cannot switch on the light. Put one sweet in each body's mouth and come back."

"What? I don't know if I can do that, Sir," Venu said.

"It's not so hard, K. Venugopal," said Dev. "In a few weeks you will be looking at dead bodies and cutting them up everyday. This is just so you will get used to it."

There was no way for him to get out of the situation. So on trembling legs, he opened the door and went inside. The trollies were neatly lined on either side of the room. The bodies were covered so only the faces were exposed. The room was refrigerated and very cold. There was a small blue light on the ceiling that allowed him see everything clearly even though it was rather dark and scary inside.

He took out a sweet and put it in the mouth of the first body. It was an old man with sunken cheeks. The next was that of a young woman who was rather pretty even in death. He kept going down the line; he finished one row and went on to the next. The first body was that of a fat middle-aged man; the next was an old woman. He started hurrying now; there were only three left. The second to last body was that of a young man with what appeared to be a gashing head wound. He put a sweet in his mouth and moved to the last body. Just then the supposed dead young man behind him sat up. Venu thought he would have a heart attack. He was scared and horrified.

"Can I have one more toffee, please?" the corpse asked.

The door opened and all the seniors came in laughing. It was actually one of them lying in the trolley and pretending to be dead.

"See, just red nail polish on my head. It looks real, right?" asked the joker on the trolley.

They all hugged Venu like he was a long-lost brother and told him he had passed his initiation to the college. That weekend, the seniors threw a big party for all the new students and greeted them as their peers and fellow members of the future medical profession.

Venu, however, had disliked this rite of passage immensely. *"This is cruel and silly. I will never rag a junior,"* he told himself.

Chapter 17

A Dream Comes True

The next two years passed by quickly for the Scrimshankers. Venu was completely immersed in his studies at the medical college. Swaminathan was now a full-time reporter for *The City Register*. He covered politics, crime, and even entertainment news occasionally when there were events he loved taking place in the city.

George still worked full-time with Kal at Dimensions and performed two sets a week at Melody Restaurant. He kept writing a steady stream of songs even though he really did not have a market for them yet. His goal was to make a record soon. However, it did not appear that he would be able to do it in India.

George had tried to put a band together, but he was having a hard time finding musicians that were willing to only play his songs. He did not want to play covers of popular songs, and most of the musicians in the city did not feel they could make a living by just playing original songs written by a young local talent. So he continued to perform on his own. He had a small following at Melody. Occasionally a few other musicians he knew sat in with him during his performance playing bass, keyboards, drums and guitar. However R.T., the owner of Melody, had made it clear that he would not pay for any additional musicians.

After a couple of years at *The City Register*, Swaminathan was also contemplating his future. The paper had continued its downward spiral, and circulation had been steadily falling. The Unwallas did not appear to know what to do to turn things around. It was rumored in the office that the paper would soon go bankrupt.

Swami had often considered getting a job in another publication. He had the talent and experience for it now. In fact, he had already received several offers from news editors at some of the largest newspapers in the city, who had begun to notice the quality of his writing. However, Swami had become quite attached to working at The *City Register*. He genuinely liked most of his co-workers and felt that the reporters at *The Register* could match the work of any newsroom in the country. He wished the management were different, though, because he felt the Unwallas were holding back the potential of the newspaper with their unpredictable policies and poor handling of the finances.

■

Swaminathan was having coffee at Koshy's a little after noon on December 9, 1980, when George rushed in. The friends usually met up every day around that time for a chat, coffee and a cigarette or two. Sometimes they had lunch together.

"Have you heard the news, bugger?" George asked.

"No, what?"

"John Lennon had been shot… he's dead."

"Oh no, when did it happen?"

"I just heard the news at the office. I tried calling you at work but you must have come here already."

"I have to get back to the office; this is a big news story as well."

Swami rushed outside, got on his scooter and drove straight to *The City Register*. He was now driving Venkat's old Vespa. When he got to the paper, he found that Javed Iqbal, the entertainment editor, was already in the process of collecting facts for the story.

"Swami, do you want to take on this feature?" he asked. "I'd like two pieces: one will be a news story about his death, and the other should be a more extensive feature on John's life and music. We'll need it for the next issue. It goes to press in three days. Can you manage that? I'll work with some photo agencies to get some photos, but you know how it is here — we may not be able to afford any exclusive photos from yesterday, so we might have to use stock."

Swami started work on the story at once. He already had an extensive knowledge about Lennon and The Beatles, but he refreshed his memory by pouring over every source he could find: newspaper archives in the library, books and magazines at the British Council Library, as well as his own collection of JS magazines from the past ten years.

His one-page news story, *"Death of a Beatle,"* as well as his six-page feature titled, *"Imagine There Is No Lennon,"* was by far the best coverage on the iconic musician's life and death in any newspaper in the city.

In addition to one image of John along with his assassin, Mark Chapman, a couple of hours before the murder, Javed had also been successful in finding many photos of John when he had come to India with The Beatles in 1967. Swami highlighted his visit to the country and created a narrative that was relevant to the readership of *The City Register.* He closed on a personal note:

"John Lennon has been one of this reporter's biggest influences for over fifteen years. I love his songs, but even more than that, I admired and respected him for his bravery and concern for humanity. I never had the privilege of meeting John or even attending one of his concerts, but I feel I knew him intimately just through his music and words. Rest in peace, John. Thank you for the timeless songs!"

The issue had one of the largest news stand sales in the history of *The City Register.* Many readers wrote letters praising Swami's tasteful coverage of the sad event.

■

One morning, several months later, Swami was at the office of *The City Register* when he heard rumors from the staff that the paper would be closing down soon. No one had any concrete details yet, but some of his co-workers said that there had been auditors from the bank looking through the books and taking away files. The Unwallas had not been seen or heard from in over a week. There was a foreboding in the office and everyone was afraid of what would happen if they lost their jobs.

"I wish I had the youth and the finances to take over this newspaper. It has everything that is needed to succeed in place: talent, set-up, location and respect of the readers. Even our circulation and advertising isn't bad actually," said Ram Murthy, the news editor. "Unfortunately, I don't have the money or the strength to take it on anymore."

He added, "Swami, you should consider buying it. I am certain you can turn it around."

"How much will it take to buy it?" Swaminathan asked.

"I don't know. I've heard talk that the Unwallas owe the bank 50,000 rupees plus their other creditors another 50,000. So, if you had about one lakh* plus some loans for operating expenses you could buy it, I think. But I am not a lawyer or accountant, so I don't know for sure."

Swami felt a surge of excitement run through his body. Was this the moment that he had been waiting for? The opportunity seemed perfect. Everything was in place already — all he needed to do was take over. He was confident in his abilities as a writer. He had no business experience, but so far he had succeeded in almost everything he set his mind to. This would be more than just a job — it would be his passion. But he also had no money of his own.

Just then, one of the auditors from the bank, a short, overweight man holding a scooter helmet and a worn-out briefcase in his hands, arrived to talk to Deepak Joshi, the accountant of *The City Register*. Swami saw them converse softly and seriously. The auditor stayed for about an hour and left.

Swami followed him out and caught up with him as he was taking his scooter out of the parking area. "Excuse me, sir," he said. "Which bank are you with? My name is Swaminathan, and I am a journalist here. I heard some rumors about the paper being closed down. Is this true?"

"I can't talk about it, but I am with the State Bank of India, Double Road Branch. We are the creditors for this newspaper. That's all I can say for now." He put his briefcase into his scooter's carrier and left.

Swami pulled his own scooter out and drove quickly to his father's office at the Unity Building. Venkat was surprised to see him.

"Kanna, what's the matter? Did something happen?"

Swami quickly told him the situation at *The City Register*. "Appa, I think the bank is going to take over the paper and liquidate all their assets. The staff will lose their jobs, and the paper will close down. Can you find out how much money is required for someone to settle all the debts and buy the paper? The bank that owns the debts is the State Bank on Double Road."

*100,000 rupees

"Swami, what do you want to do?" his father asked. "You don't have the money to buy the paper."

"But you do, Appa — at least some of it. I can ask George to be my partner, and he can put in half. I know it's a lot of money, but it's not much more than what you would spend if I went off to IIT or did my BCom and an MBA. Can you at least find out the situation? You have contacts in State Bank. Please ask."

Venkat was swept up by Swami's enthusiasm. It was true that he had built up quite a bit of savings over the years with his frugal living. And he only had Swami to look after. He knew how passionate Swami was about journalism. He was also very confident in his son's ability to finish what he started without failing.

"Okay, Swami, I'll ask around a bit and let you know tonight."

"Thanks, Appa. Let me go and tell George."

Swami called his friend at Dimensions and asked him to meet him right away at Koshy's. He then said goodbye to Venkat and rode his scooter there.

George was already at the restaurant with a coffee and cigarette when Swami arrived.

"What's up, bugger? What's the big news?" he asked.

"*The City Register* will be closing down, and the bank will be selling all their assets. I am thinking about buying it and running it. Would you like to join me as my equal partner?"

George was excited as well, not because he had ambitions about being a newspaper publisher, but since he knew how important it was for his friend.

"Does this mean we can get rid of the What's-His-Name-Eve-Teaser, and I can become the Art Director," he asked?

Swami laughed. "Bugger, we'll own it. We can do what we want. My father said he will let me know the details this evening — how much money we need to put in and so forth. I would say it could cost us about one-to-two lakh rupees each. Can you ask your father if he will lend you that much money?"

"Okay, I'll ask," said George.

Venkat had some more news on the situation with *The City Register* that evening. He had talked to a friend in the State Bank head office, who called up the branch and got the information. Apparently, the Unwallas had been trying to sell *The City Register* for the past six months without any success. They owed the bank

95,000 rupees in overdrafts. The mortgage on all the equipment in the office was another 50,000 rupees. Plus, the auditors calculated that another 60,000 rupees was owed to suppliers. They were asking for three lakhs, but so far no one had made an offer. If they couldn't find a buyer in three weeks, they were going to have to declare bankruptcy and turn over the newspaper to the bank.

"Appa, we can buy the newspaper from either the owners or the bank, correct?" Swami asked. "Which do you think is better?"

"From my experience, it is always better to buy from the owners — even though you may think you will get it cheaper from the bank. There is a lot of formality and red tape when a bank gets involved. It is a big institution, and no one there will care much about one small transaction like this. It may take you months, or even years, to finish the process, No, it's much better to get the owners to make a deal quickly, pay the bank and creditors what is owned and start fresh with no debts or ties to the old owners."

"Appa, I don't know anything about such matters. Is there someone you know who I can go to so we can negotiate the price and make sure we are following all the correct procedures?"

"I know one business advocate called Ragunath who may be able to help you. I will speak to him. I already spoke to your Amma. We can give you two lakhs for this venture but I may have to sell some stocks and shares first. If you can ask your friend, George, to also put in two lakhs, that will give you four lakh rupees. I think that will be enough to buy the business and leave you with a little money for running expenses," said Venkat.

"I can also put in a word for you with your branch manager after you start functioning — you will get overdraft facilities, which you can use while your account receivables come in."

"Thanks, Appa," said Swami hugging him. He was excited beyond belief.

"One more thing," said Venkat. "You must first come up with a business and financial plan before you go to the bank. List out the expenses: monthly rent, salaries, printing and paper costs, travel and miscellaneous expenses. Then write down the assets: fixed assets, approximate revenue from advertising each month, money from subscriptions and news stand sales…"

"Appa, I didn't know you were such an expert on all this," said Swami.

"I come into such situations all the time in the bank, Kanna. I will do everything I can to help you."

Swami met George the next day and told him everything Venkat had said. "Do you think you can put in two lakhs — that's 200,000 rupees."

George approached his father that evening and explained the situation.

"Have you considered all the angles?" Mohan asked. "Sometimes friendship and business do no go well together. Many good friendships have been ruined by business."

"Dad, Swami and I have been friends since the first week that I arrived in India. He's like my own brother."

"Okay, then… we have the money, so I will speak to Mummy and let you know when we can give it to you. Maybe you should get Annie involved in some way too — she's doing her BCom in the evening and working as a junior accountant at Macmillian and Company."

Annie was his first cousin from his mother's side. She was an only child like him. George was quite fond of her. Her father was Abraham Verghese, the well-known deputy inspector general of the Bangalore Police and their families were very close.

"Okay, thanks Dad, I'll tell Swami and call Annie as well."

George and Swami met Annie Varghese in Koshy's the next day. She was slim, tall and pretty. She had long, straight, jet-black hair that ran down all the way to her waist. She was a little darker than George with almond-shaped eyes and an unblemished, smooth face. She was wearing just a hint of red lipstick and no other makeup. She bore a striking resemblance to George, more like a sister than a cousin. Swami had known Annie for many years through his association with George but he was still a little intimidated by her. He was very attracted to her, but in the past, he had tried not to think about her in a romantic or sexual way because of who she was to his best friend.

She was wearing tight blue jeans, a short white silk kurta and sandals. Like most Indian girls, she had narrow ankles and wrists but unlike most, she also had slim thighs and breasts that were full and round. The top two buttons of her kurta were open, and Swami could see her bra and the top of her breasts quite clearly. She had a thin gold chain with a cross on it that nested tantalizingly between the "V" of her breasts. He tried not to stare.

"So Annie, Swami and I are thinking about buying *The City Register,* where he's already a top reporter. Apparently, it's going bankrupt," said George. "Daddy suggested that we bring you in as well to help with the accounts. We will have a lot of work, even from right now, because we have to look at the financial statements and other bank documents. Swami and I don't know anything about that."

"Yes, Annie, George tells me that you are working at Macmillian as an accountant and also going to evening college at St. Joseph's for your BCom," said Swami. "If you join us, we can pay you more than you are getting now. We really need someone we can trust with the accounting. It's going to be a bit hard at first."

"Don't worry about money. If G is part of it, count me in," said Annie. "I don't like my job at Macmillan anyway — it's too boring. Only thing is that four days a week, I have to leave at four-thirty in the evening so I can go to my college. Also, don't expect me to work on weekends, because I need to study for my class. So if those terms are acceptable, I will join you."

"Thanks, Annie," said George.

"That's great! By the way, have you learned how to write a business and financial plan in your college?" Swami asked.

The next day, the three of them went to meet with Ragunath, the advocate recommended by Venkat who specialized in business law and sales of corporate and business entities.

"Your father already phoned me and told me you were coming," he told Swami. "Yes, I will be happy to be your advocate in this matter. My secretary will type up an agreement, and you can pay me a token advance of one hundred rupees. After that, I will take up your matter with the bank and see how we can buy this newspaper at the best price."

In a week's time, Ragunath had negotiated a sale price from the Unwallas. They agreed to sell if they got 75,000 rupees over and above all their debts. They had invested more than that into it, but now they just wanted to get out of their obligations with their creditors. There were no other buyers as well.

Ragunath was also successful in reducing the payments they

would need to make to creditors who were owed money by the Unwallas. When all was said and done, Swami and George would have to pay out a little less than two-and-a-half lakhs for the privilege of owning *The City Register* lock, stock and barrel.

The bank wanted their money quickly, so they acted fast on all the paperwork. It took only about a month to get the formalities done. Mohan and Venkat transferred two lakhs each into the bank account of Friendship Limited, a company Swami and George had started and registered.

They signed the ownership documents and partnership agreements ten days later. After that, the newspaper was theirs. Swami decided to continue publishing *The City Register* exactly as it was for a few months until they found their bearings and decided on what they wanted to do with it.

Because of Venkat's influence, the bank had given them an additional one lakh in overdraft facilities. The paper was operating at a net profit, so the important thing was to keep advertising revenues and circulation at least at the existing levels.

There were a few news articles in some of the other publications in the city about the sale of *The City Register*. V. Swaminathan, the new managing partner, was quoted as saying that, "*The change in ownership is purely administrative and will not affect the quality of the newspaper. We are going to make it even better as time goes by.*"

Swami and George met with the staff of *The City Register* and explained the situation to them. The employees were relieved. Everyone, except for a few people, would get to keep their jobs.

Rajendra Prasad, the art director had quit as soon as he had heard that Swami had bought the paper. He did not like Swami either and couldn't imagine taking orders from him. They had also fired the accountant, Deepak Joshi. After looking over the books, Annie had discovered several discrepancies. It appeared Joshi had been working with the Unwallas to adjust income and profits to avoid taxes and inflate the expenses, as well as siphon off money into their personal accounts.

In addition to being the managing partner, Swami also took over the role of Editor-in-Chief. George made it clear that he would take Swami's lead in administrative and policy decisions and mainly focus on his role as Art Director. He was only there to help his friend realize his dream. This was not something he wanted to do for the rest of his life.

The City Register continued to be published with almost no change to its content for the time being. However, although he hadn't even told George yet, Swami had big changes planned for it.

∎

Swami and George now spent all their waking hours at *The City Register*. The paper was printed on a web offset press. Layout was handed over to the printer in negative form. All the line art such as type and illustrations were done on boards using phototypesetting and bromides, and then converted to negatives. The typesetting came in rolls set to the width of a column, which was three centimetres wide. This was then pasted using rubber cement onto large boards, pre-printed with a light blue grid that would not show up on film. Oversized headlines were created using Letraset type pasted together one alphabet at a time or enlarged and printed from phototypesetting. Halftone photos and tints were imposed directly as negatives so as not to lose detail. The final step was to combine the line and halftone negatives on a large light table into final, full-page galleys that were sent to the printer for platemaking and printing.

After examining the layout, graphics, fonts, illustrations and photographs in an average issue of *The City Register*, George had listed several visual enhancements he could make to it. When he showed Swami his recommendations for improvements to the layout, he was surprised, because Swami didn't appear too enthusiastic about making the changes.

Instead he said, "George, I would like you to not just make improvements — think about starting from scratch. If you could design a newspaper from the ground up what would you do?"

"What do you mean?" George asked.

"Bugger, I'm thinking about creating a new newspaper out of *The City Register*. I have a name for it too — *Bangalore Baloney*! That's a word you use a lot. I was lying in bed last night thinking about it, and suddenly everything began to take shape in my mind. But if you don't like the name, we can change it."

"No... no... no... I like the name a lot. In fact, I love it, Swami!!"

George often used the word "baloney" when he disagreed with something or when he wanted to say "nonsense." When Swami was thinking about renaming the newspaper, he had decided to add *Bangalore* to the name because he wanted to link the city to the publication but he also wanted another word after it that was a little different and unusual. Once he added *"Baloney"* to Bangalore, it seemed like the perfect name for his newspaper. There was a slightly irreverent aspect to the name *"Bangalore Baloney."* It would also stand out among the sea of papers that ended in *"Times,"* *"Register,"* *"Statesmen,"* *"Record,"* *"Daily,"* or *"Dispatch."*

"I was looking up baloney in the dictionary, and it said it is was also another word for bologna or smoked sausage. You don't think it will sound funny, do you, George?" Swami asked.

"No, I think the name will separate us from the other newspapers. People may mispronounce *Baloney* at first, but once they get used to it, no one will even think about what it means. Everything sounds strange when you first hear it. Think of Coca Cola. When it first came out, no one knew what coke or cola was. Now it is such a generic name. The same with Xerox."

So it was decided by the two owners that the new name for *The City Register* would be *Bangalore Baloney.* However, for the time being, they would continue to publish under the old name until they had revamped the paper and come up with a plan for launching *Bangalore Baloney.*

"Let's go to Vellore this weekend and see Venu," said George. "I wonder how the bugger is doing."

The two of them had only seen Venu a few times since he went off to medical college. He had come to Bangalore on a couple of very brief visits. George and Swami had also gone to Vellore twice and stayed the weekend there. However, their lives were now very different. Even when they were all together, occasionally, they would inevitably end up discussing serious topics. Those days of carefree abandon were now a thing of the past.

■

Swami and George decided to take a well-deserved weekend break from the newspaper and board the Friday night train from Bangalore to Katpadi Junction in Vellore. They had a thali dinner in the train and then smoked, chatted and drank steaming cups of coffee all the way there. They arrived in the middle of the night and asked the auto driver outside the train station to take them to some accommodation that was close to the CMC.

He dropped them off at Gokul Lodge. It was within walking distance of the medical college. Their room was small, but it was clean and had two beds. It was after 3:00 AM, so they went to sleep right away.

In the morning, they called Venu at the hostel. He was delighted to know that they had arrived. He directed them to an Udupi restaurant a short distance from their lodge and told them he would meet them there in an hour.

The Scrimshankers were delighted to finally get together again. Swami and George filled Venu in on their purchase of *The City Register*.

"Wow, this is so exciting," said Venu. "I can't believe you buggers are big-shot newspaper publishers now."

"Yes, it's really exciting," said Swami. "I am living my dream. Thanks, George, for coming in with me. I couldn't have done it without you."

"You're welcome, bugger," said George. "But you do know that once the paper is doing well, I'll move on. *Bangalore Baloney* is all you, Swami. It suits you perfectly; you were born to be a journalist and publisher."

Venu told them about his life in medical college. He had settled into a routine of class, hospital rotation and studying. There was no time for anything else.

"There are lots of pretty nursing students here," he told his friends, "and I know many of them, but so far I'm still a virgin. What can I say! What about you, Swami?"

"I'm still a virgin, too," said Swaminathan. "It looks like George is the only one who's not. George, did you tell Venu about Vanita? Venu, this bugger had another girl after Jennifer... brief affair again... Mount Carmel College girl... now back in South Africa... no lingering ties. He's like James Bond, this bugger," he said affectionately.

"Well, that's all there is to say, Swami," said George, laughing. "I really don't have anything more to add to that."

The Scrimshankers spent the whole day together. They saw a Tamil movie that starred MGR that night at an open-air tent theater close to the lodge. They sat cross-legged on the mud floor of a huge canvas tent with a fellow audience that included laborers, farmers, drunks, medical students and families with children. Swami and Venu translated the story for George from either side, yelling over the loud and harsh-sounding audio system. After the movie, they had a tasty dinner of chicken fry and Ceylon parotas, along with several long necked bottles of Kingfisher beer, at a roadside restaurant on Ira Scudder Road.

It was past midnight when they walked back to the lodge groggily. They joined the two beds in the room, and all three of them slept together on it. The next afternoon, Swami and George said goodbye to Venu and took the Bangalore Mail back to the hectic life they had left behind for a couple of days.

■

Swaminathan spent the following week compiling facts and figures for the bank. Since he was going to change the name as well as a lot of other things about the paper, he knew there would be a degree of uncertainty in how it would be received by the current readership. He realized he needed additional capital so he could operate the paper without worrying about collecting every rupee of each month's revenues to pay for the next month's expenses.

Working with Annie, he put together all the fixed and variable expenses on one side of the sheet and the income from subscriptions, news stand sales and advertising revenue on the other, as his father had suggested. He also listed the tangible assets of the company. When he totalled it all up, he was happy to see that they were still currently making a small profit overall.

Annie used a sample format from one of her textbooks and typed up the information as a proper business and financial plan. It detailed Swami's vision for *Bangalore Baloney* and provided hard data regarding circulation, advertising, costs and projected profits after a year of operation.

In the meantime, George had been busy creating an exciting new look for *Bangalore Baloney*. *The City Register* had been modelled after a typical daily newspaper even though it was a weekly. It was set in the standard broadsheet format with eight columns of tightly packed news stories on every page. George reduced *Bangalore Baloney* it to a tabloid size in a five-column format. Instead of twenty-four pages like *The City Register*, it would have forty-eight pages. Advertising space would be increased by twenty-five percent. Until such time as all the ad spots could be sold, it would contain house ads and public service announcements.

George and Swami decided that the cover would have the masthead on top with a two-inch strip ad running across the bottom. The four columns on the left would feature one large photo and headline in big bold type and a few lines of copy. The last column would be divided into five boxes highlighting the most important stories inside that particular issue.

The back cover would have two strip ads running along the whole width of the top and bottom of the page. The rest of the space would be devoted to just one large entertainment or sports photo with a prominent headline with a few lines of copy. George borrowed this idea from some of the popular tabloid publications in England and the U.S.

Swami had decided exactly what he wanted in terms of content. "*Bangalore Baloney* should be the definitive weekly newspaper for the city," he said to George and his news editors. "I like the fact that the name '*Bangalore Baloney*' sounds irreverent. However, the quality of our reporting and writing should be top-rate. People should take us seriously. As a weekly publication, it should offer more detail and insight than the daily papers. I don't want to use any stock photos unless it is absolutely necessary. The photographs should have quality. In a weekly, immediacy is not as important as depth and quality. The various sections can stay almost the same as it is now but I want it to have content our readers will not find anywhere else. We all love this city. That should also come through in the paper and every article in it."

George created several designs for the masthead by hand in painstaking detail using a thin paintbrush, rapidograph and Letraset font sheets. He tried heavy block san-serif designs, knock out type treatments, type with photographs of Bangalore inside, another variation of the same idea with line drawings of easily recognizable landmarks inside the type, and many more.

He chose the three that Swami liked the best and mocked up entire spreads that showed both sides of the proposed publication. *The City Register* used the traditional Times font in 9 point. George decided to change the body copy to the Garamond font family. It was more stylized than Times and was recognizable by the small bowl of the "a" and the small eye of the "e." He had read in a font guide when he was working at Dimensions that Garamond was considered to be among the most legible and readable typefaces.

For headlines, George decided to vary the font dramatically to Helvetica, the stylish san-serif typeface. Developed in 1957 by two talented Swiss typeface designers, Helvetica had become very popular in European advertising and graphic design. It was also very easy to read from a distance and added style and sophistication to a layout. It had four thicknesses: light, regular, bold and black. He was also considering using the font for body copy in sidebars and as sub-heads.

After working ten to twelve hours a day for two weeks, George finally had the dummy layouts for Swami to look at. He had greeked in the copy but used real headlines and photos from new stories to convey the tone of the paper. Finally, he made bromides of each individual page and created impositions by pasting the prints together so it looked like a real newspaper. Swaminathan was thrilled with the results.

"These layouts are absolutely fantastic, George," he said in delight. "Annie, look! Don't you think it's the best you've seen? I can't decide which one I like better; they're all so good."

Annie and Swami had been working very hard for several weeks, preparing the business plan for the bank as well as running the day-to-day operations of *The City Register*. The two had become very close, and Swami had gotten to know Annie quite well. He realized that she was very smart and had a good sense of humor. She was also very devoted to her family and fiercely loyal by nature. The two usually had all their meals together. Swami even dropped her home sometimes in his scooter when it got late and then came back to work at the newspaper with George.

Contrary to her earlier demands that she would have to leave at four-thirty each afternoon and not work on weekends, Annie had also got caught up in the excitement of launching *Bangalore Baloney*. She still went to her college classes, but otherwise spent all her free time with Swami at the paper. When he was in a creative frame of mind, George tended to be in his own world and did not like to interact much with others. He was completely focused on creating the new design for the paper, so he usually declined Swami and Annie's invitations to join them for coffee or meals.

After spending a few weeks with her, Swami realized that he

was falling in love with Annie. He tried to fight it at first, forcing himself not to think of her or focusing only on the newspaper when he was with her. But soon he realized he was thinking of her more than the newspaper he had wished to publish for so many years.

One Saturday evening, after working the whole day, Annie said suddenly, "Who wants to go for a walk with me? I'm going crazy being inside all day. You chaps are also smoking too much — it's giving me a headache!"

"Count me out," said George. "I need to finish something for *The City Register* and then work on *Bangalore Baloney*." They were going to present the business plan as well as the mock layouts the next week to the bank.

"I'll come with you," said Swami. "George, are you sure you won't join us? We can walk to Commercial Street and have jelabis at Haldiram's."

"No, you two carry on without me," said George.

Knowing his friend as well as he did, he had realized a few days ago that Swami was very interested in Annie. He wanted to at least give his friend the opportunity to woo her on his own.

"Knowing the bugger, he'll probably keep at least a foot away from her at all times and just eat the jelabis and come back," he thought to himself.

■

Swami and Annie walked down Infantry Road, to Cubbon Road and then to Commercial Street. It was a pleasant evening, and they talked non-stop the whole way. Swami had never been so comfortable talking to a girl on his own before. He felt something for Annie that he had never experienced until then. It was so much deeper than mere lust. He wanted to be with her all the time, doing anything — it didn't matter what. They discussed work at first, but then they slowly began talking about themselves.

"What is your biggest dream?" asked Annie.

"For the past few years, it has been to be a journalist and own a newspaper; that's come true now, I guess. My biggest dream since I was a boy was to go to the U.S."

"I went there once a few years ago. It was nice, very modern compared to India, but I'm an Indian girl at heart. I wouldn't want to live anywhere but here."

"I'd like to visit and travel all over the U.S. I've heard so much about it from George," said Swami. "I still have a small model of the Statue of Liberty that he gave me in the fifth standard."

"You chaps are very good friends, aren't you?" asked Annie. "G is great, he's my favorite cousin. He's a very sweet person. There is no hatred or anger in him at all. I don't know how he can be so calm and relaxed all the time. Me, on the other hand... I have a temper Swami; I warn you..."

"I don't believe you. I think you are very much like George in nature. More like a sister than a cousin I would say. You have the same mannerisms and a good attitude about everything... and the same mischief in your eyes. But both of you are willing to take responsibility for your actions. Once in the seventh standard George hid inside the desk of Mr. Bhutt, the Sanskrit teacher, because I bet him he wouldn't do it. He kept slowly opening and closing the desk while Mr. Bhutt was teaching. It made a creaking sound and everyone was giggling. Finally, Bhutt went and opened the desk and there was George curled up inside smiling at him. Bhutt kicked him out of class for three periods. I think he even gave him a couple of whacks. But George didn't mind, he was willing to pay the price for his prank."

"You boys are so crazy," said Annie. "We girls are so boring that way, even though we love to gossip."

"What do girls gossip about?" Swami asked.

"Mainly about other girls, clothes and boys."

"Well boys gossip too, but it's about stupid things... girls and sex...."

"What was the worst gossip you've ever heard about girls and sex?"

"Well, when we were in the eighth standard, George, Venu and I were in class during the short-break when this chap, Sanjay Bhatija, said he had heard from someone that they never served full bananas or whole cucumbers to the girls in boarding schools," said Swami.

"And why is that?"

"You know... because they would use it to masturbate. I've been waiting for years to ask a girl if this is true."

Annie laughed so hard that she had to sit down on the brick

wall of a compound they were going past.

"I've been in a boarding school in Ooty, and I know friends who were boarders in a lot of other schools. I have never heard of this rule. In fact, we used to masturbate with bananas and cucumbers quite often in my school..."

Seeing the shocked look on Swami's face, she laughed and said, "Just pulling your leg. The whole idea is quite ridiculous. You're right; boys do gossip and spread rumors too, but about the most idiotic things."

They reached Haldiram's on Commercial Street. It was a small roadside shop that was famous for its Indian sweets and savories. They ordered two plates of jelabis, the small crispy bright orange pretzel-shaped hollow dough pieces that are deep-fried and soaked in sugar syrup. Jelabi is considered the national sweet of India. It was served to them in small cups made from thick, coarse leaves that were stitched together with little twigs.

Swami and Annie sat on a small table in the narrow gully that was off the main road and ate the hot jelabis with their hands while they talked. They were oblivious to the time that went by. It had been over two hours since they had left the office.

"We'd better get back," said Swami.

"Yes," said Annie. "George will wonder where we are."

They parceled an order of jelabi for George and started back. As they were walking, without thinking about it, Swami put his right arm around Annie's shoulder. He realized what he had done only when he felt her tense up for a few seconds... then she relaxed and leaned into him. He was about to pull his arm away but now he left it there as they walked. Neither of them spoke for a while as they kept walking.

Soon they had left the brightly lit shops of Commercial Street behind and were on the dark Infantry Road. It was past nine o'clock, so it was deserted except for an occasional car or two-wheeler going by. Swami felt Annie shiver. He gently turned her around to him. She lifted her face to his. Her hungry lips found his. He was amazed by how soft they were. He could taste the sweetness of the jelabi on them. Then she slowly pulled away.

"Sorry, I don't know what came over me," said Annie.

"Yes, me too... do you regret it?"

"No, I think I like you a lot Swami... and I am attracted to you."

"*I am crazy about you,*" Swami wanted to reply, but he kept quiet.

They walked back the rest of the way silently. When they got inside the office, George was still hunched over his light table with a paintbrush in his hand.

"Did you go to get jelabi, or did you run off and get married?" asked George mischievously.

They both turned red with embarrassment. Later, when Swami returned after dropping Annie home, he told his friend, "George, I think I'm in love with your cousin, I kissed her. I feel we will get married. Are you okay with that?"

George punched his friend lightly on the shoulder. "Bugger, you're my best friend, and Annie is my favorite cousin. I couldn't be happier. But marriage is heavy stuff. Think about it before you go and propose. I can't believe it, you go out for jelabi and come back thinking about marriage!"

"I know. You may not believe it, but something tells me I'm going to marry Annie," said Swami.

"I hope you do," said George.

■

Swami and Annie were both a little embarrassed and awkward with each other the next morning at work. Everyone was busy putting the next issue of the paper to bed that day, so there was not much time to talk about anything but work. Swami and George shared the big office that the Unwallas had once occupied. It was in the middle of one side of the large basement room. The three walls facing out to the rest of the room were made of thick glass.

Their office had blinds that could be closed, but Swami liked to leave it open so he could see all the activity that was going on outside. There were two executive desks inside, but George usually sat outside with the layout artists on an inclined light table. Swami saw Annie look at him from her desk at the other end of the room. He smiled at her and she returned it, almost shyly — which was quite unlike her. Like George, she was not easily embarrassed and always spoke her mind.

Swami had spent most of the previous night thinking about Annie. He had begun to have misgivings about kissing her. She had turned out to be an excellent accountant and business manager. He didn't want her to quit working with him because of any personal issues that may arise if they had a relationship. He decided to resolve the issue with her that day itself somehow.

The day went by quickly: editing copy, adding headlines, tweaking the layout, filling all the advertising holes, updating news stories with last minute information, checking the boards, making film and finally taking it to the printer.

"Annie, would you like to come with me to the printer?" asked Swami. It was late in the afternoon.

"Yes, I don't have class today," she said.

They rode together on Swami's scooter and stopped at Mysore Printers on Kasturba Road to drop off the roll of negatives. They would have to come back after two hours to check the proofs.

"Let's go somewhere and have coffee while they make the plates, load the press and print proofs," said Swami. "We are not too far from Cubbon Park, let's go there."

They drove the short distance and parked Swami's scooter at the two-wheeler parking lot. Cubbon Park was created in 1870 and named after Sir Mark Cubbon, the British Commissioner at the time. It is located in the middle of Bangalore City and has over three hundred acres of natural rock outcrops, thickets of trees, massive bamboo plants, grassy areas, walking paths, carefully cultivated flowerbeds and lots of monuments.

As they walked through the park, Annie quietly slipped her hand into Swami's. They reached the outdoor restaurant in the center of the park and ordered coffee and snacks.

"So, what do we now do about us?" Annie asked, when the waiter had left.

"I told George," said Swami. "He's my best friend and partner in the paper. I don't want to do anything behind his back."

"What did he say?"

"As expected, that he's happy for us."

"What else did you tell him?"

"That I think I love you and I would like to marry you someday."

"So quickly, just like that?" Her eyes were bright.

"Annie, I know what I want. I have been like that since I was a child. When I met George and Venu I knew we would be best friends. From the time I got to know you I have been in love with you. You are just what I want in a woman. So why should I pretend otherwise? But how do you feel about me?"

She thought for a moment before replying. "I like you a lot Swami but I don't know if I love you or not. Maybe I will as time goes by. I think it's too early to talk about marriage. Why don't we go away somewhere together for a few days? I am very attracted to you as well."

"Thanks, Annie, you are the first girl who has ever told me that. I know I am not like George. He is so handsome and stylish — all the girls love him. When I am with him, no one notices me."

"Swami, I find you very attractive. Yes, George is very handsome but you have a certain distinctive look as well. I like the bone structure of your face, your slim body and the intelligence in your eyes, as well as the fact that you are a kind and gentle person."

"Wow, thanks for saying that Annie. I don't know how to respond. As for going away, we can't leave for a few months, because we need to present the business plan to the bank and then launch *Bangalore Baloney*. We have to organize a nice party."

"Then for the time being, let's continue to be like we are now, until the launch of the paper. After that, we can go away together for a few days, maybe to Ooty. Then you and I can then decide if we want to continue our relationship, get married or whatever. Either way, I will continue to work for you. You are a fantastic editor and publisher. I haven't had the chance to tell you that."

She pulled her chair close to his and put her hand in his. Swami had never been happier or more content in his whole life.

Chapter 18
The Launch

Swami and George decided that they would launch *Bangalore Baloney* in the first week of September. It was almost the end of May. In the next three months, they would have to ask the bank to loan them more money... finalize the layout and content... meet personally with all the advertisers and explain the situation... write to all the subscribers and tell them about the changes... ask the printers to order paper in a different size... create a campaign to promote the new publication... order new signs, business cards and stationery... organize the launch party... and so much more...

First, Swami and Annie met with Raman Prasad, the bank manager. They had moved the newspaper's bank account to National Bank, the same bank that Venkat worked for. It had been a few months since they had taken over *The City Register* and their banker was very pleased with their performance so far. They had taken in more money than they spent each month. When Swami explained that they were going to change the name and format of the paper, the bank manager was a little surprised and concerned.

"You are doing very well running the old paper. Why do you want to change it? You may lose subscribers and advertisers."

"I know, sir," said Swami. "But the old paper was not my dream. The new one is."

He showed the manager the layout that George had put together and then presented the business plan that Annie and he had created.

"Sir, you will see here in detail how we plan to launch and grow *Bangalore Baloney*. We are going about it in a very scientific way. Two months ago we did a survey of people in the eighteen to fifty-five age group about what they would like in a weekly newspaper that focuses on Bangalore City. Based on their answers, we have tailored our look, style and content. We will have articles and information for this group that they will not find anywhere else, in any other paper. We will present this fact to our existing advertisers. I am certain we will keep all our old advertisers and subscribers and maybe even increase them slowly."

Raman Prasad looked at the layouts and the neatly typed business plan. He was impressed. Although the couple in front of him appeared to be in only their early twenties, they both seemed very capable. Most importantly, he also knew Swami was Venkat's son.

Everyone at National Bank held Mr. Venkatasubramanian in the highest esteem. He had a reputation for being scrupulously honest and straightforward. Even though he was now very high up in the bank's hierarchy, he still kept in touch with most of the clerks, cashiers, secretaries and subordinates that he had worked with in the past. When he visited a branch, he always went around shaking hands with everyone and listening to any issues they might have. He never forgot that he had started off as a cashier. He was still very humble and treated any older worker as his senior, no matter what their position was in the bank. It was rumored that he sometimes asked the peon who brought him his afternoon coffee to bring another cup and sit with him in his office and chat about how things were at the bank.

"Mr. Swaminathan, I have only the highest regard for your father. However, that's not the reason I will sanction an additional five lakhs loan for your company. I think you have created a very good business plan and I am very impressed with how it is going to look. Good luck with the new paper... how you say it... Boloney?"

"Baloney... thank you, sir," said Swami.

Annie smiled happily next to him and gripped his hand in excitement under the table.

"Of course, our people will have to come to your office and make the required inspection and check the facts and figures... but it is just a formality," added the bank manager.

Annie and Swami left the bank feeling very relieved. They were now guaranteed to have enough money for at least the operating expenses and to even make some purchases and modifications to the office.

■

The next step was to create a campaign that would generate interest for *Bangalore Baloney*. Swami, George and Annie, along with their editors, Ram and Javed, had decided on the final logotype and layout for the newspaper from the several mock-ups.

George had also designed the new letterheads, business cards and other stationery and they had sent it off for printing. They had ordered a fifty-foot wide by ten-foot high sign for the side of the building that could be illuminated at night. The partners had also decided to spend 20,000 rupees on some much-needed renovations to the office.

"This place reminds me too much of the Unwallas... like a failing newspaper, not a successful one. Let's make it modern and youthful looking. Annie, can you take on this project?" Swami asked.

"Yes, Annie, add some color please," said George. "Also, some cool posters and art will be nice too. Do you think we can we get in a decent stereo and some music? We can take the one from the club room in my house and some records was well."

"What do we do about a campaign?" asked Swami. "We need to make people curious about *Bangalore Baloney*... starting right now! I was reading a while back about how the word 'Quiz' came into existence. A theater owner in Dublin, Ireland made a bet in the late 1700s that he could introduce a new word into the English language in twenty-four hours. He hired a group of street urchins to write the word 'Quiz,' which was a nonsense word, on every wall in the city. Soon, everyone wanted to know what it meant. People thought it was some sort of test, and that's how it got its meaning."

"That's a great idea! Let's make posters with the word *'Baloney'* running diagonally up the sheet and *'Coming in September'* under it," said George.

"It's exactly what I was going to say," said Swami.

"That's a very clever idea, or at least it is clever of you to steal an old idea," said Annie, hugging Swami.

Swami and Annie had become much closer since that day in Cubbon Park. They often went to movies and sat in the back row huddled together holding hands and kissing. But that was as far as Annie let Swami go.

"Do you really want to wait until we go to Ooty? We could go to a nice hotel in some other part of the city," Swami begged Annie.

But she was adamant. "Let's make it special, Swami," she said. "Good things come to those who wait," she added mischievously.

Swami explained his predicament to George one evening when they were alone in the office. "I don't know if I can take it anymore, bugger," he told George. "I am shagging in the morning and night just so I can come and concentrate on my work, otherwise I would only be thinking other thoughts. As it is, I can't stop thinking about her."

George laughed, "Let me see if I understand your situation: she lets you kiss and hold hands with her, but nothing else, until you go away together on your pre-honeymoon in two months. It is very cute and romantic, if you ask me. Where are you planning to go?"

"She wants to go to Ooty."

"So you go there, have sex like rabbits for a few days, come back and decide if you want to get married, correct?"

"Yes, she said that if either of us didn't want to get married after that we could decide to call it off, but she would continue to work here."

"I have to hand it to my cousin — she's a classy girl. Don't ever hurt her, bugger."

"George, I give you my word she will never be sad because of me."

■

The following week, George designed and printed 5,000 "*Baloney*" posters. They hired a vendor to get it pasted on walls all around the city at night. The next morning, the residents of Bangalore, like those in Dublin over three hundred years earlier, woke up to find an unfamiliar word pasted on almost every street in the city. It garnered quite a bit of interest. Many people though it was a rock band from England or the U.S. Others assumed that it was a new restaurant. Some newspapers even covered it as a news story — until they got wind that it was a new competing publication.

Once the poster had lost its element of curiosity, Swami decided to put up the new sign outside and reveal the news that *The City Register* would soon become *Bangalore Baloney*. He devoted a lot of ink in *The City Register* extolling the virtues of the new weekly paper. He started a Q&A column where he invited readers to write and ask questions about the changes. He ran ads that told subscribers that if they weren't fully satisfied with *Bangalore Baloney* he would refund their money. He offered old subscribers an additional three months of free *Bangalore Baloney* if they did not cancel their subscriptions.

Behind the scenes, everyone was working really hard to meet the launch date. George had completed new templates for all the sections. They printed fresh art boards, based on the new tabloid size, for each page and section. Swami wrote several articles for the first issue. The rest was similar to what they were doing earlier, but Swami instructed his reporters and editors to use a more youthful voice in the articles.

He gathered the entire staff one morning for a breakfast meeting. Annie ordered dosas, idlis, vadas and coffee from Kamat Restaurant. After they had eaten, George went over the new format with everyone. Then Swami spoke.

"As I have said earlier, this is not your father's newspaper," he said. "It is new... it is mod... it is exciting... it is *Bangalore Baloney*... not *Bangalore Times, Bangalore Courier or Bangalore Statesman*. I have taken all the information from the survey we did recently and put it into bullet points. I asked Annie to type and Xerox it so everyone has a copy. Here's what it says..."

Annie handed him a sheet of paper and he read from it.

"The readership of *Bangalore Baloney* is:
- Between 18 and 55 years of age.
- It is primarily male, especially in the above-30 age bracket. However, the women-to-men readership in the under-30 age bracket is 35/65 and there is also secondary readership of women in the over-30 group.
- Since we publish only in English, we can conclude that our readers can read English fluently. Many of them are educated in missionary and convent schools.
- The bulk of our subscribers are middle class with about 15% belonging to the wealthy.

- According to the survey, our pass-along readership is about 2.5. This is the number of additional people who read the paper. For example, if our circulation is 60,000 and our pass-on-readership is 2.5 then our total readership is 60,000 + 150,000 = 210,000. This is the number we can show our advertisers."

He paused and said, "Please remember this information when you are writing articles, editing news stories or approaching advertisers. Let us create a paper that fits our readership perfectly — then there will be no reason why they won't buy it. Thank you all, and good luck to us."

■

The launch for *Bangalore Baloney* was a gala affair. It took place the day before it hit the stands. George and Swami rented Copacabana, a spacious multi-cuisine restaurant on the floor above them in the same building. They invited advertisers, business people, public figures, bankers, advertising agency staff and even other reporters and publishers. Venu came down from Vellore to attend the big event. They also invited all their families, friends and relatives.

It was estimated that over five hundred people attended the party that went on until the wee hours of the morning. Swami, George and Annie organized small groups of guests and took them downstairs to the offices of *Bangalore Baloney*. Everyone was impressed with the new décor and renovations to the office. Visitors were given a copy of the still unpublished first issue of *Bangalore Baloney*.

"Swami, this is fantastic," said Venkat to his son after looking over the issue. "I am very proud of you. God bless you."

"Thank you, Appa, I'd like you to meet someone... This is Annie, George's cousin and our accountant. She will finish her BCom from St. Joseph's in a few months."

"Hi, Uncle," said Annie. "Swami has said so much about you. He really admires you."

She was dressed in a thin red and gold sari and a low-cut red blouse with long, tight sleeves. Her long hair was down to her waist and she had on dark lipstick. She looked ravishing.

"Hello, Annie," said Venkat. "I am very pleased to meet you.

Look after this chap. He's smart, but sometimes he forgets the reality of things; he thinks anything is possible."

"I will, Uncle," said Annie. "I know you will be very proud of Swami. He's doing a wonderful job."

Later as Venkat was sitting down with his wife and drinking a mango lassi, he watched Swami and Annie standing closely together. She leaned into him and held his arm briefly as she smiled and talked to him. Venkat touched his wife gently on the shoulder and said softly, "Amma, you may be looking at your future daughter-in-law. She's a Christian, but so what?"

His wife put down her glass and stared open-mouthed at Annie. "What? She is so beautiful, don't you think?"

George was wooing all the advertisers and agency account executives with his charm. When things started to quieten down, he brought out his guitar and started singing Beatles songs. Everyone joined in the sing-along.

Mohan watched his son with pride. He had never imagined that George could be so focused on anything. He had seen his son's layouts for *Bangalore Baloney* as well as all his work for the launch. He had also met Kalinga Rao at the party. Kal had told Mohan about the work George had done at his advertising agency. Watching him in his work environment had given Mohan a new perspective of his son. He saw the adult he had become. Then later, when he saw him play his guitar and sing, he realized that George was truly blessed to have the looks and talent few people did. Everyone was drawn to him instinctively. However, the thing that Mohan loved the most about George was his innocence and loving nature. *"Don't change, son. Stay this way always,"* he thought to himself.

Venu had come to the party with Krishnachandra. They sat together in the back of the restaurant and talked about all sorts of things. Venu would be finishing the MBBS program soon. After that he would have to spend two years as a doctor serving in the poorer rural areas of the Tamil Nadu. This was something he had to promise in writing before he started his medical classes at CMC.

"Appa, once I finish my voluntary service, I am going to apply to study overseas, maybe in England or Canada. They accept our medical board and exams standards."

"I know you can do anything you decide, Venu," said his father.

"We are all very proud of you and what you have done. If you go overseas, you will be the first person to do so in our family. Your brother Ravi is also a very good student now. He has top marks in all his exams."

"I know. I saw his exam papers. He wants to do engineering. Give him all the encouragement he needs at home, Appa."

Just then Venkat walked over. "Venu, how are you? I have heard so many wonderful things about you from Swami. Soon to be a doctor, eh… God bless you. Look at all of you! Krishna, did you ever think our children would be so smart?" he asked Krishnachandra.

"No, never… they are all smart boys, but more important, they are also good boys," said Venu's father. "They have all done us proud."

■

Bangalore Baloney hit the news stands the next afternoon. Swami, George and Annie were monitoring sales. By ten o'clock at night, after phoning around and visiting several kiosks and agents, it appeared that sales had far surpassed the past week's sales of *The City Register.*

"It looks like there is a forty percent increase in sales. It's a good thing we printed 100,000 copies instead of 65,000, like we did for *The City Register,*" said Swami to the others.

"Let's wait and see until the end of the week and the following few weeks. This could be just because *Bangalore Baloney* is new and people just want to see what it is," said Annie cautiously.

"I'm an optimist," said George. "I predict our sales will increase when people see how good our newspaper is," said George.

"We've done all we could. Whatever happens, I am proud of what we have done, and I am happy to be with both of you this evening," said Swami.

The three of them were sitting outside on the lawn at the Bangalore Club eating kebabs and drinking beer. Annie's father was also a member there. It was almost midnight. Annie got up from her chair and stood behind Swami. Then she leaned down and put her arms around him from the back. He could smell the subtle fragrance of her perfume mixed with her own special body scent. It excited him like nothing else.

He felt shivers down his spine when she whispered in his ear, "Let's go to Ooty."

■

It took Swami another week before he could leave Bangalore for a few days. The newspaper was performing splendidly so far. He organized the next issue, and then asked George to take charge in his absence. He booked a room at the Savoy Hotel in Ooty for four days.

"I'll try to call you from there," he told his friend, "but I don't know how the trunk calls are. I may not get through."

"Don't worry, bugger, have a good time and forget about everything here. I promise I won't run it into the ground in your absence," said George, laughing.

Swami told his parents he was going out of station for a few days. Ever since he had become a reporter, they were used to him travelling around the state to cover events. Annie had gone to boarding school in Ooty, so her parents assumed she was going for a reunion with her classmates when she told them she was going there.

They met in the morning in the office and said goodbye to George. He hugged them both and slipped a box of condoms into Swami's jacket pocket — reciprocating what his friends had done for him some years earlier.

"Don't see what's in your pocket until you are alone... and use it," he whispered.

Swami had booked two tickets on a luxury bus that left from the City Market bus station. Annie had asked him to pack a sweater and jacket because it was quite cold up in the mountains of Ooty. They took a taxi from the office to the bus station.

Soon they were on their way in a comfortable bus. Annie sat next to the window. She had brought a small Yashika camera with her. The journey would take approximately eight hours.

After driving a few hours they stopped at Channapattna, a small town that was famous for handmade wooden toys, for a short break. Swami bought a couple of wooden tops while Annie went to use the toilet. She came out quickly with her face wrinkled in disgust.

"Swami, that toilet is absolutely filthy and smells so bad. I held my breath the whole time."

"Here, see what I got, Annie — George, Venu and I used to play tops every morning before class. Venu was the best at it. He could do so many tricks with it. I bought four tops, one for each of us. Maybe we can teach you to play too."

The bus started off again. They stopped in Mysore for lunch at a Kamat Restaurant. Annie slept most of the way there with her head on Swami's shoulder. He felt happy and contented to have this beautiful girl next to him.

The last stage of the journey was the most scenic and exciting but it was also a very bumpy road. It went through Bandipur, a wildlife sanctuary that had an abundant population of deer, elephants, peacocks and monkeys. Annie took photographs from her seat by the window.

They arrived in Ooty late in the afternoon and took a taxi from the bus stand to the hotel. When they got to their room, they both felt a bit strange and embarrassed. They had never been together like this before. Swami could see that Annie was a bit nervous.

"Let's go out for some tea and sightseeing," he said.

Ootacamund, or Ooty as it is called, is located in the Nilgiri Hills of Tamil Nadu. It is a very scenic region with a mild, spring-like climate throughout the year. The mountains are known as The Blue Mountains, because of the blue smoky haze emitted by the eucalyptus trees that cover the hills and valleys, as well as for the blue flowers that abound in the area and form colorful blankets on the flat land.

The British Raj developed Ooty and constructed a solid infrastructure of railroad tracks, train stations, guest homes and bungalows so they could use it during the summer months when it got too hot in Madras. They left behind a legacy of several beautiful man-made structures: a quaint rack-and-pinion railway built in 1904 called The Nilgiri Mountain Railroad, which winded its way up the steep slopes; a twenty-two acre botanical garden laid out in 1842; a lake with a boathouse constructed in 1824 by John Sullivan, the first collector of Ooty; St. Stephen's Church, which was constructed in the nineteenth century; and Stone House, a huge bungalow also constructed by Sullivan during his tenure.

Swami and Annie walked around the grounds of the upscale Savoy Hotel. It was a beautifully landscaped property. The hotel had been in existence since 1845 and offered both independent bungalows as well as large suites set in the midst of luxuriant lawns, flower gardens and ponds. They went to the restaurant at the hotel and ordered snacks and tea. It was certainly a very romantic location. After they had finished their tea, Annie reached across the table and held Swami's hand.

"Let's go back to the room," she said.

They closed the curtains in the room and undressed slowly and stood naked in front of each other.

"Annie, I have never done this before," said Swami.

"Neither have I," said Annie. But she stood proud and straight in front of him. She had a slim and beautiful body with firm breasts and medium-sized nipples. She had neatly trimmed and shaped her pubic hair so it looked like a little black triangle.

Swami's erection stretched straight out in front of him. She stepped forward and kissed him gently. He put his arms around her.

"One minute," he said and took out the packet of condoms from his suitcase. He slipped one on. Then they were on the bed making love furiously. Swami didn't want it to end. She achieved orgasm first; after that, he ejaculated. They lay, spent, next to each other. Her face was covered in sweat and passion.

He kissed her gently and said, "I love you, Annie."

"I love you too Swami," she said. Then she noticed the blood between her legs. She was alarmed.

"I have some bleeding, Swami, sorry. It was my first time."

Swami kissed her again. "Thank you for making me your first."

After an hour the made love again. Like his friend had years before, Swami also mused, "Capstan is wrong!"

"What's that?" Annie asked. She laughed loudly when he told her.

They spent the next three days in Ooty. They saw some of the sights and walked around the beautiful parks and pathways, but mostly they made love over and over again and delighted in getting to know each other's bodies.

"I went to boarding school here for five years," said Annie one morning. "I want to show you where."

She took Swami to St. Hllda's School, which was nested in the Blue Mountains. They looked through the big gates at the schoolgirls walking around in their dark-gray uniforms and dark blue blazers.

"We can go inside, I am an alumna, after all, but I don't want any nosy teachers who know me wondering who you are and what I'm doing here."

"I can't believe you were one of those schoolgirls," said Swami. "You must have looked so cute in that uniform."

"I can still wear it and show you. I have it at home," said Annie.

"Yes, please. Now you will just look sexy in it. I am turned on, Annie! Let's go back to the hotel right now," said Swami. So they did...

They had dinner at Shincow's Chinese Restaurant. They ordered sweet chicken corn soup, noodles and American Chopsuey. Annie loved Chinese food. Swami was also developing a taste for it.

"You know, I just remembered another stupid rumor from when we were in school," said Swami. "Narandra Prasad, a chap in Cotton's, once told George and me that if you are looking for prostitutes in Ooty, all you have to do when you go to any restaurant is to take your empty water glass and turn it over on the table. It is a code for the waiter or restaurant-owner to call a prostitute... and they come to the restaurant in half an hour."

Annie laughed. "That is the silliest rumor — more silly than the girls masturbating with bananas in boarding school. Let's try it out..." She took her glass and turned it over.

They were having dinner, half an hour later, when a young girl wearing a lot of make-up came inside the restaurant. She was alone. Swami nudged Annie and said, "Still think it's a rumor?"

She kicked him on his shin. Just then the girl's boyfriend came in and joined her at the table.

Swami and Annie took a night bus to Bangalore and slept holding each other the entire way back. They had breakfast together at Woodlands before going home.

"Annie, I still want to marry you. That hasn't changed at all. In fact, I love you even more and cannot live away from you," said Swami as he was dropping her home in a taxi.

"I'm warming up to you too," said Annie. "Actually, I love you Swami... and James, your little friend," she added smiling.

Swami went home with a song in his heart.

Chapter 19

Happy And Sad Events

Work was hectic at *Bangalore Baloney* in the months that followed. The circulation and advertising numbers continued to hold and even rise slowly. Swami, George and Annie worked over ten hours at the office every day. Annie had graduated from college, so she could spend all her time at the newspaper without worrying about classes or tests.

After their Ooty trip, Swami and Annie had both decided that they would like to get married as soon as possible. They couldn't live without each other anymore. Swami told his parents first. He sat them down in the drawing room and broke the news gently.

"I have some news I want to tell you about. This may come as a shock to you, but please don't be angry with me for not telling you earlier. You know Annie, George's cousin? We have been in love for a while now and would like to get married."

His mother and father smiled. "Kanna," said Venkat. "We have known all about your romance for many months. Our only concern is that she is a Christian, but other than that we don't have any objection. Have you thought about the religious aspect? What will happen if you have children?"

"She is a very beautiful girl," said his mother. "As long as you are happy, we will be happy too. But your Appa is correct. Have you discussed your religion and what will happen after marriage?"

"Yes, we spoke about it. As you know, I am not religious but I am a proud Hindu by heritage and culture. She is an Orthodox Christian and she is religious. However, she will not force me to convert. If we have children, she would like them to go to church.

But I can also teach them about Hinduism and other religions. She is not a fanatic about Christianity."

"Have you spoken to her people?" asked Venkat. "They may have some objection to her marrying a Hindu boy."

"No, I haven't, but I am going to do it," said Swami.

Annie had already spoken to her mother about Swami. "Mummy, he's the kindest, handsomest and most intelligent man I have ever met. He is also George's best friend. I have known him for over a year now. We would like to get married."

"He's also a Hindu boy, Annie, I don't know… have you told Daddy? He will be disappointed. He wanted you to marry a Mar Thomma Christian groom and have the wedding in our church."

"Mummy, you must talk to him. Swami wants to come and meet him and ask for my hand in marriage. He will not do it any other way. He's a very brave chap. He has his own business, and he is well known in the city as a fearless journalist."

"Okay, I'll talk to Daddy. Ask Swami to come on Saturday evening."

That Saturday, Swami showed up at the Varghese residence on Race Course Road. He bought a Black Forest cake from Sweet Chariot on Brigade Road and took it with him. He rang the bell. Annie opened the door. It was the first time he was coming into her house. He usually just dropped her off outside.

It was a big bungalow. The gardeners from the police department maintained the outside impeccably. The inside of the house was also spotless and the furniture was arranged very evenly and neatly. The quarters was owned and furnished by the state government and it looked more like in a hotel or guesthouse than someone's home. He entered the drawing room. On one wall was a large wall carpet depicting "The Last Supper" mounted in a wooden frame. There were lots of plaques, awards and trophies in the shelves and scattered all around the room.

Annie's parents entered the room. Her father was a tall and muscular man in his mid to late fifties. He had the obligatory short mustache that most middle-aged Indian men were inclined to have and short gray hair that was combed back. Swami shook his hand and said Namaste to his wife, an attractive, tall, slim woman.

"Come, sit," said DIG Varghese. "Annie tells me you are the editor and publisher of *The City Register*."

"Yes, sir, we changed the name recently to *Bangalore Baloney*."

They chitchatted for a while about crime, politics and the state of the city. Annie helped her mother serve coffee and snacks. Then she sat down next to Swami with her parents.

"The thing is," Swami began, "I have come to ask you for Annie's hand in marriage. I know I am not a Christian, and I am not going to convert, but I love your daughter very much. With your permission, we would like to get married. This is not a sudden romance. We have been friends for a while now. I know her well, and she knows me. I come from a good and decent family. My father is R. Venkatasubramanian, the Assistant General Manager of National Bank. I have already asked my parents, and they have agreed."

Abraham Varghese sat silently for a while. His face was stern when he said, "Mr. Swaminathan, you seem like a good person but we were hoping for a Mar Thomma Christian boy for our daughter. It is going to be very difficult for you both in the future. Love is very good at first, but we have to think about the future of our only child. She's a smart girl, but she is also very innocent about such things. We don't want her to make a mistake."

"Sir, I understand what you are saying, however I am helpless. I love your daughter more than my own life. I am not rich, famous and what not, but I am a good and decent person. I will never cause any sadness to your daughter."

"But that's not enough," said Annie's father.

"Daddy..." said Annie.

Swami continued, "I cannot say anything that will convince you of the fact that I am the best suitor for Annie. She is so beautiful and smart that I am sure you will find many Christian doctors, engineers and lawyers lining up to be considered. Your daughter and I are both above the legal age. We could have run away and got married. But I promise we will not do that. I will wait until you have considered my proposal. Please don't just say no without thinking about it. Annie has told me so many wonderful things about your family. I hope that someday, I can be a part of it. I have been one of your nephew George's best friends since the fifth standard. Please talk to him about me if you like. All I ask is for you to give me a fair chance."

He stood up suddenly and shook a surprised DIG Varghese's

hand. Then, he said goodbye to Annie's mother and left. As he was walking out of the house, Annie came running out behind him.

"That's all? Why didn't you wait for me to also talk?" asked Annie.

"I came to ask your parents for your hand in marriage, not to beg for it. I want to give them some time to think about it and get used to the idea. It must have come as a shock to them."

After Swami had left, Annie's parents talked about him at length.

"He seems like a nice boy," said her mother.

"Maybe, but he is a Hindu. What will all our relatives think?"

"I have seen him with George for years. These days, what is Hindu or Christian? The children today, they don't care. Don't we always say that our ancestors used to be Brahmins?" asked his wife.

"Yes, Rema, but this is our only daughter. If we had a few children, then it would be okay, but to have our only son-in-law be a Hindu is difficult."

"Talk to Mohan-Achayan*, Sheila-Kochamma** and Georgie," said Annie's mother. "You are in the police: investigate the boy. If he is a good person, I am willing to accept him into our family. Annie is very much in love with him. Her happiness is all that matters."

DIG Varghese knew it was futile to talk his wife out of something when she was like this. "I'll check up on the cherikan***. You are right; I have the resources of the entire police department at my disposal."

The next day he visited Mohan and Sheila Chandy early in the morning. George was at home as well.

"Ah, Ebby, what a nice surprise," said Mohan. "Come on in, we were just about to have breakfast."

"Just some coffee, thanks. You know, Annie told us she wants to get married to that boy, Swaminathan, Georgie's friend, What do you think?"

George had already told his parents about Annie and Swami's romance, so they weren't surprised at the news.

"I have known that boy for many years. He practically used to live here. He's a very good boy... nalla cherikan ah... penay Hindu ah... athe ollu..."

"I know," said DIG Varghese. "Rema says Annie is very adamant about marrying him. What to do?"

*elder male relative
**elder female relative
***boy (Malayalam)

238

"Yes, Swami is a very nice boy — very respectful and kind. I am very fond of him," added Sheila Chandy. "Ebby, you had a love marriage as well, just like Mohan and I did. Let the children decide for themselves."

George, who was having breakfast at the dining table, spoke up, "Ebby-Chachan, he may be a Hindu, but he's the best boy Annie will ever meet. I can guarantee you that his character is good. He is also the smartest person I know. He came first in the ICSE and ISC exams. He could have walked into IIT or any school in the world, but he followed his dream of being a journalist."

"But what about his religion? Koche*, these things will matter in the long run. Now they may be in love… what about when they have children? Which religion will they follow?"

"Everything will be fine, Ebby-Chachan. Swami is not religious; he's a rationalist, but he respects all religions. I am sure he will have no objection to Annie taking their children to church. He comes with me to St. Mark's for services and events," said George.

When DIG Varghese got to his office, he asked his assistant, Shivshanker, to find out all he could about V. Swaminathan. He gave his address as well as the details he knew about his schooling. A week later, Shivshanker came to him with a file.

"Sir, I have investigated this boy Swaminathan. He seems to be a good chap — no complaints are listed. He was a top student in school and junior college. His father is one Venkatasubramanian, the Assistant General Manager of National Bank. He is a very important and respected man, sir. Swaminathan was a reporter at *The City Register*. Then he bought the paper along with your nephew George Chandy. Now he is the managing partner and editor. They say he is a fearless journalist. He's the chap who wrote the investigative report of bribery in our police department. You remember, we had to fire ten sub inspectors and twenty constables."

"That chap, eh… didn't he have some problem with some goondas as well?" asked DIG Varghese.

"Yes sir, he wrote another article about the goondas* in the Bamboo Bazar area about two years ago — how they were extorting money from poor shopkeepers and that the police were doing nothing. Some goondas went to *The City Register* and tried to beat him up. This was the time your nephew George called you and we sent a police jeep there right away."

*child (Malayalam)
**thugs (Hindi)

"Yes, yes, I remember," said DIG Varghese. "Brave chap, is he? Anything else, Shivshanker?"

"Only one more record of him, sir. He donates blood every six months at Bowring Hospital. He is Type O-Negative. It is in great demand always — that is why he gives so regularly. He must be a good-hearted chap. But why are you so interested in this boy, sir?"

"Because Shivshanker, he may soon become my son-in law!"

"Congratulations, sir. I think you are lucky. He's not like the grooms you hear about these days: dowry deaths, wife beating, abandoning them and going away. But he's a Brahmin boy. Is that a problem, sir?"

"I thought so at first; now I am not so sure. Thank you, Shivshanker. Keep all this to yourself."

DIG Varghese's next stop was at Venkat's office in the Unity Building. He went in plain clothes because he didn't want to cause a stir. However, many people recognized him in the bank. His photo was often in the newspapers and magazines. They wondered about it even more when he asked the receptionist if he could meet Mr. Venkatasubramanian. He was directed to Venkat's office on the eighth floor.

"Please come in, sir," said Venkat. "So, you are Annie's father. Swami has told me all about their plan to get married. I met Annie a few times as well. She is such a lovely girl."

"Thank you, nice meeting you, sir," said DIG Varghese. "You may know that I am in the police department. Annie is our only daughter. So I checked on your son, He seems to be a very good boy. However, there is the issue of religion. You are Brahmin, and we are Orthodox Christians. This may be an incompatible mix. What will happen when they have children?"

"Sir, when Swami told me this was my concern too. But after I thought about it I realized that maybe it is a bigger issue for us than it is for them. We have lived most of our lives already — whatever prejudices and opinions we may have should not be passed on to our children. Therefore, Swami's mother and I have no objection to this marriage."

"Aren't you concerned about the differences in our religion?"

"No, not at all. We are Brahmins, but our son is his own person. He has the right to follow any religion he wants. If Annie becomes our daughter-in-law, we will welcome her into our house with open arms. She can practice Christianity if she wants. We only want our son to be happy, nothing more."

A surprised and thoughtful DIG Varghese said goodbye to Venkat and left. *"At least his father seems reasonable,"* he said to himself. He went home and narrated all he had learned to his wife.

"I knew he is a good boy and comes from a nice family," said Rema. "Our Annie is not a fool. We must give her credit for her choices. She has never disappointed us in her life."

DIG Varghese stayed awake most of the night thinking about this issue. In the morning, after breakfast, he went to the offices of *Bangalore Baloney*. Swami was writing a news story on his typewriter. Annie and George were in the office as well.

"Daddy, what are you doing here?" said Annie seeing her father.

"Hi, Ebby-Chachan, come to beat Swami? Don't touch his face though. Otherwise, Annie be very sad," said George mischievously.

"Eda... neneke uru adi kodakandia... you children have given me so much worry last week. Is your Swami free?" he asked Annie.

Swami came out. He shook DIG Varghese's hand.

"Come in, sir," he said.

Annie's father looked around the newspaper's office. There were over twenty people working there. He had picked up a copy of *Bangalore Baloney* from Annie's room the previous day. He was quite impressed with it.

"This chap is quite talented," he told himself after reading the editorial written by Swaminathan.

"I'll let you all talk," said George. "I need to finish this layout."

They went into Swami's office and closed the door. DIG Varghese got to the point at once, "Swami, if you ask Annie, she will tell you that I am a straightforward sort of chap... I speak my mind, and I don't like to hold things inside. After you came and asked for Annie's hand in marriage, her mother and I talked about it. I even sent my assistant to check up about you."

"Daddy, what? You checked up on Swami?" said Annie.

"Yes, Annie, you are my only daughter, and I don't want you to make a mistake. I even met your father, Mr. Venkatasubrimanian."

"You went and met my father?" asked Swami. "Why?"

"I wanted to see how he was — and to understand his position on this matter."

"What did he say?" asked Swami.

"He said that he is willing to welcome Annie with open arms to his family."

"And what about you, Daddy?" asked Annie.

DIG Varghese paused for a while and then said, "Swami you asked me to consider you. So, I did everything I could to find out about you. From what I can tell, you are a very smart, talented and nice boy and my daughter loves you very much. So, just like your family is ready to welcome our Annie, I would also like to welcome you to our family. God bless you both."

Annie cried and hugged her father. Swami hugged him as well. "Is it okay if I call you Daddy from now on?" he asked.

George seeing what was going on rushed in and hugged everyone too. "See, Swami? I know my Ebby-Chachan. He's tough on the outside, but he's a softie inside."

"Come for dinner again with your parents," said DIG Varghese to Swami. "Let's all meet and get to know one another. Annie, fix a date with mummy and let me know."

■

Swami and Annie got married three months later. They had a registered marriage first. After that, they had token ceremonies in both the Hindu temple and in the Mar Thomma church. Swami had been clear that he would not be converting to Christianity — not because he was religious but rather because he wasn't. Many of Annie's relatives were aghast.

"At least he can become a Christian if he wants to marry our Annie," said Valsamma Aunty, her mother's sister.

"Aunty, Swami is not religious. He will not ask me to become a Hindu but he will not convert to Christianity either. He has said that if we have children, I can baptize them in our church if I want. His parents are religious... so when I am in their house I will respect their religion. Why should our religion be more important than theirs?"

People from both the bride and groom's sides shook their heads sadly as they attended one of the ceremonies. However, Swami's parents were gratified when Father Elias, the priest of the Mar Thomma church, as well as several of Annie's relatives, attended the Hindu ceremony as well. They sat through the entire event and Father Elias even shook the pujari's hand and talked with him afterwards.

Venu came from Vellore to attend all the wedding events. He had completed his MBBS and was now officially a doctor. However, he was being posted to Chennimalai, a small village in Erode district, for two years to complete his volunteer program.

The Scrimshankers met for dinner the night before Swami and Annie got married. They decided to come to Koshy's restaurant for old time's sake. After a few beers they were all a little tipsy.

Venu raised his beer glass and said, "I officially disband the Scrimshankers. From now on, Swami will have other priorities in life with his lovely wife, Annie. I am going away to God-knows-where in the middle of nowhere for two years. George will be too busy moving from one beautiful woman to the next to have time for us."

"No, Venu," said Swami. "The Scrimshankers are forever. We may all go away and do separate things, but in our hearts we will always be best friends."

"Yes, buggers, the Scrimshankers are forever. I love you chaps like my own brothers. No matter what happens, we'll be friends," said George.

"Then here's to us, the three Scrimshankers and the start of a new chapter in our lives. Good luck, Swami — may you and Annie have everything you wish for," said Venu.

"Yes, bugger, all the best," said George. "But don't forget about me — at least call me for dinner now and then. By the way, how's your love life, Venu?"

"I'm sorry to report that I'm still a virgin," said Venu. "I will probably get an arranged marriage. My parents will look for a girl after I finish my volunteer service. But enough about boring old me, George, you tell us about your adventures. I heard you had four girlfriends already!"

George narrated a few humorous stories regarding some of the girls he had known. He was currently going around with a young divorcee who was a few years older than him.

"Older women can teach you so much," he said. "Not just about sex, but also other things. Sandhya used to live in England and France. She's a very interesting woman. Her husband was a top diplomat for the Indian government, and she used to throw parties for prime ministers and royalty. Unfortunately, her husband left her for a French model, so she came back to India."

"I saw you both on your motorcycle on M.G. Road yesterday," said Venu. "She's a knock-out woman. You are a lucky bugger, George."

"Yes, here's to George, the luckiest bugger on earth," said Swami lifting his glass. "But tonight I feel a little lucky myself."

After their wedding Swami and Annie moved into a two-bedroom house in Koramangala. The next months were the happiest in Swami's life. He loved waking up with Annie and being with her morning, noon and night. He also had his best friend George in the office next to him during the day.

Annie encouraged them to go out for lunch and coffee alone so they could spend time together. She understood how important their friendship was. Whenever George was not spending the evening with Sandhya, the three of them had dinner together. George also sometimes spent weekends with them in their house, and the two friends would stay up half the night playing chess, cards or caroms.

Bangalore Baloney had become a successful publication. Circulation had climbed to over 150,000, and there were no shortage of advertisers. Swami bought a used Ambassador car. George sold his Jawa motorcycle and bought a 350cc Yamaha instead.

Everything seemed to be perfect, then tragedy struck.

■

Annie heard the news first. She and Swami were at home one evening when she received a phone call from her father. Her face turned white and she looked like she would faint. Swami saw her and rushed to her side.

"What happened, Annie?"

"Mohan Uncle… had an accident…"

Swami picked up the phone. It was his father-in-law.

"Swami… terrible news I'm afraid. Our Mohan-Achayan was in a road accident while returning from Mysore. He's dead. Rama is with Sheila-Kochamma now but we haven't been able to trace George. Do you know where he is?"

"I'm not sure. He may be with that girl, Sandhya. Let me try to find him." He hung up the phone. He was in shock but mind was racing.

"I have to go and look for George," he told Annie. "You go and be with Aunty."

It was past nine at night. He thought about all the places that George usually went with Sandhya. He tried Canopy Restaurant on M.G. Road, then Papillion Restaurant on Brigade Road, Copacabana above the office… finally he went to the Bangalore Club. He was not a member there, but he knew all the guards and attendants because he had been coming with George and then Annie for so many years. He explained the situation. They all knew Mohan Chandy. He was friendly to them as well as a generous tipper, so they were genuinely shocked and sad to hear the news. Swami saw George's red Yamaha motorcycle in the parking stand.

He walked to the lawn. He could see George sitting with Sandhya on a round table. They had beer mugs and kebabs on the table. George saw Swami approaching, and he knew right away that something was wrong. He stood up.

"Swami… you're here. What's wrong?"

Swami went up and hugged his friend. "It's your father, George. You have to come with me." He pulled his friend aside and told him the news quietly. George was too stunned to react.

He turned to Sandhya: "I have to take George home. Something bad has happened to his father. We can drop you home on the way."

They drove silently to Sandhya's house, which was close by. After that Swami told George what little he knew.

"I don't know much of the details. I'm so sorry, George."

"He must have been returning from his conference in Mysore. He took the little Fiat car. If it was the big Landmaster, nothing would have happened," said George.

They got to the Chandy residence. There were a lot of people there. Their soft voices were filled with confusion and disbelief. They saw George and ran to comfort him.

"Where's Mummy?" he asked.

"Upstairs… the doctor has given her some tranquilizers. She was very upset, as you can imagine," said her second cousin, Matthew.

George ran up the stairs. His mother was lying on the bed. Several female relatives were surrounding her. When she saw

George, she raised herself. "Georgie, Daddy has gone… he is no more, koche!"

He sat down on the bed and put his arms around her. "I know, Mummy. You must be strong. I am here."

He felt numb all over. He could hardly comprehend what had happened. He could see the relatives all around. He wanted them to leave so he could be alone with his mother. He didn't know what he could tell her, though. She had been a devoted wife. Her life had revolved almost entirely around his father. He had no idea how she would be able to adjust to a life without him. He couldn't even bear to think of it.

He saw DIG Abraham Varghese and went to him. "Ebby-Chachan, what happened?" he asked.

"Your father was driving back from Mysore. Near Srirangapatna a lorry hit his car… head on collision. He was thrown out — death was instantaneous. There was no one else in the car with him."

"It was the Fiat… allay… if it was the Landmaster he would be alive, Ebby-Chachan," said George crying. His uncle hugged him.

"Be strong, Georgie… for your mummy. She needs you now."

Annie came over and hugged him. "I have arranged for some simple food downstairs for everyone. Why don't you come and eat something."

A few hours later, George was alone in his room. The doctor had given his mother a sleeping pill. Her elder sister, Valsamma, was staying with her. He still could not fathom the news that his always-laughing, cheerful father would not be coming home. Even though he had been dead on arrival, his body had been taken to NIMHANS, the National Institute of Mental Health and Neuro Sciences. It was in the morgue there.

He thought of the gregarious, warm man who always loved company lying alone on a cold trolley in an ice-cold freezer in the morgue and he cried. He could not remember crying before. There was no need: he had never had a reason to be sad. But now the tears came, slowly first, then he was sobbing quietly. He sat hunched in a corner on the floor.

Then he got up, wiped his eyes and picked up his guitar. He did the only thing he knew how to do in times like this. He hadn't written a song in a long time — not since he had started working at *Bangalore Baloney*. But now he felt a need to unburden himself of emotions that were tearing him apart. For some reason he found himself playing an arpeggio of D and C. The words came easily and clearly as he began thinking of his father. He wrote them down. He didn't know if he would ever sing it again, but it was cathartic.

I see my life passing by
Today I feel the need to cry
I see you smiling through my tears
I hear your laughter in my ears
So I look up to the sky, and I wonder why
As I sing this elegy and say goodbye

I thank you for your gifts to me
I love you for everything you've been
I wish I could see you one more time
I know I'll always keep you in my mind
So I look up to the sky, and I wonder why
As I sing this elegy and say goodbye

I'm grateful for the years I had with you
I never knew that they would be so few
You taught me grace and right from wrong
You made me proud; you made me strong
So I look up to the sky, and I wonder why
As I sing this elegy and say goodbye

Swami was lying in bed with Annie and holding her tightly. He was crying too. He had liked Mohan Chandy enormously and always looked up to him as one of his role models.

"You know Annie, I feel that Venu and I jinxed George. We used to always say that George was the luckiest bugger on earth. He seemed to always have everything... looks... money, unbelievable talent. Now, the poor bugger is so sad. I am worried that he does not know how to handle sadness... he's not used to it at all."

"We'll be there for him and get him past this, okay Swami? Now, you go to sleep. I am concerned about you. I know this may be a bad time to tell you this, but I missed my period. I may be pregnant."

Swami sat up and turned on the light. Then he hugged Annie and kissed her belly.

"I love you Annie, I can't believe what a lucky chap I am. I feel bad for being happy at such a time, but I can't help it."

"Okay, go to sleep," said Annie kissing him. "I am pretty lucky too. Let's not tell anyone until I've gone to the doctor."

Three hundred kilometers away, Venu was at a village railway station boarding a train for Bangalore. Swami had called him a short while earlier and told him the news. He had also liked Mohan Chandy a lot and he wanted to be with George during this difficult time. There was no reserved seating left, so Venu bought a ticket in the general compartment.

When the train arrived, he managed to find a window seat and was soon squished there as more passengers filled the car. He would reach Bangalore only by noon the next day. He was very tired after looking at patients at the small village clinic all day, but he couldn't sleep. He kept thinking about everything: his life, his family, his friends, Mohan Chandy and George.

Like Swami, he also remembered that they always referred to George as the luckiest bugger on earth. But tonight his friend wasn't, he thought to himself. Venu wasn't religious, but for some reason he found himself saying a silent prayer,: "*Jesus, I am not one of your believers, but if you are there, please help George and his mother deal with this. Thank you.*"

■

The next few days were ones that no one would ever want to go through but sadly all must, because life by its very nature relegates death as its ultimate destination. George woke up disoriented. For a moment he thought that he had a very bad dream. Then hearing the uncharacteristic bustle of people in the house and the whispered voices in Malayalam, he knew with a sinking feeling that it was not a dream.

There were arrangements to make. George had discussed them with DIG Varghese the night before. The body would be brought to the house in the afternoon, after which it would be taken to St. Mark's Cathedral for the funeral service and then to Hosur Cemetery.

George's mother was in no state to do anything. He was grateful when Swami, Annie and DIG Varghese told him they would take care of all the arrangements. He maintained his composure and stayed near his mother. She was inconsolable. For twenty-eight years, Mohan had taken care of everything. This was too unimaginable for her to deal with.

She fainted when they brought the body to the house. George could barely hold himself together. Even though the accident had been horrific, his father's face had been spared. The mortician had done his best. Mohan looked like he was sleeping, but he had a slightly wincing look... like he was having a bad dream. Some of the relatives had gone to the mortuary to wash and dress the body as was required by their religion.

They brought Mohan for the last time to his drawing room. The women in the family, all wearing plain white cotton saris, had spent the morning getting the room ready. They had placed a long table against the far wall and draped it in a white bed sheet. On the middle of the table was a printed reproduction of Warner Sallman's "Head of Christ" painting that one could find in most Christian homes in India. On the other two ends of the table were headshots of Mohan, smiling and looking into the camera, as well as several lighted candles. The body was positioned so it was perpendicular to the table, with the head just below the picture of Jesus.

After they had finished arranging everything, George walked up to his father's body. He kissed Mohan's forehead. It was as cold as ice. The mortuary had frozen the body since the previous night so it would last until the burial.

His mother had been revived with some smelling salts. She came on unsteady feet to the room and hurled herself against the body, sobbing. Relatives had to gently hold her back. She sat there stroking her husband's hair and sobbing.

Although the Chandys had been members of St. Mark's Cathedral, most of Mohan's and Sheila's relatives belonged to the more orthodox Jacobite and Mar Thomma churches. The priest of St. Mark's, M.M. Koshy, was there, but so were several other orthodox priests. As was the custom, the furniture in the room had been removed, and all the relatives, parishioners and friends were sitting on the floor on large bamboo mats. The priests passed around English and Malayalam hymn books, and everyone started singing. They alternated between English and Malayalam hymns. In between each hymn one of the several priests would read from The Bible, recite a prayer or say a homily.

George was sitting on the floor next to Mohan's body with

his mother. All the incense, singing and praying was beginning to make him feel even worse than he already did. He got up and caught Swami's eye and walked outside. Swami joined him.

"I need to get away from this," he said. "Let's go to the roof for a fag." They went upstairs and lit up cigarettes. Just then, they saw Venu pull up in an auto rickshaw. They waved to him, and he joined them upstairs.

"Sorry for your loss, George. I came as soon as I could," he said hugging George.

George hugged him, "Thanks, Venu. It means a lot to me."

The Scrimshankers sat together on a little ledge on the roof smoking. George went downstairs and got three cups of coffee. He felt glad he had his two best friends with him. He didn't think he could have coped with the situation otherwise.

Soon it was time to transport the body to the church. George went in the car with his mother. Venu rode with Swami and Annie. The service was relatively short. Reverend M.M. Koshy delivered a fine sermon and praised Mohan Chandy for living a good life. Several relatives and friends came to the front of the church and delivered eulogies. Despite the sadness he was feeling, George was surprised and even amused by the many stories about his father that were narrated by his relatives and friends — some that he was hearing for the very first time.

"Once we were travelling together in Vynad district many years ago," recalled Joseph Mathan, one of Mohan's cousins. "We stopped at a small roadside vendor to have our food. The fellow served it on dirty aluminum plates. I was so hungry I started eating with my fingers right away. But Mohan reached into his coat pocket and pulled out a fork and knife that he always carried with him. Then, like a proper Englishman, he sat down on the roadside table and ate his food slowly with his fork and knife. Even those days he had so much style and class..."

After all the eulogies were over, everyone was asked if they would like to view the body. George's mother was too distraught to move from her seat in the front row. The church was packed, and there were even people standing outside. They streamed down the aisle in single file, walked around the coffin and went back to their seats. Friends and acquaintances touched the body lightly or made a sign of the cross. Close relatives kissed Mohan's forehead.

The coffin was closed after that, and the hearse left for the Hosur Cemetery, which was about five miles away.

George was in the car behind the hearse with his mother. All along the way, he was surprised to notice passers-by stop and make the sign of the cross as they went past. He realized that only a small percentage of those people could have been Christians. For some reason, George was very touched by this simple gesture.

Reverend Koshy met them at the gate of the cemetary. He prayed and concluded the service at the graveside. The coffin was lowered. George threw a handful of dirt on it and stepped back. He looked around at the other graves and made a note of the location so he could find it again if he visited the cemetery.

"Between Samuel Mathai and Sally Joseph, in front of M. T. Mathew, close to the water tap," he told himself.

After that everyone went back to the house for a traditional Malayalee Christian funeral dinner: boiled rice, parippu, aviyal, thoran, kachya moru, papadam and lime pickle.

George stayed awake for most of the night. He tried to sleep, but he was too wound up to relax. So he took his guitar and went to the Scrimshankers' clubroom. He rarely went there anymore, but it was away from the main house, so he could play his guitar there without disturbing anyone. He strummed his guitar and thought about everything that had happened recently. He knew that life was going to change drastically for both his mother and him without Mohan there to take care of them. He realized that earning a living was no longer optional, but a necessity. However, he wasn't sure of what he wanted to do anymore.

Bangalore Baloney was in good hands. Swami had Annie at his side now. Even though they always made him feel welcome, George knew they needed to be alone too. A plan slowly began to take shape in his head, but he put it aside. Tonight he only wanted to think about his father and remember everything they had done together. He went back to the house and got some photo albums from his room. He returned to the room and sat smoking and smiling sadly for a long time as he flipped through pictures of Mohan and him from the time he was a child in the U.S.

"I'll always love and miss you, Daddy," he said aloud.

Chapter 20

Hello And Goodbye

It had been a few months since Mohan Chandy had passed away in a tragic road accident. George still did his share of work and more at *Bangalore Baloney*. But he had changed as well. There was a sort of sadness in him now that those close to him had never seen before. Both Swami and Annie tried their best to cheer him up and share their lives with him. Annie had not only found out that she was pregnant, but a few weeks later she was also given the news that she was carrying twins. Swami was ecstatic.

"See, my little James is a fantastic worker. Just like that, in one shot, he got two kids. Annie, I am so happy."

His wife, however, had been anything but happy for many weeks. She had terrible morning sickness. It started after the sixth week and went on until the thirteenth week. It was so bad that she had to take anti-nausea pills and stay home the entire time. Swami felt really sorry for her but there was really nothing he could do.

"You and your little James don't have to suffer like this. It's easy for you; everything is like it was before. I have to stay home and throw up ten times a day," Annie said sadly. "But it's okay. I don't mean to complain… I am so happy."

By the fourth month, however, she was back to normal and in fact seemed to have even more energy than before she was pregnant. She worked the whole day at the newspaper and then went home and started cleaning the closets and dusting the furniture.

"Come, Annie, sit down with me. Just watching you running around like this is making me tired," Swami would say.

As the months went by Annie's belly began to grow considerably.

Soon, they experienced the babies' first kicks, then the heartbeats. Swami loved kissing her bulging belly and saying, "Hi, guys, daddy loves you."

One day George was with them at home when he saw Swami kiss Annie's belly and whisper, "Daddy says, 'I love you.'"

It triggered off something in his mind. He borrowed Swami's guitar and began strumming some chords and writing on a scrap piece of paper. He was completely absorbed in his task for over an hour.

"What are you doing?" asked Swami finally.

"Here's my gift for you and your babies," said George. He started singing…

"The horse goes neigh, neigh, neigh
It sleeps in the hay, hay, hay
The cow goes moo, moo, moo
And daddy says, I love you

The bell goes ring, ring, ring
The children all sing, sing, sing
The train goes choo, choo, choo
And daddy says, I love you

So many things to learn
So many things to see
It's all so easy
Like counting from one to three
1-2-3

The baby goes waa, waa, waa
The clown goes ha, ha, ha
The lady goes shoo, shoo, shoo
And daddy says, I love you"

Once he had become familiar with the song, George took a tape recorder that Swami used for interviews, along with his guitar, to the garage. He slipped in a new cassette and recorded himself playing guitar and singing the song. He then labeled it, *"Daddy Says I Love You — by Uncle George"* and gave the tape to his friend.

"Play it for them and tell your kids that their Uncle George wrote it just for them," he said.

"You sing it and tell them, bugger. In fact, we won't be happy with just the tape. You must sing it for them every day. It's not like you're going somewhere."

George just smiled but didn't say anything.

■

Since Mohan's passing, life had changed for George and his mother. The first thing they needed to do was to vacate the company bungalow and move into another residence. George rented a modest three-bedroom house in Indira Nagar.

Mohan Chandy had earned a high salary at his job and had saved a lot of money over the years. He had also invested in stocks and shares. It took George many days to look through all his father's assets. The company Mohan worked for had also been very helpful. They had invited George to the office and a human resource officer had gone over all the death benefits. Mohan had a provident fund that was quite healthy, as well as a life insurance policy for ten lakhs.

George was relieved. His mother had given up her job at Air India when she married his father. She had never worked since then. He was glad that there was enough money for her needs and to live comfortably for the rest of her life.

Since her husband's death, Sheila Chandy had changed drastically as well. She had started dressing in only a plain white cotton sari and white blouse without makeup or jewelry. She had always been a happy and carefree person, but she had been unable to reconcile to the situation of Mohan's sudden passing. She was not particularly religious before, but now she appeared to look for some consolation in religion. She spent most of her time going to various churches and praying or just sitting there on the pew like someone who was completely lost. Sometimes George had to go out and look for her and bring her back home.

One day, she had taken a bus on her own and gone four hundred miles away to the sea town of Velankanni for the feast of the Nativity of Mary. The town is known as the Lourdes of the East and is one of the most frequented religious sites in India. It usually attracts more than a million pilgrims during the festival months. George had been frantic looking for his mother in Bangalore. He called DIG Varghese, but there was nothing he could do. Finally, late that evening, a neighbor came to the house and gave him a note his mother had left with her.

"I am going to Velankanni. Ackamma will be meeting me there. I will be back in three days... Love, Mummy," it said.

Ackamma was her cousin who lived in Madras. She had lost her son in a drowning accident two years ago. She had never been the same ever since, and like George's mother spent her time looking for answers in churches all over the region.

"I don't know why she couldn't call me at the office and tell me," George told DIG Varghese.

"Be patient with her. She is still very sad and distraught. Poor Sheila-Kochamma. It is too much for her to handle," said his uncle.

His mother returned home safely in a couple of days, but after that George made sure that he kept track of her activities. She had also become absent-minded and forgetful as well. As the days went on, she sank further into a world of her own. George got even more worried. He became afraid of leaving her alone for too long and made it a point to come back home early every evening. His father's death and his mother's erratic behavior were having their toll on him as well. He became gaunt and lost the cheerful optimism that he always displayed before.

In addition to visiting various churches all day, Sheila Chandy had also stated attending the rallies of a local evangelist named Brother Albert Rajshekar. She had heard about him from some of the other Christian women in the neighborhood. Soon, she was attending a meeting almost every week and sending in contributions for his ministry.

Brother Rajshekar had been born a Hindu, but when he was in his early twenties, he claimed that the Holy Spirit had appeared to him and commanded him to spread the word of Jesus Christ. So he had converted to Christianity, changed his name from Anand to Albert and begun preaching a message of forgiveness and redemption that he professed was possible only through the acceptance of Jesus Christ. Albert soon realized that the nascent evangelist movement in India was also a lucrative endeavor. Before he became Brother Rajshekar, he had barely earned a living working as a ticket collector for the Indian Railways, but as his followers grew, he found a steady stream of donations coming in as well. He made it a point to read the Bible over and over until he was an expert in its various books and teachings. However, because he had no formal training in the Christian scriptures, he often misunderstood much of its content. But that did not stop him from preaching what he thought it meant. He found that most people needed something bigger than themselves to cling on to and believe in. Life was hard, and everyone needed hope. He could provide it for them. He held his meetings in open-air venues all over the city, and it usually drew thousands of believers.

"He's a crook," George told DIG Varghese. "Can't you do something about him? Mummy is sending him hundreds of rupees every month. I checked the bank book."

"I will speak to her," said DIG Varghese.

However, it didn't do much good because Sheila continued attending the gatherings and donating to Brother Rajshekar's ministry. George finally decided to accompany her for one of his events just to see what it was all about.

The rally he went to was held at the Shivaji Nagar grounds. A big tent was set up and long fluorescent lights had been tied to the many bamboo poles that supported the structure. The crowds squatted on the grass and on the low granite walls of the grounds. A temporary stage about thirty feet wide had been erected. There were a handful of microphones and a large public address system on it. A choir was on one side of the stage. They began by singing, *What A Friend We Have In Jesus*. George and his mother sat cross-legged on the grass in the middle of the field.

"Mummy, why do you feel the need to come here?" he asked her.

"I feel at peace when I come and listen to him, koche. Since Daddy passed away, I have been looking for answers."

"Sometimes there are no answers, Mummy. Random bad events happen to people every day all over the world. People like this Rajshekar character are taking advantage of unfortunate people who are going through some crisis or the other."

"George, I thought you wanted to come with me to keep me company, not to criticize Brother Rajshekar. You sound like your uncle Ebby. Have you been talking to him? I am not a child. You sit and keep quiet. You will also feel God's grace if you listen to his sermon."

The choir was now singing *When I Survey The Wondrous Cross*. George would normally have sung along because he liked the hymn, but he was too annoyed to do so that night. When the song was over, Brother Rajshekar appeared on the stage. He was a tall, handsome, dark-skinned man in his mid-fifties with thick black hair and a short black mustache. He was dressed in a cream-colored leisure suit and a pink shirt with big collars.

He started his sermon by quoting from the scriptures and explaining what it meant. "The Lord Jesus Christ says in the Gospel of Luke, *'If anyone would come after Me, he must deny himself and take up his cross daily and follow Me.'* What does that mean? It means that a person who follows Jesus must not worry about money and property. They must give up what they don't need and live a simple life in Christ."

Brother Rajshekar spoke in Tamil-accented English for the next hour to the thousands of people who had gathered there. His message was a general Christian message of hope, love, and most importantly, giving. George had to admit that he was a very gifted and passionate speaker. Throughout his entire sermon, he had uplifting music playing softly in the background, and he effectively maintained the cadence of his words in time with the music. It was a very effective technique and the crowd was mesmerized. They watched him in rapt attention.

George looked at his mother. She was also listening to the preacher intently with a sad smile on her face. His heart went out to her. Maybe he had not been there for her when she needed his strength. Her whole life had been torn apart. She had loved his father passionately and had deferred to him on everything. For the past months, she had been cast adrift into a life she was unfamiliar with on her own. She had just been coping with it the best way she could. He reached out and held her hand. She squeezed his hand gently and smiled at him.

"This week we will be sending you our beautiful cross pins for your offerings of one hundred rupees or more to the Divine Service ministry. For those who give over 1,000 rupees, we will send you these one-of-a-kind Bibles which has a cross on the cover inlaid in real pearls with a handwritten personal message from me inside," continued Brother Rajshekar.

He paused for a few moments and said, "Today, I would also like to mention one individual who has had a lot of suffering in her life recently. She wrote to me a few months ago and I have been praying for her since then. I think she is here tonight. Mrs. Sheila Chandy, please come up to the stage if you are here."

George was surprised to hear his mother's name mentioned and shocked when she got up shyly. "George, please come with me," she told him. "I don't want to go up there on my own."

Even though he didn't want to go, George went up to the stage with his mother. Up close, Brother Rajshekar radiated even more charm than he had from a distance.

"Come, Mrs. Chandy, please… who is this next to you… such a handsome boy… must be your son, who sings beautifully and plays the guitar. What is your name?"

George told him… and the preacher shook his hand warmly. "Your mummy has written several letters about what happened — it is all in God's plan. A great man once said that we are merely actors in God's play," he said. Although Brother Rajshekar used the expression frequently, he wasn't sure who had said it.

"That was Shakespeare, from *As You Like It… All the world's a stage. And all the men and women merely players. They have their exits and their entrances. And one man in his time plays many parts*," said George, elaborating sarcastically. He had studied the play in his eleventh standard English class. He wanted to show that he was not like all the other followers at the rally.

"Ah, yes," said Brother Rajshekar, "A very godly man, that Shakespeare."

He appeared not to notice George's sarcasm… or had chosen to ignore it. He went to the microphone and started speaking to the crowd again.

"Brothers and sisters in Christ, please join me in praying for Mrs. Sheila Chandy and her son George, who are here with me. Some months ago, they lost their husband and father in a terrible road accident. Mrs. Chandy has been writing to me for several weeks now. She says that coming to our rallies and receiving our newsletter every week is giving her hope and strength."

He paused and lifted his face up and said, "Lord Jesus, please grant your mercy to these your children Sheila and George, and give them your bountiful blessings so they may look above all their adversities and see the true meaning for their existence, which is to serve you."

Brother Rajshekar beckoned Sheila and George towards him

and placed a hand on each of their heads and said "The Lord make his face to shine upon thee... grant his gracious presence, the manifestations of himself, communion with him, clearer discoveries of his love, of interest in him, and an increase of spiritual light and knowledge of his Gospel and the truths of it, and of his mind and will." He had memorized this paragraph and recited it quickly and forcefully. He was not sure if he even understood what it meant fully but he had been told by several people that anyone who heard it were suitably impressed.

George was thinking to himself that maybe Brother Rajshekar was harmless after all. He seemed genuinely caring. The couple of hundred rupees that his mother sent now and then was not a lot of money. Then Brother Rajshekar started speaking again.

"I wrote to Mrs. Chandy last week and asked her if she could contribute to the construction of our new church in Whitefield. Her husband was an important and wealthy man. Yesterday, this dear woman called my wife Elena and promised to give 10,000 rupees to our ministry! Do you have the check, Mrs. Chandy?"

George stood dumbly by her side as his mother dipped into her purse, took out the check and gave it to Brother Rajshekar.

"Thank you, Mrs. Chandy. God will bless you in abundance. Once again, let us pray for Mrs. Chandy and her family as the choir sings *How Great Thou Art*. Our ushers will be coming around with the collections baskets. Please give generously whatever you can afford — no amount is too small or large. God will bless you for helping to spread his word."

George was seething silently as they walked back. He knew he had to do something to end Brother Rajshekar's influence on his mother. He had already decided that he was going to do something different with his life. Maybe he could change the circumstances in his mother's life as well.

■

Annie gave birth to twins, a boy and girl, in October. There had been some complications in the last week. One of the babies had stopped growing in-utero and the doctors had decided to do a C-section. Annie had been calm, but Swami was a nervous wreck after they set the date and time.

"Swami, why don't you go to the office? You are making me

nervous, walking up and down the house," said Annie.

"Never, how can I relax? This is big, Annie. We are having two babies. I am nervous about you, and I am thinking about our life once they are here. Will you promise to show me attention — not a lot of course, but at least once in a while?"

"Of course, you buddhu. How can I not show you attention? I love you. Just watch… once you get your babies from me, you will ignore me."

"Never, Annie… I promise. You will always be my number one." He hugged and kissed her on the forehead.

They went to St. Philomena's Hospital at eight the next morning. After filling out the required paperwork, Annie was whisked away. Swami had to wait in the lounge until he was called. He phoned George and gave him the update.

"I don't want you to wait alone. I'll be over in thirty minutes," said his friend.

Swami was outside smoking when George arrived. He had left instructions with the nurse to look for him if his presence was required. As a matter of policy, family members were not allowed inside the operating theater. George went to the canteen and got two coffees. The friends sat outside in a bench outside and talked for a while. Then they went inside. After another half-an-hour, a nurse came and asked Swami to go inside. A doctor met him there.

"I am happy to tell you, Mr. Venkatasubramanian, that everything went off fine. Your wife and children are all doing well. Your wife is in the Recovery Wing. Your children are in the Infants' Unit. Would you like to see them?"

"Yes, of course! Thank you, Doctor."

His first moments with his children were ones that Swami would never forget. They were in little transparent plastic trays at the Infants' Unit.

A few months after their wedding, Swami had decided to change his name from V. Swaminathan to Swaminathan Venkatasubramanian. It was the Brahmin custom to have the initial of the father's first name in front of the offspring's given name. This practice made it quite confusing for subsequent generations to maintain a family name.

"Let's start a new family with the last name Venkatasubramanian," said Swami to Annie. So you will be Annie Venkatasubramanian."

They had also picked names for the twins in the last month of Annie's pregnancy, once they had discovered the sex of the babies in the ultrasound. The girl would be named Anindita, meaning beautiful, and the boy Nikhil, meaning complete.

Swami walked up to his children in their little trays at the Infants' Unit. Each tray had "Venkatasubramanian" on a card pasted on the bottom. The babies were wrapped in white cloth and looked so small and vulnerable. They were asleep. Both had wrinkled faces but they were beautiful to him. Swami felt a lump in his throat.

"Do you wish to hold them?" asked the nurse.

"No, I don't want to wake them," he said.

"It's okay. At this age they sleep a lot," said the nurse.

She picked up one of them and handed the little bundle to Swami.

"Say hello to your daughter," she said.

"Hi, Anindita, nice to finally meet you. I promise to love you and take care of you always," he said. He kissed her gently on her cheek. She stirred and moved her head towards him. She had a milky new-baby smell that he found very pleasing.

"See, she knows I'm her daddy," he said. He then handed her over gently to the nurse. Then he picked up his son.

"Nikhil Venkatasubramanian, extremely glad to meet you. I love you, my little boy," he said and kissed him on his forehead. He realized he had tears in his eyes.

"I'm sorry, I tend to get a bit emotional," he told the nurse. "Has Annie, my wife, seen the children?"

"No, she was sedated. She will be waking up soon."

Swami went into the private room that Annie was in. She looked beautiful, lying there. She had a glow on her face. He bent down and kissed her lips. She stirred and woke up.

"Swami, the babies... is everything okay?"

"Yes, everything is okay. I saw them... they are beautiful. They both look like you, thank God."

"I want to see them at once."

Swami called the nurse who came and took Annie to the Infants' Unit in a wheelchair.

"Can I also bring their uncle to see them?" he asked.

When the nurse agreed, he went to the lounge and took George with him inside. Annie had both babies in her arms and was talking softly to them.

"G, they are so beautiful," she said.

George took little Nikhil in his arms. "I am going to teach you how to play the guitar as soon as your little fingers are big enough," he said.

"What about her? She also wants to learn," said Annie.

"Yes, she will also have all the advantages that boys have," said Swami. "I have never been happier, Annie. Thank you for carrying them for nine months and going through all you have. I will love you all forever."

The nurse came in and said, "The grandparents and other family members are also outside. We can only allow four people at one time."

"I'll go outside with George and send the grandparents in," said Swami.

■

Three weeks later, family and friends celebrated the birth of Swami and Annie's babies at a big get-together at DIG Varghese's house. They had erected a small shamiana in the backyard to accommodate all the people who were attending.

George found Swami inside the house, playing with his babies.

"Swami, come outside for a few minutes. I'd like to talk to you."

"What's up George?"

He asked his mother-in-law to look after the twins and went out with George.

"I wanted to tell you first, Swami. I'm going back to the U.S. next month."

"Wow, this is a surprise George… why?"

"Lots of things. It's not been the same since Dad passed away. I've been feeling the need to change my life. *Bangalore Baloney* is doing well. You have Annie; you don't need me. I don't have anyone special here. I want to try to do something with my music in the States. In a few years I will be too old."

"I understand, George. You have the talent to become a great musician there. You are wasted here but I will miss you terribly. We take people close to us for granted. For so many years I always knew you were always there. I was looking forward to you being here for my kids as well."

He hugged George. "I love you, bugger. You're the brother I never had. Remember, no matter where you are, that you have a home here with Annie, the kids and me."

"Thanks, Swami, that means a lot to me," said George. "I have also convinced my mother to come with me. As you know, her elder sister, Molly Aunty, lives in New York, and when we called her last month, she was so excited. She wants us to stay with her for as long as we choose to do so. Both her kids have left home, and it's only her and my Uncle Sam in the house now."

"When are you planning to leave?"

"In a few weeks, most likely."

"So soon, bugger, we won't even have a chance to say goodbye properly. I forgot to tell you, Venu called yesterday. He's coming next week. We can have a nice evening on our own... just the three of us. Bugger, I was so happy today, but now you've gone and made me sad thinking that you won't be here in Bangalore anymore," said Swami.

Venu arrived the next week. He had some big news to share as well. The friends met at Koshy's for dinner.

"Guys, I have something important to tell you both. I am getting married in three months. It's an arranged marriage. Her name is Shantha, and she's from the same caste as me. Her family is originally from Madras but they have now settled down in Canada. She's graduating with a degree in pharmacology there. I will be going to Canada after our marriage," said Venu.

"That's great news, bugger," said George. "Unfortunately, I don't think I will be able to attend your wedding. I have already bought tickets to leave for the U.S. in three weeks. I wish I could be there, Venu. Where is the wedding?"

"I don't think any of you can attend. The bulk of their family lives in Madras, so we are having the wedding there. Of course, we will also have a reception here. I will finish my voluntary service in two months, so we are planning the wedding after that."

"I will try to come to Madras, but with the paper and the twins... I don't know," said Swami.

"Don't worry, chaps. Such is life. We are not kids anymore. We have to think about our families now," said Venu.

He had lived an extremely hardworking and lonely existence for the past few years, first at medical college and then at the little village running the medical clinic, working from morning to night six days a week. He had learnt a lot about being a doctor and taking care of a variety of people and illnesses. However, he was glad his tenure would soon be over. When his mother had sent him the details of the proposal, as well as the girl's photo, he had accepted.

Shantha's family lived in Brampton, a suburb of Toronto. Like him, she was a bit dark but quite pretty, he thought. Even though the family had been there for five to six years, she appeared to be rather traditional in her dressing and outlook. He liked this in her. He had planned to go abroad and study further after his voluntary service. Marrying Shantha would solve two issues: finding someone to spend his life with and going abroad. Having residency status would also make it much easier and cheaper to study in Canada.

Venu felt he was making the right decision. He knew he wasn't like Swami or George. The two of them would not even have considered an arranged marriage. But he was more traditional in his views on women and marriage. He felt it was important to let the families work out the details and find out if they were compatible for each other. He liked Annie a lot, but he'd been very surprised when his friend had married her. The families were so different — even their religion was different. However, it appeared that everyone got on well with each other. Venkat and DIG Varghese seemed to like each other, and Swami appeared to be very comfortable in the world of his in-laws.

"Buggers, this time the Scrimshankers are really going in three different directions," he told his friends. "Let's drink to us, to our success and happy lives to all of us!"

"To the Scrimshankers," said Swami. "Good friends for life!"

"The best friends for life," said George.

Three weeks later, George flew to New York with his mother. A few days before he left, he came to Swami and Annie's house one evening. He had a folder in his hand that he gave to Annie.

"I have a little gift for you," he said. "I met with the lawyer this morning and transferred my share of Friendship Limited and *Bangalore Baloney* to Annie. I don't want you both to have any restrictions with whatever you choose do with the paper."

"But George, it is worth a lot of money, now" said Swami.

"I know. Don't worry about it. If I am ever homeless, I will come to your house, in the meantime, it is all yours. I love you both. You are lucky: you've found your passion, and you've found each other. Live your dream, and be happy," said George.

Swami and Annie hugged him.

Venu got married two months later. Swami went alone to Madras for the wedding. They also had a big reception at Hotel Ashok in Bangalore that everyone attended. It was a gala affair that was paid for by the bride's family. It took Venu six months more to get his application for immigration to Canada. He worked at CSI Hospital in Bangalore while he was waiting. He rented a house in Ulsoor, close to his parent's home.

Soon it was time for Venu to leave for Toronto. Swami came to the airport to say goodbye. He stood alone at the observation deck on the first floor and watched sadly as the plane took off.

"Goodbye, Venu. I am the last and only Schrimshanker here now," he said to himself. *"Wonder what you're up to, George?"*

Chapter 21

New York

George looked out of the window of the Boeing 747 plane as it approached New York City. It circled around the island of Manhattan as it settled into its descent for landing at JFK Airport. The view was magnificent. Those that had never seen Manhattan before stared in wonder at a skyline that was unlike any other in the world. It featured some of the tallest buildings on earth: the Empire State Building, the World Trade Center, the Chrysler Building and so many more. Even those that had seen it before, like George, couldn't help but stare in amazement at the results of some of man's most notable architectural achievements of the twentieth century.

"Welcome back," said the immigration officer, looking at George's U.S. passport. He spent a little more time examining Sheila Chandy's green card and passport. Then, they were outside.

Sheila's sister, Molly, and her husband, Sam Matthew, were waiting for them. They cried and hugged her. It was the first time they were seeing her since Mohan's death.

George sat quietly in the front passenger seat of Uncle Sam's car on their ride home from the airport. It was a new white Ford Taurus that was very roomy and comfortable. His uncle and aunt spoke to his mother in Malayalam. He understood it well enough but could only speak it sparingly. So, he looked out of the window as they took Interstate 678 to the Whitestone Bridge and then the Hutchinson River Parkway to Westchester.

His uncle and aunt lived in a large, four-bedroom house in the Village of Elmsford. It was within the Town of Greenburgh in Westchester County and next to White Plains, the biggest and most important city in the county. They had moved there from Bloomfield, New Jersey, a few years ago. Molly worked as a registered nurse at Westchester Medical Center. Sam was a maintenance supervisor at the County Airport.

The story of Malayalee nurses that emigrated to the U.S. from India is a heroic one. In the late 1960s, the U.S. was facing a severe shortage of nurses. So, they began looking for English-speaking nurses from other countries to fill the vacancies.

This happened to coincide with the establishment of several nursing schools in Kerala at the time. They had been started by Christian Missionary organizations that wanted to provide young women in the state with employable skills that would benefit society as a whole, as well as give them a chance to work in the quickly developing oil-rich Arab states. Many of these Malayalee Christian nurses who could speak English were recruited to come to the United States instead.

The first wave of nurses from India arrived in the late 1960s and 1970s. They were some of the early pioneers of Indian immigration to the U.S. They came alone and without any safety net in place. Most of them had never travelled in an airplane before. They had no friends and relatives in America. They did not get paid the same as their American counterparts and had to face racism, bigotry and ridicule. Many could not afford to bring their husbands and children with them.

But still they persisted. They worked hard, saved their money and managed to finally reunite with their families in the U.S. As soon as they became citizens, they petitioned for the immigration of their brothers, sisters, fathers and mothers. They liked their new life in the U.S. and had no intention of going back to India.

These nurses were the primary breadwinners in their families. They usually worked an extra shift or at another hospital on their days off. They sent money home to take care of parents and siblings. Their husbands were often incapable of earning as much as they did because most did not have professional degrees. They got token jobs in stores, worked around their wife's schedule and took care of the children. Those who were more ambitious took civil service exams and found government jobs. Still, it was the nurses that moved the family forward in the U.S. and paid for the above-average lifestyle their families enjoyed. In less than ten years, many were able to purchase homes in the suburbs. But it was a hard life for these women. They usually worked a twelve-hour night shift, often six days a week. The extra hours paid time-and-a-half overtime rates. This additional income put many of them in six-figure salary bracket, or at least close to it.

Molly Matthew was one such Malayalee nurse. She had arrived in the U.S. in 1966. However, what made her situation a little different from the other nurses was that her younger sister, Sheila, and her brother-in-law, Mohan, were already in New York at the time. Until Molly's husband, Sam, joined her two years later, the Chandys were her only family in the country.

Mohan had completed his post-graduate studies in engineering at Rensselaer Polytechnic Institute in Troy, New York. After graduating, he got a managerial-level job at the Long Island Power Authority and the Chandys moved to Hicksville where Mohan's office was located. George was born at North Shore University Hospital in Hicksville.

On long weekends, the Chandys' would drive from their home in Long Island, New York to Newark, New Jersey in Mohan's beat up old Pontiac. They would pick Molly up from the little apartment she shared with two other Malayalee nurses and drive back to Long Island. A couple of days later they would make the two-hour drive again to drop Molly off in Newark.

Molly was able to bring Sam to the U.S. two years after she arrived. They became members of the Mar Thomma congregation in Dover and were very active in the Church.

Even though Sam did not have the relevant education required to land a desk job, he was very outgoing and soon managed to find work as a maintenance worker at the Westchester County Airport. It was a long drive there from New Jersey but he liked his job. He moved up the ladder slowly until he became a supervisor ten years later. The couple lived in Newark for a while. After the children were born, they bought a house in Bloomfield, where they stayed for several years.

Then Molly got a better-paying job at Westchester Medical Center, and the Matthews sold their house in New Jersey, and moved to Elmsford. It was much closer to Sam's workplace. By then, their children had already left home.

Molly and Sam held a special place in their hearts for Mohan and Sheila. The families had been very close until the Chandys returned to India. They had been very sad to hear of Mohan's death but because they couldn't get time off from their jobs at such short notice, they hadn't been able to travel to Bangalore for the funeral.

"Sheila, you and George must stay with us for as long as you want. Sam and I are alone now. The children are both far away. Sophie lives in Maryland with her husband Roger, who is in the Army, and Solomon is studying for an MBA in Chicago," Molly said.

Their house was certainly very large. It even had a swimming pool in the backyard. George was given the room that his cousin Solomon sometimes stayed in when he visited. His aunt put his mother in the large guest room.

"George, treat this as your own house," said Uncle Sam. "Your father was very kind to us when we first came here. He took me to the Social Security office, taught me to drive, went with me for the road test and helped carry our first mattress. He even gave your Molly Aunty money for the advance for her first apartment."

He wiped the tears from his eyes as he reminisced about Mohan Chandy and their early days in the U.S.

"Now that we are well settled, please allow us to be there for you," he said.

George was relieved that his mother had a place to stay temporarily while he made something of himself in the U.S. He did not plan to be with his uncle and aunt for more than a few weeks. He would find a job and move out. Then, once he was established, he would bring his mother to live with him.

■

George started looking for work right away. He applied to jobs at advertising agencies in New York City as a graphic artist. However, after a few weeks of sending out resumes in reply to job postings in *The New York Times* he realized that without a Bachelor's degree in Art, he would not be considered if he applied through the mail. The letters of rejection started coming in everyday. He was disappointed but still optimistic. *Maybe if they saw his portfolio they would consider him.*

He decided to go to Manhattan and search in person. It was a very exciting place but also very daunting and unfriendly when one didn't know anyone there. He usually spent the morning applying to jobs from home. After lunch, he would catch the Route-13 bus from Elmsford to White Plains train station and then take the Harlem Line of the Metro North Railroad to Grand Central Station in New York City. The journey took about an hour.

He photocopied a list of all the advertising agencies in the City at the Greenburgh Town Library. With his portfolio in hand, he went around from building to building, up and down Madison Avenue and its environs. He didn't have much luck with this unsolicited approach. The buildings that had doormen in them wouldn't even let him in without an appointment. If he managed to get past the doorman and make it to the correct floor, he had no way of meeting an art director or someone else of importance. The receptionist at the office there would usually turn him away at the door. Sometimes one of them would take pity on him and ask him to leave his portfolio behind but he did not feel comfortable doing that. He only had one set of comps and layouts that he had brought with him from India showcasing his work at Dimensions and *Bangalore Baloney*.

After spending a few hours wandering the streets in his quest for a job, George would take respite at the New York Public Library on 42nd Street. He liked sitting outside on the steps near the statues of the Patience and Fortitude lions, smoking and watching the people there. Attractive and fashionable women in business clothes, apparently oblivious of everyone else around them, hurrying past... Homeless men and women sleeping on park benches with pitiful plastic bundles at their feet... Executives striding quickly and purposefully with cold determination on their faces... Tourists of all ages walking around looking up at the big buildings in wonder and taking photographs... Cops with benign but tough expressions keeping a watchful eye on everyone... Greek and Arab roadside vendors selling gyros, shish kebabs, hotdogs and hamburgers from their carts... Old men playing chess on little granite checkered tables on the sidewalk... Street hustlers slyly engaging tourists in games of three-card monte and pocketing their money with apologetic smiles... Drug addicts, pushers, hookers all making brief appearances and disappearing before the cops noticed their presence...

As the sun went down, he occasionally walked west to the blocks near Port Authority Bus Terminal at the corner of 42nd Street and 8th Avenue, where the seedier side of life was on full display. Movie theaters that played pornographic films with vulgar-sounding names which were similar to that of popular Hollywood movies... Live peep show halls with several circular stages, where fifty cents would buy two minutes watching nude girls walking around, two dollars a quick feel of breast, buttocks or genitals, and a fast hand-job for ten... Adult video booths where three minutes cost twenty-five cents and where cleaning staff roamed around mopping semen off the floors with disinfectant every few minutes... Live sex theaters that featured threesomes, foursomes, midgets and other strange acts that seemed more pathetic than titillating... Specialty houses, where transexuals in curtained glass cages allowed people to see them naked for five dollars, touch them for ten and performed BJs for twenty... Emaciated, tired-looking prostitutes with bad teeth, beckoning passersby from entrances of decrepit tenement buildings... Little stores selling pornographic magazines, videos and sex aids staffed by Indian and Bangladeshi immigrants reading incongruous Gujarati, Hindi and Urdu books with bored expressions on their faces as they rang up the hard-core porn purchases of furtive customers...

As an artist and songwriter, George reveled in the experience of watching all these disparate specimens of humanity that were on display so readily in a city that was unlike any other he had known before. Sometimes he tried to imagine what the lives of some of these people he saw were.

He went home and wrote long letters to Swami narrating his observations and experiences but he then put them away in a folder and sent shorter, edited versions instead – or nothing at all. He realized that his friend was probably too busy with his twins and managing the newspaper to have time to read or reply to long, drawn-out letters. He called him a few times but spoke briefly because he didn't want to run up the long distance charges on his hosts' telephone bill.

■

Often George felt defeated and disillusioned after wandering around all day trying unsuccessfully to get a job. Coming from a life where he knew a lot of people everywhere he went, it was very lonely being in a place that was so crowded but yet where everyone was a stranger to him. One day, while he was sitting in Bryant Park late in the evening on his own, he wrote a song that expressed how he felt. He called it "My *Crazy World*."

> Took a plane from Bombay
> Made it here to the USA
> But I know I'm still on my way
> No doubt about it
> And the life I came here to find
> Is still only in my mind
> But I'll be okay, I'll be fine
> No doubt about it
>
> It's just my crazy world going round
> One day I'm happy, next day, down
> Life is like a roller coaster
> Now I'm going down
> My crazy world will come around
>
> So now I'm here in New York City
> And those Broadway lights don't seem so pretty
> When you're alone and feeling blue
> No one to talk to
> But I'll make it here someday
> I'll sing and my guitar I'll play
> I ain't Bob Dylan, but I got things to say
> Oh yeah... yeah... yeah
>
> It's just my crazy world going round
> One day I'm happy next day down
> Life is like a roller coaster
> Now I'm going down
> My crazy world will come around
> Crazy world... crazy world

However, there were other times when he felt excited and empowered just to be in Manhattan. Anything seemed possible there. The hustle and bustle of thousands of people moving around purposefully gave him strength. Even the people enjoying themselves in the parks and cafés seemed different than the residents of other cities. They looked as if they were resting so they could go out the next day and work twice as hard. In spite of his loneliness and frustration, he also felt a sense of hope. One day, he sat at a diner on 42nd Street and wrote another song he called *"New York City"* over a cup of coffee and a few Marlboros:

Standing at a corner
On 8th Avenue
Watching the world go by
Feel a little blue
There's no one here with me
But I am not alone
So many people here
In this place I call my home
You can call me on the phone

New York City is my kind of town
New York City is my kind of town
You could be pretty or wearing a frown
New York City is my kind of town
Won't you come on down

See the colorful people
In the Village down
You can be who you want to be
Without feeling like a clown
It makes no difference who you are
You got to pay your dues
But it's so liberating
To live the life you choose
A life that you can use

New York City is my kind of town
New York City is my kind of town
You could be pretty or wearing a frown
New York City is my kind of town
Won't you come on down

Finally, after a few months of trying to find a job in an advertising agency, George tried another possible approach. One day while he was photocopying his resume at a PIP Printing store, he realized that all printing companies also had graphic designers on staff. He copied down a list of all the printers in a fifty-mile radius from the yellow pages in the library. Rather than visit them all, he tried calling them first. A few showed interest. He checked them off on his list and visited them one by one with his portfolio. After a few days of futile wandering in the many boroughs of New York City, he was finally lucky.

He walked into BQE Printers on Atlantic Avenue in Brooklyn after covering the Manhattan downtown area all morning. One of the partners there was Vinnie Calvano. He looked through George's portfolio and was very impressed by it. He hired him on the spot for $350 a week. He wanted George to come in from the very next day itself.

"Of course, we are a printing company, so when you don't have layout and design work, you will have to help out in other things: photography, typesetting and even bindery operation," said Vinnie.

BQE Printers was named after the Brooklyn Queens Expressway that ran on an elevated section a short distance away from the shop. It was a reasonably sized operation that offered customers sheet-fed and web printing services. It occupied a large single-story, warehouse-style building. Paul and Cindy, the other designers, were quite friendly, and in a couple of weeks George was pulling his own weight in the art department.

Vinnie realized that his new designer had a much more sophisticated sense of design than the others. He was pleased because he wanted to offer his customers design services that were compatible with that done in advertising agencies, which had a much higher profit margin.

George traveled back and forth from Westchester to Brooklyn for the first few weeks. It took a lot of time and cost almost fifteen dollars a day for his commute. He spoke to his mother and aunt about possibly moving to Brooklyn.

"It's taking me over an hour to get to my job. Is it okay if I found a small apartment in Brooklyn?" he asked. "Mummy, if you want, you can come and stay with me."

"You can go and live there if you want, but Sheila is staying with us," said his aunt quickly. She had got used to having her sister with her. They went shopping everyday, chatted, cooked together and went for walks every evening.

"What will she do alone in your apartment while you work and come back home at all hours? No, she will stay here. You first get married to a nice girl, then she will come and live with you," Molly told him.

■

George found a furnished basement apartment for four hundred dollars per month in Bay Ridge. It was a forty-minute bus ride from his job. He would have liked to live in Brooklyn Heights, under the shadow of the Brooklyn Bridge, but the rents there were more than he wanted to pay.

Uncle Sam helped him move. Since the apartment was furnished, he only had to buy a few items. It was a partial-basement apartment and had a narrow strip of windows that were at street level. The rest was below ground level. It had a living room, bedroom, kitchen and bath. The boiler for the house was right next to the kitchen.

George had arrived in the United States in the beginning of February and it was now the first week in May. Spring was slowly giving way to warmer weather. It had been raining on and off for the past few weeks. He gradually began settling into this new phase of his life. He took the B63 bus everyday from Bay Ridge to Brooklyn Heights coming all the way down on 5th Avenue to the corner of Atlantic Avenue. George made friends easily and soon got to know several of his co-workers. He started hanging out in the evenings near his job with Paul, one of the other designers, who was of Polish descent, or with Ricardo, the AB Dick press operator, who was from Jamaica.

Paul played drums and had a couple of friends in the neighborhood that played guitar and bass. One day George rented a rehearsal space at King Studios in Bay Ridge and they jammed together for five hours. Paul and his friends were impressed with George's songs and vocal abilities.

"Your songs are very good," said Jeff, the lead guitarist. "You should look into getting a recording contract."

George thanked him but he had no idea how to go about taking his music to the next level. The truth was that he barely had time to do much more than just go to work and come back home. He usually spent weekends with his mother at his aunt's house. He was getting tired of using public transportation. He decided to buy a used car.

George's mother had given him 20,000 dollars from his father's assets a few months earlier. He opened a bank account with it, but other than spending 1,000 dollars as a deposit on his apartment he had not touched it so far. He felt it would be a good investment to purchase a reliable automobile. He knew how to drive but decided to go through a driving school for his license. In addition, they provided the car for the test and his instructor also appeared to know the officers that conducted it.

Once he got his license, he visited a Polish used car dealer on Ditmars Boulevard under the F train line where he found a dark green Ford Escort that appeared in good condition for $2,500. He took Paul with him the next day and had him speak in Polish to the dealer. It resulted in his lowering the price to $2,150 and throwing in a detachable Benzie Box for free. The car gave him freedom. He loved the sound system in it. He could now come and go as he pleased. It took him only twenty minutes to get to work. That was the time it took him just to wait for the bus before.

The third month after he started working at BQE, he slept with Liz, the receptionist. She was Italian and had been attracted to George from the moment she saw him. One day after work she had asked him to drive her to Prospect Heights. She flirted with him the whole way there. They parked near the Brooklyn Botanical Garden and walked around a bit. Soon they were kissing. George drove to the Sleep Inn in nearby Sunset Park and they spent a few hours there making passionate love. Afterwards, they had pizza for dinner and he dropped her off outside her apartment building in Bensonhurst, where she shared a studio with a roommate.

His relationship with Liz was not one that was bound for something much more than a series of hot and heavy, one-night trysts. She had a regular boyfriend who was a salesman and away most of the time. She was pretty and slim but dressed a bit too loudly and talked a little too coarsely for George's tastes. She acted as if nothing had happened between them at work in the days following their evening together. He reciprocated and ignored her as well.

A week later, she asked him for a ride again. They drove to the same hotel without talking much and they had sex like animals for a couple of hours before he took her home. He never considered taking her to his apartment. He didn't want her to know too much about him or where he lived. They didn't have anything other than casual conversations during their time together. This weekly rendezvous went on for a few more weeks. Then, one day, she stopped asking him for a ride.

He never wondered why. One night, lying in bed, he decided that in the near future, he would only have relationships that were free of any commitment.

"I am a rock... I am an island," he sang softly to himself.

Ricardo, the pressman, was a big friendly Jamaican. He spoke English with a noticeable Jamaican accent with the colorful Jamaican Patois lingo sprinkled frequently in between. George sometimes walked with him to the Chinese restaurant at the end of the block. Paul, his graphic designer friend, did not like Ricardo much. He warned George about him.

"Be careful of Ricardo. He may appear to be a nice guy, but don't trust him. I've heard some crazy stories. He does drugs — not just any drug, but crack. That's some serious stuff, guy!"

Paul also told him that a drug dealer had tried cutting Ricardo's throat from ear to ear with a box cutter — but he had not cut deep enough. George did notice that Ricardo had a scar that ran across the front of his throat. However, it was in his nature to be interested and curious about colorful characters, so he sometimes spent time with the Jamaican pressman.

One evening Ricardo asked him, "George, duh yuh want to come wid mi to East New York fah some Jamaican curry?"

George was curious about Ricardo's life, so he agreed to go. They got into his Ford Escort, and he drove into a world he had never experienced before. It is claimed that East New York became a ghetto because of what was later termed as "blockbusting."

In the early 1970s, some unscrupulous real estate agents in New York realized that white residents were getting nervous about black people moving into their neighborhoods. So, they sent flyers to the white homeowners warning of an impending black takeover of the area. They even paid for some unsavory looking black people to loiter around on the streets. This resulted in a majority of white families hastily returning their homes for much less than they were worth to their banks and moving out.

The real estate agents then resold these homes to black families for more and collected their commissions. The banks charged higher interest rates because of the risk involved. Soon, the neighborhood was almost entirely black and many of these new homeowners were unable to pay their mortgages, partly because of the high interest rates. In a decade, it became a wasteland of crime and drugs and was even portrayed as such in one of the popular *Death Wish* movies starring Charles Bronson.

George was mostly ignorant of the history and reputation of East New York, or he would have declined the pressman's invitation. He drove up Atlantic Avenue in his Ford Escort with Ricardo beside him. He looked curiously at the decrepit buildings in neighborhoods that were almost devoid of people that were not black or Hispanic. Ricardo directed him to a street in the Cypress Hill section.

"I haffi stop here fah a minute," he said to George in his thick accent.

They were next to a large tenement building. The New York City Housing Authority had created such buildings all over Manhattan and the other boroughs in the 1950s, 60s and 70s to provide affordable housing for working families. This was replicated in other big cities in the country. As the years went by, these housing projects were occupied mainly by low-income families and were rife with crime, drugs and prostitution. They were seen as the housing of last resort and known commonly as "Projects."

"Yuh wait here I'll come bak soon," Ricardo added.

George looked around. There were tough-looking young people hanging around on the street corners. Some were looking directly at him. He had second thoughts about coming to the neighborhood. He quickly made up his mind.

"No, I'll come with you," he said.

"Okay, but I ave sinting to tek care of here."

He led the way into the doorway of one of the big buildings. There was a sign that said the elevator was not working so they climbed the narrow stairwell all the way to the eighth floor. They walked past what George thought were scary-looking teenagers in jeans and sneakers, smoking at landings and entrances.

One of them asked, "You looking for some action, man?"

George declined their offer. Ricardo knocked four times on a door at the end of the hallway. A woman opened it. She was a very slim and attractive light-skinned, black woman.

"What gwan Monica, dis is mi friend George. You ave di stuff?"

Monica smiled at George politely. They entered a small living room. A girl of ten or eleven was sitting on the sofa watching *The Cosby Show*.

"Yuh sidung an watch some TV, mon," Ricardo told George. He went into one of the rooms with Monica.

George was very uncomfortable being there, but he sat on the sofa with the young girl and watched TV for over an hour without talking to her. She acted like he wasn't even there. After *The Cosby Show*, they saw an episode of *Family Ties* and were in the middle of watching *Who's The Boss* when Ricardo and Monica came out of the room. Monica's clothes were a bit disheveled and she had a wide-eyed appearance. Ricardo had a glow on his face and a slightly glazed look in his eyes as well.

"Okay, mon, let's go," he said.

George followed him down the stairs and back to his car. He was glad to see it was still there. Ricardo gave him directions to Pine Street where there was a good Jamaican restaurant. George didn't feel much like eating now. He just wanted to return to the safety of his apartment in Bay Ridge.

Ricardo was also not very talkative. He just sat there with a distant expression, like his mind was elsewhere. They ordered oxtail and curried goat with rice. The food was excellent, but George barely ate. He was relieved when, after dinner, Ricardo asked him to drop him off at the subway on Atlantic Avenue.

He drove quickly back home. He wasn't sure what Ricardo had done inside the room with Monica but he decided that it was the last time he would hang out with the Jamaican pressman after hours. He wondered what would have happened if the police had raided the apartment or stopped them outside. He vowed that he would be more careful from now on.

A few weeks later, he had another strange experience with Eric O'Malley, the operator of one of the large roll-fed web offset presses. It made him even more wary of spending time with his co-workers from BQE.

George usually had lunch in one of the many low-priced food establishments around the lower end of Atlantic Avenue. They ranged from American fast food to Chinese, Arab and Greek. It was not unusual to find other BQE staff eating wherever he went in the neighborhood. He kept running into Eric at various restaurants. Not wanting to be rude, he usually ate at the same table as the pressman.

They hit it off because they both liked music. Eric was in his late fifties and a big fan of Elvis. One day George brought in his guitar in to work and played some Elvis tunes. Eric was very impressed by his ability to play guitar and sing. After that, he would seek George out during his lunch hour and ask him to go with him. One afternoon, he asked George to join him at a local bar for drinks and dinner after work.

They walked to John's Ale House on Court Street and ordered beer. After a couple of hours, Eric was quite drunk. His enormous red face became even more flushed. He was a large man with big shoulders and arms, a large potbelly, unkempt long hair combed back and an untidy reddish-brown beard.

"You're a good fella, George," he said. "Not like those bastards who are taking over my neighborhood." He didn't use the word "black," but George knew what he meant. He didn't want to encourage Eric to continue talking about race or ethnicity so he just kept quiet.

"I'm sick of these fucking people," Eric said. "They don't want to work… just collect welfare or steal from us, fucking bastards!"

"Let's order some food," said George. "I'm hungry." He called over the waitress.

"You go ahead," slurred Eric. "I'll just have another beer."

George ordered a hamburger and sipped his beer. He was beginning to regret socializing with another of his co-workers. Eric talked about his life and family. He had a wife, who was also Irish, and three children. They lived in Far Rockaway in a house along the beach. It had once belonged to his grandfather, and he had grown up there.

"When I was young, it used to be a great area… only white folks. Now it is full of those bastards… crime, drugs, prostitutes everywhere… I hate them… motherfuckers!"

George tried to steer the conversation to music or work, but Eric kept coming back to his rant about black people. Then he narrated an incident that shocked George completely.

"I'll tell you something I have never told anyone, George — anyone for ten years… you wanna hear it?"

Actually, George didn't, but he was now committed to the conversation. He didn't know what to say, so he tried another strategy.

"I need to use the restroom, Eric, I'll be back soon." He took his time getting back. His co-worker was slouched on the table with a slightly annoyed look on his face.

"Boy, look at some of the women in this place. I'd like to fuck them all... but they'll want nothing to do with me. You're a good-looking guy, George. You get a lot of pussy?"

"I do okay," said George.

"You do Liz yet? She bangs all the good-looking guys I heard. You fuck her yet, George?"

This was another area of conversation George wanted to stay away from. He didn't answer and acted like he hadn't heard Eric clearly.

A black homeless man, who appeared to be drunk or on drugs, stumbled past outside. Eric saw him and began ranting again.

"Bastards, these people. They don't wanna work. They want everything for free. We pay for them with our taxes... they collect through welfare, or they steal from us." Then a cunning look appeared on his face, "I haven't told anyone this in ten years... you wanna know what happened...?"

He lowered his voice to a conspiratorial whisper. "One night, many years ago, I woke up suddenly around midnight in my house and heard a noise downstairs. My kids were just babies. So I crept down and I saw this black bastard in my living room, trying to steal my VCR. I crept back to the bedroom and got my Louisville Slugger. He turned around just when I was almost at the bottom of the stairs. He was a thin little guy — only about five feet tall or something, but I didn't know if he had a gun or anything with him... you know? I swung the bat with all my strength at his head. It cracked open like an egg. I hit him a couple more times. I was so angry. The sonnuvabitch was in my house. There was blood all around. He wasn't moving. He was dead as a doornail. My wife came down. She was as angry as me, but she was scared. We didn't know what to do. If we called the cops, they would probable arrest me. So I phoned my brother who lived nearby... he's dead now... heart attack... but he came over right away. The kids were too young, thank God. We talked it over and decided to bury the bastard in our backyard. It's all sand, so it was easy to dig. My brother and I dug down almost fifteen feet down and buried him there. The next week we put up a gazebo and added cement and stone. No one came looking for him. It's like he never existed but he's still there. No one knows about it... you hear... you unnastand, guy?"

George didn't know what to say. He couldn't even be sure if it was a true story. He just nodded. He just wanted to leave now. Eric finished his drink and asked George if he would give him a ride home to Far Rockaway. It was over an hour away.

George had no intention of driving in the middle of the night to an unknown location with Eric, who had just confessed to killing a man — or maybe even a young boy, from his description. So he lied that his car was giving some trouble and it would not make it there and back. He dropped Eric off near the A-Train station and drove home as quickly as he could.

After these two incidents with his co-workers, George realized that he needed to be careful of whom he hung around with from now. In India, his social circle had been the upper crust of society. Now, in less than a year, he was almost at the bottom of the social ladder. Nobody knew, or cared, if he had gone to elite schools in India or had lived a privileged life there. He was blue collar now like everyone else at BQE.

George knew that he would have to slowly change his life. That night he decided he would go to college and register for a liberal arts degree like his father had wanted for him.

The next day, it appeared that Eric had been completely drunk the previous night because he did not seem to remember anything he had told George. He went about his work like nothing had happened and even asked George to join him for lunch. But George was wary. He was actually mulling over what to do with the information he had. Should he go to the police if a murder had really been committed... or had Eric only been spinning a tall yarn to impress him?

Whatever the case, he had seen a side of the pressman he did not like at all and decided that didn't want to spend time with Eric anymore. He tried to avoid him and went out for lunch with Paul or took his break at a later time for the next few weeks. The issue was resolved a month later when Vinnie fired Eric for coming in drunk to work. George never saw him again, but he often thought about the body buried in Eric's backyard for several years.

■

A month later, George took the SAT without much preparation and scored a respectable score in it. As a New York resident, he was now eligible for reduced tuition at any city or state institution. He registered at Hunter College for a broad Liberal Arts education.

The college was located between 67th and 69th Streets on the East side of Manhattan. He struck a deal with his boss, Vinnie, where he could work around his college schedule. The truth was that after a few months there, Vinnie needed him more than he needed the job at BQE. George had raised the design standards and added a very profitable offering to Vinnie's customers. Vinnie gave George a key to the front of the shop so he could come in after hours and work.

It was a convenient arrangement for George. Having a regular job while he was in college meant that he didn't have to dip into his father's money too much. It also ensured that he had medical insurance that cost thousands of dollars to purchase on his own. Now that he had a car, he was able to visit his mother anytime he wanted. He always drove back to his own apartment, even if it was past midnight. He preferred to sleep in his own bed if he could.

George soon got quite familiar with the little stretch of Brooklyn that he lived and worked in every day. Bay Ridge, where his apartment was located, was at the Southwest corner of the borough. It was a middle class neighborhood inhabited primarily by Italians, Norwegians, Irish and Greeks. At its tip was the Verrazano Narrows Bridge, which connected Brooklyn to Staten Island. When it was built in 1964, it was the longest suspension bridge in the world.

George's landlords were an old Greek couple. They had taken almost a parental interest in him and often left homemade Greek food for him in his kitchen when he returned home. Living in Bay Ridge exposed George to the Greek culture and cuisine. He liked both. He was very attracted to the beautiful Greek women in their tight mini skirts and coiffed up hair that walked around the shopping districts of 5th Avenue and 92nd Street or gathered in groups at the cafes and restaurants. The Greek men, however, were very possessive of their women and not very welcoming to single men from other ethnic groups. The same was true of the Arabs in the neighborhood. Their women were quite beautiful as well, but completely out of his reach, because it unthinkable for them to sit alone with a man, especially someone who was not Arab.

Brooklyn Heights, where he worked, was all the way downtown at the opposite end of the borough. It was right next to the Brooklyn Bridge, which connected it to Manhattan. The raised promenade along its edge offered magnificent views of New York City and the Statue of Liberty. The residents of Brooklyn Heights were mostly upper-middle class. The main commercial area, Montague Street, contained boutique stores, antique shops, booksellers, bars and small cafes. Depending on his mood, George would hang out in Brooklyn Heights, Bay Ridge, or cross the bridge into downtown Manhattan. When he wanted female companionship, he would go to a singles bar in one of these neighborhoods.

He found that he was quite desirable to women and usually found an attractive female who wanted to leave with him. He tried to keep his relationships uncomplicated and at a physical level. The women tended to be older than him and usually divorced. He always took them to a hotel, never to his own apartment and made it a point to use a condom. In a little over a year, he had slept with several beautiful women of varying backgrounds and ethnicity. He enjoyed the company of women enormously, but he liked being able to go back to his apartment at some point in the evening and sleep in his own bed.

He missed his old life in Bangalore and the company of his friends more than he could bear sometimes. Swami corresponded regularly, but George knew things had changed. Swami had a family now, and Annie was his best friend — as it should be, George realized. They talked now and then on the phone, and George narrated some of his adventures to his friend.

"George, your life is like a Hollywood movie as far as I am concerned," Swami said incredulously. "But be careful, bugger, New York is not like Bangalore. It's a dangerous place. Be careful of jealous boyfriends and the like, okay?"

Venu had called both Swami and George a few times, but the truth was that they had generally lost touch with him. His life was very hectic. He was both studying and working as a doctor in a Toronto hospital.

"Poor chap is probably going crazy. I admire him for how he has made everything work," said George.

"Yes, but I miss our Scrimshankers days too," said Swami. "Life just gets more and more complicated as one gets older."

George agreed with him. He was a little jealous of his friends now. Both Swami and Venu seemed settled in their lives. Meanwhile he was still right at the start of his new life in the United States.

Chapter 22
Handsome George

Hunter College exposed George to a different life than the one he had known until then in the U.S. It took him out of the blue-collar work environment of BQE printing into one of abstract thought and academics. He was almost ten years older than most of the freshmen undergraduate students in his class. He found it relatively easy to do well in most of his courses. George especially enjoyed subjects such as philosophy, psychology and art history, which he had been largely ignorant about before.

"You were right, Dad," he thought to himself after the first few weeks of college. *"Everybody needs to have a broad view of life before they specialize in something."*

One day, George was in his "Introduction to Philosophy" class when a new song came to him. It was his first in many months. The topic that day was the work of Zhuangzi, the Chinese philosopher from the fourth century BCE.

Professor Emma Roth read the pertinent passage from the textbook, *"Once Zhuangzi dreamt he was a butterfly... a butterfly flitting and fluttering around, happy with himself and doing as he pleased. He didn't know he was Zhuangzi. Suddenly he woke up, and there he was, solid and unmistakable Zhuangzi. But he didn't know if he was Zhuangzi who had dreamt he was a butterfly, or a butterfly dreaming he was Zhuangzi."*

For the next half an hour, Dr. Roth discussed epistemology, relativism, cognitive rationalism and existentialism. George, however, couldn't get Zhuangzi's dream about the butterfly out of his mind. The words and melody came to him together right there in the classroom. He wrote *"Butterfly's Dream"* at the top of the last page in his notebook and started writing:

Am I dreaming... or is this reality?
Am I flesh and blood... is this really me?
Look into the mirror... what do I see?
Just another stranger... longing to be free
But do I see the butterfly... or am I just... a butterfly's dream?

There is a feeling... that I have inside
It makes me feel happy... just to be alive
I feel love... I feel pain
I can see the sunshine... I can feel the rain
But do I see the butterfly... or am I just... a butterfly's dream?

I see the bad... I see the good
I've been forsaken... I've been misunderstood
I've been lost... I've been overrated
But do I see the butterfly... or am I just... a butterfly's dream?
A butterfly's dream

George soon got to know several of his fellow students at Hunter College. He sometimes hung out at the Fig & Olive, a small restaurant on Lexington Avenue, where he was bound to run into a few of his classmates. Other times, when he wanted to be alone, he went to a Greek diner a few blocks away.

In the two years he had been in New York, George had lost most of his Indian accent and reverted back to the way he spoke in his first twelve years as a child in the U.S. He was brown-skinned but he had sharp features, probably from some ancient Greek or Jewish ancestor, both of whom the Syrian Christians in Kerala claimed lineage from — a strong jaw with a cleft in his chin, high cheekbones and expressive eyes.

Ultimately it is the proportions of a person's facial features: hair, lips, nose, chin, cheekbones, eyes, ears, forehead, eyelashes and they way they are situated in relation to each other that make a person attractive, striking, ordinary-looking or ugly. George was fortunate that his features seemed to have been put together perfectly. He was also tall and slim with a sinewy build. Both men and women found him attractive.

One evening when he was walking to his car in Brooklyn

Heights, an expensive Lincoln car pulled up alongside him. A well-dressed man in a tux got out and hailed him over.

"Do I know you?" he asked George.

"No, I don't think so."

"Are you a student?"

"At Hunter College, not here."

"Do you know Professor Randall in the Physics department?"

"No, I'm in the Humanities department."

The man came over. He was middle aged. He looked like he was rich and was on his way home from some social event. He had been drinking a little. He held out his hand.

"I'm Jeff. What's your name?"

George put out his hand. The man held it for a second and then moved his hand to George's crotch.

George stepped back. He was a bit startled.

"I'm sorry, but I'm not gay," he said.

"Are you sure?" asked the man.

"Quite sure," said George.

"Okay then, sorry." He got in his car and drove away. Brooklyn Heights had a sizable gay population, but it was the first time he had been propositioned by someone.

In his second year at Hunter College, George decided to start performing seriously and find a way to get into the music business. He had already begun playing at college events and small venues when he got the chance. He only performed his own songs now and called himself George John. He felt that Chandy was too ethnic, and since John was his second favorite Beatles, after George, he decided to use his name instead. By changing his last name, he also got rid of the baggage of ethnicity and preconceived ideas people had of his Indian heritage.

George's above-average and exotic looks usually got him through the door when he went to the clubs in downtown New York to audition. Most of the owners and managers were attracted and intrigued by him when he walked in with his beat-up guitar case in hand. They gave him the opportunity to audition for them at least. He did not disappoint.

The club owners realized right away that George had a charisma and stage presence that was rare in most of the hopefuls that walked through their doors. His original material was quite outstanding and reminiscent of some of the stalwarts to the early folk and rock scene. It was the late 1980s, and most of the newer acts were electronic, alternative rock, pop or heavy metal. But George's music was a blend of classic rock and acoustic folk that reverted to an earlier era of meaningful lyrics and strong melodies.

Soon he was playing open-mics and gigs at the many small clubs and showplaces in and around Greenwich Village and New York such as the Bitter End, CBGB, Pyramid, Continental, Street Level and others. What was remarkable about these places was that in addition to some of the most famous names in music playing there, they also showcased upcoming singers, songwriters and acts no one had heard before, like George John. The audience was usually quite encouraging and comprised mostly of people who genuinely came to hear good new music as well as their favorite bands and singers.

The clubs were also a venue for musicians to get the respect of their peers and meet people who could possibly further their careers. George went there on his own, but he soon got to know several other songwriters and musicians that performed there. One day after he had finished his set at the Bitter End, a short, slightly built man met him backstage and handed him a card.

"Sol Levin," he said. "I'm a music manager. Do you have a manager already?"

When George said he didn't, Sol said, "Good, then come and see me next week."

A month earlier, George had quit his job at BQE Printing. He was now able to make almost as much playing his songs at the various clubs. He became a member of ASCAP, the music performing rights organization, and was able to buy group health insurance at affordable rates through them.

He also started copyrighting his songs at the Library of Congress. He created volumes of ten to fifteen songs each that he sent together under one title. It cost thirty dollars. He included a cassette tape with just guitar and vocal renditions as well as a hard copy of the words and chords in an envelope. By the time he started performing regularly at the clubs, he had three volumes of almost forty songs copyrighted with another one in the works.

Sol's office was located on 7th Avenue and 25th Street. George walked up to the second floor after being buzzed in. It was a small suite with a reception area outside and an office for Sol inside. He came out and shook George's hand enthusiastically.

"George, great to see you again. Thanks for coming. Do you have your tape and lyrics with you?"

When George had phoned him a few days earlier, Sol had asked him to bring a tape of his songs and a copy of his lyrics. He led George into his office and told him to get comfortable on the reclining chair while he listened to the tape. Sol put on his headphones, closed his eyes and heard both sides of the tape completely. After he finished listening, he read through the lyric sheets. Over an hour went by before he spoke.

"George, you are quite good. I can see a lot of talent. However, your music and songs are dated — maybe ten years ago, you may have had a hit album. Today, the records that sell are not classic rock or folk. They are current synthpop and hairbands. When I saw you at the Bitter End, I thought you had something special. You have star quality, but your songs need a lighter theme and a more contemporary arrangement."

"I don't know; I write songs from the heart — this is what comes out," said George.

"Tell me, do you want to be a great songwriter that no one has heard of, or do you want to be popular entertainer?" asked Sol. "From what I can tell, your songs are definitely good enough for you to play at small clubs. You may even develop a faithful following, but it will be hard to get a recording contract or airplay or a music video on MTV with the music you have here. I hear the music and songwriters that have influenced you in your songs — The Beatles, Dylan, Van Morrison — but those guys belong to a previous era. Now tastes have changed."

"Okay, so why are you interested in me?" asked George bluntly.

"Because I'm trying to put together a music act… a new band that I can sell to a record executive that I know well. He is looking for something specific. I already have four musicians: lead, bass, piano and drums. I'm looking for a songwriter and frontman. When I saw you, I thought you would be perfect."

"What kind of music would I have to write and perform?"

"The arrangement will have to be contemporary pop. You will have to write songs that are easy to understand — love songs with catchy lyrics, repetitive hooks and edgy melodies. Listen to some of the hit artists today: Fine Young Cannibals, Tears for Fears, The Human League, Depeche Mode, Duran Duran, The Cure. Nothing too complicated. Songs about girls, love, automobiles, city life — anything catchy with a lyrical or musical hook!"

George wasn't sure about changing his musical direction. He was rather fond of his songs and the genre of music he played. But Sol was quite adamant and forceful.

"Let me tell you something," he said finally. "There are lots of singer-songwriters who would jump at an opportunity like this. I think you have something special to offer. That's why I'm willing to spend my time and resources on you."

Sol paused for a moment. He looked at George intently and said, "If you can write ten great new pop songs, or even change some of your songs so they are more current, I will invest my own money in your success. I have an idea for a band name as well as how you should look and sound. Come back in a month with ten songs I can use. I will be responsible for getting them to the right people and getting you signed."

George left and spent the next few weeks, when he wasn't attending classes or performing at the clubs, writing songs for Sol. It was the first time he was creating songs that didn't come to him naturally. He looked through Billboard magazine at the titles of the songs that were currently in the charts. Then he came up with titles of ten songs that he thought would fit Sol's expectations.

He composed catchy melodies and wrote simple lyrics based on the song titles he had created: *Someone Like You, Manhattan, Bright Eyes, Yvette, Party Song, Best Friends, My Lover, Just You, Outside Your Window.*

They were some of the hardest songs he had ever written because they didn't just flow out of him like all his other tunes. He spent several days writing and creating the melody for the first song, "*Someone Like You.*"

I've been walking down this road for so long
What hasn't made me weak has made me strong
I've been a stranger so many times
And I've heard all those worn out lines
Though I was looking for answers in my life
As I wandered through this world with my books and my knife

And all my searching only helped me prove
In the end it don't matter what you knew...

If you don't have someone like you
Everyone needs someone like you
And you show it in the things that you do
Everyone needs someone like you... like you

Never turned to God or some religion
Only believed in truth and reason
In my life I've never asked for much
Been satisfied with a stranger's touch
It's all the same in this foolish game
Cos tomorrow no one remembers your name
Stand up for the red, white and blue
But only one thing is true...

It's the love of someone like you
Everyone needs someone like you
And you show it in the things that you do
Everyone needs someone like you... like you

It had a very upbeat tune, a catchy melody and a repetitive chorus. George was sure Sol would like it. He got a talented keyboard player he knew from the club scene to play pop piano while he played guitar on the demo.

He then wrote and recorded the rest of the songs with just guitar and vocals in the next few weeks. The instrumentation was simple, but he thought they conveyed the feel and intent of the songs quite well. When he was finally done, he went to see Sol in his office again.

As he had done before, Sol asked George to sit in his office while he listened to the entire tape completely from beginning to end with total concentration. When he took out his headphones and smiled, George could tell that he liked the songs.

"These are good songs," said Sol. "Very catchy tunes, nice hooks, good variety, surprising interludes and bridges, clever lyrics... Good job! I think we can do something with this. The lyrics are still a bit wordy, but they are good."

"Thanks," said George. "I'm glad you like it. Now what?"

"Now we do the fun stuff: write up a contract... and you promise me your first born, blah, blah, blah! Do you have a lawyer?"

"Yes," said George, even though he didn't, actually. But he did not want Sol to think he was dealing with a naïve amateur.

"Okay, ask him or her to contact my secretary tomorrow, and we can work out the details. After that, we can get to work."

When George thought about it later, he realized that he did know a woman who worked at an entertainment lawyer's office. He went home and looked through his desk drawer and found her card. Her name was Deborah Shapiro, and she worked as a paralegal for Baker & Skilburgh, an entertainment law firm in New York City.

George had met her at a singles bar in Brooklyn Heights. She was in her late-thirties and separated with two children. They had slept together a few times. She was attractive and very smart. George had liked her a lot. When she found out George was a songwriter and musician, she had given him her business card and asked him to contact her if he ever needed a good entertainment lawyer. A few weeks into their relationship, she told him that she was getting back with her husband for the sake of the children even though he had cheated on her.

He called Deborah at her office the next day. She was a little surprised and wary to hear from him at first. When he explained the situation, however, she was more receptive and asked him to meet with her boss, Geoff Baker, as soon as possible.

George went to see him that afternoon itself. Geoff was a handsome, sun-tanned man in his sixties, with silver hair and steel-blue eyes. His firm was quite successful. Normally he didn't take on new clients who just walked in, but he made an exception in George's case because of Deborah's recommendation.

"So you are signing with Sol Levin?" he asked. "I don't know him personally, but I've heard he's a good guy. You could do worse!"

George paid him a retainer and the lawyer said he would call Sol later that day. On his way out, George hugged Deborah and chatted with her briefly. She was still together with her husband.

A few days later, he met Geoff and Sol at the law firm and signed his first music contract. It was relatively simple. Sol would get twenty percent of all his songwriting, publishing and performance revenues for the next five years, with a provision to extend the contract at the end of the period. For his part, Sol would pay for the expenses of creating a product that could be shopped to the record companies, expenses that he would recoup from future revenues.

George wasn't sure if he was doing the right thing, but he signed on the dotted line with the appearance of confidence. Sol shook his hand and said, "Welcome to Levin Management. We're going to be a great team — you'll see. Come to my office tomorrow afternoon at three o'clock and meet your band."

The next day George showed up at Sol's office on time. His new manager came out of his office as soon as he heard George's voice outside.

"Welcome! I'd like you to meet some people."

He led George to his office. There were four men there.

"Folks, meet Handsome George. And George, meet the Ugly Ducklings!"

George had no idea what he was talking about… and neither did the others in the room. Sol laughed.

"Ha… ha… ha… I have told all of you that I needed you for a band I'm putting together. Well… it is going to be called Handsome George & The Ugly Ducklings! So once again everyone, this is Handsome George… also known as George John on vocals and guitar," he pointed to George…

He went on, "And The Ugly Ducklings are Steve Popp on lead guitar." He gestured to a slightly built man with blond hair. "Jack Cross on bass." A tall lanky man with long black hair nodded. "Dee Williams on keyboards." He pointed to a slim man with a ponytail and horn-rimmed classes who was lounging against the window frame. "And last but not least, Derek Love on drums." A big, well-built black man in jeans and a cut-off T-shirt pointed his index finger at George and smiled.

The five of them were a motley bunch. George wondered how they would fit in as a band. He wasn't sure that he was thrilled about the name that Sol had come up with.

"Can we call it something other than Handsome George & The Ugly Ducklings? Are you guys okay with being called The Ugly Ducklings?" he asked.

"I don't care," said Derek. "I just want a gig, man! You can call me Ugly Derek for all I care."

The others also said that it didn't matter to them. So, the band

Handsome George & The Ugly Ducklings was born that day in Sol's office in New York City.

■

The next step was to get five strangers to become a band of musicians that sounded and looked good together. Even though George and the others had no idea of what the final outcome of the band would be, it appeared that Sol knew exactly what he wanted. He gave each of them five hundred dollars a week for their expenses.

"Remember this is going to come out of your future revenues," he said. "I am confident that we will all be rich."

Sol hired a room at Smash, a rehearsal studio in midtown Manhattan, for a few months so the band could practice anytime they wanted. He also brought in a fashion stylist one day to the studio who showed drawings of the clothes that the band would wear. George would be dressed in bright, shiny suits, padded jackets and tight pants, coiffed-up hair, a touch of eyeliner, frilly shirts or synthetic T-shirts and boots with studs. The "Ducklings" would all wear tight-fitting black suits with white shirts, narrow black ties and fedoras. At first everyone laughed when they saw the sketches. It looked almost antithetical to what they were like in real life.

"Seriously, Dude?" asked Derek. "You want me to play drums in that?"

"Yes, Sol, that's not my style at all," said George.

"Fellers, you have to fit the part if you want the gig," said Sol. "My goal is to get you signed with a Major. To do that, you need to be what they are searching for. My friend is an A&R man at Starlight and he's looking for talent. However, I don't want to expose you to him until I think you are ready. That means the way you look, your songs, how you sound and your chemistry as a band."

George and the others had to admit that Sol had a point. They decided to give him a chance, at least until he got them signed with a record company. So they listened patiently while the fashion consultant — a slightly built flamboyant man — gave them advice on dressing and make-up so they could play their roles as Handsome George & The Ugly Ducklings. Lastly, he took their measurements so he could order custom clothes for all of them.

"Okay, now that we have your appearance out of the way, you can spend your time playing the songs George has written for this project," said Sol.

"Tomorrow, Ted Bennett, one of the hottest producers of today, will be coming to the studio so he can help you in arranging the songs. I want you all to keep practicing until you are really tight as a band and have a sound that is current and appeals to the young people of today."

Ted showed up the next day. He had worked with several of the popular bands and built up a reputation of being someone who had a golden ear for producing hit songs. He listened to all the songs and nodded approvingly.

"These are good songs, George. I think we can work with them. Okay, here's what we are going to do. I'm going to play some songs I compiled from other bands so you get a feel for the genre of music I'd like you to play. We won't use labels okay? Let's make music that sounds good and that people will buy."

For the next two months, George & The Ducklings practiced their songs for hours on end, over and over, with different tempos, instrumentation, and melodies until Ted decided they had exactly the sound he wanted. As soon as he had started playing with his band, George realized that Steve, Jack, Dee and Derek were all top-notch talent. In a few weeks, they had perfected all the songs and sounded like a band that had been together a long time. They were also getting to know each other as people since they spent so much of their time together and soon even became friends.

Steve Popp was of Hungarian descent and married with two small children. He had attended the prestigious Berklee College of Music, where he majored in composition with a minor in American Roots Music. He was an excellent guitar player and could read and write music, but after he graduated he wanted to play and compose contemporary music. He soon realized that he wasn't very prolific as a composer of music, and his lyrical abilities were rudimentary at best. He was hoping to tag on to someone who could write great songs so he could just play guitar. He lived in Forest Hills and worked in construction when he was in-between gigs or couldn't find work as a session musician. When he met George and heard his songs, he was impressed. George appeared to be a great front man. He was handsome, charismatic and an excellent songwriter.

Maybe this was the break he was looking for — the band that would anchor his career.

Jack Cross had played bass since he was fifteen years old in various bands. He had learned to read and write music in school and spent several years training under Eddie Roque, a legendary bass player from New York City. Like Steve, he had worked as a session musician and played with various bands on tour. He was gay and lived with his partner on the Upper West Side. He was a quiet man who didn't speak much but played his Steinberger headless bass with style, precision and creativity. The bass guitar anchors the sound of a band, and Jack, in addition to doing that musically, also usually provided a calming presence in the studio.

Dee Williams had studied classical piano at Juilliard in New York City. However, after he graduated, he was also drawn to the world of pop and rock music. He saw music more in commercial terms than as an artistic expression. He didn't care what he played or in which genre as long as it was popular and made money. He worked extensively with advertising agencies on jingles and music for commercials and corporate videos. He was single and lived with his mother in Staten Island.

Derek Love had grown up in the Bedford-Stuyvesant section of Brooklyn. His early influences were gospel, R&B and funk, but he had later turned to jazz. After high school he went to William Patterson College in New Jersey for a Bachelor's Degree in Jazz Studies and Performance. He played both sax and drums proficiently. His first love was jazz, but he had also worked as a drummer with several pop and rock bands on tour. He was just looking for a steady job as a musician with maybe the opportunity of something much bigger. He had responded to Sol's ad in Billboard and passed the audition easily. George liked him instinctively. He was open, friendly, very professional and a solid drummer.

■

Sol soon got the band gigging at clubs along the Jersey shoreline, Long Island, Westchester and New York City. It allowed them to get familiar with playing in front of audiences and with each other. They performed mainly originals written by George as well as a few covers. Sol and Ted would be present on most nights. They guided the sound of the band so it matched what Sol knew he wanted. The were now in character as Handsome George & The Ugly Ducklings and playing a unique blend of pop, rock and dance music.

George was not very thrilled about the sound or the direction his music and career appeared to be heading towards. He longed to play classic rock and acoustic folk, which were the genres he like the most. However, he was also curious to see if Sol could get them a recording deal with a major record company. In the past two years, he had sent several tapes of his demos to other agents and record companies without any success.

The band was warmly received in some venues, but rejected for the way they looked and their synthpop sounds in others. The clubs where the crowd was younger and had a dance hall were more receptive to the music that Sol and Ted had instructed them play. Other places, like bars and rock n' roll saloons, wanted a harder sound and a more rugged appearance from their performers.

"Go back to Greenwich Village, you pansies," yelled a drunk one night at a bar somewhere in New Jersey. George & the Ducklings were dressed in their costumes and were even wearing a bit of make-up and eyeliner. Other patrons started yelling similar epithets. Then, someone threw the cap of a beer bottle at Derek. The drummer stood up, took off his jacket and fedora and pointed his drumstick as a warning gesture to the crowd. They were quiet when they realized how big and muscular he was.

George took off his jacket, rolled up his sleeves and the band launched into a blistering rendition of *Johnny B. Goode.* He followed this up with two of his own songs that were hard hitting rock n' roll numbers. The crowd went wild but Sol wasn't happy.

After the show was over, he admonished George and the band sternly, "Never go out of character. This is who you are now — a contemporary synthpop band, not grungy rock n' rollers."

"Well Sol, this is not the place for a synthpop band to play. You almost got us killed," he said defensively.

"Okay, that was my fault, I guess," said Sol. "But I think you are ready for your big audition. Next week you're playing at 1018, and you will have a special spectator, Rodney Brown from Starlight Records. If you impress him, you'll have a contract."

The 1018 Club was located where the old Roxy Theater was on 10th Avenue and 18th Street. They opened their doors for the night precisely at 10:18 PM. It was a very popular spot and sometimes hundreds of people lined up outside for a chance to get inside. It featured a variety of live entertainment. Handsome George & The Ugly Ducklings were given a forty-five minute slot at 11:15 PM.

They started the set with *Someone Like You*, which was an excellent song to dance to and followed it up with most of the other songs George had written for the band. Everyone was playing excellently, and the crowd appeared to enjoy their performance tremendously. After their set, Sol approached them with a man who looked like a well-dressed banker.

"This is Rodney Brown. He's an A&R man at Starlight Records." The man nodded and smiled.

"Rodney, this is George John, Steve Popp, Jack Cross, Dee Williams and Derek Love, also known together as Handsome George & the Ugly Ducklings!"

"Great set, fellas," said Rodney. "Good energy and connection with the audience. I was just telling Sol that I'd like to get you into a studio and record. I think we can do something with you. Do you write all the songs, George?" he asked.

When George replied that he did, Rodney's face lit up.

"Excellent! Come with Sol to my office next week."

The band and Sol met together at Rodney's office at the appointed time. He had a lawyer with him. Without any preamble, he handed out contracts to everyone.

"I spoke to Sol about this already. We have prepared individual contracts for each of you. George, you have two — one for songwriting and the other for being in the band. Please look it over, discuss it with your attorneys and get back to us."

George met with Geoff Baker the next day and went over the contracts with him. He had three documents to look over. The first one had been prepared by Sol for the distribution of total revenue that the band generated. They had already discussed this earlier and agreed to it. George would receive thirty percent and each of the other four members would share the remaining seventy percent equally.

The second contract was between Starlight Records and Handsome George & the Ugly Ducklings. The record company would be responsible for creating a master recording to acceptable commercial standards. They would pay for the studio costs and other expenses associated with the creating and marketing the album and recoup these costs from gross income later. The rights to the songs would belong to Starlight Records. The record would have to be produced in six months' time. The band would also have to tour and promote their album as deemed necessary by the record company for up to fifteen months after the record was released. The band would receive twenty percent of all revenues from record sales after expenses.

The third contract was for songwriting. George would receive twenty percent of all revenues from the sale and distribution of his songs on the album. Rodney had said he wanted the band to do a couple of covers as well as a few new songs by other songwriters.

Geoff tweaked the details in various places and sent it back to the record company's lawyers. He negotiated an up-front advance for both the recording and songwriting contracts. The next week George and the band met at Starlight Records and signed the papers.

"Welcome to Starlight," said Rodney. "Let's make a great record together and all get rich."

■

The next six months were a hectic time for George. He had finished his last semester in college a few weeks ago. He attended the graduation ceremonies at Radio City Music Hall. His mother, uncle and aunt were in the audience.

George had been very busy with his classes and his music for the past two years. However, he had made it a point to visit his mother at least once a week at his aunt's house. Other times they went out together for a movie, a Broadway show or dinner. He had noticed that his mother looked very tired recently.

"Mummy, are you okay?" he asked one day. "You look very tired. Are you sleeping well? Do you want to go to a doctor?"

"No, koche, I am okay. Since Daddy passed away, I haven't slept properly. I feel a bit weak, but I am getting older, so it must be expected."

"Mummy, you are only fifty-eight years. That is not old," said George. He was very concerned but he was also too busy with his own life to dwell on the subject for long.

When he received his diploma, he paused on the stage, looked up and said, *"This is for you, Dad. I wish you were here."*

After the ceremony they all went for dinner to the famous "21 Club" on 52nd Street, where George had reserved a table a week earlier. He was feeling flush with money at the moment. He had received a hefty advance payment from Starlight for signing the two contracts.

During dinner, he had an idea. He hadn't been back to India since they had left six years ago. Handsome George & the Ugly Ducklings were scheduled to start recording in three weeks. He still practiced with the band every day, but he felt he could get a bit of time off.

"Mummy, let's go to Bangalore for two weeks," he said. "Let's all go," he told his uncle and aunt. He was very grateful to them for taking care of his mother. "First class, my treat."

He bought tickets the next day on Air India, and the four of them flew out of JFK two days later. His uncle and aunt had both been able to convince their employers that they had to leave for two weeks on short notice. The truth was that they had reached a point in their lives where they were not afraid of losing their jobs anymore. They had put both their children through college and had even saved a little for their retirement.

"I can't wait to surprise Swami," thought George as he sat in the plane on the way to India.

Chapter 23

Back in Bangalore

The years had passed very quickly for Swaminathan in Bangalore. His life was everything he had ever dreamed of and more. The newspaper had succeeded beyond his wildest imagination. In just under six years, it had become one of the most popular weekly publications in the city. Circulation had climbed to over 400,000, and advertising revenue kept increasing every year. He had added sixteen pages to the paper to accommodate the demand for advertising.

There had been a few changes in staff over the years as well. Sadly, Ram Murthy, the news editor, had died of a heart attack two years ago. Swami was very fond of him. Javid Iqbal, the entertainment editor, had retired and moved to Australia where his son was living. Swami had hired Deepak Malhotra, who had worked for the *Calcutta Times,* to replace Ram as news editor, and Asha Gupta, who had worked at *Femina Magazine*, to take Javid's place as entertainment editor in the newspaper. He was very pleased with his recent hires because they were both doing an excellent job.

The preceding six years had been almost a blur to Swami. Things were hectic but they were also the same: working long hours at the newspaper and spending the remaining time with Annie and the twins; visiting his parents and in-laws over the weekend... His life had got into a routine. Each day was like the next in many ways. Yet, he knew he was very lucky to have the life he did.

He felt envious of George sometimes. His friend appeared to be having a very exciting time in the U.S. He wrote candid letters regularly to Swami in which he talked about college, women, music and living in New York City.

George's life and career appeared to be on an upward trajectory. Swami had no doubt that his friend would be successful with his music someday. He wished he could enjoy a few weeks with George, just like in the old days, without any obligations to his family or the newspaper. But he was not complaining. Life with Annie had been so much more than he could have imagined. She was beautiful, smart and a wonderful mother. She got on especially well with his parents. Annie had become the daughter they never had, and her religion had never been an issue at all.

The twins had brought so much joy to their lives. Both sets of grandparents doted over them. When they were younger, Annie left them with one of the grandmothers and went to work at *Bangalore Baloney*. Now that they had started going to school at Bishop Cotton, Swami would drop them off, and Annie would leave work early and pick them up.

He was surprised, late one afternoon, when Annie called him and asked him to come home.

"Is everything all right, Annie?" he asked anxiously.

"Yes, everything is great. We have a visitor who is waiting to meet you."

"Who is it?" he asked.

"It's a surprise. Come home soon."

Swami and Annie had moved to a nice house on Brunton Road. It was very close to any location in the Cantonment area. He was there in fifteen minutes. He had sold his old Ambassador a few months earlier and bought himself a new Maruthi car.

It was almost five o'clock. Annie and the twins were in the front lawn. Swami was always filled with gratitude and love when he saw her. She still looked exactly like she had when he married her — slim and with a beautiful, unlined face — in spite of the fact that she had given birth to twins and worked harder than him, taking care of the accounts at the paper and then coming home and looking after the needs of the children. He parked his car on the street and then ran and hugged her.

"What's happening, Annie? Hello, kids."

"Daddy," yelled the twins together. "Uncle Jo is here."

"Who? We don't know an Uncle Jo," he said.

Just then George stepped out.

"George, I don't believe it!" Swami rushed and hugged him.

"Bugger, why didn't you tell us that you were coming? I would have come to pick you up at the airport."

George looked the same, but his hairstyle was different. He had cut it so it was long in the front and short in the back. He was also clean-shaven now. He still looked very handsome but somehow more fashionable.

"Don't worry, I wanted to surprise you. Ebby-Chachan picked us up. I told him not to even tell Annie."

"You look good, George, but different."

"It's a long story. I'll tell you about it later."

"How is Aunty? Is she with you?" asked Swami.

"Yes, Mummy is with me. She's been a bit tired and not sleeping well recently, so I thought a trip home might do her good. Molly Aunty and Uncle Sam also came with us. We are all staying at Ebby-Chachan's house."

"Wonderful, but George, you must stay with us. I will come and pick up your things tonight. This is the best news I've heard. Come let's have tea and catch up. I can't believe it, bugger, after so many years." He had tears in his eyes. "And you know what, George? In two days' time, Venu is visiting Bangalore for the first time since he left," said Swami. "I met Uncle and Aunty last week. He's coming with his wife and one-year-old daughter. This is going to be a great reunion. The Scrimshankers rise again!"

■

George was delighted to finally be with his friend again. They had shared so much together in their youth that they didn't even have to speak to know what the other was thinking. He had made many friends in New York, but he knew he would never develop a friendship like the one he had with Swami and Venu again.

Childhood is the time when a person's real nature and character are revealed to those close to them. As people get older, they usually manage to hide who they really are behind layers of social etiquette, polite conversation, carefully contrived facades and well-rehearsed opinions. Most adult friendships are thus usually very shallow. But friendships forged as children are deep and remain fast and true even years later because people rarely change who they are at the core. It only took a few minutes for George and Swami to get back to the friendship they had as children.

George looked at his friend closely. Swami was still quite thin but looked a little older. He had grown a mustache, cut his hair short and combed it back. He had a few specks of gray in his hair now. At first glance, he looked exactly like who he was: the respectable publisher of a successful newspaper. But he also still had the piercing eyes and questioning look that George remembered him for and which had made him one of the leading investigative journalists in the city.

George realized how much he had missed his friend. He was happy that Swami's life was filled with good fortune and happiness. Earlier, DIG Varghese had waxed eloquently to him about his son-in-law: the success of *Bangalore Baloney*... his dedication to Annie... how smart the kids were... the respect he showed to his in-laws...

Any misgivings anyone had before about the incompatibility of their religions or backgrounds had been completely erased. Both sides loved the couple and their two adorable young children.

The fact that Venu was coming down to visit was exciting news as well. George couldn't believe the coincidence that led to both of them being together in Bangalore at the same time.

That evening, George had dinner with Swami, Annie and their kids. It was a joyous time for everyone. Nikhil and Ani loved their Uncle Jo — he had got them all sorts of gifts from the U.S. After the kids had gone to bed, the two friends went for a walk alone to Koshy's Restaurant. Over coffee and cigarettes, they caught up on everything they had done in the years they were apart.

"Wow, I can't believe you have a recording contract," said Swami. "I always knew you would do it, George. This is great news. Next time we meet, you will be famous — Handsome George... wow!"

"Well, I'm excited to have a recording contract, but I'm not thrilled at how much I have had to change — my hair, my clothes, and even the sound of my music. The money is nice, though."

"George, your share of the newspaper is worth a lot of money" said Swami. "I know you transferred it to Annie's name before you left, but as far as we are concerned, it is still yours," he added.

"Swami, I'm doing well. I've been lucky. We still have a lot of money left over from my Dad's insurance, provident fund and stocks. Your kids are my niece and nephew. I am leaving my share of the paper to them, so don't worry. As I told you before, if I ever become homeless or destitute, I will show up at your door."

A couple of days later, George and Swami drove to the airport to welcome Venu back. Krishnachandra and his entire family were there as well. George and Swami went over to their little group at the airport.

"Hi, Uncle, how are all of you?" asked George.

"George! When did you come back? It's so nice to see you boys again together."

Krishnachandra was still embarrassed about his earlier dislike for George. He had stayed sober over the years, and his life had become so much better as a result. His medical shop was the most popular one in the area, and they had bought their own house in Langford Town a few years ago. He also bought a used Ambassador car which he had come in to pick up his son at the airport.

"Ravi is at the IIT in Kharagpur, near Calcutta, studying mechanical engineering. The girls have both finished school. We have a marriage proposal for Priya, but I told them she has to finish her BA before she gets married," he said. "It is a good match, so if they are willing to wait, we may consider it."

"The plane has landed already," said Swami looking at one of the monitors. "Let's go to the arrival hall."

They waited amidst a crowd of expectant relatives and friends of the arriving passengers. Venu's family had got garlands and balloons with them. They waited for another thirty minutes, and then the passengers began streaming out. Most of them looked tired after their long journeys but excited to be coming back home. Swami noticed Venu first.

"There he is," he said excitedly and pointed. Everyone looked in expectation and delight.

Venu was dressed in jeans, a polo shirt and sneakers. There was a woman wearing a yellow blouse and black trousers next to him. She was carrying a baby. Everyone yelled out to him. He came rushing over and hugged his family first.

Then he turned to George and Swami, "I don't believe it... you buggers, here?" He hugged them. "Let me introduce you to my wife, Shantha. Swami has met her once, but not George... Shantha, these are my two best friends."

Shantha was quite pretty. She was almost the same height as Venu and dark, like him.

"Hi, George and Swami. Venu has already told me all about you guys… all your adventures. So nice to meet you finally, George! This is our little baby girl, Priyanka."

Shantha seemed very good-natured and outgoing.

George picked up the little girl and kissed her. "She's beautiful," he told her proud parents.

"Okay, Venu, we know your family is waiting to talk to you and take you home, so we'll leave and catch up with you tomorrow," said Swami.

"Great idea. Call me tomorrow. Appa, what is our phone number at home?" he asked Krishnachandra. His father came rushing over, and wrote it down on a piece of paper and handed it to Swami.

"Uncle, maybe Venu and Mallika can come in our car so everyone has a comfortable ride back," said Swami to Krishnachandra.

So Venu and his youngest sister rode with Swami and George in the Maruthi. Mallika chatted non-stop to her brother the whole time, so his friends could barely get a word in.

However, the next day the three friends met for dinner at the Bowring Institute, where Swami was a member now. They talked for hours, and Venu told them about his life since he had left Bangalore almost six years ago.

■

Venu had arrived in Canada with only his bride and his medical degree in hand. For the next two years, he stayed with his wife in his father in-law's basement in Brampton, Ontario while he did his internship at Peel Memorial Hospital. They didn't have privacy, but they didn't have to pay rent and were able to save their money. It was a hectic period in his life but a happy one as well.

Venu had gotten to know Shantha, whom he had married based on just looking at her photograph and his mother's recommendation. She had lived in India until her early twenties and then immigrated with her family to Canada. She went to college there and worked as a pharmacist at the local Pharma Plus. On Venu's days off, they would go sightseeing all around Ontario in her 1980 Cutlass Ciera.

"We visited Toronto City and saw all the important places: Niagara Falls, where we stayed the night... I was the last one among us to find out Capstan was wrong, buggers!" Venu laughed. "Ottawa City, Montreal... we even crossed the U.S. border and went to Buffalo, New York once," he told George and Swami.

After his internship was over, Venu had done his General Surgery Residency at the University of Ottawa. He had moved to Sandy Hill with Shantha and rented a studio there. It was a very diverse and international neighborhood, full of workers from the several embassies nearby and students from the university there. Shantha had got a job right away at a Shoppers Drug Mart close by. They had lived there for four years. Priyanka was born at the Ottawa Hospital.

For Venu, it had been a relief to move out of his in-laws' basement and finally have the privacy of their own apartment, even if it was only a studio. They had moved from there to a one-bedroom recently, so the baby could have her own room and not be disturbed by the unpredictable hours of Venu's rotations. They would be moving again in a few months. He was about to complete his residency soon and then go on to do a Fellowship in Vascular Surgery at the University of Toronto. Fortunately, it was relatively easy for Shantha to find a job as a pharmacist almost anywhere.

"My immediate goal is to become a cardiac surgeon," Venu told his friends.

"Wow, I can't believe that you are the same guy who once put our dissected frogs into the pocket of Mr. Jairaj's coat that he had left hanging on the back of his chair. Now you're going to be a heart surgeon soon. If only he knew," said George.

"Yes, I liked dissection even then, — and if I ever see Mr. Jairaj, I will apologize to him," said Venu. "He was a great biology teacher. We all did so many stupid things as kids."

Then George told his friends about his life in New York. They were amazed at his experiences. "Bugger, you are still just like James Bond," said Venu.

He added, "My life seems so boring compared to yours: women, clubs, drug dealers, murderers, famous musicians. I will be able to tell you my whole life for the past six years in one paragraph. I worked in the hospital every day until I could hardly walk... spent the nights with my lovely wife... saw a few places nearby... had a baby... don't have time to sleep anymore... and that's all. Bugger, you on the other hand, can write an exciting book already!"

"Well I think the best is yet to come," said Swami. "This bugger is going to be a big star. He'll forget about us."

"Never," said George. "Venu, you are only six to eight hours away from me in Toronto. Why don't you come a visit me in New York?"

"I will come, but I don't know when. I am technically still a student. I barely get time to sleep, and I am living off my wife." He laughed. "She's a great wife and mother. I know you guys may find this funny, but I have got to love her, possibly as much as you love Annie, Swami, even though yours was a love marriage and mine was arranged."

"There are no degrees in love," said Swami. "I am sure your love is every much as valid as mine and Annie's. You either love someone or you don't."

"What about you, George?" asked Venu. "Have you ever met a girl you fell in love with?"

"To be perfectly honest, I haven't," said George. "I've met a lot of very beautiful women, but I never felt I wanted to live with just one person for the rest of my life. Maybe I haven't met the right woman yet. I like my independence too much, but who knows?"

"How do you juggle all these women?" asked Venu.

"I don't lie or deceive anyone," said George. "I try to be monogamous while I am dating a particular woman, but if someone else catches my eye, then I don't feel guilty for going off with them. I am always honest with women, I tell them the truth and let them decide what they want to do. You'll be surprised, but many women also like relationships without complications. Sometimes they have boyfriends or husbands that they are separated from and are just looking for some sex on the side. I never chase after married women, but if they come to me, that's a different matter."

"Well, be careful, George! Jealous husbands and boyfriends can be dangerous," said Swami.

"Don't worry, I'm always careful," said George. "But enough about me. Tell me about your kids. That's one reason I may get married someday — so I can have the experience you buggers are having with your beautiful kids."

"It's not all fun and games," said Venu. "Just one kid is a lot of work. Swami, I don't know how you managed with two."

"If it wasn't for my parents and in-laws we would have died — or got divorced," said Swami. "The first two years were very hard. When one fell asleep, the other would wake up — different meal times, poop times, colic and tantrums — you name it! But it has also been the best times of my life. I love them so much I choke up just thinking about them."

"Same here," said Venu. "Priyanka is the light of my life."

For the next two weeks, the Scrimshankers saw each other every day. They spent time at old haunts, met other friends, had lunch and dinner on their own or together with their families. Mostly they just chatted about the past, the present and the future, like they had always done.

"When you look at your life, where do you see it going in the future?" asked George one day. "I'm curious. Do you guys have a plan for your lives?"

"I can see it all quite clearly," said Swami. "Running the newspaper for the rest of my life, watching my kids grow, getting old with Annie — nothing remarkable. But that's the way I prefer it to be. To me, life is made up of the small events: everyday moments with my wife and family, attending Nikhil's cricket match or Ani's dance program, having dinner with my parents, going for a walk alone with the dog, lying in bed and talking to Annie, reading a good book, walking on a beach, hugging my kids, chasing a good story... I don't want anything more than that."

"I would like to make something of myself in my field," said Venu. "I want to be a famous surgeon, I have the talent for it… I'm not bragging. I also want to be very rich someday. I come from a very humble background, so I suppose that's the reason for my ambition. After I finish my studies, I would like to move to the U.S. and go into private practice. The opportunities are more there. I will work hard and try to be a good doctor, but I would also like to make a lot of money. There's nothing wrong with that, is there?"

"No, Venu, there's nothing wrong in wanting to make money. It's how you make it and use it that matters," said Swami.

"You know, buggers, I still can't see my future clearly," said George. "I'm envious that you both know exactly what you want. For now, I'd like to be a songwriter and musician but I'm not sure if just being that always will keep me happy. Sometimes, I try to look twenty years into the future but all I see is just black. I can't envision anything actually. Maybe I'm going to die soon, so I don't have a future. I look for my mother and even she's not there. There's no one; it's all just dark!"

"George, of course you're not going to die or anything," said Swami. "It's just that you are a for-the-moment sort of guy. You live in the present and take each day as it comes. But don't ever think you'll have no one. We will always be here for you, even fifty years from now if we are alive."

"This is getting morbid, buggers. I can tell you some really sad stories from my experiences as a doctor in the hospital, but I won't. Let's have a good time instead. George, why don't you share another one of your exciting New York adventures?" said Venu.

◾

Then, before they were ready for it, their vacation together was over. George was leaving first. Venu would be in Bangalore for one more week. Swami and Venu came to the airport to see George off. DIG Varghese, had driven them there in his government-issued Contessa, which was a big roomy car.

"George, see to it that Sheila-Kochama is eating and sleeping properly," he said. "She is getting very thin and frail. I though people went to the U.S. and became fat. She is getting thinner day by day."

"I will try, Ebby-Chachan," said George. "I've asked her to go and see a doctor, but she refuses and says nothing is wrong with her."

"Ebby, I keep telling her too," said Molly. "Sam and I will have to take her to the hospital when we get back if she goes on like this."

"There's nothing wrong with me. Don't worry, Ebby," said Sheila Chandy. "I am okay."

"Good luck with the music career, George," said Swami. "We will be looking out for your new record and seeing you on TV."

"Yes, bugger... or should I say Handsome George," said Venu. "I'm sure I will see you on MTV soon."

They hugged him and watched him sadly as he walked away with his mother, uncle and aunt into the security area. George turned and waved to his friends. The Scrimshankers all wondered when they would ever be together again like this.

Chapter 24

A Star Is Born

T he week after George arrived back in New York, he went into the studio to record their first album as Handsome George & The Ugly Ducklings. The band had played most of the songs together for many months already, so they were quite familiar with the material. Sol also added a few covers to the track list, in addition to George's songs. They would be recording fifteen songs, and then culling it down to ten songs for the album. It was George's first exposure to professional multi-track recording. In the beginning, it was hard for him to play along in time to a metronome and lay down the initial guitar track, but he soon got the hang of it.

Ted Bennett was producing the album. He worked closely with Steve Rudd, the recording engineer. Once the guitar or piano track was recorded, George sang a scratch vocal track. Then the band all recorded their parts individually. With a rough mix in place, George recorded the final vocal track and the background vocals.

Ted usually mixed the track on his own. After recording a few songs, George began to understand the process clearly. He was very interested in everything that Ted did: coaxing a superior performance from the band, placing microphones at different spots to get the drums to sound better, mixing the tracks so each instrument or vocal had its own unique space in the mix, sweetening tracks with post-recording wizardry, and mastering the final mix.

It took six weeks to finish recording, mixing and mastering the tracks. Sol got in a film crew to shoot some of the time the band spent in the studio and to make a scripted music video for *Someone Like You*. It featured Tracy Bell, a B-list Hollywood actress, who played George's love interest in it. The band flew to Arizona for three days to shoot the video. This was inter-cut with footage of the band in the studio recording the album. The director, Randy Rosen, had made several videos for some of the top bands, including REM, Van Halen and Jefferson Starship. When it was completed, the result was quite remarkable. George realized that he liked being in front of the camera. He was a natural actor, and everyone who saw the video in post-production thought it was very good and perfect for MTV.

It took another three months for Starlight to finally release the album. The video was launched on MTV at the same time. The response was almost immediate and overwhelming. In less than three weeks the album was #10 on the *Billboard* charts. The video of *Someone Like You* became a Top 5 Video for over three months and even knocked out The Red Hot Chili Peppers, Faith No More, and Depeche Mode from their top spots. On radio, two songs from the album made it to the pop charts and were in constant rotation for several months.

For George, it was a roller coaster ride that lasted for more than a year. The band was suddenly in big demand. They performed at colleges, clubs, TV and radio stations, including an appearance on Howard Stern where the incorrigible host asked George if he had ever had anal sex or been a participant in a ménage à trois. He was a guest on late night television talk shows including Letterman, Arsenio and Leno.

After a few months, the band was performing in large stadiums. They travelled all over the United States, Canada, Europe and Japan. Each day just rolled into the next.

On most days, George had no idea where he was. He just went where Sol asked him to go. It was usually from airport-to-hotel-to-show or appearance... then, back to hotel-to-airport-to-another city... and then repeating it, over and over again.

There were perks as well. They lived a life he had only heard of before: five star hotels, limousines, private jets... hobnobbing with famous musicians and Hollywood stars... hoards of fans and admirers wherever they went... and of course, the beautiful women who were always available for company. He started smoking marijuana regularly, drank a little too much and took sleeping pills to get a good night's rest.

After several months of this type of living George realized he had enough of it. He was tired, bored and restless, as well as desensitized to almost every thrill and excitement he could imagine. It was almost as if he had nothing more to look forward to. Every carnal desire could be fulfilled easily. He had reached a point where he just wanted to go back home and slow down the pace of his life.

The other members of the band were also feeling the strain. They had got along well together before, but now, after touring for over a year, they could barely tolerate one another. As the fame and money began pouring in, egos started getting bigger. There was some resentment from the band that George was getting all the attention and a lion's share of the earnings. He got paid for both songwriting and performing.

Even Sol and Ted were no longer happy with just being behind the scenes. They also wanted to be acknowledged and visible in the media as a critical part of the band's success. The print and television reporters, however, only focused on George, because he was the best looking and fronted the band. They usually ignored the others.

He was interviewed by *Rolling Stone* magazine and the writer, Jonathan Rider, did a Q&A type article on him. The piece ignored the rest of the band as well as Sol and Ted's contributions. Actually, George had answered the questions truthfully and made it a point talk about the role that the band and his management played. However, much of that was edited or left out entirely.

"Great job of taking all the credit in *Rolling Stone*, guy," said Dee to George.

"You've got to believe me, that's not all I said. They left out a lot of stuff."

"Yeah, George, we work as hard as you but as far as the press and the public is concerned, it's all only you, Handsome George. You're the singer, the songwriter, the spokesman and the best looking guy in the band. We are all just here to be extras in your life," said Jack.

"Yes, I've worked so hard to create your look, the sound, the whole package," said Sol. "In your interview, you almost seemed like you didn't like the music you were playing or the way I made you dress… in toy costumes? Here's what you said…" Sol took out the *Rolling Stone* magazine and read from it: *"I'm just a singer and songwriter. The rest is Sol Levin, my manager. He has created the toy costumes, the haircuts, the pop sounds… If I could, I'd take all that away. I just want the music, man."*

"Sol, that's how I feel. This is like a carousel that is not stopping," said George.

"We are also on the same ride but only you are getting the credit. It may be your songs, but we create the sound and play our hearts out every night," said Steve.

Derek Love was the only one who did not join in the criticism of his band mate. He got along well with George, and the two spent a lot of time together playing cards, chess, or just talking when they were closeted in their hotel rooms for hours on end before their shows.

"Dudes, leave George alone," he said. "We know what we signed on for; we all knew who was going to be the star of this band. Maybe none of us thought we'd become so famous so quickly. But I just want the money. As long as it's coming in like it is, why should we suddenly become jealous of the guy? He's doing a heck of a job. The crowds are coming in for him, and we are such a hit mainly because of George. If he is interviewed by the media, he can say whatever the heck he wants, Sol."

The others backed off then but the episode left George with a bad taste in his mouth. There had been differences between all of them for a few months now. He wasn't sure how long he could continue with the endless touring, interviews and appearances. As part of his recording contract, he had agreed to tour for up to fifteen months to promote the album — and more, if both parties decided it was mutually beneficial. He still had a few more months of touring left to do before he could get out of it.

Other than for brief visits now and then, he had not seen his mother much. One afternoon, while he was waiting in his hotel room and just killing time before the show, he decided to call his mother. He dialed his aunt's number. His uncle picked up the phone.

"George, thank God you called. We were wondering how to get in touch with you."

"What happened?" asked George with a sinking feeling in his

stomach. "Is Mummy all right?"

"You have to come home," said Uncle Sam. "She is not well. She's at Westchester Medical Center."

"What happened to her?" he asked.

"She had severe abdominal pain, so we took her to the hospital a few days ago. They did all the tests. George, it is pancreatic cancer," he said softly. "Your Molly Aunty is with her. We don't know what else to do."

"Have they told Mummy what she has?"

"Yes George, she is taking it very bravely. I don't know what has been going on in her mind since Mohan passed away, but it is almost like she wants to die. Please come here as soon as you can."

"I will leave tomorrow itself," said George.

He didn't know how he managed to perform that night. He did his best but he was overwhelmed with the news.

"The show must go on," he thought to himself as he remembered the words of a song performed by one of his favorite singers, Freddy Mercury, recorded while he was dying of AIDS recently. He managed to give a good performance in spite of the turmoil he felt inside.

After the show, he approached Sol and explained the situation. They had two shows the next week as well as several appearances scheduled.

"I have to go home, Sol," said George. "This is not negotiable. It's my mother."

His manager knew he didn't have a choice but to reschedule or cancel those dates. He was also not heartless. Maybe he had become a little more ambitious and greedy over the past year, when he realized that Handsome George was also his golden goose but he genuinely liked George as well. He was still the same person as he was before. Sol knew that for George, it was always only about the music. He enjoyed the trappings of wealth and luxury like anyone else, but to him they were all merely amusing distractions and not meant to be taken seriously.

"Okay, George, you go and be with your mother. I'll buy us two weeks. Don't worry about it. But you have to come back and finish up the rest of the shows. The promoters have already spent a lot of money."

George met with the band before he left. They all felt bad for him when they heard the news. Everyone liked him and they had gotten along well for most of their time together. They had also begun to realize that George probably did not need them for his success anymore, but that they still needed him. Steve, Jack and Dee apologized to him for their outburst.

"Sorry for the heat we gave you on the *Rolling Stone* article," said Steve. "I guess we lost perspective for a while."

"Yes, we all did. Remember, we got into this career for the music. Let's keep it that way," said George.

"You take care, bro, and all best to your momma. I will pray for her," said Derek, who was quite religious. "We'll cool our heels here for a couple of weeks. I think we all need the time. It's been crazy."

They were in Halifax, Nova Scotia. George did not usually even pay attention to which city he was in anymore. They were all the same to him. Two days ago, he had been in Boston and two days before that, in Portland. At first he thought he would ask Jessica, Sol's assistant, to get him a flight to New York, but then he decided to drive. He wanted a bit of time on his own to think about everything. So he called and rented a car from Hertz. He had it delivered to the Prince George Hotel, where they were staying.

It was a dark Ford Explorer. He had selected an SUV in case it snowed, since it was the second week in December. But looking at the weather forecast that night, it appeared that it wasn't expected to snow for the next few days. So, the drive wouldn't be too hard. The rental agency had also sent along a route map. It was 904 miles to New York City and the journey would take him approximately fifteen hours.

He left the next day after breakfast. He drove straight through to Bangor, Maine with only a few short stops on the way. It was ten-hour journey. The traffic was heavy while crossing the St. Stephen-Calais border into the United States. He was travelling incognito from his stage persona. In the past year he had achieved a substantial level of recognition among young people because of his exposure on MTV and other interviews and appearances on TV. But he didn't think he would be easily recognized during his journey by one of his fans. His passport was still in his actual name, George Chandy, and he was dressed unobtrusively in blue jeans, sweatshirt, leather jacket and aviator glasses.

He thought about his mother for most of the trip. He wished he had spent more time with her over the last few years. But his life had been hectic since he had arrived in the U.S. He wanted to call her at the hospital but didn't know what to say over the phone. It would be better to see her in person and talk to her.

It was almost nine o'clock at night as he approached Bangor. He decided against staying at an expensive hotel, even though he could afford to do so now. When he was alone, he preferred the smaller places that ordinary people stayed in rather than the sanitized world of five-star hotels, replete with fawning staff and pretentious fellow guests. It also offered him the opportunity to observe the lives of average individuals and their families at close quarters. He found that it inspired him to write songs which people could relate to... that cut through to the very core of human experience.

When he was five miles from for Bangor, he saw the sign for a small motel off the freeway. He took the exit and pulled into the parking lot of The Restful Motel.

"From Bangalore... to Bangor... I've been everywhere, man," he sang to himself as he parked the car and walked to the reception.

He wasn't surprised to see a middle-aged Indian man at the front desk. An Indian woman, probably his wife, was arranging the free travel brochures for the area on the stand against the wall. George had read in the *New York Times* recently that said approximately fifty percent of all motels in the U.S. were owned by people of Indian origin. Most of them belonged to an Indian Gujarati sub-caste with the surname of Patel. A large number of them had come from Uganda via England.

In 1972, the dictator Idi Amin had expelled all Indians from the East African country at short notice — offering them little more than their lives in exchange for their property. Indian businessmen who lived there were the most affected by what they considered a betrayal by the black Ugandans. Most of the Indians had been born there and considered themselves as Ugandans and equal citizens. As a community, they had been rich and important members of society. They had owned stores, offices, factories, banks, and even airports but overnight they were reduced to destitutes without a home or country.

Like Hitler had done with the Jews, Idi Amin had made a wealthy minority the scapegoat for the economic problems of the majority. While it could be argued that it was hard for the people to stand up to a dictator, from the perspective of the Indians not many of their fellow Ugandans had even tried — most of them just pillaged and took the lands and property of the Indians — justified in the explanation of their leader that Indians were greedy and conniving.

The exiles sold what they could and withdrew as much cash as possible before the banks were shut down to prevent them from getting their money. The lucky ones escaped to England with bags full of dollars. Others had to bribe their way out of the country and escaped with barely their lives. Those that had money with them settled down in England or came to America. The rest went back to India.

Earlier to this cruel expulsion from Uganda, a handful of Gujaratis had arrived in the U.S. in the late 1940s and become very successful operating small motels. Their stories became legends in the Gujarati communities of Africa and India. So, many of Patel refugees from Uganda who had a bit of money to invest and had bought motels of their own.

"Welcome to The Restful Motel. I am Sanjay Patel, the proprietor," said the man behind the desk. "How many days will you be staying?"

"Just the night," said George. "Are you originally from Uganda?"

"Yes, we had to run away and leave everything behind because of that bastard Idi Amin. You know I once had my own airport? Our rate is forty-five dollars for the night, but because you are Indian I will give it to you for forty. We serve a free continental breakfast as well."

George thanked him and took his key. His room was on the ground floor, close to the parking lot. He went to the car and took his overnight bag and his guitar case inside with him. It was his old Martin that had been his constant companion since his youth.

He noticed a McDonald's across the street. He left his luggage in the room and walked over. The girl at the register looked at him closely because she thought he looked familiar, but she couldn't place him. After dinner, he bought a coffee to go and went back to his room.

There was a chill in the air because it was the middle of December. A few of the houses on the street had Christmas lights. In one house he could see a large Christmas tree through the big window. Suddenly he felt lonely and all alone. He had been so busy for the past year that he didn't have time to pause and examine what he was missing in his life. There were always people around him to keep him company and things that needed to be done to keep him occupied all the time. When he wanted to sleep, he usually popped a couple of pills and went out like a light.

But now, sitting alone in a chair on the porch outside his hotel room on a cold December night, he felt an overwhelming sense of loneliness, sadness and despair. He felt tears run down his eyes when he thought of his mother and her illness. What would he do without her? She was the only person left in his immediate family. He wished he could talk to Swami or Venu, but they had lives of their own now. It wasn't like it was before.

He would just have to find the strength to be there for his mother and get through this on his own. He was envious of people who could take refuge in religion. Derek, his drummer friend, seemed to believe in Jesus and God unquestioningly. He often said that if something was more than he could handle or beyond his control, he would leave it in God's hands and stop worrying about it. This was similar to Venu philosophy of leaving things to the Universe when it went beyond what he could control on his own.

George had tried to believe in God several times in his life since he was a child. He had studied all the religions: Hinduism, Christianity, Judaism, Buddhism, Islam, but, like Swami, he was too much of a rationalist to accept any of them unquestioningly. He wished he could. It would be easier. But he had somehow always been unable to make that leap of faith, to accept the premise that other mere mortals just like him were somehow privy to information of a supreme being that was denied to everyone else.

The saying, *"There are no atheists in foxholes,"* came to his mind. *"Was he considering the possibility of God because he was faced with a scary event in his life,"* he wondered.

He went inside the motel room. There was a funny odor in it, as if someone had sex in it recently and a lingering smell of some woman's cheap perfume. He opened his guitar case and picked up his guitar. He began strumming and a pattern began to emerge… C-G-F… He added an Am-F for the rise before the chorus. He started to sing:

As I sit here in my hotel room

Which smells of sex and cheap perfume
Through the open window I can see
The lights of someone's Christmas tree
Everyone's happy, but I'm alone
A million miles from who I was
And ten thousand miles from home

Let your light shine on me
Let your light shine on me
'Cause I'm lost... lost as can be
Let your light shine on me

I wandered through paths unknown
And what I've seen has turned my heart to stone
So I never let anyone in
And I've done my share of sin
But if you're God up in heaven
That's looking out for me
24/7

Let your light shine on me
Let your light shine on me
'Cause I'm lost... lost as can be
Let your light shine on me

Maybe I'm a sinner who needs salvation
Or maybe I'm a man with no hope for redemption

Let your light shine on me
Let your light shine on me
'Cause I'm lost... lost as can be
Let your light shine on me

If you're there...

He was pleased with the song. It expressed what he was feeling at the moment precisely. He washed up in the little bathroom, took out his jacket and shoes and got into bed dressed in the clothes he was wearing. He couldn't fall asleep for a long time. He had sleeping pills with him, but he decided not to use them. The next morning, he work up early and made the rest of the journey to New York City in less than seven hours.

■

George crossed the George Washington Bridge and took the Henry Hudson Parkway to the West Side Highway. He wanted to have a quick bath and change his clothes before he went to see his mother. He took the 79th Street exit. Six months ago, he had moved from his Brooklyn apartment to a two-bedroom duplex on the Upper West Side. The rent was high, but he realized he now had a lot of money. The payments from record sales, touring and songwriting royalties was slowly beginning to come in. It was a lot more than he had ever known or could spend easily.

He was not stingy or frugal, but he had never been one for living extravagantly. He liked good things but never bought something just for the sake of acquiring it. Though he earned a lot more than the rest of the band because of his songs, George realized that all the others spent much more them him buying Rolex watches, expensive cars, designer clothes, antiques, jewelry and even real estate. They lived off their advances from the promoters and the record company, not thinking about what would happen when the accounts were tallied or if their contract was terminated.

He pulled into a parking garage on 74th Street and 6th Avenue. He rented a monthly space there but he had already parked his red Mazda Miata in his spot. So, he left the Explorer with the parking attendant and walked with his guitar and carry-on to his apartment complex on the next block. It was a renovated historic eleven-story, pre-war, luxury building. His apartment was on the top floor.

"Good evening, Mr. John," said the doorman. George used his stage name almost exclusively now.

"How are you, Andy? Any mail for me?"

While he was waiting for the doorman to go to the back and retrieve his mail, he ran into Isabel Williams. She was a vivacious brunette in her mid-fifties. Her husband was a well-known TV personality. They lived down the hall from him. George had gone to their apartment a few times for drinks. He liked them. They were childless and doted over their little Shih Tzu, "Miffy."

"How's Paul?" he asked. "That was a great feature by him on the homeless last week. I watched the whole thing in my hotel room."

"Paul's in England on assignment," said Isabel. "Are you still on tour?"

"Yes, I'm taking a few days off, but I have to go back."

"Paul will be back tomorrow. Stop by."

George promised he would. Andy returned with the mail.

"Andy, can you do me a favor? When you get off from work, or tomorrow... I have a rental parked at the garage next door. Can you return it to the nearest Hertz?" He took out the key and handed it to the doorman.

"Sure thing, Mr. John," said Andy. George was a very good tipper, and he knew he would be more than adequately compensated.

George put the mail into his carry-on and went to his apartment. He was barely there for an hour. He had a quick bath, changed clothes and went out again.

He took the Miata and got back on the Henry Hudson Parkway. He crossed into Westchester, merged into the Saw Mill, got on to the Taconic and exited in Valhalla, where the hospital was located. He had already called his aunt from his apartment and gotten the floor and room number.

"I will be there by the time you get there, koche, I will tell Sheila that you are coming," she said.

George got a visitor's pass at reception and took the elevator to the sixth floor, where his mother was. It was past visiting hours, but since he was a direct relative, he could be there anytime he wanted. He walked into Room 618. He could see Molly Aunty sitting on an armchair next to the bed. His mother was sleeping.

"Georgie," said his aunt. She got up and came to him. He hugged her. She had tears in her eyes. "She is sleeping, koche. They are giving her all kinds of medicines... pawam*."

George went to the bed. He felt a lump in his throat. His mother looked so frail. He hadn't seen her in a month. Maybe it was just from being in a hospital for a few days but she seemed to have aged a few years suddenly.

She stirred. Her eyes fluttered awake. "Georgie... ne annao..."

"Yes, Mummy, I am here." He leaned over and kissed her. There was a mild odor that he couldn't place: a mixture of the hospital bed linen, medicines, chemicals and what he concluded was terminal illness.

"Mone*... how are you? I was just dreaming of Daddy... you know when we went to Mysore Zoo? You were a small boy. You saw the elephants for the first time... the lion was so thin in the cage..."

*poor thing (Malayalam)
**son (Malayalam)

"Yes, Mummy, I remember. That was a fun trip."

"The doctors are saying that I have cancer, koche, but don't worry. I am not frightened."

"Mummy," he had tears in his eyes. "I am here for you."

"Georgie, take me from here. I don't like being in a hospital. Also, I don't want to cause trouble for anyone. Get me a small apartment and I can live there alone..."

"Mummy, you can't live on your own now... I will take care of you, I promise."

She drifted off to sleep with a smile on her face. He sat down on the chair next to her bed.

"Aunty, I'll stay here tonight," he told Molly. "You go home. Uncle Sam must be lonely. He told me you have been staying here every night."

"Yes, fortunately, my nursing duty was on this floor as well, so I have been able to keep my eye on her during my shift. Most of the nurses are Malayalees and my friends, so we are taking good care of her. Don't worry, Georgie, I know how busy you are. All the young people here know you from TV. So many of the staff have asked me to get your autograph. I told them you are my nephew. You don't mind?"

"No, Aunty, of course not. You are one of my favorite aunts as well." He hugged and kissed her. "I won't forget what you have done for Mummy all these years."

"She's my younger sister. It is my duty and privilege."

George sat next to his mother's bed on the armchair the whole night. He drifted in and out of sleep waking up to the activity in the hospital and the room: announcements on the intercoms outside... nurses and doctors coming into the room and taking fluids and checking vital signs... medications being administered to his mother... emergencies taking place in the hallways...

The TV in the room was on with the sound turned off. "*The Soviet Union is slowly dissolving... Gorbachev's resignation imminent,*" said the chyron at the bottom of the screen. George watched with interest. It was unbelievable that the Iron Curtain was being demolished almost overnight.

"*Nothing is permanent... nothing is absolute,*" he thought to himself.

In a span of less than ten years, his life had gone from a happy childhood, to the responsibility of working, to the sadness of his father's death, to the uncertainty of emigration, to scraping by as a recent immigrant in obscurity, to wealth and fame as a rock star, to tragedy again with his mother's illness. He had no idea what tomorrow would bring. He went outside for a walk and a cigarette. The receptionist downstairs recognized him and asked for his autograph as he was coming back inside.

In the morning, he met with his mother's doctors. They didn't have any good news for him. She had Stage IV pancreatic cancer. It had spread to her other organs.

"I'm sorry, Mr. John. If we had caught it early, we may have been able to do something," said Dr. Richardson, the cancer specialist. "Apparently your mother did not like visiting doctors or hospitals. I am very sorry, there's not much we can do now."

"We can try to make her comfortable and treat her for the smaller issues, so she has a decent quality of life for some months at least," said Dr. Silver, her primary care physician. "She is also quite insistent that she doesn't want surgery or any other invasive treatment."

After speaking to all the doctors individually and pressuring them to give him a definitive answer, George realized that his mother probably had no more than six months to a year left to live. He had prepared himself for the worst over the past few days but it was still more than he could handle.

He sat alone in the hospital cafeteria with a cup of coffee. He tried to imagine life without his mother. He couldn't. It was too painful. All the memories of her over the years came rushing out: he could see her sitting with him doing his homework; waiting for him in school after his sports practice; putting a towel with ice on his forehead when he had a fever; teaching him to dance the waltz; watching him proudly from the audience as he sang and played guitar in public for the first time.

He went back to the room. His mother was still asleep. He kissed her on her forehead and sat down on the armchair next to the bed. For the next few hours he sat there thinking. Finally he got up and walked outside to the parking lot for a cigarette. He had decided what to do.

■

Two weeks later, George went back to Canada to complete his tour. But by then, he had already set his plan in motion.

He rented a fully furnished, four-bedroom house in Scarborough. It had a backyard view of the Hudson River. He got his mother discharged from the hospital and took her there. He contacted an employment agency in Tarrytown and hired a full-time health aide, a housekeeper and a handyman. He asked the doctors to tell him what equipment he needed and got Carlos, the handyman, to purchase it and bring it to the house. The house was relatively close to where his aunt lived and only minutes away from Phelps Memorial Hospital where Dr. Silver, his mother's primary physician, worked as a staff doctor.

He spent five days, including Christmas Day, with his mother in their new home before he left on tour again. Sheila had started receiving various medications, including painkillers, so she had become more active again. She was able to walk around, eat a little, watch television or sit in the backyard and enjoy the view. On impulse, George purchased a real tree on Christmas Eve from a roadside seller on Route 9 and brought it home in his Miata with the top down. Then he, Uncle Sam, Molly Aunty, Carlos and Naomi, the housekeeper, decorated it with lights and ornaments while his mother sat on the sofa watching happily.

They had a mixture of Indian and Western food for dinner and watched the lights of the Tappan Zee Bridge from the backyard. It was a lovely evening. His mother was in good spirits and for a few hours George forgot that she was even sick. She seemed so full of energy and life. Uncle Sam and Molly Aunty stayed the night in the spare bedroom.

The next morning, his aunt made appam and stew for breakfast and they ate outside in the backyard. It was unseasonably warm for the time of year, and they all sat outside for many hours enjoying the winter sunshine next to the patio heater. His mother, bundled up in a blanket on a comfortable armchair, talked to everyone while they all fussed over her. Later that afternoon, his uncle and aunt went back home.

When he had a few minutes to spare, he called Swami in India and told him all the news. His friend was shocked and upset about it. He had already heard the information from his father-in-law. George couldn't believe sometimes that Swami was now related to him by marriage.

"Why don't you get Aunty and come here for a while?" asked Swami. "We have very good doctors and hospitals here now. Anything you can get there is also available here."

"I will ask, but she may not want to come. She told me she doesn't want to be a burden on anyone. That's why I got this house and some hired help to take care of her. This way there is no obligation to anyone. She wants it that way."

"Any news of Venu?" asked Swami.

"I tried calling him, but I think his number has changed. We spoke a few months ago. He told me he was taking up a post in Montreal."

"I'll call his parents and get his phone number," said Swami. "You take care, George. We are all very proud of your success. We watched you on TV here once. The kids were so excited. Here's Annie. She wants to speak to Aunty."

George took the phone to his mother. She spoke to Annie for almost an hour. She was very fond of her niece. When Annie was young she spent every evening after school at the Chandys' residence. She had been at Bishop Cotton Girls' School until the seventh standard before going to Ooty as a boarding student. Sundar, the Chandys' driver, would usually pick up both George and Annie from school and bring them home. The two would sit side by side on the big dining table and have tea together — and later dinner. Sometimes DIG Varghese would pick up Annie only after nine o'clock at night if his wife hadn't returned from the hospital where she worked as an administrator. Even after Annie went away to boarding school, she remained very close to her Sheila Aunty.

George had a chance to talk to his mother alone later that night. They were alone. George had given Naomi and Carlos the night off. The nurse's aide that he had hired, an Indian woman named Alka, was starting work only the next day.

"Mummy, are you afraid?" he asked. "I am very scared." They were sitting in the spacious living room. It had big bay windows that faced the backyard and the Hudson River.

"No, koche, I am not scared of being sick or dying. We all have to die sometime."

"I wish I had rented a small place near here instead of in

Brooklyn so you could have lived with me all these years. I never thought you would get sick, Mummy," he said.

"No, Georgie, you have always been a very good son. You struggled so much since you came here, but you still visited me at least once or twice every week. God knows you are a good boy. That's why He has been so generous to you. He gave you so much talent and now money and success. Always be a good boy, Georgie... don't go astray. Turn to God once in a while. It is only through His grace that you have so much."

"Mummy, I never cared much for just money or success. If there is a God, I would be angry with him for taking Daddy away and for making you sick."

"Georgie, don't ever say that and do not question God's plans. He has his own reasons, koche. You will see."

"Until Daddy died, I used to feel like I was so lucky," said George. "I suppose I have to be thankful... I had such a happy life."

"Yes, I have had a wonderful life as well, when your father was alive. He was the handsomest, kindest and most gentle man I have ever met. You have taken after him. I am sure he is waiting for me in heaven. You know, we had a love marriage. I was working for Air India. He had just graduated from the IIT. One day, he came to the office to inquire about the price of an airline ticket to the U.S.A. He had applied for graduate studies. He didn't have admission or money or anything, but he was so confident. I fell in love with him right away. Six months later, we were married. One year after that, we came to New York. He had a full scholarship."

George felt a lump in his throat when he thought of his father and his sick mother. He went and sat next to his mother and held her tightly. They sat silently watching a repeat of It's A Wonderful Life on TV.

Early next morning, Alka, the nurse's aide, showed up along with Carlos and Naomi. She was a thin, no-nonsense, Indian woman in her fifties with a noticeable British accent. She looked very capable. She had lived in England for over twenty years before divorcing her errant husband and emigrating to the U.S.

"Don't worry, sir, the agency has explained your situation. I will take good care of her." Her face softened when she smiled and looked at Sheila. "We'll get along well, Mum."

His uncle and aunt had told him they would keep an eye on

things until he got back. In fact, Molly Aunty had decided that she would be sleeping in the house on most days.

George left that evening, heavy in heart, but knowing his mother was being cared for. He returned to his tour that was still in its Canadian leg. He took a flight from JFK to Toronto.

He was surprised to see Derek waiting for him with the limo at the airport. "Sol was sending the limo, so I decided to come," said the drummer. "Thought you could use a friendly face at the airport."

George hugged him. Derek's simple gesture meant more that anything anyone could have done for him that night. They stopped at a small steakhouse on the way and had dinner and shared a bottle of wine together. The next day the tour started again.

■

George's contract for touring to promote the album lasted three more months. It took him all over the U.S. and Canada: to big cities, small towns and college campuses. Every time he got more than a couple of days to himself, he would fly back to New York. He also made it a point to call his mother every night on the telephone, no matter where he was. Considering her dire diagnosis, she was still doing quite well. Because of her medication, she was eating a little more and had put on a bit of weight. The painkillers also helped her live a relatively normal life. She went out almost every day with her sister, accompanied by Naomi or Alka. Molly stayed most nights with her. Sometimes, Uncle Sam would join them as well and they would all sit in the backyard talking and reminiscing about life. They were good days, in spite of an ever-present threat of the deterioration in her condition at any time.

As soon as he had fulfilled his obligation to the record company, George decided to quit. He was tired of his role as Handsome George. The music they played did not inspire him. He wanted to play only the kind of music he liked, whether it was popular or not. Sol was very upset when George told him that he was quitting touring as soon as his contract with Starlight was up.

"George, you can't just walk away in the middle of a successful career. You know how many musicians would kill to be in your shoes? Starlight is willing to spend more on marketing if you extend your promotional tour for another year. The album is still flying off the shelves. You can't quit now. I have too much invested in you. It's in our contract!"

"Sol, our contract was for you to manage me, I'm not firing you. However, I'm not going to do the Handsome George act anymore. I'm also taking a break from everything to be with my mom. Maybe, after a few months, we can do something else, but not now."

"George, I may have to sue you for breach of contract," said Sol.

"You do that if you want, Sol. I have made more money for you in the past two years than you could have imagined. Don't spoil what we have, okay?"

George met with the band again. They were disappointed and most of them were upset. They liked the steady income they were making from touring and the lavish lifestyle they had become used to on tour. Only Derek understood George's situation.

"You go on and do what you have to do George," he said. "Anytime you need a drummer, or a buddy to have dinner and share a bottle of wine with, call me."

George returned to New York. He decided to keep his apartment in Manhattan but he moved most of his clothes and personal items to his house in Scarborough. His mother was overjoyed to have him back.

There were news stories about his departure from the band in several magazines as well as on entertainment and music television. It was reported that he had been fired for drinking too much. Some articles in the tabloids said he had a drug problem and was in rehab. A few weeks later, he read that Sol had hired another singer to replace him and continue touring with the band. George smiled. He was happy to move on.

However, a month after that, he was notified that Sol Levin was suing him for breach of contract. Apparently the public had not warmed to the new singer and the tour was losing money. Sol had decided to blame it all on George. He wanted him to come back and continue the tour.

George called Geoff Baker, his lawyer.

"Does he have a case?" he asked.

"I don't think so," said Geoff. "I think he's just trying to rattle your cage so you will go back."

"Well I'm not going to. Try to get me as much time as possible if we have to go to court," said George.

■

It was spring now. George spent almost all his time with his mother. He bought a Range Rover and they would go on long drives by themselves or with his uncle and aunt whenever she was feeling up to it. Other times they stayed at home talking and looking at old photographs.

Carlos, Naomi and Alka had all turned out to be excellent choices. When George had to go out for a short while, he knew his mother was in good hands. Every night, after his mother had gone to bed, George would go to the basement with his guitar and write songs.

They came to him as soon as he picked up his guitar. He let some of them go if he thought they weren't good enough. Some he wrote down. Others, he recorded on his cassette player. His songs were different now: sadder... more nostalgic... and even existential. He wrote one that he called "*Pages From My Book Of Memories,*" as he was reminiscing about his early life at home with his mother and father in Bangalore... He played a progression in E-Minor... Em-D-C-D-Em... and C-D-G-Bm7 for the chorus. The words came easily because they were real and described his past:

Splashes of color on a painting in the hall
I see my reflection on a mirror on the wall
Somewhere in the distance, I can hear my mother call
I'm ten years old and I think I know it all

If I close my eyes I can almost see it now
Those pages from my book of memories
So I close my eyes and I turn another page
Of my book of memories

He moved forward in time to the days after his ICSE exam and spending the days with Swami and Venu:

I'm seventeen years old and hanging with my friends
We try to meet some girls, but you know how that ends
Laugh about it later when our broken hearts have mend
And share cigarettes until there's no more left to lend

If I close my eyes, I can almost see it now
Those pages from my book of memories
So I close my eyes and I turn another page
Of my book of memories

George though of Jennifer, the first girl he had kissed and made love to and the times they had together. Was she still in Dubai? He thought of Kal and his first job. He thought about Sandhya, the beautiful young divorcee from London and riding through Bangalore with her on the back of his Jawa motorcycle. He remembered that there had been a total solar eclipse in the City one day, and the two of them had sat in the park next to Ulsoor Lake holding hands and watching the event slowly unfold. He wondered where she was now.

I'm working for a living and I'm twenty-one
Have a girl, and back then, I thought she was the one
Ride my motorcycle in the rain just for fun
Look at an eclipse with my eyes to the sun

If I close my eyes I can almost see it now
Those pages from my book of memories
So I close my eyes and I turn another page
Of my book of memories

When he lived in an apartment in Brooklyn or in New York City, George had been unable to bring any of his gear home because of space issues, and also due to the fact that he couldn't play loudly. So he usually kept his guitars, amps, speakers and microphones in storage. One of the things he liked about the house in Scarborough was the fact that it had a small sound proofed room in the basement. Whoever had built it had obviously enjoyed listening to music loud or was a musician who liked playing electric instruments at home.

George moved some of his music gear to the house: his American Strat, a Fender Jazz Bass, his Marshall amp, some speakers and microphones. He got Carlos to strum his Strat loudly with the volume turned up while he went upstairs to see if it could be heard. He was pleased to know the soundproofing worked perfectly.

One night, he plugged in his Strat and came up with a catchy riff on his guitar. He was excited and aware that creating a memorable guitar or keyboard hook wasn't easy. Most bands, including The

Beatles and The Stones, only had few at most – *Satisfaction, Smoke on the Water, Sweet Home Alabama, Pretty Woman, Day Tripper, Johnny B. Goode, Sunshine Of Your Love, Light My Fire*, and *Beethoven's Fifth*. It was the Holy Grail for musicians... seemingly easy once you had it... but it was very hard to create an original musical hook. George's riff revolved around the Am chord, and he built the rest of his song from it. The lyrics reflected his recent foray into his past — looking at photographs, discussing long forgotten events with his mother and just reminiscing on his own. He called his song, "*Can't Go Back:*"

It feels good to remember those good old days
When I was young and didn't care at all
For those grown up ways
And everyone I ever loved was alive and in no pain
Now looking through these old photographs
It all comes back again
You can climb a mountain and think of what you lack
Or polish those mementos you keep in a gunnysack

But you can't go back
Can't go back... can't go back
We're moving forward so we can't go back
Can't go back... can't go back
We're moving forward so we can't go back

Time keeps on moving it all goes by so fast
This little boy is aging, since nothing real can last
Up ahead in the distance, there's a newer day
Through the mists of time it's always been that way
You can spit into the wind or take another crack
To make sense of your life or call yourself Jack
But you can't go back

Can't go back... can't go back
We're moving forward so we can't go back
Can't go back... can't go back
We're moving forward so we can't go back

Wonder where I'm going when will I get there
Is this all there really is should I even care
Are there more years behind me than I'll ever see again

Is everything I've ever known part of a larger plan
I'll figure it out someday and follow that beaten path
To the place where everyone goes it's a matter of fact
That you can't go back

Can't go back... can't go back
We're moving forward so we can't go back

Sheila Chandy lived for nine months more. It was much longer than her doctors had expected, and most of it was relatively free from excessive suffering. The end came quickly. Once she had taken a turn for the worse, nothing could be done. She never complained. Dr. Silver visited her at home almost every day in her last two weeks. He adjusted the pain medication so she was comfortable and as alert as possible. Alka took care of all her other needs. George sat by her side faithfully after she became bed-ridden. He read her favorite Agatha Christie novels aloud to her or played softly on his guitar. She died peacefully one afternoon with George, Molly, Sam and Alka around her. George and Molly were each holding one of her hands. They didn't know the exact moment when she died, but she had a small smile on her face when she did, as if she had seen what was on the other side and was happy about it.

George had prepared himself for this moment, so he had already planned what to do. He contacted a funeral home in Sleepy Hollow to make the arrangements for taking the body back to India. The next day, he boarded a plane for Bangalore with his uncle and aunt. He had considered staying in India for a few months, but the day he was leaving Geoff, his lawyer, called to say that he had a court date in ten days and that it would be important for him to be there.

The funeral was held at St. Mark's Cathedral. The burial was at Hosur Cemetery. When he had arranged for Mohan's grave at the cemetery, DIG Varghese had also bought the plot right next to it. It was cordoned off from the rest of the graves neatly with little raised bricks. Sheila was buried there next to her beloved husband.

George spent a week in Bangalore. He stayed with Swami, Annie and their children. It was a bittersweet time. He visited *Bangalore Baloney* and was surprised to see how much it had grown. They now occupied the fourth floor as well. It had become a very popular and well-respected publication in the City.

George loved being able to talk to Swami every day during his time in Bangalore and being able to spend time with Nikhil and Anindita. They were ten years old now and very smart for their age.

"Uncle George, are you a rock star?" asked Ani.

"Yes, I suppose so," he said.

"Then your head must be a rock," she said laughing.

"Uncle George, knock-knock."

"Who's there?"

"Ani."

"Ani who?"

"Ani one who knocks!" She laughed again. "Ani is me... you get it?"

George laughed too. It was great being in the world of children again. He thought back on the years when Swami, Venu and he were children.

"Hey kids, do you know what your daddy and used to like doing when we were just a little older than you?"

"Tell us, Uncle George," said Nikhil.

"G, be careful what you tell them," said Annie. "They will want to do the same thing."

"Don't worry Annie, it's all good, nothing bad," said Swami.

"Most Saturday afternoons, Uncle Venu, your daddy, and I would ride our bicycles from Ulsoor to Bangalore Dairy," said George. We used to sit outside the milk booth and drink a bottle of cold rose milk. Sometimes we had two or three if we had money, it was so tasty. After that we'd be too full and tired to cycle back but we did."

"Oooo, can we go?" asked Ani.

"Not on your cycle," said Annie. "It's not like before when Uncle George and Daddy were children. Now it's so crowded, full of cars and trucks. I will take you in the car, okay?"

So they all went together and had cold rose milk straight from the bottle at Bangalore Dairy. It still tasted wonderful. Swami put his hand around George's shoulder and hugged him.

"Brings back memories, bugger," he said.

George nodded. "Yes, they were the best days of our lives, but we never knew it then."

Chapter 25

In A New York Minute

G eorge returned to New York in time for his appearance in
court. He met Geoff outside the Court building on Pearl
Street in downtown Manhattan.

"We're just meeting with Levin's lawyer and the judge today,"
said Geoff. "I still think he's bluffing and wants to work it out."

The judge met all of them in his quarters. Sol looked straight
ahead of him and avoided meeting George's eyes.

"Have you gentlemen discussed this matter amongst yourselves
to see if you can reach a solution to this without taking it to court?"
asked the judge.

He looked at the file. "It says here, Mr. Levin that you are suing
Mr. John for breach of contract for refusing to tour and promote
the album, *Someone Like You* by Handsome George. You say that
you will lose a lot of money because your client refuses to tour. You
will agree to drop the lawsuit if he agrees to continue touring for
six more months. Is this correct?"

"Yes, your Honor," said Sol's lawyer.

"Your Honor," said Geoff. "My client has fulfilled all his
obligations to the record company and to Mr. Levin. There is
nothing in the contract that stipulates that he has to continue
touring indefinitely as Handsome George just because it will
generate money for Mr. Levin."

"Would both parties like to discuss this again before we proceed
with a court case?" asked the judge.

Sol nodded to his lawyer. George nodded too.

"Your Honor, my client would like to speak to Mr. John," said
the lawyer. "We'll see if we can come to some understanding."

"Okay," said the judge. "I am postponing this case by two weeks so you can try to resolve it amongst yourselves."

They met the next day at Geoff's office. Sol's lawyer, Howard Wineberg, got to the point right away.

"Mr. Levin has decided to drop his lawsuit against Mr. John," he said. "We can end this now."

"George, I'm sorry about your mother," said Sol. "I didn't know she had passed away. Let bygones be bygones. I was thinking about it last night. You're a great artist and I'm a great agent. We have so much more to do together. When you are ready for your next project, let's talk." He held out his hand.

George was a little surprised but he took Sol's hand. Now that he had left life on the road behind for several months, he could also appreciate everything Sol had done. He had been true to his word about making Handsome George & The Ugly Ducklings a successful band. George had become more famous and wealthy that he had ever imagined in a span of just two years.

"Don't worry about it, Sol," he said. "I never got the chance to tell you this, but thanks for everything. However, the fact remains that I'm not the Handsome George character with the padded jackets and the make-up that you created. In fact, I hate that guy... I'd just like to be plain George John, who likes to write and perform the music that comes from the heart."

"I am sorry, I never realized how much you disliked it," said Sol. "I guess that's the difference between a true artist and someone who just wants to be rich and famous. Most bands today don't care what they do as long as they make money. That's the world I know. I'm sorry, George. You're a good guy. I always thought so."

"Thanks, Sol," said George. "You're still my agent, so don't sue me over that, okay?" he laughed. "I still want to make music, that's all I ever wanted to do."

"Then let's do it together," said Sol. "Let me know when you are ready."

"See, that wasn't so hard," said Geoff Baker. "Let's all have lunch together and celebrate. Sol is buying. Since there is no case, let me at least win lunch for my client!"

■

George had continued living at the house in Scarborough after he returned from India. It was a nice town, and the people in the surrounding area had got to know him slowly. Many of the residents knew who he was but they generally left him alone. They nodded to him in stores or restaurants but respected his privacy as well. George had noticed several other celebrities in the towns and villages of Westchester County who, like him, appeared to be living normal lives in the beautiful Hudson Valley region.

George had retained the services of Carlos, as a general handyman, chauffer and helper around the house, as well as that of Alka, the nurse's aide who turned out to be an excellent cook and housekeeper as well. Naomi, the woman he had hired originally as the housekeeper, had decided to move to South Carolina with her husband. Alka had asked for her job. She had gotten used to working for George and didn't want to go back to being a nurse's aide. She also knew he needed someone to take care of him.

George still had his apartment in New York City. He sometimes spent a few days there if he had something to do around Manhattan. However after a short while, he longed for Alka's home cooking and came back to Scarborough just so he could have her homemade chapattis and chicken curry.

He missed his mother terribly as well. Until the last few weeks of her life, when she had become bed-ridden, George had enjoyed the months he had spent with her in the house. He was grateful that he had got the chance to become close to her again and show her how much he loved her before she died.

He had abstained from women in the months that his mother was sick. However, since he came back from the funeral in India, he began to get that familiar longing again for some female company. One day when he was shopping at a supermarket in Tarrytown, he ran into Maria Lopez, a backup singer who had toured with the band for a handful of shows in the New York region. He had got to know her a little then. She was dark haired, of medium height and very pretty. She had a lithe dancer's body with great legs and a beautiful smile.

From what he remembered of her, she had some issues with her husband, who was a veteran of Operation Desert Storm. He had been an infantryman at the Battle of Khafji, where there had been brutal fighting. He had returned from the war with an honorable discharge and a mixture of illnesses that was later termed collectively as the Gulf War Syndrome: post-traumatic stress disorder, chronic fatigue and cognitive dissonance. Doctors and psychologists concluded that it was caused by a mixture of being exposed to depleted uranium, Sarin gas, burning oil wells, army vaccinations, combat stress and the general anxiety of living each day with the fear of death. Maria told once George that her husband had always been jealous about her and other men — even before he had been deployed. When he returned, he had become paranoid. He had once followed her to Albany, where they were doing a show to see if she was unfaithful. It was one of the reasons why she had quit her job as a singer and returned home.

It had been over a year since George had seen her.

"Maria, so nice to see you," he said hugging her. She looked very good. She was wearing tight jeans, a white blouse and knee-high boots.

"George, Handsome George! I didn't know you lived around here."

"Just George now," he said. "I have an apartment in the City, but I got a house in Scarborough last year. Where do you live?"

"Scarborough! You live with the rich people. I live here in Tarrytown, in an apartment complex close to here."

"How's everything? Last I knew, you were having some problems," said George.

"Yes, with my husband. We're separated, soon to be divorced. He was getting to be too much. I have a restraining order against him, too. Hey, I'd like to start singing again. George, are you going to be on tour soon? Tell Sol that I'd like to be one of the backup singers?"

"I don't know," said George. "I'm just laying low for the moment, writing songs and getting my breath back. It's been a crazy year and a half."

"Yeah, I know what you mean," said Maria. "Hey, you married or seeing someone?" She looked at him directly.

"No, I'm still single and not seeing anyone right now," he said.

"Then maybe we should hang out together, seeing we are almost neighbors and everything..."

"Yeah, sure," said George. He could feel Mr. Johnson perk up with interest.

"Wanna meet tonight for dinner?" asked Maria. "There's a nice

Japanese place right here in town."

"Okay," he said.

George met her that evening. They had a bottle of wine and sushi for dinner and talked about common acquaintances from the world of music. She was currently working as a fitness instructor at a spa in town. After dinner, he walked with her to her apartment complex on Washington Street. She invited him in. As soon as they were inside, she grabbed him and kissed him hungrily.

"I've always wanted to do that," she said. "You are a very handsome man, Handsome George."

"Just George," he said as he picked her up and carried her to the bed.

They sent the next few months together whenever she was free. They liked each other, but it was mainly about the sex. They both needed it and enjoyed the time they spent together in bed. They usually went to Maria's apartment. He still enjoyed going back home to his own bed and sleeping alone. He took her a few times to his apartment in Manhattan, but never to the house in Scarborough. Alka and Carlos were usually in his house during the day, and he didn't want any awkwardness. Alka came in every morning at eight o'clock from her home in Yorktown Heights whenever he was home, and Carlos lived nearby in Ossining. They both left at around six in the evening.

One day he was lying alone in bed in Scarborough around mid-morning, after a late night out with Maria, when the phone rang. He picked it up and was surprised to hear a familiar voice.

"Venu!" he said excitedly. "Where are you, bugger? Swami and I have been trying to reach you for months."

"What can I say, George, I'm so sorry. It's all been studies and work for several years," said Venu. "I was even in England for six months completing a course. I am now a cardiologist at McGill University Hospital in Montreal. It's what I've always wanted."

He had developed an accent now that was a mixture of Indian and Canadian. He sounded very confident and sure of himself.

"That's great," said George. "I am really happy for you, Venu. You've come a long way."

"Thanks, George I heard about Aunty. I am so sorry. I tried calling you at your New York City apartment as well as this number as soon as I heard the news from my parents, but no one picked up. I just want to say how sad I was to hear of her passing. She was always so nice to me all those years, when we practically lived in your house. Both your parents, George… I can't believe they're gone. They were the best."

"Thanks Venu… sometimes I can't believe it myself. But I tell myself that I was lucky to have them for so many years."

"George, I want to apologize for not staying in touch. We're not so far from each other now but I have really been so busy working and doing my higher studies that I have barely had time even for my own family. Poor Shantha, she's been raising Priyanka almost entirely on her own. I've been to India only a couple of times since we came here. My parents come and visit every year."

"How are Uncle and Aunty?" asked George.

"They're doing well. My father still runs the medical store. My mother always asks about you. She is very fond of you, George!"

"Your mother is a remarkable woman Venu — most mothers are," said George. "Please convey my regards to her."

"I will," said Venu.

"George, I almost forgot why I was calling… I'm coming to New York for a medical conference next week. I thought we could spend some time together. I have about a week. Shantha and Priyanka are in India for a relative's wedding, so I am here alone. My conference is next Monday and Tuesday at the Hilton in Port Chester, New York. After that I am free. I can stay until Sunday. Are you free during that time? If you are doing something else, it's okay. Don't change any plans. We can meet some other time."

"No, I'm free, Venu. I'd love to meet you. Your hotel is not too far from where I live, actually. You can stay with me, I have a big house; it's just me."

"Same old George… still going solo but enjoying the company of very beautiful women, I bet! We hear about you on TV and in the papers. You are a big star now, George. People don't believe me when I tell them we are good friends and grew up together. Although, no one who knew you when you were young could be surprised by your success as a musician and singer. You always had so much talent even as a child. How is the music business?"

"Well, I've been taking a break since my mother got sick. I've been writing songs but I'd like to get rid of the Handsome George persona and just be George John."

"Not George Chandy?"

"No I prefer George John. There's no ethnic baggage attached to it. People here, especially in show business, change their name all the time. Bob Dylan is actually Robert Zimmerman."

"Yes, you are right. I am still Dr. K. Venugopal, although now that I'm a surgeon, when I'm in England they call me Mister… surgeons are not called Doctor there."

"Yes I've heard of that," said George, chuckling.

They spoke for a while longer. George was very excited to hear that Venu was coming the next week. He gave Alka instructions to prepare the spare bedroom and stock up on extra food. When he was by himself, his needs were few, although Alka always had delicious food waiting for him. If it was after six, she left dinner on the table in thermal containers, so it was still hot when he came home.

George was grateful to Alka for looking after his mother and then being there for him in the weeks and months after her passing. She was a calming presence in his life, almost like a mother figure now that his real mother was gone. She was in her late-fifties now, but she was very energetic. The house was spotless and there was always the aroma of some delicious food. In addition to Indian food, she also cooked Italian, Greek, and French cuisine. She also served as his secretary, answering the telephone in her distinctive blend of clipped British and North Indian accents.

The next week, George went to pick up Venu from the Hilton in Port Chester. Venu looked fit and healthy in a white Polo t-shirt, khakis and a dark blue blazer. He had a French beard now, and he looked very distinguished.

"You're looking very good, bugger," said George. "Just like I would imagine a successful doctor would look like."

"Yes, it's been a lot of hard work, but life's been good to me. You look the same, George," said Venu. "In your videos on TV you had cut your hair shorter. You looked different, but now you look the same as before — long hair and beard."

"Yes, that was the character I played for a couple of years. Now I'm back to being me."

He put Venu's bag in the back of his Range Rover, and they drove home. He was very happy to be with his friend again. In half an hour they had caught up on each other's lives and were back to being the close friends they were before. It was almost as if the last fifteen years had not happened. They were still the same kids from high school having fun and hanging out.

George called Swami and put him on speakerphone. He couldn't believe Venu and George were together.

"I wish I was there with you chaps," he said. "We could have a nice Scrimshankers reunion."

"Why don't you come here, Swami?" said George. "The paper is running smoothly; your kids are older... bring Annie too. I have a big house. You can stay for as long as you want."

"I suppose I could. I've thought about it, but you were always so busy before. Now that you have stopped touring for a while, I could come for a couple of weeks with Annie. But we'll have to make arrangements for the children, the paper and other things. It will take a few months to organize, but I promise you we will come."

"If you come, I will find the time to come to New York as well when you are here," said Venu. "If you come with Annie, I will also bring Shantha with me."

The next morning, George took Venu to his apartment in Manhattan. They stayed there for a couple of days while they visited the landmarks, museums and even took in a couple of Broadway shows. In retrospect, the persona of Handsome George that he had begun to despise was also literally a blessing in disguise.

Now that his hair was much longer and he had grown a beard, didn't use makeup and dressed in jeans and t-shirts, most people on the street did not recognize him as Handsome George, the pop star. This meant that he could live a relatively normal life that was free of scrutiny from the general public. Occasionally, a fan or two would make the connection and he would pose for pictures or sign a few autographs.

George was always very nice to fans, even though he had never understood the need to venerate any other human being. He had the obligatory rock star posters in his room as a child but he had never looked up to any musician or famous personality in his life. When he had got the chance to meet several of them during his roller coaster ride as a rock star himself, he had not been surprised to find that they were very much like everyone else — with the same pettiness and insecurities as average individuals. He signed autographs and posed for pictures for fans, because he didn't want to be rude or deny someone whatever happiness it bought them, but he always felt embarrassed and uncomfortable doing it.

It was Saturday night, and Venu was leaving back for Montreal the next day. The two friends were sitting together in the backyard and drinking beer. It was December again. George remembered, sadly, that a year earlier he had been sitting right there with his mother.

They had the outdoor heater on so, even though there was a chill in the air, they were very comfortable. The Hudson River flowed along peacefully a short distance away. The sun was going down in the distance. Everything looked so beautiful.

"Hey Venu, remember the time the three of us went to Jog Falls? You rode with me on my motorcycle and Swami came on his father's Vespa."

"Yes, we had to stop several times, because the cable on his scooter's clutch kept breaking. The bugger hadn't learned how to use it gently without jerking it all the time. Fortunately, there were little roadside auto-repair shops everywhere on the way."

"That was a fun trip. We met some pretty Mount Carmel girls there."

"Yes, you went off somewhere with the most beautiful one. We buggers just sat there doing nothing until you came back."

George laughed. "I remember her... Divya. She was a Bengali girl... so young and pretty! I think she called me once when we got back, but I was with Sandhya by then."

"Swami and I were always so jealous about you when it came to girls," said Venu. "But we've done okay now, I guess. Both Annie and Shantha are beautiful and smart."

"Yes, I sometimes envy you buggers now. You have wives who love you, children who are adorable, families, in-laws, predictable lives... you can relax. I am still all alone — maybe it's by choice, but I have never met any woman yet that I have wanted to spend the rest of my life with."

"You have to be ready for it, bugger," said Venu. "I don't think you are ready to settle down. You are not like us, George. You are an artist. You need to be free to observe the world so you can write songs about it. Your pop record is nice, but I have always liked your other songs. Last time, when we met in India some years ago, you made me a tape with your songs, just with guitar and vocals. I've been listening to it since then in my car. I know all the words by heart. There is so much feeling… it's so real. The one you wrote for your dad, 'Elegy'… I cry when I listen to it. You have a rare talent — there are very few like you."

"Thanks, Venu," said George. "That means a lot to me. But you are the one doing an important job and saving lives. How does it feel to operate on people?"

"I have done hundreds of operations over the years. My specialty now is heart surgery. It's delicate but very rewarding because the results can be immediate and life changing for the patient. Still, every now and then you lose a patient, and that can be very traumatic for all the doctors who are involved in the surgery. I take what I do very seriously, George. I eat properly, exercise and get enough rest. I make sure I am physically and mentally prepared for each operation I perform. If something goes wrong, it is not because I made a mistake or that I was negligent, so I don't sit around blaming myself. There are other patients who require my skills, and I can't operate on them if I don't have confidence in what I do."

"You had told me when we are in Bangalore that you were thinking about coming to the U.S. because the money was better," said George.

"Yes, that was my plan," said Venu. "Coming from my background, without money, I also wanted to become very rich. But in the past two years I think I have changed my mind. I have begun to see what I do as a higher calling — remember my answer for the medical college interview that you guys helped me with? I just said it then, but I think I believe it now."

Venu paused and added, "George, I also feel an obligation for the countries that have made me who I am now — that is India and Canada. I'd like to practice in Canada and try to do something in India as well. Maybe set up a free clinic for heart patients or something in Bangalore in a few years."

"Hey, that's really cool, Venu," said George. "I am so happy for you…"

They were interrupted by the sound of the telephone. George picked it up.

"George?" It was Maria. She sounded frightened. "George, can you come to my apartment?"

"Why, what's wrong? Is everything okay? My friend Venu is here. It's his last night. He's going back tomorrow. Can I see you after a couple of days, Maria?"

"George, I am frightened… please come now," she was pleading.

"Okay, I'll come for a short while but I have to come back right away."

"Thank you George… I'm sorry," she said sobbing and hung up the phone.

"Venu, I got to go out for a short while to the next town. You relax and make yourself at home. Watch TV or just sit here and have a beer. I'll be back soon."

"No, I'll come with you. I can just stay in the car."

"It's this girl I'm seeing. Her name is Maria… she has some family issues. It's very close. We can come back and have dinner. I don't normally like driving after a few drinks, but we'll drive slowly. The cops around here are quite vigilant, especially on Saturday night!"

George took the two-seater Miata. It wasn't expected to snow that night but it was cold, so he had the top up. They got to Maria's apartment complex on North Washington Street in a matter of minutes. George pulled into a parking spot that was reserved for residents on the street right outside the complex.

"She's in a garden apartment on the ground floor. It's 11G — see that window there? Just in case the person this spot belongs to shows up. I'll be back in a few minutes."

"Okay, I'll be waiting here," said Venu. "Don't start getting romantic inside and make me sit here for two hours — not even a quickie, okay, George?"

"Okay, bugger, I promise," said George, laughing as he rushed away.

He ran to Maria's apartment and knocked on the door. There was no reply from inside. It was slightly ajar, so he pushed it open and went inside.

As soon as he had entered, he felt alarm bells go off inside his head. He heard Maria's muffled scream and found himself being pushed forward into the room. He fell down on the floor and turned around on his back. He could see a man holding Maria from behind. He had the palm of his left hand around her mouth.

He had a gun pointed at her right temple. It was a small gun. It looked almost like a toy, dwarfed by his hand.

"What… w-who are you?" asked George as he stood up.

"So you're the guy who has been fucking my woman, right?" snarled the man. He was wearing army camouflage pants and a black t-shirt. He was very muscular with close-cropped hair. His eyes were flat and almost lifeless but his face was angry.

"I've been watching and following Maria for the last few weeks. I know what you've both been doing." He took his hand off Maria's mouth.

"Tell him, bitch… tell him who I am!"

"Gerry, please, don't hurt us… he's just a friend. He doesn't know anything."

"Shut up, you slut. I am her husband, motherfucker… Do you know what that means?"

"Please, don't do anything stupid. We can work this out," said George desperately. "Maria told me you were in Iraq. You're back home now. There's no need for guns."

He was very scared. He had never been in a situation like this before. Maybe the closest he had got to it was when he accompanied Ricardo to East New York. He didn't know what to do.

"Let me ask you, motherfucker… what do you like best about this bitch?" He moved the gun up and down Maria's body. "Is it her tits… or her ass… or the fact that she opens her legs so easily?"

Then Gerry's concentration wavered a bit. He appeared to be disoriented. George realized that he was probably high on drugs. He had seen the same look in Ricardo's eyes that night a few years before.

"Look, Gerry, let her go. Then we can sit together and talk like men. Maybe have a beer together." He had no idea what he was saying.

"It's too late, motherfucker. This bitch is going to call the cops again and they're going to put me away… no, this ends now." He suddenly turned the gun in George's direction and pulled the trigger.

Everything seemed to happen in slow motion… He saw Gerry point the gun at him and shoot. He could see the bullet coming towards him. He wanted to get out of the way, but couldn't. He felt a sudden, searing pain in the middle of his chest. Then, he was falling backwards. He hit the wall and fell to the floor. He heard Maria scream. In horror, he watched Gerry turn the gun and shoot her through the side of her head. Just before he blacked out, he saw Gerry put the gun to his own temple and pull the trigger.

■

In the car, Venu heard the shot, followed by a woman's scream, then two more shots. It was coming from the direction of the window that George has pointed to as the apartment he was going to. He had the radio on softly tuned to a news station but the sounds of the shots were unmistakable. He got out of the car and ran towards where the sound of the shots had come from. Maybe the shots have nothing to do with George, he told himself, but he kept running. He remembered 11G, the number of the apartment. He saw the door was shut. He tried the knob. It was open. He rushed inside. He knew he was being foolish. He should wait for the police. But it was his friend inside.

It was a small apartment and he saw the three bodies right away. He didn't know if there was anyone else in the bedroom. George was at one end of the living room on his back. His chest was covered in blood but he was moving a little. A man and woman lay on the other side of the room. They both had head wounds and were not moving. Venu ran to his friend.

"George, I am here. Don't move. I'm going to call an ambulance."

"Venu, he shot me, then he shot her in the head. Maria... check on her... I saw it." He had tears in his eyes. "He shot her, Venu."

"Let me look at you first, George," said Venu.

Fortunately, during his four years at Toronto General Hospital, Venu had seen his share of patients with bullet wounds that had come to the emergency room while he was on call. He knew the protocol and what had to be done right away.

He looked across the room at the gun. It was a small caliber handgun, probably a .22. That was good. The damage would be less than if it had been a heavier caliber. He unbuttoned George's shirt and looked at his bare chest — the bullet appeared to have missed his heart. There was blood in George's mouth, so it had probably penetrated a lung. He lifted him up gently and looked at his back. He could see a hole. The bullet had passed through. That was good as well.

He ran to the bathroom and got a towel. He folded it a few times and held it to his friend's chest.

"George, if you can hear me, keep this pressed as tight as you can. I'm going to call for an ambulance."

He used the phone in the kitchen to call 911.

"I'm in 11G in Tarrytown." He had no idea where he was. "Can you trace this call?" he asked the operator. "I don't know the address."

Then he noticed the mail on the kitchen counter. He read the address from one of the envelopes.

"Please send an ambulance. Three people have been shot. One is my friend. He has a bullet wound through his chest. It is a .22 caliber. It has penetrated his lung. I am a doctor, a thoracic surgeon."

He hung up the phone and looked at the man and woman on the floor. He felt for a pulse on both. There was none. He ran to George. He pressed the towel to the wound. George had passed out again.

"George, wake up," he said urgently. He patted him lightly on his cheek. George's eyes fluttered open.

"Venu, I'm cold."

"You're going into shock, George. The ambulance is coming soon but you need to stay awake. It's only for a few minutes more."

The door opened suddenly. There were two uniformed policemen with drawn out guns in their hands. Apparently, someone in the building had called the police after hearing the shots.

"You!! Step away from him and put your hands in the air," said one of the policemen. He was a tall, gray-haired, white man. His partner was a younger, short and stocky Latino.

"Officer, I am a doctor. This is my friend. He's going to die if I don't keep pressure on his wound. The other two are dead, I think."

The policeman kept his gun pointed at Venu while his partner checked the other two bodies.

"They're dead, Stan," he said. "Let me call it in."

"I've already called for an ambulance," said Venu.

"Do you know what happened here?" asked the gray-haired policeman.

"I was waiting in the car. My friend came here because the

woman phoned him and asked him to come over because there was an emergency. He was here for a few minutes and then I heard the shots. So, I came running inside. This is what I found."

"He looks familiar," said the other policeman.

"He's a famous singer. He's Handsome George," said Venu.

"We need to handle this carefully," said the gray-haired policeman to his partner. "If the press gets wind of this, it's going to be a circus here."

The ambulance showed up just then. Venu identified himself as a doctor.

"The bullet appears to have passed through him but it has punctured his lung," he said. "You need to put an endotracheal tube so he can breathe before you take him to the hospital. I don't know if the bullet has gone through both lungs or not," he said. "The other two are both dead. I checked."

"We got it, Chief," said one of the EMT men. He checked the two bodies for signs of life and then examined George.

"Good job of applying pressure on the wound. We've already called it in. They're waiting for us at Phelps. It's only minutes away."

"Officer, can I ride in the ambulance? He's one of my best friends. Here's my driver's license and hospital ID. I am a thoracic surgeon from Montreal."

The gray-haired officer looked at Venu's ID. He thought for a few seconds and then said, "Okay, since you are a doctor… but Jeff, you ride with them," he said to the Hispanic officer.

Then he turned to Venu, "And you, Doctor, we will want to talk to you again tonight, so don't go anywhere, okay? I'm going to hold on to your ID."

In the ambulance they started the IV and were about to put in the ET tube when George regained consciousness for a few moments.

"Venu, call Swami. Tell him what happened… you are my brothers. Maria… I saw Gerry shoot her in the head…"

Venu held his friend's hand and whispered to him soothingly. Jeff, the policeman, wrote what George had just said into a little notebook. The two paramedics worked on their patient as the ambulance sped towards the hospital with sirens blaring.

Chapter 26
Together Again

S waminathan walked away from the immigration counter at JFK airport. He had wanted to come to the U.S. since he was a young boy. He had always dreamt of traveling all over the world but somehow he had never been able to go too far from Bangalore. When he was young, his family didn't have the means. After the newspaper had become a success, he found he couldn't leave because of his commitments to his work and family.

He checked the monitor and looked for the carousel where his luggage would be delivered. It hadn't arrived yet, so he found an empty chair and sat down. It had been a hectic and tiring three days.

Venu had called him at the paper. Swami was surprised because he had spoken to his friends only a few days earlier.

"Swami, bugger, George's been shot. He's in the hospital," said Venu without any preamble.

"What? I don't understand, Venu. What do you mean, shot?"

"I was there. I went with him to the hospital. They are doing surgery on him now. I was outside the building when it happened. Swami, he asked about you in the ambulance. He wanted me to tell you."

"Venu, I don't know what you are saying. George has been shot? Who shot him? Is he going to be okay?"

"I hope so, Swami. He was shot in the chest. The bullet missed his heart, thank God, but it pierced his lungs. I think he will be okay but the first two days are critical."

Swami sat down. The whole room was spinning. He was in

an editorial meeting with Deepak Malhotra and Asha Gupta, his news and entertainment editors. They heard his side of the conversation and were beginning to realize what had happened. Everyone at *Bangalore Baloney*, as well as the paper's readership, knew about George Chandy — Handsome George. In addition to George's direct connection to the paper as a founder, Swami had also written several insightful articles on his friend and his music in *Bangalore Baloney*. He was very proud of his friend's success over the past two years.

"Call Annie, please," said Swami to Asha.

She ran out of his office. Annie's office was on another floor of the same building now. Deepak went to the kitchen and got Swami a glass of water. He had never seen his boss so upset before.

"Venu, I'm coming there. I don't know what the procedure is, but I am coming — you tell George I am coming, okay?"

Annie rushed in. She was breathing heavily from running down four flights of stairs.

"Swami, what happened?"

"It's George. He has been shot. Venu is on the phone."

He handed the telephone to Annie and sat down. She spoke quietly to Venu for several minutes and then hung up. Swami was still in shock but his brain was working furiously.

"Annie, I am going to New York. I have to go."

"Yes, you have to go, Swami," said Annie. "You will need a visa. It's only eleven o'clock in the morning. You can take the night train to Chennai, go to the U.S. Consulate straight from the station and get your visa. I will arrange for your ticket from Chennai to New York today before you leave."

With her usual efficiency Annie went about doing what was needed to get Swami to New York. She called up a travel agent and got a round trip ticket first. She then compiled a list of documents that Swami would need to take with him when he went to the U.S. Consulate for his visa: passport, ownership documents for the newspaper, bank records and property deeds. She even got her father, DIG Varghese, to get a letter from the Governor of the State testifying to Swami's character.

Swami tried to set things in order at *Bangalore Baloney* before he left. He didn't know how long he would be in New York. Annie could easily manage the finances while he was away and he trusted his editors and staff to bring out a good issue every week. He met with the entire staff that afternoon and explained the situation.

"George is my best friend and also one of the founders of this paper. There are going to be many stories coming out about what happened. Because it is so personal, I am going to recuse myself from it. Deepak and Asha, I leave it to your discretion to decide how you want to cover it. I will tell you what I know, or you can speak to Annie but I can't look at this as a reporter, only as a friend."

Swami went home in the evening and spent a few hours with his wife and children. He told Anindita and Nikhil that he was going to New York because Uncle George was hurt.

Nikhil asked, "Is Uncle George going to be alright?"

"Yes, he's going to be fine. Uncle Venu is with him now, and Daddy will be there in two days."

Annie drove him to the Cantonment Station after dinner. She had paid an agent a premium to get him a first class ticket. He was grateful. It had been an exciting and tiring day. He sat in the air-conditioned compartment and smoked for much of the journey. He had a berth, but he was too tense to sleep. He dozed for a few hours in his seat waking up every half an hour or so to the hustle and bustle of vendors and passengers on the platforms as the train stopped in the various towns and villages in Tamil Nadu State on the way to Madras.

The train arrived at its destination a little after six in the morning. Annie's cousin, Alex, was at the station. Swami knew him quite well. He was ten years younger that Annie. He lived with his parents in Nungambakkam and was a student at the Madras Christian College.

"Thanks for coming, Alex," said Swami. "You shouldn't have troubled yourself. I could easily have taken a taxi."

"No trouble at all. After all Annie-chechi and you did for me when I was in Bangalore, this is nothing."

They went to Annie's uncle's house. He was her mother's younger brother and had settled down in Madras, or Chennai as it was now called, with his family for decades. They lived only a short distance from the U.S. Consulate. Swami had a quick bath, changed his clothes and was in line outside the consulate by seven-thirty in the morning. He had to wait for it to open at nine o'clock. He waited in line again inside the building for two more hours.

Finally, a female consul officer interviewed him and asked him several questions about why he was going, as well as proof that he would not overstay his visa. He was surprised because the woman appeared to be familiar with Handsome George, had heard the news of the shooting and even knew many of his songs. Swami presented his bank and ownership documents as well as pictures of George and him together. She seemed particularly impressed with the photos.

He was relieved when she looked through everything and finally said, "Mr. Venkatasubramanian, please come at 4:00 PM and pick up your passport with the tourist visa."

He spent the day with Alex and his parents. He called Annie on the phone in the evening before he left for the airport.

"I miss you already, Annie. This is the first time I am going so far away from you and the children. But you understand, I have to go. George is your cousin as well, but he is like a brother to me. He asked for me, Annie. He needs me now."

"I know Swami. You go and take care of our George. I will manage everything here. Remember I love you... you come back safe home to us, okay?"

"I love you too, Annie, and I love our kids. I am going to miss all of you."

◼

He saw Venu waiting for him in the arrival lounge at JFK. He ran and hugged him. Venu looked tired. The last few days had been very stressful. He was supposed to have left on Sunday, but it was Tuesday, and he was still in New York. Shantha and Priyanka had returned on Monday, but he had been unable to pick them up from the airport in Toronto. Instead, his father-in-law had met them and explained the situation.

Once the police had processed the crime scene, they had concluded that Venu had nothing to do with the shooting and was merely an innocent bystander. The doctors at the hospital had credited him with possibly saving George's life. It turned out that the trajectory of the bullet was such that it had punctured both lungs. The ET tube as well as the steady pressure on the wound had been vital to George's survival.

The press had caught wind of the story, and there had been

reporters and news crews everywhere. In the past two days, a steady stream of news stories — most of them completely untrue — about the handsome rock star, his girlfriend and her jealous husband were on the front pages of every newspaper. A few reporters had found out where George lived and even tried to break into his house to look for photographs or other juicy morsels of details for their stories. A police car had been stationed outside on the street, but intrepid reporters had even tried coming in by boat on the Hudson River to George's backyard.

Venu had decided to stay in the house in spite of the constant barrage of reporters outside. It was very close to Phelps Memorial Hospital, where George was, almost within walking distance. Alka made sure there was enough food always for him. Carlos pulled all the blinds down in the house, but Venu could see the reporters and photographers outside all the time, peeping through hedges, waiting on the street and even camping out on the river in boats with long-range telephoto lenses photographing every movement inside the house.

"Good you see you, bugger," said Venu to Swami.

They walked to the parking lot of the airport. He was driving George's Range Rover. He put Swami's luggage in the back and they started their journey to the house. On the way, he filled Swami in on what had happened and all the latest developments.

"The surgery was successful. They had to repair both his lungs, but the bullet was a small caliber and exited completely which was fortunate. Normally, these small bullets get lodged in the chest cavity and can cause other complications. He was very lucky that it missed his heart."

"Thank God you were there, Venu," said Swami. "I can't imagine what the outcome would have been if he had gone there on his own."

"Yes, I've been thinking about it for the past two days. It is as if my entire life and training somehow prepared me for that moment. I have treated dozens bullet wounds when I was on call at the hospital in Toronto, so I did not panic."

He went on, "Swami, I was so cool and calm the entire time, you won't believe! It was only the next day that it hit me. I was lying in bed yesterday and I started to tremble uncontrollably with an anxiety attack. Thank God I was calm the day it happened.

Sometimes I also think about what would have happened if that guy, Gerry, hadn't killed himself but had waited and shot me as well. What would have happened to my family?"

"You can't think like that, Venu," said Swami. "You were there, and you saved George's life. That's all that matters now." He squeezed his friend's arm. "Did you tell Shantha everything?"

"Yes, I called her last night and spoke to her for over an hour. She's okay. She's been a doctor's wife for many years, so she is used to emergencies but never one where I could have been in danger as well. I have to return soon to my family. The police said I'm free to leave. Now that you are here, I can go without worrying too much. I'm thinking of leaving in a day or two, once I have seen George. They're still not letting anyone visit him yet."

It was rush hour, so it took them over an hour to travel from the airport to the hospital. There were police officers stationed outside George's room. The nurses and officers all knew Venu since he had been around right from the first time George had been brought there.

The doctor was still not allowing any visitors. George was on a ventilator and there was the danger of potential infections at this stage of his recovery. They had performed another surgery on him earlier that day. Molly Aunty was outside the ICU. She smiled wanly when she saw Swami. She had met him in Bangalore two years earlier.

"The doctor is not allowing any visitors for another forty-eight hours. So you boys should go home and get some rest. I am also going to my house. I have many nurse friends here. They will keep an eye on George and phone me if the situation changes. After they remove the ventilator, the doctors will put a chest tube. Only after that they will allow him to receive visitors. So, for at least two days, you will not be allowed inside."

Venu and Swami could see George from the outside. It was very scary to watch the ventilator moving up and down and all the tubes and monitors that were attached to him.

"Come, Swami, let's go home," said Venu. "We can't do anything here."

It was a two-minute drive from Sleepy Hollow, where the hospital was located, to George's house in Scarborough. At any other time, Swami would have been thrilled to be in the hometown of the novelist Washington Irving, but that day it didn't matter at all.

There were a few photographers waiting outside on the street. They took pictures of the car. They had got the numbers of the license plates of all cars registered to George from their moles at the DMV. Some even yelled out questions. Venu didn't stop to talk to them.

"I know you are the press, Swami," he said. "But the reporters here are like parasites."

They went inside the house. Carlos had placed a screen across the entire length of the backyard so that photographers on boats in the water would not be able to see what was going on in the house.

Swami called Annie as soon as he was inside the house. It was in the middle of the night in India, but she was glad to know he had made it safely to New York. He promised to call her again in a couple of days.

Venu decided to leave only after he had seen and talked to George. For the next two days, the two friends stayed in the house and caught up on their lives and discussed the future. George's surgery had been successful, but the long-term prognosis was still uncertain at this point.

"I think he will be okay in a few months, if he can get through the next week without complications," said Venu. "I have seen many cases like this before. He's young and healthy, so he'll be okay. Don't worry, Swami."

"I hope you are right, Venu," said Swami. "I feel much better now that I am here."

That afternoon, he was down in George's basement when he came across an old box full of letters that were addressed to him from George. They were written over a span of two years when George had first arrived in the U.S. It read almost like a diary. Each one was addressed to him, but they had never been mailed. He remembered that George had sent much shorter and more optimistic letters instead.

Reading the letters, Swami could see the struggle that his friend had gone through in his first few years in the U.S: dealing with the death of his father, his difficult quest in finding a job, being all alone in New York, insecurity in his abilities as a singer/songwriter, worrying about his mother, sadness in the fact that his friends no longer had the time for him. He found some lyrics, simply titled "*Morning Light*," that explored what George was feeling then — melancholy, but followed by hope as well:

> *Morning light... wakes me up to another day*
> *Feel its gentle glow wash all my blues away*
> *I'm living through... changing day by day*
> *Made it through the night again*
> *But morning light makes me feel all right*
>
> *When I was young... I thought I could make it on my own*
> *As I'm getting older I find my fears have grown*
> *I'm living through... changing day by day*
> *Made it through the night again*
> *But morning light makes me feel all right*
>
> *As night time comes... I turn and look for a friend*
> *But I was born alone and that's how it'll be in the end*
> *I'm living through... changing day by day*
> *Made it through the night again*
> *But morning light makes me feel all right*
>
> *And I know I will be all right*
> *By morning light*

Swami felt a lump in his throat when he read through the letters and the lyrics.

"*George, why didn't you send it to me? I always had time for you*," he said to himself. But he knew his friend was right. Since he had got married, Annie had become his priority, and after the twins were born, he had lost touch with George on a deeper level. They had still written to each other every few months, but it had always been on the surface, not the way they were before. He put the letters away carefully.

"What's the matter, Swami?" Venu asked from across the room.

"Nothing, just some old letters George had written to me and never mailed. The bugger had a hard time here on his own during the first few years. I'm only finding out about it now."

"Don't be too hard on yourself, Swami. We all had hard times. Some of us get our share of sadness early in our life. Others get it later. Remember how we used to always say that George was the luckiest bugger on Earth? He was, during those days. But then he hit a bad patch in his life. I hope he has seen the last of it. I am convinced that he will be okay. He is still a handsome and talented bugger. As soon as he is better, all the girls will follow him again, and he will write beautiful songs — just watch."

In spite of how he felt, Swami had to smile. Yes, George was still George — a handsome and talented bugger.

The next day, they went to the hospital. Molly Aunty had called to say that the doctors would allow them to visit George in the morning. He was awake but covered in tubes and wires when they went to see him. His eyes brightened when he saw Swami and Venu.

"Swami, you are here? The Scrimshankers are together again," he said weakly.

"Yes, I came as soon as I could. Everyone in Bangalore sends their love to you: Annie, the kids, my parents, your Ebby Uncle and Rema Aunty. We were all so worried."

"I'll be okay, don't worry. Venu, thanks for saving my life. The doctors told me." George had tears in his eyes. "I'm so sorry for putting you through this. It was supposed to be a happy reunion, not all this. I can still see him shooting her in the head every time I close my eyes."

"It will fade with time," said Venu. "George, do not blame yourself. You didn't cause it. You had no idea about her situation."

"You know something, buggers, I didn't even know her at all," said George. "I wish she had told me about how crazy her husband was. He was stalking and following us for over a month!"

"Yes, I've been reading all the salacious details in the *New York Post* for the past two days. I don't know how they can get away with publishing outright lies here. Carlos has been buying all the papers in the supermarket for me," said Swami.

"Yes, I'm sure they are writing all sorts of things about me. Have they got to the part where I am actually an alien?"

The friends laughed knowing in the back of their minds that nothing was too far-fetched for the tabloid reporters. Fortunately, George was single and didn't have any family members they could harass.

"I'm going to leave soon, George," said Venu. "I have to get back to my family and my job at the hospital."

"Yes, you should. Thank you for everything, and I'm sorry

again."

"I'm glad I was there, George, but this is more excitement that I've ever had in my life. I don't know how you handle being a star."

"It's hard sometimes. You are seeing the worst part of being a celebrity. But it will pass. They'll find something else that will overshadow this soon."

George was right. A few days later, a famous Hollywood actor in his sixties had a heart attack and died while in bed with two naked starlets in his penthouse apartment in New York City. The reporters all rushed like vultures to feed on that event instead, and George's story slowly made its way to the back pages. Venu went back to Montreal but promised George and Swami that he would be back in a few weeks.

Swami did not have a license to drive in the U.S., so Carlos was also on duty as the resident chauffer. In the last week he had performed over and above what was expected of him: keeping the press and gawkers at bay, taking care of all the needs of the house, handling security in the house and being always on call in case George needed him.

After a week, George had been moved into a chair from his bed to speed up his healing process. He also began respiratory therapy with deep-breathing exercises to help the lung stay inflated and heal more readily. After another week, the doctors made him walk slowly so he could gain his strength.

George's progress was good. He had always been very strong and in good health. In less than three weeks, the doctors told him he was ready to go home. They said he would recover completely in two to three months.

Swami decided that he would stay with him for a little while. They missed Christmas but George was home in time to celebrate New Year's Eve. His wounds were healing but Swami could see that the psychological trauma of seeing someone shot through the head would take a lot longer to forget.

In January, Annie and the children came to visit for two weeks. It raised George's spirits to have the sound of children in the house. Uncle Sam and Aunt Molly stayed over as well, and they all had a good time for several days. For George and Swami, it was also a time to renew their friendship and catch up what they had missed in each other's lives.

It snowed almost every week in January that year. It made going out difficult, but it was beautiful as well. The children loved playing in the backyard and building snowmen. It was the first time they were seeing snow.

George enjoyed sitting inside the house with Swami and watching Annie and the children through the big bay windows playing outside. The press appeared to have gradually lost interest in George, although occasionally a reporter or photographer would show up outside. Carlos would politely ask them to leave. Other times, some photographer with a telephoto lens would manage to get a shot of George when he was outside and publish it in the tabloids along with any story they could concoct about George, Maria or Gerry, the shooter.

The police came a few times to the house and took statements from George. But since both Gerry and Maria were dead, there was really no case for them to pursue. Gerry's violent past and drug use, as well as his prints on the gun, had made it almost an open and shut case.

Many of George's friends and business acquaintances also dropped in now and then to see him. Sol was one of the first ones to visit George in the hospital. He came several times to the house with flowers and chocolates. Derek was a frequent visitor as well. He always made everyone laugh with his stories of life on the road with the band. Swami enjoyed meeting all the people that were in George's life in New York.

Now that his friend was getting better, he started thinking like a writer and journalist again. He had been keeping a journal since he arrived, but now he started writing longer pieces. He visited Sunnyside, the home of Washington Irving in Tarrytown, which was located only a few miles from where George lived. He had always enjoyed the author's novels, and it was fascinating to see where he had lived and worked. He wandered around the town of Sleepy Hollow, which had a headless horseman as its icon, the Old Dutch Cemetery, where he visited Irvin's grave, and Christ Episcopal Church, were the famous author worshipped and often served as a godfather for many of the local infants.

When Annie and the children returned to Bangalore, he sent along several of his articles about his experiences in the Hudson Valley with her for publication as human-interest pieces in

Bangalore Baloney. Whenever he called the paper, he spoke to his editors about George and his progress, but he abstained from writing anything about the incident or his friend himself.

George had bought a new Apple Macintosh computer recently and had signed up for America Online as his Internet and e-mail provider. Swami was fascinated by the possibilities of the World Wide Web, e-mail and desktop publishing for *Bangalore Baloney.* Instead of taking over a week for him to send a letter or story to his editors, he could do it instantaneously via e-mail. Of course, they would need computers and e-mail in India, as well, to make it possible.

George knew a local printer and publisher who used computers for layout and typesetting. He was still recuperating from his wounds, so Carlos drove Swami there in the Range Rover. He was amazed at the scope of what could be done by desktop publishing on a Macintosh computer.

A software company named Aldus had produced a suite of programs that handled the complete design and layout process: Photoshop was an amazing program for photographs and scans; FreeHand could be used to create illustrations, line art and logos; and PageMaker was a layout program that put it all together along with type. Everything from flyers, brochures, and posters to novels and full-sized newspapers could be created directly on a computer.

"Swami, the only issue now is that pre-press technology has not caught up with computer technology," said Bruce Goldstein, the owner of Rapid Printing. "We can put everything together on this wonderful machine but we can't produce film for printing directly from it yet — certainly not as good as the photo negatives we use now. But it's all going to change as soon as they perfect postscript and scanning technology. I predict that in less than five to ten years, all layout and publishing will be done only on computers."

Swami thanked Bruce. The trip was an eye opener for him. He decided that he would buy a Macintosh when he returned to India and explore the possibilities of this new technology as soon as possible.

George's condition was improving quickly. By March, he was well enough to join Swami for short trips to New York City. Carlos drove them there and waited around — or they stayed the night at George's apartment.

Swami visited Pearl Paints on Canal Street, which had the largest selection of commercial art supplies, including Letraset sheets, Pantone books, rapidographs, fine art brushes and drafting tools. He bought as much as he thought he could carry back with him in his suitcase. He also went to B&H Photo, where he bought a 35mm Pentax K-1000 and an additional telephoto lens. It was a completely manual camera and very easy to use. Photography had become one of his favorite hobbies. They had a well-equipped darkroom at the newspaper, and Jacob, the photo-technician, had taught him how to develop black and white film and make enlargements.

Now that George was recovering nicely, Swami decided he would be going back to Bangalore soon. He reserved his ticket for the first week of April. Venu said he would come down from Montreal for a few days before Swami left.

George has begun playing the guitar again. He was slowly regaining dexterity on his left hand. His wounds had almost healed, but it was an effort for him to play and sing for extended periods. The doctors encouraged him to use his hands, as well as sing, so he could make his lungs stronger. He spent a lot of time in the basement, playing his many guitars, writing songs and singing for his friends.

Venu arrived during the last week of Swami's stay, driving his red Mercedes-Benz 500E.

"Wow, that's a nice looking car, Venu," said Swami. "Mercedes eh… looks like you've made it, bugger."

"Yes, it is something I've dreamed of from when I was young. People who were successful always drove Benz cars… don't laugh, buggers. There was a popular South Indian movie character called Benz Vasu. I guess I am Benz Venu! It's a pretty good car as well," said Venu.

The Scrimshankers were thrilled to be together once more. They spent their time just hanging out together in George's house and talking as well as making day trips to Manhattan or other places nearby.

"Hey buggers, do you want to go for a great party in the City?" asked George one day. "I got an invitation in the mail today. But we'll need to get dressed up for it. I think I can get a couple of additional passes."

"What is it?" asked Venu?

"It's the annual Met Ball. It's at the Metropolitan Museum of Art, and it is organized by Vogue magazine. You'll see some of the most beautiful women in the world there, buggers. I donated a lot of money to some charity or the other last year, so I am on the list."

"Wow, maybe I can do a story on it for *Bangalore Baloney*," said Swami.

"Let me make some calls and get you invitations," said George. "We'll need to rent tuxedos."

A few days later, the three friends showed up at the Met on Manhattan's Upper East Side in their tuxes.

"You chaps look good," said George.

"This is the first time I am wearing a tuxedo," said Swami.

"I've attended a few events in a tux before," said Venu. "I was a speaker at a Cardio Conference in Denver last year."

The walked up the red carpet and mingled with models, actors, rock stars and celebrities. Many people knew George — especially because of his notoriety in the news media recently.

"You may see a lot of famous people here," said George to his friends. "Don't be overwhelmed. They're just like you and me… maybe more rich and famous but not any different."

They enjoyed cocktails and hors d'oeuvres and walked around the Met. It was wonderful to be able to see the priceless art at the museum in such a private setting. George saw a group of men standing in the Greek section.

"Buggers, I'd like to meet some guys I know. Don't act too shocked, especially you, Venu, okay?"

He walked over to the group.

"Hey, fellers," he said approaching the men.

They turned around.

"Hey, George! It's Handsome George! Haven't seen you since the benefit concert last year. Heard about all the stuff that went down. You okay, man?" said one of the men. He was a slightly built, handsome man with straight long hair who Swami recognized at once.

"Jackson, how are you?" said George. "I'd like you to meet my childhood friends from India. This is Swami, a journalist and publisher… and this is Dr. Venu, a cardiologist, who is now in Montreal. Chaps, this is Jackson, Don and Glenn… you may recognize them from somewhere…"

"Wow, great to meet you all," said Swami. "Love all your songs."

They talked for a few minutes. Venu was too star-struck to speak much. But Swami took a few pictures and spoke to them about music and what they were doing now. He couldn't wait to phone Asha, his entertainment editor at the paper and narrate his short interview. He also walked around taking photographs of other guests at the event. He was sure that he had enough for a whole feature.

The next night was Swami's last in New York. It was also George's first public performance since he had left the band over a year ago. Sol had got him a forty-five minute gig at The Player's Theater in Greenwich Village as part of an acoustic concert featuring several performers.

George was going on stage at nine-thirty. He had practiced in the house for several nights in preparation for the show. The Scrimshankers drove into the City late in the afternoon and had dinner at a bar close to the theater. They sat backstage, half-an-hour before George went on, and watched the other performers. It was Swami and Venu's first exposure to this aspect of George's life in New York. It was very exciting. Swami took a lot of photographs.

When George went on stage, he was absolutely wonderful and had everyone in the small venue mesmerized right from his first song. He still had a bit of difficulty with his left hand and could not hold his breath for a long time, but he had taught himself to compensate with his current limitations and still put on a good performance.

"Ladies and gentlemen, I would like to close my set with a song I wrote only a few days ago. It's the first time I'm playing it in public. I'd like to dedicate it to my two best friends, Swami and Venu… I'm fortunate to have them in the audience tonight. The song is called *Friends*. I hope you like it."

He strummed his Martin and started singing…

I was looking through some photographs
Some were more than 25 years old
We all looked so young and happy
None of us knew what lay in store

You are my friends

Broken souls on the mend
Wasted years... time well spent
Stick together until the end

Some of us made a lot of money
Others lost everything they owned
Some of us tried to find a new life
Some of us never came in from the cold

You are my friends
Broken souls on the mend
Wasted years... time well spent
Stick together until the end

We've lost some good friends along the way
We remember them and those good old days
Grade school pranks and teenage romances
We've lived our lives and taken our chances

You are my friends
Broken souls on the mend
Wasted years... time well spent
Stick together until the end

You are my friends

It was the first time his friends were hearing the song. It bought tears to their eyes. As he was watching George perform, Swami suddenly had an epiphany that everything was once again the way it should be. He glanced at Venu. He was so different from who he had once been as a boy. Swami smiled when he remembered Venu's trademark crumpled shirt and worn-out slippers. Now he was a dapper, successful and confident surgeon. He had undoubtedly come the farthest of the three of them.

George's eyes were shining as he performed; he was doing what he loved and was born to do. Swami realized that George was going be okay, too. "*Yes, they would all be fine.*"

The next afternoon, Venu drove George and Swami in his car to the airport. The sat in a restaurant at JFK and had a beer together. In a few hours, they would all return to their separate lives. The past four months had brought them together again in a way that had renewed and cemented their friendship for the rest of their lives. They sat there without talking, sipping their beers. Each one of them was thinking of the years and experiences they had shared together.

"Swami, I know it's always been your dream to travel all over the United States," said George. "I'm sorry you couldn't do it during this trip."

"Don't worry, I'm glad I was here with you both," said Swami. "Anyway, I realize now that I am not indispensable at the newspaper. The editors have done a good job of running it in my absence. I can leave it in their hands for a few weeks now and then if I want."

"Let's do a road trip next time," said George. "You come with Annie and the kids, Venu, you come with Shantha and Priyanka. We'll rent an RV and drive from coast to coast," said George.

"Tell me when you're coming, Swami, and I'll plan it too," said Venu.

"That's a great idea. I promise I'll try to come soon," said Swami.

George raised his glass. "Okay, then here's to the Scrimshankers, the best friends ever," he said.

"Yes, here's to the Scrimshankers," said Venu.

"To be continued," said Swami, raising his glass…

Epilogue

S waminathan leaned back in his seat at 36,000 feet. He was in an Air India flight on his way back home to Bangalore. It was the second leg of his journey. The Boeing 747 had first flown from New York to London. He had slept most of the way there.

He was exhausted after the non-stop activities of the past few days with George and Venu. There had been a five-hour stop at Heathrow Airport. He walked around a bit and did a little shopping at the duty-free stores: English chocolates for his parents, Annie and the kids; Johnny Walker whisky for his father-in-law.

He still had an eight-hour journey ahead of him to Bombay and then another two hours on the domestic Indian Airlines flight to Bangalore. He was wide awake because of the change in time zones. He tried to watch the in-flight Hindi movie but was bored by it in a few minutes.

He looked in the seat pocket in front of him and found *Namaskaar*, the Air India in-flight magazine, as well as a small brown bag for airsickness. He opened the magazine and flipped through the pages slowly. Then something caught his eye.

At first he couldn't believe it. He looked closer at the photograph and read the article. There was no mistake.

"After all these years... imagine that," he said to himself. He laughed out aloud.

The middle-aged Indian woman who was sitting next to him was startled and glared at him disapprovingly. He smiled at her apologetically.

"Sorry, I just read something funny." He turned back to the article...

Beautiful Flowers:
A Blooming Success Story

Beautiful Flowers is a local Indore business that is about to be franchised all over the country. It was started under the staircase of a decrepit office complex in Saket in 1975. Since then, it has grown to over ten locations in the City of Indore. The BF stores are distinct in décor, style and product offering. It now appears poised for the national stage with over fifty franchises already sold in fifteen cities all over India. *Namaskaar* spoke to its owner, the enterprising C.K. Ganguli.

When and how did you get the idea for Beautiful Flowers?
Ganguli: *You see, many years ago, I had some trouble in my life... hoodlums, gangs and such in some far away city — I won't say which one. One day, to escape all that, I bought a ticket on the first train that was leaving from there. I didn't know where I was going or what I would do. I had a little money with me but nothing else. The train stopped at a small station in Madhya Pradesh. I was standing on the platform and thinking of my future when I saw an old woman selling flowers from a basket. Just as I was about to board the train again, she came up to me and gave me a Gulmohar flower. "You can change your life, beta... go from gang to gul," she told me. Those were her exact words! To this day, I think that was God speaking to me through that woman. How could she have known my name was Ganguli or that I used to be in a street gang? The train was going to Indore. When I got there, I started my first flower shop in Saket. Over the years, I have been very fortunate. The business has grown, and now we have ten Beautiful Flowers stores in Indore alone...*

Swami read through the rest of the interview with interest. There was a photo of C.K. Ganguli standing next to one of his stores. He looked older. His hair was thinning and he had a paunch, but it was unmistakably the CK who had once terrorized them as boys.

He tore out the page and put it in his pocket. He wanted to Xerox it and send it to George and Venu. He closed his eyes and thought of C.K. Ganguli, Walter Broom, Ram Murthy, Mohan Chandy and all the other people that had shaped his life.

"On straight on! On Cottonians on!" The first lines of their old school song came to his mind... *"Life was about moving forward, not looking back!"*

Venu had an expression he used when things were beyond his control. *"The universe will take care of it,"* he would say.

The Scrimshankers had often wondered what had happened to C.K. Ganguli. Had he gone to Australia? Did he die a heroic death in the French Foreign Legion? Had he joined the pirates in the South Seas? Was he a notorious Don in the Bombay underworld? The answer appeared to be much simpler and infinitely more benign. The universe had taken care of it.

– The End –

The Theme Song

BANGALORE

There's a city that I come from
It's in the East if you follow the sun
I lived there till I was twenty-five
It's a part of me until I die
It was a sleepy little place until somebody said
"Let's bring in more people and let them paint this town red"
Bangalore… Bangalore… Bangalore… Bangalore

They started by cutting the trees
And building big factories
Until there was no more room to grow
But the people they wanted more
Now they've got CNN; they've got KFC
They've got beauty queens; they've got global reach
Bangalore… Bangalore… Bangalore… Bangalore

It's the same old story wherever I go
From Bangalore to Baltimore
Everything's changing in the blink of an eye
Makes a man like me want to break down and cry!

Now I go back when I can
And even though I'm still the same man
Everything I know has changed
My town's has been rearranged
Everyone I know is living on a wing and a prayer
Traffic policemen wear masks because you can't breathe the air
Bangalore… Bangalore… Bangalore… Bangalore

Thomas Itty

(Photo by Chris Kelly)

Thank You

for reading this novel.

Please visit www.thomasitty.com to buy
songs featured here as well as others by
Thomas Itty.

Life is hard. Be kind to others.

www.ingramcontent.com/pod-product-compliance
Lightning Source LLC
Chambersburg PA
CBHW030548180626
46816CB00005B/1454